WHEAT

WHEAT

White Castles on the Plains

Dorothea Condry-Paulk

Library of Congress Control Number:		2011901939
ISBN:	Hardcover	978-1-4568-5659-5
	Softcover	978-1-4568-5658-8
	Ebook	978-1-4568-5660-1

This novel is a true history of the times from the late 1800s to now and of a
fictionalized family that loves wheat country, the land, and the grain itself.

Any resemblance to situations or persons that are not historical is purely coincidental.

This book was printed in the United States of America.

To order additional copies of this book, contact:
Xlibris Corporation
1-888-795-4274
www.Xlibris.com
Orders@Xlibris.com
90366

CONTENTS

DEDICATION

To my mother, Pearlie Lee Upton,
who was born in 1902 in the shadow
of the Ouachita Mountains and who
told me stories of those early days and
dreams.

Acknowledgments

I gratefully give recognition of the interview and resource materials given to me by Ferdie Deering of the *Daily Oklahoman* when the story had just begun to "germinate" for me in the late 1970s.

Besides the Indian Territory stories told to me by my mother, Pearl Upton, I owe much to the Canadian County Historical Museum's collection of Joseph Danne information and to the generous interview granted me by Joe Penwright, a Calumet elevator owner, operator, and manager for the past half century. I have included a brief bibliography of other resources.

My years of experience while employed by the Oklahoma Flour Mills in El Reno before it consolidated with the owner, Colorado Milling, during the 1950s proved advantageous to the storytelling as well. These years were followed by more than fifty years in agribusiness on both leased and owned farms.

Perhaps the crowning information arrived in 2009 and 2010. The Q and A meeting at Redlands College in El Reno with Secretary of Agriculture Tom Vilsack supplied information regarding some of the new technologies and funding available to generate and sustain agriculture here and around the world. Then in September 2010,

Brad Tipton, Canadian County agent, supplied data on the wheat belt and production bushels of the varieties across it, and Jordan Mincke of Minnesota supplied transit information from Oklahoma and beyond.

I also owe many thanks to my assistant, Marilynn Penwright, who gave me both apt story advice and prepared the manuscript, and to Tanner Fisher and Loretta Hobson who read for the overlooked errors in spelling, punctuation, and typing.

CHAPTER I

Born for Adventure

Upton arrived in the pristine southeastern area of Oklahoma's Indian Territory in time for the land run. But from the moment he saw the rugged hills and mountainous region, he wanted to stop here, live here—here where the spring-fed streams ran into the Washita River. After watering Horse, his pony with no name, he tethered him to a young sapling.

Tired, dusty, and hungry, he waded into the clean shallows. A winter chill alerted him to a cold night ahead. A north wind rattled the willow's branches nearby.

He looked around for a campsite after he had splashed his dusty face and hair clean with the soft water. The young buck deer in the shallows northeast of him lifted his head from a cool drink. *A deer steak will set well on this empty stomach tonight,* he thought. Basically a fisherman or a rabbit and bird hunter, Upton had never killed a deer, but he'd seen it done. *What luck to see one,* he thought, for his food supply dwindled to nothing but berries and a few hard biscuits.

He carefully stepped to the shore and Horse for the bow, one arrow, and his hunter's knife from the saddle bag. With the knife between his teeth, he drew the arrow taut, aimed, and let it fly. "A hit!" he exclaimed, racing eagerly to the buck. Water sprayed from his boots as he ran, the flying droplets red as blood in the sun's reflection.

The animal gazed at him as if bewildered before it staggered in an attempt to flee. Red blood spilled over the downlike hide and spun in the pale eddies of the river's flow as if writing a warning there in blood. Upton shivered.

It was done. He couldn't take it back. Across the river he saw two larger deer, a doe and an older buck, watching. An ache clutched at his throat as if grief gathered there. He swallowed, and the pain eased. The bloody water reached for his boots and leggings. He must move, though he wasn't certain that he could.

At last he dragged his prey to the bank and hung it from a branch to gut and dress. He built a fire of wood with stones around it to both restrain the fire and to add heat. The smoke bit at his nostrils and teared his eyes as he leaned over it to stoke it with ample wood sticks and chips. He staked a site nearby with four saplings and tarped it to sleep beneath. Then Upton dressed the young deer and carried the waste into the woods for scavengers to find.

He scooped dirt over the spilled blood near his camp, then salted and wrapped large pieces of meat in burlap. He emptied his leather saddle bags to store it there until the morrow when he would cook it over a spit. Cooking in daylight rather than moonlight would deter varmint intruders that searched for food under the cover of night.

When he finally lay with his head on his knapsack, he recalled the deer's great eyes, its gentle demeanor, its stunned expression—the blood circling his legs. *The first and last time,* he thought. For he knew he hadn't the heart to kill another deer.

Then Upton's mind sped back to his childhood to climb up the years that led him to this place. Such memories often coaxed him into sleep and dreams.

Born in 1872, Upton Rush arrived upon a continent reeling with excitement, hardship, and change. His father, Morgan, home to Ohio from the Union Army after five years, secured a teaching position in the university's school of architecture.

His mother, Maddy, managed the house's three levels for his five siblings and Maddy's mother and father, Joseph and Emily Hines.

The whole family, as he soon learned while still a toddler, cultivated the orchard, fields of corn, gardens, and manners.

"Sit up straight, wipe your mouth, say 'please'" commonly tortured all six of them, forever eager to finish chores. For then they became free for croquet, for the stables, or for hunting rabbit and squirrel. Even Kate, his sister, could shoot.

The youngest boy, Upton lagged behind or found himself in front of a rider, hanging tightly to the saddle horn. Still, they rarely left him behind, nor were his parents protectionists—not even for Alice, the baby, two years younger than he.

He learned survival skills early. Often it fell to him to lie awake with a rifle in hand to prevent raccoons from stealing corn before prime ear gathering.

Summers, his auburn hair turned red as fire; winters changed it back. His eyes were black as castor beans. By the age of six, Upton guided a plow behind Sally, their mule, and rode horseback three miles to school behind Todd, his oldest brother.

His siblings sported the black hair and hazel eyes of Morgan Rush, though Maddy had hair of gold and gray-blue eyes that spoke to him from a beautiful face. Her fair cheeks flushed easily from heat or cold beside the small, straight nose and heart-shaped mouth. Upton adored her.

He'd handled the team and plowed for half a dozen years by the age of twelve, curried the horses, and cleaned the stables. He'd shocked grain into sheaves the years they'd raised it, milked over ten cows before breakfast, yoked oxen, and walked behind Maddy, her hoe in hand, dropping garden seeds or finger furrowing the rich black soil for planting the spinach and lettuce. He loved the feel of earth. The smell of it smarted his nostrils as pleasingly as the freshness of the new-mown hay or cut grass.

Upton felt he understood the earth and animals and loved all of nature as a source of enormous energy and beauty. He felt akin to *it*, belonged to *it*. Even the sharp scents of the horses' breath and sweat pleased him as he fed, watered, and brushed the animals.

He hunted the dense woods across the hay field and gathered wood there. Tree bark revealed antler marks and cat clawings more often than not. He had learned to be still, to listen, to watch. He would not have done any animal harm unless there was need. Still, he regarded the snap of twigs or the crunch of leaves with his rifle at his side to fend off some wild thing if he must while he reveled in discoveries of wild berries and in identifying the various songs, appearances, and demeanors of birds habited there. His eyes were as likely to follow the diamond glint of sun that invited bits of sky as to follow a scurrying brown lizard through the dry leaves upon the ground.

"You've won a prime position in my heart," Maddy told him. "You assume the responsibility for your behaviors easily and take instruction well. From your first steps, you've been eager to learn and experience. You eat life like you devour chocolate cake." Then she hugged him tightly. "Like me, you are," she murmured and kissed him. "No matter if life's gift is bitter chocolate or sweet."

Then she brushed a tear from her cheek, a tear that confused him.

Always eager to help, cautious yet basically unafraid, he had quickly aroused the competitive hostility of his siblings. He pretended not to notice; his natural affection for them prompted avoidance of their grievances so as not to spoil his joy. At sixteen, Upton overheard his parents' conversation about him: "Upton is the child who knows no guile, only a pure heart. He's so sure of himself, it scares me for him," his mother said.

"A man needs confidence. That's good," his father responded. "I'll speak to him about caution. Don't worry."

His father repeated that opinion to him while they chopped wood the early March day he turned sixteen. Then he reinforced the advice with an approving slap on the back. "But your mother worries," he added. "You have developed an adventurous spirit at sixteen, a spirit that would says 'Come on, let's go for it' if it could be heard."

"Why should Mother be scared?" he asked. "She knows God walks with us."

Morgan gave him a long thoughtful look. "She's taught you well. Still, life isn't always kind, Upton. Recall for yourself the story of Job. It has a side as harsh sometimes as a March blizzard." Morgan regarded the ominous snow clouds that gathered.

"That's true, Father, perhaps to make the better life he found."

Morgan shook his head. "And will our life be better with fewer cattle?"

Upton said nothing for he felt his father's life must be between himself and his god—whatever or whoever that god might be. He hoped his father believed in Job's God. For the falling temperature and harsh wind would drive them to the house soon and could indeed kill stock that could not reach hay and shelter through blinding snow.

The blizzard came in much faster than anyone had supposed. Morgan and all the boys worked to corral the stock but could not succeed in the face of driving north wind and the stinging sleet that accompanied snow.

"My good luck and God's will to have you all back!" Maddy cried, shaking out wet clothes and giving them warmed flannel before the fire.

When the blizzard finally ended, half of their herd lay frozen to death. Only a few calves had survived. Morgan fell ill with pneumonia due to his exposure.

"Thank God, the horses survived," his father muttered two weeks later when they could finally check the farm.

"Thank God *you* survived, Father," Upton said.

Besides Upton, there was Todd, John, Neal, Noah, Kate, and Alice, who was now five. All of them (except Alice) reveled in their various achievements at the local Washington public school. But Upton had persuaded his mother to teach him at home after his second year at Washington, a thing that delighted them both.

Besides the McGuffey Reader, geography, history, Latin, math, spelling, and writing, he learned about food preservation, home remedies, and dyes. School no longer bored him.

Nor did Maddy leave out art and music, for the arts and literature pleased them both more than others of the household. She often played and sang "Flow Gently, Sweet Afton" for them in their parlor after the evening meal and his father's Bible reading. His father doted on the song "Annie Laurie" for his own mother's kin, William Douglas, a Scot, wrote it. If Morgan Rush whistled a tune, it was that of "Annie Laurie."

Morgan had built the kitchen and dining area with a breezeway between it and their bedrooms and parlor as a fire-safety measure. Nights were cold for sleeping, but safe from fire. Still, many January nights found them on the warmer kitchen floor.

Early in 1889 when flyers were posted on shop windows in Dayton announcing land openings in Oklahoma Territory, it surprised no one that Upton, now seventeen, prepared his saddle bags to go. He threw them over the back of his sorrel, Horse, and announced that he intended to stake his claim. Besides, Kate was engaged to marry, and Todd and Noah had gone to the university. Neal opened his smithy in town, so only John and Alice remained at home. Alice still attended the public school, and John prepared to graduate.

Upton knew that John clearly hoped to farm with Morgan. Increase divided among the three of them would make paupers of them all. Times remained hard in Ohio due to the great blizzard. It would take years to restore the herd and replace all the fences their frantic terror and snow blindness destroyed when they broke through them.

Upton knew much about home remedies, languages, math, and even Shakespeare. Moreover, he could build outbuildings from logs or timber. For better or worse, he knew no reluctance—no fear. He dreamed of an empire of wheat and cattle. His purse jingled with a few coins of silver and gold. It would not buy books for the university but a team and plow for his farm in the territory.

—

So with the self-confidence that Maddy's teaching and trust had grown in him and with the outdoor skills Morgan had taught him, he set out for the free land where a man could be king at seventeen.

Rumor had it that Indians were giving up lands in the southern Indian Territory to join other tribes in Kansas. He thought he would like to see that land before going on to Oklahoma Territory and the run. The maps revealed mountains and rivers across an area that looked made for him. When he wasn't farming, he could hunt and fish—live off the land. *There would be deer and rabbit in those hills and near water for certain,* he thought. *A veritable heaven on earth.*

His father's warning that the world was not always kind flitted across his memory like a lizard over a rock. Later, he would learn more about the lawless bad lands of the Indian Territory. Some of the national articles sounded exaggerated to him, like fodder for saloon talk to deter young men from leaving home.

Following trail, river, or rail, Upton and his sorrel, Horse, picked their way across country. When he could, he moved in the shadows or along wooded trails. He forged some creeks and rivers. Wary of currents, snakes, and unknown depths, he tested the waters with a cane staff. It was early spring 1889.

Mostly, he looked for shade and slept during the warm afternoons to conserve clean water and his energy. He had heard that the rivers harbored typhoid and malaria. When moonlight allowed, he traveled nights. The sun compassed the days; the star configurations, the night.

He'd left Ohio mid-March, figuring on reaching the Territory long before summer. He wondered about the Unassigned Lands—the land run. But the mountains and water toward the southeast continued to lure him. He draped his rubber slicker over the north side of his tent of sticks in early April where night air still chilled from the north. He slept on a saddle blanket. He'd left wearing warm clothing and carrying salt-cured meat and dried beef. The several skins of water over his saddle horn that assured safe drinking water needed replenishing; he must boil water soon.

Maddy had packed dried fruit and hard tack for him. A couple of pans dangled from Horse's sides. Periodically, Upton felt for the matches buttoned into his shirt pocket to verify they remained dry. Foolishly, he hadn't worried about food, figuring he'd fish and hunt a little along the way. He'd forgotten how the cold discouraged some furry critters and could ice over the fish, making food harder to garner.

Now picking his way along the Arkansas River after three weeks on the trail and depleted food reserves, Upton hoped for a fish supper. He dismounted and tethered Horse to a willow tree up the bank. The sprigs of grass among the dry leaves announced spring. The smell of the river's fish encouraged a successful catch. Rivulets of evening sun shot arrows through the willows. The breeze wafted their slender branches as if to welcome him. Horse whinnied and dropped his head to forage the rust-red and yellow leaves for a snack.

Until now, Upton had not considered the possibility of meeting renegade Indians unhappy over being removed again from their home. Nor did confronting any outlaws whose names were now famous in all the states bother him when he remained far away. The newspapers back east told stories of the Daltons, the Youngers, and the Starrs, which he thought about now. He fastened a bit of dried beef to the hook and plopped his line into the river. *Waste of energy to think on those stories,* he thought, admiring the river. Still, nostalgia for the rivers back home overtook him. *It looks like creamed coffee today instead of the Ohio's deep blue water.*

Could he shoot a legend like Belle Starr should she want him dead? he wondered.

Could he fire before a Reed or Younger fired? He felt a tug and saw the fish flop in the sun. Looked like a golden perch, a big one. The Youngers and Reeds and Belle Starr were forgotten while he reset bait for another bite.

Soon, he'd built a small fire, cooked, and eaten his two perch and decided to travel on under the night's full moon. For the more he'd thought about Arkansas's famous Judge Parker and the random

8

chance of getting into trouble before he'd made his fortune, the more cautious his adventurous spirit became. Still, those outlaws and the judge had aged, he concluded. Maybe even died. The thought relieved his anxiety as he kicked dust and dead ashes over the campfire.

After he had come about thirty more miles across country and made camp, he met up with three riders as he strode down to a stream for water. He regarded them with quiet suspicion while their horses drank.

Now Maddy had judiciously sewn most of his money within their singular-stitched places along his undershirt armholes in the event that he met up with thieves. She had shrewdly sewn the garment of white muslin herself. Still, thieves could take Horse and leave him stranded—or dead. He straightened his shoulders and looked them in the eyes without speaking. Only a few coins still jingled in his pockets.

The three volunteered no information of their own but asked Upton a dozen questions or more. After he had answered them honestly and briefly, he had the presence of mind to mention his fine supper of fish. "Ran out of food for my trip," he said. After that bit of information to influence their thinking as to his probable poverty, he asked if they knew if he might hire on to the Santa Fe or Baltimore and Ohio, if either was in these parts, as he surely needed funds if he was to prove up land he hoped he'd be lucky enough to claim.

He laid a gaze of humility on them that did not waver.

"Can you shoot?" one of them asked. He was tall and lanky with blond hair and blue eyes.

"Rabbits," was Upton's brief response, skirting any hint of aggression.

They looked prosperous to him, so he gradually lost his notion that they would rob and kill him. After a while, the tall blond asked, "Maybe you could ride with us. We can use an extra hand to cook a little, curry the horses."

Upton sensed he shouldn't respond too soon. It was after supper as they rode along together in silence that he said he had thought over their offer. He intended to locate land in Indian Territory, he told them; build a cabin and plant corn and wheat, cotton, maybe, prove it up. "I'll need work close by," he explained. "I hope to marry in a few years, raise a family.

"So as much as I need the work, fellas, I just don't have the time to change course for it now. I'm hoping to find it in the territory. There's rail to build, a north and south to connect for a country moving west."

After more silence, the one who looked part Indian spoke in low tones. "You expect to live that long, do you?" Then he spat a stream of tobacco too near Upton's face for comfort. Moist brown specks of it dotted Upton's hand that held the saddle horn. He turned toward the speaker.

"Who should I look out for?" he asked, intentionally avoiding the word *fear*. Nor did he choose to reveal that he thought the last speaker looked like the Younger's picture on a poster he'd seen. He had read that he was half-Shawnee or Apache—or was it Cherokee? Whatever his tribe, this member's looks were as dark as his comrades' were blond. He knew there were all five civilized tribes on the plains and other smaller tribes as well that had been driven to the territory so that others could take their lands in the northeast. He had heard that there were fair-haired blue-eyed Cherokee Indians.

Adding literal fuel to an already volatile period, oil had been found. A speculator from the east had hit it. What would the next fifty or one hundred years bring to the land, especially if a gusher came in? Great wealth and more violence, he supposed.

Upton looked at the supposed Younger beside him as if to say, *Are you going to try something?*

"Much," the dark one finally responded. "Malaria, typhoid, renegades looking for a free place someone else has *proved up*. If that or horse thieves don't kill you, when you've proved up your place, someone will invent another way. There's no law yet. Just a marshal that rides through now and then and perchance catches someone to drag into Judge Parker on the Arkansas side. You should just give up the struggle and ride with us. It's an easier way to get rich fast."

"Another cut won't hurt us, eh, Jim?" the blond agreed with a laugh, looking at the darkest of the three. "Besides, rumors are that Judge Parker's dead."

The warning look the dark one threw him carved the long silence that followed.

"God willing," Upton finally ventured, "I'll be across Arkansas and in the territory in under twenty more days. I'll have to stop for hunting, of course. Gotta eat. Hope to see a deer, something to make enough meat to last for a while. Stopping for smaller game and fish slows me down too much."

They parted company after he'd killed and cooked them a rabbit for supper. He fell asleep under a star-filled sky of navy blue and with the scent of wild honeysuckle reminding him of home, now miles behind him.

Chapter II

The Claim

Upton filed his 160-acre claim at Guthrie for land near the Ouachita Mountains and near the bank of the South Canadian River. The mountains were near enough to ride into and find wild game. The river yielded fish. Often, he found duck, geese, wild turkey, or quail nearby. But he loved the week or two away to hunt near Winding Stair Mountain where he felt alone with absolute beauty.

That first year, he hewed logs for his dirt-floor cabin, chinked them with mud and straw that he mixed together. Because of a kitchen fireplace, he built two bedrooms separated from the cooking, dining, and sitting area by a breezeway for safety from fire, just as he had learned from his father. Maddy had survived a fire in their Ireland home due to her father's method of home construction and told Morgan of it.

Early on, he fashioned bow and arrows from river willows in order to save rifle shells. He railroaded and farmed, his earnings purchasing tools, supplies, and feed. At spring seeding time, he planted corn, cotton, and a garden. Before the following fall, he planted the orchard. Upton figured he could turn winter's dead grass stubble under in moist soil, then siphon water from the river to sow fall pumpkin, squash, and beans. It was rich bottomland that he'd spotted a safe distance west of the South Canadian River. During heavy rains when the river would surely crest its banks, his garden would not be washed away.

Before his first winter ended, he had made a firm start. Prosperity seemed certain.

He hired on at the CRI & P to lay rail more than fifty miles west of his farm during the idle months before the second spring planting. With that increase, he purchased a team of work horses to pull the plow and retired himself and Horse from the more arduous farm labor. Upton no longer needed to wear the leather plow straps on his own shoulders to follow along behind Horse. He could sit atop the plow and guide his team. He had ridden six hours on Horse to the rail site and six back to his farm.

He finished the barn in April. He had no stock except his recent purchase of a Jersey milk cow. He nurtured two dozen baby chicks that he cooped in his warm kitchen, safe from skunks, snakes, or fox that might get them. He'd seen bobcats try for the fowl near the river, but they usually failed to capture any. The wild ducks and geese fluttered into the water and swam fast to the middle, a thing he loved watching.

He hammered the last nails into a finished barn on May 1 when a marshal coming through told him Al Jennings and his gang had held up a train on the line he'd helped lay south of Minco.

"Missed me by a month," he told him. "I left on horseback the last of March."

The second year on his claim, he finished a stable large enough for his team and several riding horses. The horses no longer had to stomp around a small corral and open-front shed, commonly referred to on these homesteads as a lean-to. A spacious split-rail corral encircled the stable.

A pen of young heifers and a new bull munched hay in the corral that encircled the barn by summer's end. So far, Upton had not revealed that he had money to passing cowboys and near neighbors. Though passersby stopped from time to time as if to monitor his progress, they could take one look at the skins hanging on poles to dry to surmise that he sold them for his increase. Locals knew he traded cream and eggs for groceries, tonics, salves, and seed.

The way he lived, he didn't need to buy much. He burned goose-fat tallow and made rag-wick candles, and he made his own soap from Maddy's recipe of tallow and lye. He caught his own meats and gathered his own wood for heating and cooking. The mountains provided good hunting. The river provided varieties of fish, just as he'd surmised. Soon, he thought, he'd find time to make his own tonics and salves from Maddy's recipes to treat the winter chills and coughs, the skin with dry scales or scabies.

"I hope you can come see my heaven here in Indian Territory," he wrote home. He told them of his stock, the garden, the new orchard, the house. He sketched the buildings and hills around the craggy knolls where he hunted and the river where he fished. Soon he found that he could wander nine miles on Horse in only an hour. He had made the almost 150-mile trek to Guthrie and back in three days by staying in the saddle after nightfall and rising earlier than the sun.

Some silent and curious traffic passed by—ordinary cowboys looking tough or unkempt and groups of Indians on ponies. He waved; they waved. No *real* problem occurred to write home about. Yet he did not sense a friendly, generous spirit in their stony, hostile expressions. This vexed him at times, but not enough to warrant alarming his family in Ohio. Besides, a marshal had passed through just last week—a warning to outlaws who would wrest his achievement here from him.

He dreamed of buying more land. He wondered if he should head for the rumored lottery lands in Oklahoma Territory and away from these mountains and the river he had come to love. He felt he would wear his youth away pushing and dragging the plow and rakes wherever he settled. Though his back reminded him daily that the hoe was far inferior to the square dance, a thing he aspired to attend, his soul required this spot. His vision of wheat and cattle had bent to poultry and hogs, to cotton, fruit, eggs, and self-reliance.

The best wheat country lay west of him. He had seen it that season of railroading near Minco, and his heart leaned toward it. But these rivers and mountains seemed to nourish his soul.

Flyers at the trading centers nearby announced the dances, box suppers, and church socials. Time for recreation neared for Upton, for his farm lay picture-perfect, complete, and productive. His recently purchased team of mules shortened his workdays. Even wood for winter fires rose in stacks before October's end, and his home medications that he conjured in his kitchen now lined a cabinet shelf.

Maddy had taught him the square dance tunes and calls back in Ohio. The steps had crossed the ocean with the colony settlers and followed them here. He had no clothes for socials yet; no new boots.

This winter, he thought, *I'll make a fiddle, and come spring and produce sales, I'll shop for clothes.*

He *could.* He had decided it. It would take some doing. The bow for his fiddle was no obstacle either. He'd pull a few of Horse's tail hairs and resin them, then tie them tight to a slender hardwood bow. He fashioned it all in his mind as he had his future here. For when all was built and bought, Upton intended to purchase more land with the coins, hidden now, shirt and all, under the false bottom of a small kitchen cupboard.

Further, he'd not only go to the dance in new clothes and boots, he'd play his fiddle and call the square dance. He smiled widely, revealing gleaming white teeth as he dreamed of it. "Once you dream a thing, Upton, you, God willing, can make it real." Maddy's voice followed him up and down his river of dreams.

It was on such a perusal for land two years later and four after he'd staked his first claim that he and Horse followed a narrow canyon trail past several caves in search of quail. There he spotted a lone young woman and her paint horse on the prairie near one of the caves and in a small clearing. No fence hindered him from a cautious approach through the sea of tall yellow-green native grasses for he saw she wore a holster over a skirt made from tanned leather.

―

"Don't shoot," he said on his approach. "Truly, I mean you no harm. Indeed, I approach to offer you any assistance or protection you may need for wherever you're bound."

"You live around here?" she asked bluntly and with what seemed wary regard to Upton. "You sure talk funny."

He felt he had spoken the King's English and merited her grateful response. "Four years," he said, stretching himself taller in the saddle. Those four years had tanned and muscled the twenty-one-year-old Upton, who now sat on Horse.

She smiled, but he noted the question in her blue eyes, her raven hair lifted by a breeze. He noticed as well the shapely figure that appeared tanned and strong where skin could be seen.

He tipped his hat. "Upton Rush, at your service."

She shaded her eyes against the bright afternoon sun. Her felt hat had fallen back against her shoulders. She silently drew it back on, then pushed up the bead that tightened the strings beneath her chin. She knelt to place the small bouquet she still held on the grave site at her feet. Then she fetched a rose rock from her saddle bag and placed it beside the marker, as if to comfort the stone.

Without another word, she deftly swung astraddle the saddle-free paint, leaned to grasp the reins, kicked the animal sharply in its flanks with small boot-moccasined feet, and rode away in the direction of the hills that flanked the south side of the river.

Upton stared after her for a long time as if she were a vision. Finally, he dismounted and walked up to where she'd laid the things to read the marker of Belle Starr.

Six months later, the first week of June, Upton finally walked through the country schoolhouse door where desks were pushed aside for the box supper bids and a scheduled square dance. He carried a small wooden case at his side. He'd been strongly motivated when he'd carved the violin from balsam priced at over $2. The violin had a mellow resonant tone he admired.

On his feet were the new boots he'd swapped six bushels of early peaches for at the traders' store. His shirt and trousers were new as well, and he carried silver dollars to spare in his pocket from a cattle sale to spring traders passing through.

Lean, tanned, and strong, his tall stature, clean shave, and auburn hair over black eyes that matched the black sideburns turned more than one young lady's head when he arrived. But Upton's eyes sought out only the one across the room. To his dismay, an escort sat beside her.

Upton thought the boy spindly and pale, hardly a match for one as strong and independent as his lady, as he had begun to think of her, and he thought of her a lot.

Never mind, he thought. He'd have her attention before the evening ended.

"No guns allowed," another rancher advised, approaching to take the violin case.

"It isn't a gun but a violin," Upton replied, handing over the case for inspection.

"Our fiddler may want a break. Keep it handy."

Upton smiled and nodded.

They scheduled the dancing first, and sure enough, he was asked to relieve the fiddler, an older man with a shock of gray hair who had spun them around and do-si-doed superbly for over an hour.

"And it's ladies to the center and it's gents around the row. And we'll rally round the canebrake and shoot the buffalo. The girls will go to school, the boys will act the fool, rally round the barn and chase the old gray mule. Oh, the hawk shot the buzzard and the buzzard shot the crow. And we'll rally round the canebrake and shoot the buffalo."[1]

Upton played and sang while he watched the girl of his dreams spin and skip in a blue calico dress and dainty blue slippers. She wore no boots tonight. He had fallen hopelessly in love with her without even knowing her name.

---

[1]   As remembered by Pearl Upton from early 1900's square dances in Pottawatomie County.

Nor could he buy her box of food, for he bid all the ten silver dollars in his pocket, knowing he'd thought half of it would buy oat seed for a bit of calf pasture north of the cabin. Still, as she moved to a table with the gangly sidewinder (Upton's lowly opinion of her present suitor), she glanced over her shoulder and threw him a ravishing smile. His heart skipped a beat.

He resolved to come prepared to capture her at the next dance unless he learned where she lived tonight and just happened by her place. Before leaving, he hedged a question or two about who she was and who the escort was who had ignored her most of the evening.

"Why, that's Letti Pearl McLeod, Belle Starr's foundling granddaughter. When Pearl, Belle's daughter, was only fourteen, she *found* her and her brother, Cory McLeod. Folks here say they were left in her tree house. She heard their crying one morning when she went out to chore and took them in. Most folks around here that know her think she's Belle's blood kin because of her nerve. She's afraid of nothing and stouter than she looks. Cory, on the other hand, has the consumption. Can't get over it. 'Spect he'll die when winter hits."

Having that to go on, Upton knew where the pair lived within days. He didn't keep his cure for consumption a secret from them. He knew a cure for most ailments for Maddy and Morgan Rush had passed them on to all their children with the knowledge of scriptures as well. "There's cures for the body and cures for the soul—takes both," Morgan Rush had often said.

"Knowledge is power to reap abundant life," his mother had often reminded. "But you must put it to work and never give up. Sitting on it won't hatch results. Living is an act of either your faith or unbelief, pure and simple."

Upton savored the words of Maddy and Morgan that seemed to keep them near him here, so far from home.

From what he knew of living so far, Upton believed in their maxims for success. He knew how to build and to plant, to play and to sing, and to pray and to heal. Though he wanted Letti Pearl, making her brother well was a thing apart.

Upton cared deeply for everything that lived, especially for other people. If he could help Cory and Letti Pearl with anything, he would, he thought as he approached their farm days after. Whether he won her heart or not.

A mockingbird chorused his joy from a white-blossomed catalpa tree beyond the gray split-rail corral. The paint mare nickered at him, a young colt at her side like a promise. Several tethered sorrels grazed beyond.

Under today's morning sun, he felt as he felt beneath full moons—that a new chapter of his life opened its first page.

CHAPTER III

The Courtship

Within a few days, Upton *happened* by Letti's place again, a neat house of about five rooms with whitewashed outbuildings. He greatly admired the rail corral, the fencing, the outbuildings, and the house, shored up to the shuttered windows with rock. *They'd surely gathered it by hand from the hills behind their valley farm,* he thought. *Hard and tedious labor.*

When he learned they had been orphaned for over four years and that Letti was only sixteen and Cory a mere twenty years old, his amazement at their achievement here reluctantly faded over the following months.

He made a weekly visit, applying heat, giving camphor rubs, making fresh batches of bark teas, and placing kerosene poultices to Cory's chest. He supplied them with canned rhubarb and fresh as well as homegrown bunches of carrots that Letti was to cook soft and mash. "These are healing foods," he explained as he handed Letti more quarts of canned chicken in broth.

Before fall, Cory's color had returned, and he had gained weight. At best, he could work longer hours with the animals or in the field without exhaustion. Letti, in the meantime, had filled the dug cellar with fresh eggs, sweet and Irish potatoes, and crocks of pickles and kraut. She had placed the turnips, cabbage, and apples in holes dug there and lined with straw before she covered the produce with loose dirt.

Maddy taught Upton preserving in glass, but Letti built cooling racks in a narrow closet with a dirt floor to keep some things for short or long periods, depending on both the climate and spoilage risk. When he saw the smokehouse for curing wild turkey, fish, pork, and beef, he wasted no time making his own and working up piles of hickory chips for it, though he knew he would still dry, salt, or cover meats with fat too.

"You did all this yourselves?" he asked her.

"Of course we did." Then she added, "With the Lord's help, of course. And other families helped. Most that lived around here are dead now. There's a few that live a day's ride away. Sam Starr died about five years ago. He weren't really family, he just seemed like it."

"Of course. You had close friends."

If one would work, he thought, *hunger would never come here.*

Due to Cory McLeod's uncertain health and the distance of their farm from his, the McLeod farm sold for $250 when Upton and Letti McLeod married. A couple from the east named Beck purchased it. Their parents were emigrants from Germany. The Becks had a beautiful blond-haired blue-eyed girl of ten called Ida and a chubby dimpled baby boy named Lester, barely two years old.

They exchanged vows at Upton's home before the evangelist preacher from Briartown, who took the license to Guthrie for filing.

It had been five years since he saw the three men that he rode and camped with on the trail to the Territory. They came to his and Letti Pearl McLeod's wedding in 1894, a Reed and two Youngers. Though Upton had been raised to uphold the law and though these men sometimes rode with outlaw gangs, he could not bring himself to judge them harshly. They were Letti Pearl's friends or kin and had helped her and Cory survive hard and perilous times when orphaned.

In recent times, they hadn't seen Judge Parker. The rumor that he'd taken ill or been killed in 1889 seemed true. Fewer cases went to court in Guthrie, none lately for Letti's kin. Foundlings, both she and her brother, Cory, had fended for themselves. Upton learned that by Cory's twelfth birthday, their *volunteer* guardian, Rose, had moved to Van Buren and then on to Fort Smith without them. Letti was a mere eight years old at the time. The Reeds and Youngers assisted them then for the next four years until Cory reached the age of sixteen, and they were on their own.

"You're safe from now on," Upton assured her. Her bright laughter at the remark puzzled him.

Only an occasional marshal passed through these days. Most didn't live long enough to capture any gangster. If he did, he had to travel with his captive on the long trail to Guthrie, the legal center of the times. One or more of some gang often came out of the woods or rocks to kill him before he could arrive.

Marshalling wasn't a job Upton sought. He had hired out to lay rail and to build fences until and after wedding Letti.

Cory came to live with them, and he and Upton added two more rooms to the log house: one for Cory and another for the children Upton and Letti hoped to have.

From time to time, Youngers or Reeds dropped by for they were Letti's *adopted* uncles or cousins, if not real kin. They would break out the cider and pop corn for these guests. Often, Upton played his violin while Lettie Pearl played the french harp or danced about the room with some of their guests.

She often spent evenings listening to Upton read or tell stories of his family and their life in Ohio. When they were alone, they whispered softly to one another and clung together in love's embrace.

Eager to learn now, she had spent her younger years trying to survive. She questioned until he'd shared all he knew of math and language, of literature and crafts and of healing. She seemed insatiable for learning, so he began ordering books from the east for her with extra funds. He ordered a harpsichord for her eighteenth birthday, delighted that she could play a tune she knew or heard. She invented her own songs that they played together—she on the harpsichord and he on the violin. Often their happiness spilled over in laughter, light roughhousing, and teasing games.

"I don't say *weren't* no more," she told Cory, who labored within a year in good health beside Upton at any chore.

"When you don't say *no more*, you'll be educated for sure," he laughed.

"Hush your mouth!" she snapped back.

*   *   *

In Ohio, Maddy read Upton's letters before Morgan's evening Bible reading. Alice, the only sibling still at home now, sat on the oriental carpet at her feet. At seventeen, she looked after Morgan and Maddy with a warm, brave spirit, though they aged well.

"This life is as near heaven as I ever hope to be," she read. "Letti Pearl makes breakfasts of steaks from our own beef served up with biscuits and gravy. Often, there's even a fruit pie before daylight. She says the chores are hard and the chill of morning burns fat off bones. She intends to keep me working for sure."

Maddy knew her young granddaughter, Mary-Mary, from his letters, their house and outbuildings, the river, and woods and hills. She knew their animals, from the horses, cows, and hogs to the mongrel dog, Ralph. He had shared all but his nights with Letti.

It had been over six years since she had seen him, but he had promised that when the honeymoon was over, they'd take the train for Dayton.

"The years run by swifter than the Washita after rains. Mary-Mary's almost five years old," he wrote, "and we're expecting another. Probably for Christmas. Letti is saving the news from me still, so don't let on in your letters to her I told you."

"Hmph!" she wrote back. "Seems that honeymoon will never be over." Then she chuckled to herself. "He knows. I'm sure he does. Upton notices things."

*   *   *

Indeed, that first two years of their marriage, Upton and Letti even chored together, playfully squirting milk from a cow's teat at one another as if in a water fight. Letti always aimed a stream at old Sally's mouth, the fat yellow cat that prowled the barn for mice. They checked cattle together, mended fence together, prepared their food together, hardly ever out of the other's sight.

Even after Mary-Mary was born, she fastened her in an apron or on her back and went with him. They churned butter together, made cheese together. They often rode their horses in the afternoon, tethering Horse and Paint while they picnicked in the hills and where they might cling together on a soft mound of prairie grass, exhausting passion while Mary-Mary slept on her blanket.

Usually they bore fish home to salt down or fry if it was summer. Then near sundown, it was time to chore again: feed the chicks and stock, milk the cows, pen up the young calves and piglets. Even the work seemed play to Upton. Cory was always somewhere near to help when there was work to be done.

At four, Mary-Mary fed the chicks and gathered eggs; she swept the cabin and stood on a stool to wash the dishes. Rosy cheeked and aproned, she looked the mini image of Letti. Black ringlets clung to her head like a fur cap while her turquoise eyes watched everything.

A town had sprung up about thirty-five miles away named Wanette. Thousands of folks still swarmed to Oklahoma, plenty of them from the Wanette, Davis, and Ardmore areas. Upton knew that it was only a matter of time before Cory met someone and married too.

"If Cory marries," he said to Letti one afternoon when they were riding, "let's ask him to build on our land, and we'll share the increase. Old Mr. Haney, a mile north, says he's going to California about every time I stop to jaw. He wanted to fight Cubans in '98 too, though, and Africaners the year after."

—
24

"To pan for gold?" she asked.

"That's what he says. Should I ask him what he wants for his place? Be ready for more mouths to feed?"

"Let's do it now," she responded with a revealing glance.

That look needed no translation to Upton, for he had noticed her body's bloom and anticipated a birth near December as related to Maddy. He could read every mood, every expression of Letti's. The news from her delighted him, though he dreaded the nine-day stay of a bossy midwife again. "When?" he asked, as if surprised and wondering if he had guessed correctly about December.

"For Christmas," she laughed. "I like expensive presents. And I wanted to be sure. I didn't want to disappoint you, or I would have spoken sooner."

"Lucky that I do too," he chuckled. "But after today, you're not to risk falling off Paint or being thrown if he startles. You're on foot from now on."

Tucking Mary-Mary in front of her and reminding the child to hold the saddle horn, they headed for Haney's place, Letti's raven hair lifting in the breeze like a winged bird.

To Upton's surprise, Mr. Haney priced his eighty acres with a trade offer. He wanted their wagon, two horses, one cow, five barrels of horse and cow feed and the same of water, enough dried fruit, beef strips, and cornmeal to last him the six weeks he figured it could take him to get to the gold fields.

"I've got a rifle and bullets," he said, pulling on his gray beard. "Had to use it yesterday when a bobcat came in from the woods and killed two of my ducks. Folks in town say there's a cougar been killing calves, but I've not seen one."

"Most would stay away from folks unless they're a mite crazed with rabies," Upton added. "We'll watch out for them, keep our chicks up. You've a trade when you're ready, Haney, but in my way of thinking, you've a gold mine right here in this valley."

"Nothing and no one to set roots for," he said, glancing admiringly at Letti. "If I was young as you, I'd have gone to fight those Cubans instead of farming, joined Teddy."

Upton wasn't listening. He was thinking. Cory could replace and restock all the trade items the rest of the summer and most of the winter should Haney actually leave. But his meal request would run them short. He was going to miss Letti's Sunday morning corn cakes and syrup—their special treat. "When do you figure you'll go, *if* you go?"

"Dunno. Just stock the wagon and barn it. I can gather up the rest. You'll need to take my word to Guthrie. I'll write it all out and sign it legal. There's still no other law. I'll give you the paper tomorrow if you'll come by after supper."

"*You're* invited to supper tomorrow, Mr. Haney," Letti said with a smile. "I'll have a gooseberry pie and fry up a chicken." Mary-Mary clapped her hands with joy.

"You can plan on it. I'll bring the paper to you."

Upton could hardly believe the good luck nor could Cory when they told him. "But Sunday corn cakes and syrup—" Cory paused, his sacrifice suspended.

Letti laughed. "I've a backup stash of dried corn and nothing better to do than hammer and pestle meal. My mama taught me a few useful things too," she cajoled. Then she tucked her blushing face as if embarrassed about calling Rose Mama.

Upton reached an arm about her shoulders to draw her close for a moment until she recovered.

Soon after Mr. Haney left the next night, Cory cleared his throat uneasily. An anxious expression crossed his hazel eyes. "I've meant to mention Louisa to you." He paused, then tried again to tell them.

"There is a little filly I've set my sights on," Cory finally revealed. "A-a woman, I mean. Louisa. Guess I can screw up enough nerve to ask her to church. They've built one at Ardmore, did you know?"

They didn't know. Satisfied with the days at home, towns were only where they went when staples were needed. The wagon ride to Ardmore and back for supplies not found nearer claimed a whole day. Letti realized before Upton did that Cory could seek a life away from the land and had warned him. She darted a quick glance toward Upton, who caught her concerned expression.

———

Upton put his arm about her shoulders and, with a reassuring squeeze, said, "We're glad for you, aren't we, Letti? There's a life here for you and for her—if you want it." Cory's silence left that decision open.

In the weeks that followed Mr. Haney's visit, Cory rode into town on horseback each Sunday. He soon became the song leader for the little whitewashed congregational church, and by fall, he had married their choir director, Louisa Long, who was as blond as Letti was brunette. Opposites though they were in many ways, she and Louisa became fast friends.

Letti Pearl also realized that Louisa cared little for farm life. She liked books and music, painting and parties. She wanted a house in town. But both Upton and Cory were silent on the subject for the time being, and the order-filled wagon still waited for Mr. Haney's trip west while Louisa and Cory honeymooned in their tiny apartment above a mercantile at Briartown.

*   *   *

A month passed, and they knew nothing. Before two months passed, the wagon, an ox, and two horses with gear disappeared. Upon Upton's investigation of Haney's place, a rundown cabin with a lean-to that leaned to the north as if a strong south wind would flatten the rotting boards, he saw that it sat vacant and deserted. A table and chair, a bare mattress, and a lantern decorated the forlorn single room. A hungry cat curled its gray body around a front porch post and meowed loudly. Upton drew it a drink from the well.

Mr. Haney had *really* left this time to seek wealth in the streams of California. *It would take less time than his own place to improve it,* Upton thought, for now a sawmill run by two Swedish brothers operated six miles east where woods thickened. He looked long at the sagging cotton mattress Haney had left on the narrow iron bed and the rough-hewn table and chair of pine. *He had a single life, for sure,* he thought. *Bare necessities. Bare life.* Then he closed and boarded the door until the next spring. He'd be preparing the land (as moisture allowed) to sow winter wheat.

"You look like a good mouser," he told the gray with a chuckle as he thought about Mary-Mary's joy at having the animal to fatten.

"Cat, cat!" she squealed when she saw it.

"Won't make," Cory said. "Cotton, corn, peanuts if you can find some—not wheat. Ground's too poor. Rains too often. Smut gets it."

Upton's heart sank. Yet the thought of a son by Christmas lifted his spirits.

"Feel!" Letti laughed. "Harlin's kicking."

Upton placed his hand, fingers spread, over her belly. "I feel him," he assured her, pulling her gently into his arms. "If we get another girl, I guess we'll call her Harlinda?" he teased.

Late December 1899 Harlin arrived, bald and kicking—Upton's son.

"He's a turn-of-the-century child," he told Letti. "He'll be smack in the middle of rapid change: statehood, petroleum, the growth of cities, of universities, and of milling." He envisioned a great future for this son and for Mary-Mary.

That cold January 1900, Upton and Cory finished building a one-room consignment school across the road west on a corner lot of the Haney farm for the settlers' children and Mary-Mary. "The journey of a thousand miles begins with one step," he cajoled Letti. The four families on the adjacent farms that included the Beck children had only a mile to travel to that location. Mary-Mary and Letti could walk or ride a pony the eighth of a mile in most weather, for Letti had both organized the school and persuaded the families to support her teaching there.

She carried Harlin with her in his basket until his second birthday. Then Upton made a carrier to strap on her back. By May, she prepared and corrected lessons while Mary-Mary made the goose-tallow candles with the rag wicks. School closed for summer harvest and spring planting. Winters, the kerosene lamps and cut stacks of wood were supplied by Upton. Often, he went early to start the fire in the iron stove. They usually had to stoke it at least once before school ended at noon. Country people needed their children home to eat and then help with the evening chores.

The older children of fourteen or more could not attend if the cotton, corn, hay, or garden needed planting or harvesting or if the ground needed plowing before it dried.

One couldn't risk good seed in a clodded field. Often, they never returned due to work on the farms.

"What a heaven," Upton often murmured in spite of that sacrifice for some of the children. Life seemed good to him in fat years or lean. Late evenings he assumed further teaching of Mary-Mary and Harlin with Bible or poetry by Longfellow and Walt Whitman while Letti tended to the house. His optimism, his gratitude for the smallest things, often seemed naive to her, he knew. She could not trust life as he did. But then, she had seen tragedy in these parts that he hadn't.

Once she had said, "Promise, you'll not let the outside world change us. There are those, Upton, who are jealous of great love, of success, of other's happiness. They can be monsters. They can't spoil our life unless one of us allows it, or they kill us. Promise me you will *never* lose your faith. It's like a water well in this desert for me. I live so full of fear for Mary-Mary and for Harlin."

He just shook his head and opened his arms to her. "You silly little bird. No one could *ever* hurt someone as precious as you." With his thumb, he pressed away the warm tears from her cheeks, then kissed her. "You seemed to have no fear of anything before the children came. It's no different now."

"I'm different now," she said. "Their lives and my life are two different things."

Cory and Louisa moved to Wanette. Louisa had decided that. Letti felt sure they'd stay there, even if the Haney place were a castle. Letti didn't blame them for wanting off to themselves. Already, Louisa had fifteen piano students, and Cory had begun a made-to-order furniture business that he started with cane-yard furniture until he had the funds for the pine and oak furniture he hoped to sell.

He could create shelves, chairs, love seats, and tables with a handsaw, a sharp knife for grooving, and vine ties. When sanded smooth, he painted them, rubbed and waxed, or varnished them to order. They sold fast, especially to people passing through, and he had only been at it for six months. He ingeniously arranged to ship items using mail orders from an advertisement in the *Harper's Bazaar*, the single magazine available to them.

Louisa inferred they'd build a two-story house soon. She wanted wrap-around porches for sure, she told Letti, who didn't want to tell Upton about their conversation. She knew that he already missed Cory's company and his help. When winter weather broke, Upton needed to leave for Guthrie to file the Haney place as their own. Guthrie would be the capital when statehood came, a thing expected soon. The trip would take ten days on horseback. "Louisa and Cory need to stay with you while I'm away," he told her. "I'll speak to Cory about it."

"They're both too busy and too far away to stay with us," Letti defended. "We'll be fine. Mary-Mary is a lot of help now that she's almost seven. Don't worry. I'll have Paint and the new wagon if I need to go to town. And I have my rifle should trouble come. Besides, school families will be by most days. You're not to worry," Letti assured. "I know how to take care of us."

Late one evening on the third day that they were alone, three cowboys that Letti had seen at the box suppers stopped by the well. She put the children in their bedroom with the firm instruction to "stay quiet." Two of the men ambled toward the corral and the horses. The third looked toward the house, the water dipper at his mouth. She dropped the curtain, took the rifle from the wall, and hid it in her skirt folds as she stepped outside.

"Do you need vitals?" she asked, masking her wariness of them.

"We're lookin' to buy horses," the tallest of the three volunteered. "Already et."

"Ask at the blacksmith shop in town, they'll know where the best ones are. Ours are all up in years, need young ones ourselves. One's already let out to pasture," she said, thinking of Horse. Then she called over her shoulder as if Upton were home but busy.

"Know where a body could buy horses, Upton?" She laughed lightly. "He's chinking the north wall against winter. Gets cold here."

"Never mind," the stranger called, dumping the rest of the dipper in the dust. "Thanks for the drink," he added, tipping his hat.

She nodded, closed the door, and leaned back on it. She felt weak as a reed in the wind. The sight of their unkempt figures still saturated her mind. They wore beards and leather and soiled shirts. All of them looked tall and stout.

She dared a peek out of the muslin curtains again. "Thank God," she muttered as they rode away. She drew a deep breath of relief, then called Mary-Mary. "Bring Harlin, our supper's ready."

"Were you scared, Mama?"

Letti looked at her evenly, deciding she should tell Mary-Mary an uncomfortable thing. "Very. That's exactly why I pretended your father was here.

Your father is an honorable man who protects women. Some men only respect other men and will harm women because often they are stronger and can."

"So they're . . . they're . . ." Mary-Mary stopped as if she didn't know how to think about men unlike her uncle Cory and her father.

"There really isn't a word other than . . ." Letti hesitated.

"Monsters," Mary-Mary said softly, her voice breaking a little as a tear rolled down her cheek.

"Monsters," Letti agreed regretfully, then smoothed the tear away with a napkin.

"What are women called who don't respect men?" she asked, wide-eyed.

Letti regarded her quietly, then decided she should know. "Whores. A whore is a woman who cares nothing for a man's life, only what she can take from him if she becomes whatever he wants."

"Can a wife do that?"

Letti didn't know whether to laugh or cry. "Yes and no. When you are older, we'll talk about it. Hope that you never have to give up your very self to just survive. Life can be very hard mentally and emotionally for women, Mary. Men often suffer and die in physical struggles—even wars." She shivered, thinking of Harlin and war. "To be fair, life can be difficult, even tragic for both men and women."

"I think life's a thing to keep, Mama," Mary-Mary said, a question still in her expression like a shred of doubt.

"To keep, to save, and to share," Letti assured her with a hug.

A bright afternoon sunbeam slipped through the west wall where mud chinking in the logs had fallen away around the hole she had made. "We'll mix some mud and repair that wall after supper," she said, turning aside to replace the rifle. She hesitated for a moment, for she thought an eye peered at her through the hole in the wall. She'd made it that summer to let in more air before this chilly fall arrived.

Mary-Mary nodded agreeably. "I'll help."

Letti wanted no one peering in to see that they were actually alone. That night, she didn't close her eyes and slept fully dressed with the rifle at her side. Both the sun and Upton wakened her at dawn.

"It's Upton," he assured her. Hurriedly, she placed the rifle back on the rack and opened the door for his embrace.

"Tracks outside," he muttered.

"Several straggling cowboys came by, but they left without trouble. Said they wanted horses, but they didn't look as if they could buy any."

"Think they wanted to steal a few?"

She nodded, and an unmistakable frown furrowed Upton's brow.

"I hope this isn't the first scent of trouble ahead. We've worked so hard," he said. "Well, no use to worry. The Haney farm's legally ours now."

"You wash for breakfast, you must be starved," Letti said, and she began to mix biscuit dough. "We'll have side meat and gravy with them. Wake Mary-Mary. She's missed you so."

CHAPTER IV

The Cougar

By November '07, Upton had winter crops sown or ripening. He had gone before daylight to the Haney cabin to finish shuttering its four windows. The logs were chinked, the wood floor was installed (available now due to the sawmill), and a stone fireplace was built. An oak ladder led to the sleep area above the storage and closet.

He hoped to thatch a few spots on the roof this morning before heading on horseback for Wanette to help Cory and Louisa with the town council prepare for a street dance and supper to celebrate statehood. He expected Letti and the children to come by wagon. Cory would follow their wagon on horseback after he finished digging the potatoes. He'd been eighteen years developing the farms and establishing his family. Mary-Mary was almost twelve now and Harlin seven by Christmas.

There were banners and flags to raise, bleachers and stands to build. He kissed Letti good-bye, thinking to see all of them there later. Letti wanted to help with the food the next afternoon. Pots of stew and beans and large pans of ham, ribs, and corn bread were planned. She had promised pies. The pie dough was ready now. Cory insisted that he help her finish digging fall vegetables: the turnips, potatoes, and carrots. "I'll accompany you and Mary to Wanette in the wagon," he told her, for she had promised the rest of their garden to her brother and Louisa.

"There should be several bushels of vegetables for Louisa to can or store in the ground," she assured him.

Mary-Mary sat peeling the apples for pies under a blackjack tree, its yellow and red leaves drifting down from time to time to appliqué the burnished carpet around her. Harlin played with his carved wooden horse and plow in the loose dust nearby. "I'm planting wheat," he told her.

"Go west, young man, go west. That's where you plant wheat."

"I am!" he responded hotly.

Mary-Mary set the apples aside to help Letti carry a basket of potatoes to the house, one on either side to share its weight, when Letti Pearl saw the cougar slinking toward them.

Cory had left his rifle on his saddle, too far away to reach. Polly, his mare, nickered and flared her nostrils. She pulled at reins he'd looped and tied to the corner corral post.

"Cory!" Letti yelled, dropping her side of the basket first, running toward Harlin, who had ignored the commotion. "Run, Mary!" she screamed as Cory ran toward them from the garden plot, stumbling over spilled potatoes as he tried to reach the rifle. But neither reached Mary-Mary before the cat reached her, seeing his most vulnerable prey.

"Harlin!" she screamed, trying to jar him from his absorption in his games.

The cat leapt for Mary-Mary's upper torso as she ran toward the cabin's shelter. Letti screamed, "No!" In that instant, she saw the bright awareness flash in Mary-Mary's eyes as her arm raised in the split second of defense that saved her life but knocked her to the ground. The crack of the rifle caught the cougar in its left temple, and it fell across her.

Letti had grabbed up Harlin by the waist and dragged him as she ran. Now she put him down and grabbed Mary-Mary from under the cougar. She shielded her daughter's eyes from the bleeding stump of her arm, torn away at the elbow. The cougar lay stretched across a clump of blood-tinged dry yellowed leaves beside them. Letti jerked the kerchief from her neck to tourniquet Mary-Mary's arm.

Cory lifted her and followed Letti into the house. Harlin's attention seemed riveted on his sister now. Rushing with focused purpose to the house, Letti swept the table free of flour, pans, and dough with her free arm. "The whiskey," she instructed Cory.

"Don't die, don't die!" Harlin cried, tears making roads down his dusty cheeks.

"She's not going to die. You go around the table and hold her other hand."

After drenching the arm to clean it, she pointed high on the cupboard for the laudanum and gave Mary-Mary a spoonful. "Be brave, darling," she murmured as she told Cory to bring the flat iron, cleaning cloths, and vinegar.

"You may as well see this, Harlin. Heaven knows we can't learn too much about how to survive on this earth."

That Cory moved quickly and quietly pleased her. Her flat iron sizzled when she checked it with a bit of sputum on her finger, for she kept it ready on a raised stone in the kerosene stove for the many clean-garment needs. Grasping it with a heavy pot holder, she pushed it across the vinegar-soaked cloth to clean it.

Faithfully, Harlin stood by Mary-Mary, clutching her hand. Letti placed a strip of leather between her daughter's teeth. Mary-Mary stared at Letti and the iron, terror distorting her young face. "Turn your head away," Lettie ordered calmly. "It will be over in less than a minute. I promise. Cory, you'd better hold her still. I *must* seal the wound." Her very bowels turned at the sound of the iron on flesh and vessels as she cauterized the raw wound.

"Such a little arm," she murmured, the odor of Mary-Mary's flesh in her nostrils. Letti looked into Cory's tearing eyes, her own face wet with tears. They held the glance, sharing their suffering for a future changed—not just the day. Mary-Mary had fainted.

Harlin had begun a weeping that shook him. The trauma of the moment pulled loud wails from his depths.

Tenderly, Cory pried Harlin's hand from Mary's and lifted him up for a warm hug. He put him down for a nap with a lump of raw sugar that he'd tied inside a bit of white muslin for him to hold. His lips were soon slack with sleep.

"I should get her to the doctor in town—if he's there," Letti said. "Upton needs to know as well," she said. She saturated a square of clean muslin with kerosene and placed it gently against the fresh but cauterized wound. Then she bound it with more white muslin.

"She'll be fine until morning," Cory said. "She's so shocked by it, rest seems best."

"I'm worried about . . . about . . ." She couldn't make herself say it.

"I know, sis," he said. "And the thing's dead. We have no way to see if he will drink."

"He wasn't foaming at the mouth."

"No," he agreed solemnly.

*   *   *

Upton left before the dance began for Letti and the children hadn't come into town, and he felt concern that something unexpected had happened.

Besides rumors of cougars, rumors that ruffians were making trouble for more than a few families who had worked for over a dozen years to create prosperous farms with good buildings circulated regularly. To Upton, statehood meant law that might protect them. To thugs, it meant time was short for their thievery.

Letti had told some of the Youngers who were still around about their concerns and the rumors of farm claim jumpers in case they needed their help to pit power against power. To discourage hoodlums from stealing the farm by scaring them off would hopefully prevent them from burning them out—the common method before outright murder.

Cory had strung the cat up in a tree so no one would touch it when they passed by—a sickness prevention should it indeed be rabid. Upton saw it when he rode up, slid off the saddle without tethering his new gelding, Nameless, and rushed into the house.

Mary-Mary had wakened from her faint but had begun racking sobs, so Letti Pearl held her close the twenty miles to Dr. Rice's office. Letti thought her heart might break when Mary-Mary said, "Thank you, Mama, for fixing my arm." Nightmares plagued her off and on during the nights that followed. Upton insisted on holding her through the hours until dawn each time the nightmares came.

Cory had gone on home to Louisa after the doctor saw her. Dr. Rice told them that had they had ice and a doctor who could do the surgery near enough, the arm might have been saved.

"Someday," he had murmured, "we'll have a hospital for such tragedies. Unhappily, we're lucky to have a few procedures such as the one you used. I'd have done the same thing, Letti. There's no way to stitch the skin together now. We'll just watch it, see how it heals. Keep the stump clean until then."

The following day, instead of getting in pumpkins or melons before an expected November freeze, they left for Ardmore with Mary-Mary and Harlin. They had been told by Dr. Rice that he would telegraph their need and schedule an appointment there for a new vaccination developed by Pasteur, but very scarce. They would need to take her to that clinic each month for a series of three painful vaccinations, for there was no other known way yet to recognize or to prevent the disease of rabies when the animal was dead.

But before the second vaccination, they lived in Ardmore instead of on their farm, an event they would never have predicted. Louisa promised them she would find a teacher for the one-room consignment school in rural Briartown. For when they returned from Ardmore that first trip for Mary-Mary's vaccination, a federal marshal followed them in from Wanette where they had stopped to see Cory and Louisa before going on home. Cory told them a lawman had been around asking questions, so Upton's confrontation with the marshal wasn't unexpected. His arrest was, however.

When Upton could not explain blood on bedding and on the floor of Haney's cabin, when the old man could not be located, the marshal arrested him for murder, handcuffed him, and set off with him on horseback for Guthrie. "At least it isn't Arkansas and Judge Parker's court," Upton muttered to Letti as he swung into the saddle.

"But those crooks framed him!" Letti protested. "To steal our hard work, our land, our home!"

Late 1800s had seen the last of Parker's justice, but the marshal didn't know whether to believe Upton's plea that he had been set up by the hoodlums so that they could steal his place.

"Court at Guthrie has to decide that," the marshal insisted.

"Be gone by then, marshal," Upton said.

"You filed it?"

"I did, but that's not been a guarantee, and you know it when dollars can change hands."

The marshal looked at Letti and the children. "Saddle up," he told her. "We'll escort you as far as we can to shelter with friends or family."

Letti Pearl ignored him. She and the children tried to enter their own gate, but the three ruffians who said they had wanted horses a few weeks before bounded out of the house.

"Your man's about to be hung for murder! Maybe you helped him hide the body!" one of them yelled. The other two threw their heads back in raucous laughter.

Letti didn't blink or waiver in her response. "Mr. Haney left for the gold fields. Papers will prove it at Guthrie. You best be traveling, for I have help coming that will shoot you between the eyes if you touch us."

She fiercely hoped her bluff got them off the place.

"Oh, I'm real scared, aren't you, Harvey?" They were all still bearded and needing a bath. Looked to be in their twenties and lazy, if looks could tell.

"Like when your man was home the last time we met."

About that time, Upton turned in his saddle and yelled back at her. "Let it go, Letti. Take the children to Cory's. Do it now!"

—

She did not move immediately. She had left her land for this land. It seemed a part of her now—the land. But beside her, Mary-Mary and Harlin held her gaze, both of them still more a part of her than the land.

"You circled back and spied on us like cowards. You will reap what you have sown," she said softly, turned, and mounted one of the young sorrels Upton had brought back from Guthrie that stood at the yard fence. She pulled Mary-Mary up behind and put Harlin in front. Paint and Horse had been turned out to pasture, both over thirteen and no longer sure-footed, either of them.

"That's my horse!" the man called Harvey yelled. "All those animals are ours! And I want that rifle at your side. I seen it before or I'd have had my way with—"

The marshal had lagged behind Upton a few lengths as if to keep an eye on Letti until she seemed safely on her way.

"Let her be!" the marshal warned before he could finish.

Letti whipped the horse around, telling Mary-Mary to hang on tight. Her arms protected Harlin, who had handfuls of the sorrel's mane.

"Let her go!" another one said. "We'll pick it up later. She won't be far away."

When Upton showed up at Cory's place in Wanette two weeks later, Letti rushed into his arms. "The marshal had been shot in the back en route," he explained.

"Unarmed, I just hid from the gang that did it—I didn't know them," he said, as if assuring her none of her own had committed the murder. "They went on, and I turned myself in at Guthrie. The judge said my story was believable, that I wasn't the first person who had proved up a good claim to be run off it with such a frame. He said I could go back and shoot them, but that they have, no doubt, filed their own claim on our place and Haney's, swearing Haney dead and me hung and that no one in Guthrie cared."

"Then you *would* be hung."

"Or some of their other hoodlum friends could seek revenge on me or on you and the children. I couldn't stand that."

"Right. And those hoodlums know it," Letti argued. "What do we do?"

"Well, I'm wearing my lucky undershirt," he said without explaining the silver and gold pieces he had never spent or spoken of to her. "I didn't know what doctors in Ardmore charged. I'll explain that later," he told her with a wink.

Always lucky enough to find railroad work or to trade skins for his start on the land, he had saved them for an emergency. Then the good Lord, as he always called Him, had done the rest with bountiful crops and a market for them. Maddy's coins would provide for their new start.

"Whoever heard of a lucky undershirt! Can't be explained," Lettie said. "And what does the doctor's charge have to do with it?"

Upton smiled and caught her close to him, his arm about her waist. "The fishing and hunting, the days in the sun will be scarce too. I've had two weeks to think and to be glad we're alive. I want us to *stay* alive. We're opening a drugstore in Ardmore. The town's large enough now to prosper us. I know how to prepare the elixirs, the tonics, and the salves. We can have a sandwich counter, a gift and sweets area, tobacco. Save folks money and make some ourselves."

"And the law to back you, Upton," Cory said, walking up beside them. "Require a bill of sale for your farm. You aren't in jail or dead. Haney's place may be lost, but I think you can force them legal-like to buy yours. It's worth a try. I'll go with you. So will some friends to witness for your character and the truth."

"He's right," Louisa said, joining them in the yard. "We'll go with you for references. It will go a long way. Why, Cory's even been preaching once a month. He's real popular when he talks. People come in to hear him from all around—even from Guthrie when he preached a revival at Edmond."

"But money, Upton," Lettie said. "We'll need money." He just smiled and hugged her. "And I'd like to hear Cory preach."

"We'll do all that: get payment for our farm, open our store, and hear Cory preach." Cory flashed an appreciative smile at Upton before speaking.

"I never talked about it, but I thought I was going to die before the age of eighteen. Then Upton made me well. I wasn't the same inside when my health came back. It was as if I had something important to do yet—not a thing to talk about, to sound, well, uppity, but a thing to *do*."

She hugged him. "It seems all our lives have a new direction. Maybe I can start a consignment school for rural children in Ardmore. They say there's a normal school at Edmond that will be a four-year college when completely organized. Maybe I can get a real certificate, pass the test they give. Teachers are needed all over the state."

"I'll take you up there to check on it, sis, if you need me to help."

"Yes, we'll help you both get the farm sold instead of stolen and a teaching certificate for a country school at Ardmore," Louisa declared with certainty.

"Is Ardmore where I can grow wheat?" Harlin asked.

"No, no, son. Not west enough," Upton laughed.

"And a teacher for my little country school at . . . at home," Letti pleaded. She looked at Upton. "You're tenderhearted and a better person than I am. I wanted to shoot those hoodlums and might have if I hadn't heard you say 'Let it go.' I've been hardened. I'm—"

"You're a good woman, tough but loving. I want you and the children to live—for me and for each other. I can't always be close to protect you on the claims. I can in a store."

So their lives turned toward new directions with a courage different from Letti's, but a kind she recognized, respected, and willingly followed without protest. A man who would ride a pony from Ohio and do what Upton had done with his bare hands was no coward.

"I love you, Upton," she said.

"That says it all," he responded.

———

*   *   *

Almost a week passed after accepting Cory's hospitality when Upton said, "Let's go look for a building to buy or a lot to put a building on for our store."

Those thugs had complied with the purchase of their farm when faced with fifty local men on horseback that resembled a posse that might hang them. They got a hundred dollars from the three of them, a pittance for their hard labor. Still, it would help.

"We'll watch the children for you," Louisa volunteered.

"I want to go too," Mary-Mary said. "I want to go to Oklahoma City. I want to meet Kate Bernard. I wish I was old enough to do something so fine as help others have better lives."

"Me, too," chimed in Harlin.

"So you shall," Letti agreed. "You'll be our first employees too, so you should have a say in where we stop and how we stock our store."

"Are you serious?" Harlin asked, obviously pleased.

"I'm serious!" Letti laughed. "We're family."

Letti continued to teach six-hour days after testing well at the Edmond Normal School. She relocated in Ardmore in a one-room deserted cabin that she called Oak Grove. Her fifteen students ranged from six years to seventeen years. With donated piano and violin and canvases and paints, she soon included lessons in music and drawing with units on the great painters and composers. Late afternoons and Saturdays, she helped in the pharmacy.

She leased a carriage so that Mary-Mary and Harlin could be kept warm during the winter trips to the country one-room schoolhouse. Mary-Mary was almost thirteen and Harlin eight when they established the store in Ardmore's downtown. Upton built the shelves and laboratory, ordered the bottles, jars, and labels, then Upton proceeded to stock their store with healing spices, teas, tonics, cosmetics, and salves. He made the soaps, the cleaning solutions, the starch, and dyes, all recipes from Morgan and Maddy who had brought them to Ohio from the isles their forefathers left: Ireland, Scotland, and Wales. That first year left him little time for sleep.

"I'm going to be a teacher too," Mary-Mary said with certainty. She assisted Letti with classes at Oak Grove, then both of them, with Harlin, helped Upton at the pharmacy evenings and summers. (Letti thought the Pharmacy an appropriate name.) A daily dessert menu and pictures of their products decorated the front windows. Business thrived.

"I'm going to be a farmer," Harlin announced while still a boy. The family sat at supper. "Just wheat and cattle though," he emphasized. "I'll have white-faced cattle on a thousand acres of wheat and grass out west."

"Then you'll be a rancher," Upton advised.

"He's seen those new Herefords that came into the country from Scotland," Letti said.

"Same thing," Harlin quipped, always reluctant to give up the last word. "Farmer-rancher."

When he returned from school each day, he sprinkled sawdust on the wooden floor to catch the dust, then swept the store for Upton. The building they found for the store had adequate living quarters behind and two upstairs rooms, which Letti used for a sitting room and extra bedroom.

Upton thought Harlin's dream a fantasy to equal his own as a boy in Ohio before he understood the dark side of dreams. Still, he admitted to Letti that he loved the turn their lives had taken as much as he had loved developing the land. Harlin had the law to protect and even advance his dream.

"I imagined a wheat farm and found a paradise. Then carved the violin that lured your dancing feet to join me there. The farm we developed together grew Mary-Mary and Harlin, richer blessings than wheat could ever be. This place will provide for our future, Letti. You'll see!" Ecstatic, he grabbed her about the waist and swept her off her feet while she clung fast to him and smiled back at laughing eyes.

"Put me down!" she squealed, secretly delighted at this habit of his when his joy for living touched her.

Besides his lotions, rubs, elixirs, and poultices, he created his dyes of polk berries, turmeric, and concord grape hulls and the barks of trees. Blackjack bark and crème of tartar set the color. Women came from miles around for it to tint the bleached muslin that would become the shirts and dresses for their families.

After a few years, the store never wanted for business. The Upton Rush family prospered along with the young state. By 1910, the legal center moved to Oklahoma City, the new capitol. Those long trips to Guthrie on horseback ended.

Harlin graduated from Letti's school at sixteen. He enrolled at the agricultural college at Stillwater, Oklahoma, and stayed two years before going to France in the Great War. By postwar 1921, there was a year of celebration on Oklahoma farms. Wheat and other grains sold well, two to four dollars a bushel. European demand for it caused the price to soar. And the flu of 1918 faded in its extremes, then left the state.

"We thank you, Lord, for our spared lives and good health," Upton prayed as he blessed their bread daily, for not one of them here or in Ohio had died of that plague while almost six hundred thousand lives were taken from the country and thirty million in the known world.

Oklahoma raised thousands of oil derricks and boasted great prosperity on a land many said to be the largest and richest for growing winter wheat for a world hungry for bread. When Harlin announced he was off to wheat country farther west in Canadian County, they encouraged him to go raise his wheat and white-faced cattle.

Mary-Mary received her basic teaching certificate from the normal school at Edmond, and while Harlin fought in France, she finished a four-year degree to teach science. One year later, she earned her master's degree in medical research from the Methodist University in Oklahoma City.

Letti gave up her teaching to help with the store full-time after the children moved on with their lives. She bought calico for two cents a yard, then Upton sold it for five cents a yard. Percale that she bought for five cents a yard sold for ten cents a yard. She made pastries on the weekend by order: cakes, pies, cookies, and bread. She beaded tobacco pouches and moccasins of soft leather that sold as fast as she could make them. The years flew by as the pharmacy metamorphosed into a variety store and pharmacy with a restaurant in the back.

*   *   *

Mary-Mary let nothing—certainly not the loss of her arm—impede her confidence. She accepted a second teaching position in Oklahoma City in the chemistry department of the Methodist College, declaring that nothing, a man included, would interfere with her teaching career.

By 1929 when the world economic crash came, oil derricks rose in Tulsa.

"Some wells pump thousands of dollars a day," Upton told Lettie. "But that prosperity only comes to them. Our customers are fewer and fewer—giving up, leaving for California to pick fruit. We've plowed up a lot of land for crops, and there are no funds to maintain it, to keep up equipment, to pay the taxes. The rich are richer for it, and the poor are penniless."

"We'll manage. We'll stay, and we'll help those we can because we know how." Letti spoke softly as if grieving for others, their own altered circumstances of no real concern.

"You've outgrown your pessimism, Letti. You're a blue-blooded pioneer woman at last. You remind me of my father. He was a source of motivation for us all for his hands were never idle unless he slept. No opportunity to provide for us or others got past him. 'Consider the ant,' he would quote. 'Consider the lilies.' But Harlin. I'm so worried about him and his young family: married only four years, a young son, fifty cent wheat.

—

46

"For ordinary farmers like him and business people like us and our customers, for the local bank that holds unsecured funds, this crash means another beginning."

"Don't you worry me, Upton. Why, we're still young and strong. We have each other, and Harlin is no quitter, he'll hang on. This is another storm—like a duster. It will pass."

Upton still looked young, but Letti recognized that he had begun to feel the effects of hard labor and long hours. "I'm tired," he told her, standing there at the kitchen doorway while she kneaded a lump of dough at the table for tomorrow's bread.

At the end of something, something else must happen, she thought. *His fifty-fourth birthday had come and gone. No gray hairs had appeared, no wrinkles.* She shoved the dough aside and turned to the stack of dishes to wash and dry.

"A door will open," Letti encouraged, hoping to lift his mood, to give him the hope he seemed to have lost. "Why, you've always been the one to—" she stopped and spun about to face him, thinking nothing, sensing everything.

He reached for the open door's facing, his expression saying he wanted to reach her but could not move. "Lettie!" he gasped, his intense pain now crowding his eyes with agony. With his other hand, he clutched his chest.

Letti screamed. "No! Oh no!"

She rushed to him as if she could stop the tragedy happening before her. He slumped into her arms, pulling her to the floor. She lay there with him, weeping, knowing what was happening.

She felt for his pulse and found none.

Upton died in her arms of a massive heart attack.

Mary-Mary came to stay with her for a week. Harlin, now almost thirty, came to the funeral with his wife, Rena Lily, and their three-year-old son, Gavin.

Rena and Gavin seemed strangers to Letti for she seldom saw them. True to intent, Harlin had settled on an Indian land lease until he could eventually buy his own farm in Canadian County, a county seat and part of the hard red-winter wheat belt that exported tons of wheat abroad.

The Cheyenne owner couldn't sell this farm that Harlin loved. The agency discouraged it and handled most of the leases for the tribal members at the Concho agency. Though his own dream seemed as tarnished to Letti as Upton's dream of land, Harlin happily related a description of the farm as if it were his own. He spoke of the wild possum grapes on a canyon that skirted *his* wheat farm and of corn that grew eight feet high. "My native grass grows thigh high, Mom," he related.

He talked into the morning hours of a man named Danne who had developed a miracle wheat that produced twenty-five to thirty-five bushels more than the typical ten to fifteen bushels to the acre. They sat in the small parlor at the back of the store, Upton's body waiting for the burial site nearby.

"He grafted the plants in fruit jars at his kitchen table with a pair of tweezers! I thought of Pa when I heard it—Pa in his laboratory. Men with vision make things happen. Not much seed around yet—takes time. But there will be thirty-five to fifty bushel wheat to the acre soon, for his farm at least. There will be more seed each year to sell. I wish Dad could see it. His original goal will be lived in me, Ma."

She stood up from the chintz-cushioned rocker to hug him. *How he would miss Upton. How they all would miss the music of him, his energy, his dreams, his violin,* she thought, lavishing him with a smile. "Perhaps he passed the brain cell that spawned that dream to you at birth. Who knows! Best get to bed now so we'll be fresh for the funeral. Mary-Mary went to her room hours ago. Your father is *in* you, Harlin, you're part of him too, surely as the sun rises and sets. Remember it, and you will miss him less."

Before he said good night, he stood in the spare bedroom door to tell her, "Won't be long before you can come see the farm, Ma. It looks no better than the times, but that will change. We'll soon start building Route 66 that will lead right into Pottawattamie and Murray counties."

———

48

"We?"

"Yeah. It's President Roosevelt's idea. It was in the Sunday paper. We'll build it with a crew of men and mules. It will be extra money for the farm."

Letti knew that the two-dollar and four-dollar wheat sold now for forty cents a bushel or less. Thirty or forty bushels would flood the market and sell for even less—cost more to raise. She bit her bottom lip. Many hungry would stay hungry; she had seen the control over the flow of grain and the price for it. The motives of growers and government seemed at odds to her, but she could not discourage her son, especially now when they prepared to bury Upton.

Extra money for the farm, she thought bitterly. She would pray for the day that Harlin could realize extra money *from* the farm instead. She had not felt bitterness toward the land before, but toward the market that betrayed it. She yielded to nature's capriciousness. She loved her men and the land. Harlin must not die of hard work and a broken dream.

"I want you to have a fair reward for your labor. The price and the market are so wrong."

"Aw, Mom," he said, walking closer to hug her. "Hard work is good for me, it won't kill me young. Don't you worry. Besides, I know here," he emphasized, his fist on his chest, "that nothing ever dies. Even the dust we all run to in the end is alive."

He let her go, but not before he kissed her brow. "Maybe farmers need to play a larger role in marketing—someday, some way. Now, it takes all we can give to save and care for the land and grow the crops. Even getting them to the buyer or to storage can be a hassle. No one comes to do it for us. All I know is that I love the land, the life, and the challenge," he assured.

"You are your father's son," she said softly, reaching to touch his cheek as she retired to her room.

CHAPTER V

The New Start

The year of 1930 had just begun. The new beginning spun both Letti and Harlin like tops into a future never imagined so fine in spite of loss and economic depression.

After Upton's death, Letti moved on with her life by selling the store and sorrounding improvements for ten thousand dollars to an oil man who needed an investment.

Before his father's death, Harlin had hired on at the Rock Island rail yards' four-to-midnight shift besides building roads for the Canadian County day shift. He often farmed most of the weekends. Rena and Gavin shared the chores: the milking and feeding, the gathering of eggs, and filling the cream cans for each Saturday's selling. They hoped to save enough to buy their own land besides leasing the Indian land they lived on. From the El Reno Hotel to his dugout[2] and to the cabin on the lease when he and Rena married, Letti knew that Harlin dreamed of building his own home on his own land soon.

---

[2]   Temporary shelters were *dug out* of hills in Oklahoma by a homesteader or new comer until a permanent home could be built. If the season allowed, a *soddy* (a home built of mud and straw bricks) was built.

"Don't worry, Ma. I'll be building my own house by next crop," he told her after the funeral for Upton.

"Times are too hard for that, but I like your optimism," she said with a smile. She had decided to invest in Harlin—her secret for now. Dressed in calico of faded blue with a white lace collar that she had crocheted herself, she twisted graying hair into a bun atop her head to ride beside him to town in the one-ton truck. He was helping her settle in the El Reno Hotel, his former home, until she found her own place.

Mary-Mary had bought her own place in an excellent area of Oklahoma City near her chosen school, and she had also purchased one of the new Ford automobiles so popular in Oklahoma.

Although the Depression and the persistent dust storms and illnesses that the dust brought commonly caused calamity around her, Letti Pearl labored patiently and faithfully with an attitude of gratitude that did not waiver.

Mary-Mary spent a week with her each summer unless she attended summer school for she aspired to be Dr. Mary Rush.

"I'd like to stay in research and eventually make it my only career. There are cures for these terrible fevers in Oklahoma and for these new respiratory illnesses these dust storms cause. I'd like to help find them. I'm sure of this though, Mother," she told Letti. "Most are from river bacteria and the mosquito instead of the dust."

"Human waste," Letti said. "I wish your uncle Cory would run for the legislature. We need laws to protect health and the environment. We need to control human and animal waste and protect our water supplies. Only people who will act on their convictions change this world."

"We need to protect the land!" Mary-Mary retorted. "I know you're still angry with it, but conservation *must* come before it's *all* blown away and more children die from mud in their lungs and the hunger attacks that plague the world as well. As for Uncle Cory, he'd better hurry. He's not getting any younger."

"I'm no longer angry with the land. I understand the world's need for bread and this land's role in that need. This central

Oklahoma land could supply the world with bread. How could I stay angry knowing that? But don't think in either-or terms. Either-or attitudes defeat multiple options or are too limiting in almost every circumstance. Inclusive—that's the key to problem solving.

"Survival is like war," she continued. "Defense is on both land and sea or the enemy has an avenue to us. Both land and water everywhere in the world require our protection and care. Yes, even more: land, water, and the air that we must breathe require each individual and every company to actively guard them. Not just crops but all life depends on that active, responsible care."

"How right you are. Thanks, Mom. I'll teach a unit on it every semester that I teach from now on. Education may be the mother of conservation."

"Write articles about it. Publish. Be an activist like your idol," Letti encouraged.

"You're recalling my fascination with Kate Bernard's achievements."

"I am," Letti confirmed. "It always surprises the public when one person achieves what an army often can't."

From either her or Mary-Mary's house in Oklahoma City, Letti had only to walk a few blocks to catch the interurban trolley to or from the county seat where Harlin lived. She had been undecided about her own future until recently.

At the El Reno Hotel for only two months, she decided on an idea for a neighborhood store. None existed, and only the rich owned cars. Most of the population at the county seat walked or called a taxi.

Summer vacation 1930, when she concluded all her business in Ardmore, she felt a freedom to live wherever she chose, do whatever she pleased. *I have moved to El Reno. So in El Reno I must create a way to thrive, not just survive,* she thought.

She had gotten $10,000 for the store's stock, housing, storage, and all the equipment. She franchised Upton's recipes for the teas, dyes, liniments, salves, and tonics, bargaining for a 10 percent profit from the new owner's sales to be paid with evidence each July.

—

Besides the tonics and liniments and salves that she knew how to make, her own concoctions for beauty she packaged, patented, and sold door to door out of the hotel. Eventually, some buyer would change them a bit and patent them under their own name, but until then, she could generate tidy sums for her new life and cultivate customers for her own El Reno store when she opened it.

When Harlin suggested she go with him and Rena to look at the farm he planned to buy, she could hardly wait. Land and Letti had always gotten along well together.

The hotel had a carriage barn and stable. When he'd helped her in beside Rena, he said, "I've saved $3,000 in wages. People are leaving the land. They think the drought won't end, but it will. I can't buy too low, or the river will wash me out some seasons, nor too high or rains will wash topsoil down to the canyons. This farm lies almost level between the rivers with need for only a few shallow terraces."

"Sounds perfect, son. I've an investment in mind of my own: a store for my living," she told him, "so I can sit by the fire nights, remember, and write the stories I've seen this past half century. Those eastern hills of this state were wild and lawless.

I don't mean cowboys and Indians—I mean outlaws and heroes and people brave enough to carve a living out of an undeveloped pristine land where thugs were as common as malaria and the women knew how to ride and shoot as well as any man.

"I did laundry in a river and could skin a deer or scale a fish."

Lettie thought she saw Rena Lily shudder at such revelations. Gavin, almost six, caught her hand and laughed aloud.

Harlin reached to hug her as the ton truck traversed dusty bumpy roads. "A lot of homesteaders died doing what you and Dad did those fourteen years, murdered instead of chased off it by scoundrels."

"And he called it heaven," she said, a little smile revealing her pleasure at the memory.

"I remember it that way too, though I wasn't around as long. It's the life I want for my family," he said, smiling across at Rena.

"I want it too," Rena assured. "As much as you."

"This land's all still pretty new, just cleared and plowed after '89. Lots of it is still in native grass that will grow hip high when the rains come back. I'll show you a buffalo wallow on it," Harlin gushed with enthusiasm.

Letti caught his excitement. When her own store had replenished her investment in it and she could, she thought silently, then she would tell him her plan to help him buy his land.

"I've seen a few of those, son, but I haven't seen your buffalo wallow—an imprint of years gone by to remind us of what we took away, I suppose."

"Hope you got a good price for the pharmacy," he was saying.

"I sold the lodging too."

"You did? You come live with me and Rena, Mom. I'll get a larger house if we can't get this farm soon to build on. You might not like the cabin on the lease. That hotel gets expensive."

"Mary-Mary's got a house, a car, and she's on her way to a doctor's degree. You and Rena have a place large enough for yourselves until you build your own. I'll have my own place soon, and I rather like the El Reno Hotel until then."

"Has Mary-Mary got a beau?" he asked.

"Says she doesn't want one."

Letti was quiet then, wondering about Harlin's future. *What if this land he had his heart set on sold before he could buy it? Oil men weren't just looking in eastern Oklahoma for investments in land and business. They were looking here for land and minerals.*

"I'm going to buy a house here," she said. "One with a parlor I can stock with necessities. A neighborhood store for bread, flour, eggs, coffee, tea—that kind of thing. A small area up front near the door can be used for candies and gum, treats, you know. Children's school tablets and pencils, a line of beauty and healing products.

"I'll help you with the right land," she told him then, sooner than she'd planned. "I can look and ask around for my place while you're at work. Together we *will* be able to fund our new life. Mine should be in town. I'm getting older—*not old*," she emphasized. "You, on the other hand, should prepare a private place for the family you'll raise. You won't be over about twenty-five or thirty miles away. I'd be a similar distance between you and Mary-Mary."

"You're just independent," he said. "Housing in town is reasonable. Folks need the cash."

That seemed to settle things, so before January of '32, the two of them had made their choices. Harlin had his section of purchased land between the north and south Canadian rivers, a rich level land but elevated enough to stay safe from the river during heavy rains. Letti admired his choice at first sight.

She found a two-story eight-room house in the middle of El Reno only twenty miles east of Harlin, Rena, and Gavin. Three elementary schools were within six blocks of her in three directions. The high school rose west of her in the same distance. Neighborhoods surrounded her.

Two thousand dollars bought it; another thousand made the parlor a store.

The little bell on the parlor door jingled every few minutes with a customer opening it from 8:00 a.m. to closing at 6:00 p.m.

She wrote her stories on the Big Chief tablets she sold there.

Harlin did start their house as a home in progress for he wanted to build it himself. It was after Letti gave him half of the $10,000 for his farm that he spent the rest of his $3,000 for more equipment and stock. $7,000 paid for the half section, which he mortgaged for the other half. He and Rena worked together, hammering and nailing the scrap lumber and hauling up the rock for frontage. Six-year-old Gavin fetched and carried what he could after school. Summers and weekends, he farmed with Harlin. It took Gavin only a week to handle the tractor by himself. On the farm, no one thought it child exploitation, least of all Gavin. It would take them five long hard years, however, to finish their house.

They hauled rock for the foundation that footed six rooms with an upstairs that they completed over the next two years. The following year saw the screened wraparound porch with the tin tub in the corner for bathing. It would be the fifth year before they had indoor plumbing and electricity. Harlin had read how to build a fireplace, so the partially finished house was warmed with wood from the start. The interior wasn't completely finished until spring because of the blowing dirt that could spoil the paint and varnish.

So while the house grew and employment continued, the dust pursued them, and their crops failed. In 1934 and 1935, the dust seemed a dark curtain that no one could see through. Fields became deserted with equipment half buried in the dust. Tools waited, a useless extravagance. Cattle and other animals died. Food rationing seemed a norm they might cope with from now on.

"Nothing is certain but God and change," Letti assured constantly. "The next change can be better or worse. We shall hold on and see." She gave as much credit at the store as her own budget could carry, even more free penny candy than credit to the neighborhood children.

"Pity the poor who aren't on the land. Even as it blows away, it remains our only hope after God. God and land," Letti would mutter as if they were one and the same.

Until propane gas came to the county, Rena Lily cooked on a kerosene stove. Kerosene lanterns cast evening shadows now. While she prepared their meal, Harlin played Upton's violin.

Though their house sat on his own section of land, Harlin loved the Indian land more than his very own. It was near those woods and canyons on the South Canadian where he remembered seeing Rena Lily bathing Gavin then helping him into his night clothes in the flickering lantern light. He valued the struggle that enriched his life and made it memorable while it made him strong and kept him reaching for a future like a swimmer reaches with each breast stroke. He thought his life a thing to build like Route 66: by hand, often on an empty stomach and over a stretch of time. Overcoming had grown his manhood, and he *knew* it.

"I'd fancy your playing a polka," she told him.

"Then a polka you'll have," he said, rosining the bow.

The day that he met Rena Lily, her horse had dropped a shoe going past the leased land. She led it up his lane and asked for his help. Rena Lily Lind, only seventeen and due to graduate from Post Road school in a few weeks. Harlin knew he wanted her the moment he saw her. Tiny with raven-black hair and hazel eyes, he bet she barely weighed a hundred pounds. She reminded him of Letti.

"I want to thank you proper for fixing Venus's shoe," she said brightly. "Can you come for supper and meet my folks? They'll want to thank you too." She flashed a brilliant smile.

To Harlin it seemed his life hadn't really started until that moment. He revered the past and looked forward to their future.

"Venus," Letti Pearl mused when he'd told her that first day about Rena. "That's what Belle named her horse."

"Belle who?" he asked.

"Never mind," she said. "I can only remember such bits of things as a pony's name, too little and told less." His mother might be a foundling with a forever unknown history, he thought.

"I never even knew if Rose, Belle's daughter, lived or died," she had said once. "We were told she left Cory and me with the Reeds herself and checked on us a time or two each year."

Fame was like that sometimes, he thought, putting the fiddle away. *It disguised the facts when the facts weren't as interesting as legend.* Harlin had heard in the saloon before heading for Canadian County that Rose was a prostitute in Arkansas after leaving the territory. He hoped his mother never heard it.

"I hope one of your children will be named Belle," she said that day. If I had known I would have only two children, I would have named Mary-Mary Mary Belle."

After supper that evening while he repaired a fence along the east road of the Indian lease, Harlin had the quiet for more remembering. It seemed a need today, a thing to connect tomorrow and make this dirt that gritted his teeth bearable. Recalling life before the crash and his father's death, revisiting the richness of the year he and Rena married and the following days of celebration to today made these dusty days bearable.

For by July 1925, most family could come to their wedding. Times hadn't changed so drastically yet. Upton's fiddle playing and calls at the dance wakened the curious young lambs and competed with the chorusing cicadas. It was the last time he saw his father alive.

Rena Lily's folks supplied the large house for their reception. Letti brought the wedding cake and a handmade quilt for them.

His uncle Cory and aunt Louisa had four children by then, all girls. Uncle Cory, the evangelist, was going from town to town and sometimes to another state to start a Nazarene church. Louisa and the children went also so she could provide the special music. Harlin had felt such pride when he introduced his family to new neighbors and friends at the wedding.

Travel by train had become more affordable for most by then. Upton's brothers and sisters came from Ohio by train to give the couple a cash gift of $1,000. Maddy and Morgan had died several years before the wedding. He and Letti both regretted they'd never met them, though Harlin still felt he knew them from his father's tales of home in Ohio. Meeting Todd, John, Neal, Noah, Kate, Alice, and some of their families seemed odd after so many years. He tried to recall all their children's names again but gave up.

Maybe Rena and I will visit them in Ohio when this famine ends, he thought. "And it will," he said aloud like a prayer answered. *Life will be good again with fresh air and money to pay bills.*

Mary-Mary came, he recalled. She had her doctorate then. Most country folks knew her name for she had written and published her thesis on the two dreaded diseases that still took lives from time to time: malaria and typhoid.

Scallops edged Rena's dress of white lawn. Lace graced the throat and hem. Everyone had embraced her. The wedding attracted more family than Harlin had ever known and brought with it the joy of dancing, music, and feasting.

He put his tools in the truck, slapped the dust from his clothes, and opened the truck door.

The Younger and Reed cousins had aged, but well, he recalled. He knew that most, if not all, had died or left the territories now. Jim Younger and Carl Reed came by train to Letti's delight. They brought their guitars and banjo with them, so the old tunes and hymns filled the night.

"Farther Along" and "Golden Slippers," "Birmingham Jail," "You are My Sunshine," even "Little Brown Jug" rang out that July.

Then they were all gone again, and he and Rena settled into home alone.

He knew that Letti and Upton had witnessed the love beginning for them with quiet gratitude for she'd said that they reminded her of herself and Upton when they had fallen in love.

Married at the Lind house that July with family, friends, and pet dogs and cats all peppering the vast yard where croquet and horseshoe games progressed, they fled away after midnight to the rattle of tin cans following. Guests had tied them tightly to the bumper of Harlin's old truck, the same that he'd kept repaired and drove today.

What was it his mother said that day before she and his father left? "Heaven is what you make of your life now. Hell too. I trust no afterlife though I believe in a god. May His love give Upton and me an afterlife together. I would welcome such a bonus." Then she hugged and kissed him.

He knew her motto for successful living: "Do no harm." She lived it and, therefore, carried no guilt and no grudges to thwart great joy in loving her family. Best, he couldn't think of her without recalling her good works for them all and for others.

For a fact, she had prayed for those hoodlums who stole their land, though they finally had to pay a dollar price for it. "They need more than prayer," she'd said sorrowfully. "For a fact, I'm glad I didn't have to kill any of them."

He smiled to himself every time he recalled that remark. For he knew that night she might have to protect both himself and Mary-Mary.

After all the cost to both the buyer and seller, they heard that the hoodlums lost it: Letti learned from the Youngers that the young one had raped and killed the Beck girl while the others allowed it, even encouraged it, some said. A posse of self-appointed ranchers had tied all three of them to an arbor and set it afire.

"They'd have been hard-pressed to get them to a court alive," Letti said then. "Their lives are no longer wanted anywhere in the territory. But a wrong for a wrong can't be right."

Thank God, he thought, remembering it, *that law finally came to Oklahoma. When the capital moved to Oklahoma City and not so far from everywhere and the counties built their courthouses, the lawyers came. Oklahoma City itself was a big spread, no doubt about it, perhaps the largest capital city in the USA. It reached most places quite well, located in the middle of the state, more or less. Oklahoma itself covered almost seventy thousand square miles. No wonder lawlessness reigned until after 1935.* He supposed Bonnie and Clyde were the last of the celebrity gangsters.

He liked recalling his mother's words the first time she saw this Indian-land farm. "This land will sprout crops and melons like summer freckles from head to toe." The local businesses had also excited her. Their proprietors were Greek, Jewish, German, Irish, Scottish, and other immigrants. Their open doors and colorful clothes, their candy bins and cigar signs, even their pubs intrigued her.

The sight and scent of oil derricks stretching to the sky thrilled her as much as the Indian powwows that sported bright shawls, feathers, blankets, and delicious fry bread. She proclaimed that Oklahoma was a melting pot. "I love this variety and energy."

His father, Upton, may have come here from Ohio, but Upton's father, Morgan Rush, had come to Ohio as a child from England. *The Rush's had roots,* Harlin thought. Where did Letti come from?

"I was just lucky enough to be born here in this emerald place to someone," she'd said once. "A Scottish trapper went his own way to return once a year. I was special to him. He was a man with a brogue that always echoes down memory and lives in my heart still—a man with curly black hair and a red beard and sideburns.

"I called him Papi, but Mami Reed called him McLeod. He always brought me a present of handkerchiefs, a locket, a ring."

—

These words spoken in his childhood by his mother still haunted him. A tear had slid down her cheek when she said them.

"There was no help to be got for birthing in the hills in December with a blizzard outside," Letti had told him. "They said our ma died having me. I guess she must have, or it was a birthing that couldn't be told." Harlin knew that the man named McLeod had been unforgettable, a distant echo in the caverns of her soul. Harlin yearned to know more about his mother's earliest days by the Ouachita's woods and rivers for the bits of information that had no home echoed in his soul as well.

As for her Papi, he left for Alaska after a visit in the early '20s, and she never saw him again. Mary-Mary was at work in Oklahoma City and Harlin was already in Canadian County at the time, so neither of them ever met the man called McLeod that might have been their grandfather.

"She was born and lived and will surely die as we all will," he said, crawling into the truck to return home. "Thank God for that and may the rest—rest."

*   *   *

Late November 1935, the land lay frigid. Stinging sleet from the north covered it. There was little moisture in the sleet. Like bits of crystal, it lay loose and dry. Then after a week of the hammering wind, it crusted there in bumpy ripples over the new-sewn wheat, over the pasture and yard grasses that ran along Route 66 in mile-long hills. Each hill fell into a low meadow, slashed with canyons from north to south and lined with evergreen and chinaberry, with native elm and willows. The wild currant, sand plum, and grape bent bare with the ice now, and the canyons' streams crusted thick with ice. Beneath the ice, the black silt that blew in from South Texas waited in frozen mounds for the thaw.

The farm stock—the cattle, horses, and sheep—huddled in fenced corners or in the deep canyons, their backs white with sleet that matted their eyelashes as if frosted with granulated sugar.

They thirsted in these early-morning hours just past dawn. Each farmer of a sixty, a quarter, a half section, or a section or more of the land would walk down with his ax and cut holes in the canyon ice or pond ice near the banks so the animals could drink instead of walking on the ice and breaking through it to drown. Many had already died from the drought, but a few canyons and ponds held enough water to last until spring. Harlin credited it to a few underground springs.

Some of the men and their wives, some of the foremen of the larger ranches, would risk horses on the icy hills and plains. Others who had no ponds or canyons had tanks near their houses that they filled from a well. These would pump fresh water into the steel or concrete tanks. At these farms, the cattle lumbered up from the pasture in a straggling line toward water.

Hay stocks were low. Debt grew from necessary purchases of feed to keep animals and poultry alive. These supplied their food: milk, eggs and meat, all becoming frighteningly scarce for many families and for the local stores that bought this produce. Banks took over much of the land for taxes, and it fell into the hands of the wealthy who leased it to sharecroppers, usually for a third of the increase. Cash remained scarce; wheat at forty cents or less a bushel and eggs for under ten cents a dozen barely kept a family going.

Centipedes, black widow spiders, and scorpions thrived. Grasshoppers and jackrabbits by the thousands ate everything. And all twelve inches of Harlin's topsoil had blown away.

The hip bones on most of the cattle, especially the Holstein stock, had begun to stick out like stunted misplaced wings. Without rain soon, even the springs would fail due to vanishing ground water in the subterranean streams. With the long duration of the freeze, it became more difficult to get hay to all of them. In this Canadian County section of the long hilly valley, most of the herds were milk herds of Holstein or mixed Jersey and Guernsey. Harlin and Rena sold the cream in town for twenty cents a gallon. It bought the staples of sugar, coffee, flour, and shortening.

They fed the whey to hogs or turned it into cottage cheese. Each family daily kept enough whole milk for their own use, separating some into cream and whey for making the butter and cheese. The ominous possibility that these could also vanish inspired considerable frugality.

They wasted nothing. Even the bones of butchered meats were boiled for soups and tallow. The feet and organs were kept and carefully cleaned (as were the pork rinds) and used for food. The hides of cattle became rugs and warm covers. Feed sacks became garments, bed linens, tablecloths, and dish towels. All fabric scraps and worn-out garments became quilts.

Harlin and Rena's income from their cream and eggs and from summer corn and wheat shrank. They needed fat calves to sell, but many were now born dead due to their cows' poor nutrition.

Harlin raised melons near the river when spring broke through the cold. He siphoned river water to them in the summer and hauled the sparse extra produce to town where he sold it off the back of his wagon.

Smaller farm communities like Calumet, a town about ten miles northwest of El Reno, the county seat, and only about seven miles north of Harlin's farm had their own land, cows, eggs, hogs, garden produce, and orchards. The population of only about three hundred supported small groceries, both rural and in town, besides other necessary shops, a livery, and a bank. The North Canadian River formed the north boundary of the community.

To the north and to the south of the fertile valley, the two Canadian rivers flowed east toward Macintosh County, this side of the Arkansas border and not far from where the Upton Rush's and Cory and Louise McLeod had lived.

Western Canadian County lay like an emerald jewel where the two rivers narrowed on either side of the valley. The green-gold fields of winter wheat spoke hope for summer grass pastures. Red clay that grew cotton and peanuts lay miles farther west. Fort Reno and the Concho Indian Reservation occupied the land between Harlin's valley and the county seat, El Reno.

Oklahoma City lifted its lights and skyscrapers, its oil derricks, and industry fifty miles east of the valley and about thirty-five miles east of El Reno where Letti lived. Creek beds were less dry now and the rivers low. Wheat production still lagged due to the dry climate but looked some better than the year before. Whatever the price or demand, there remained sparse product; vast acres of land had been cleared and plowed for wheat production due to the early '20s' four-dollars-a-bushel price. Without the abundance of grass and forage to hold the soil, it blew away.

The fair price for wheat after the war years that encouraged the vision of unstoppable plenty was only a memory.

In the very heart of the valley, Rena Lily looked out of her front window. The morning sun hit the rainwater drops on it and sent sparks of light into the morning as if to celebrate winter's thaw and summer's approach.

At the end of the long lane, Route 66 lay quiet except for the roar of the government truck. It turned up the lane, its wheels spinning on the mud. Its motor groaned, then stopped midway to the house. From under the back tarp, several families and several lone men disembarked, their belongings under their arms or in knapsacks across their backs.

Rena knew that the second Route 66 crew had arrived. The road supervisor told them yesterday to expect it. The driver and his partner got out of the front seat and began to unload the tents and bundles of goods. They set them down a few yards from the lane. The first cluster of canvas homes had been erected nearer the canyon the river had cut years before, a great red gash in their farm that held sparse water about a week ago. Smoke curled out of their canvas tops this morning like blue-gray cats seeking the lavender blanket of sky.

Then Rena Lily saw the driver walk over to one of the women who had left the truck to examine the land. Three young children scampered about in the cold and meddled with the bundles upon the ground. Rena Lily saw the woman point farther down toward the canyon and up south toward the road near the other tents.

Rena knew she wanted to move on to more protection from the cool damp wind.

The man restacked the truck as the children returned to the truck bed. Wearily, the woman stooped for a bundle. Then the man took part of her burden. Hoisting the makings for a tent over his shoulder, he motioned her back to the protection of the tarp, for the sharp winds had begun to blow rain in their faces.

Twelve families now camped in the Harlin Rush's huge yard besides the bachelors and widowers far from home. They formed the WPA work crew that built the highway that stretched eagerly across country in front of Harlin and Rena Lily's farm.

They used the wood and water of the canyon, and Rena would have allowed them the house where there was room. Most had kerosene. Harlin carried down well water for drinking, firmly telling them to boil it. The small-frame house on the Indian lease had barely sheltered herself and Harlin and young Gavin. Here, the large kitchen, the two bedrooms, the bath, and the parlor seemed more than enough.

Outside near the well stood a small well house where she washed. Beside it was the dug cellar with a smokehouse on the other side of the washhouse that they used for curing pork and aging their beef away from the midnight critters and coyotes who would steal it. Nearby, the eighty acres of Indian land that Harlin loved still pastured some of their stock. There hadn't been time or warmth enough to move everything here. Summer would see their move finished for the rest of the packing was done.

She turned from the window to look at Gavin asleep on the couch. His cheeks were rosy from the kerosene stove's warmth, dry and chapped from the dryness of the air. She went to the kitchen and put a dipper of water in a small aluminum pan and set it atop the potbellied stove so that the steam would moisten the air.

Before dawn each day, she and Harlin rose and milked the small herd of Holsteins while Gavin fed the horses first and then the chickens as instructed. Harlin and Rena had never explained why horses first and chickens second was the rule.

"Wear your slicker and boots, Gavin. The rain hasn't quite stopped."

Rena Lily usually separated the milk and stored the cream in great crocks in the cellar after helping Harlin milk. This morning she prepared Harlin's breakfast of hot biscuits and gravy and packed cold egg sandwiches and an apple for his lunch bucket before going to the barn.

Gavin decided to feed the chickens first this morning. The hazy dawn hadn't broken through the cloudy morning before he came running into where Harlin and Rena milked, tears streaming down his face. "The chickens are dead," he cried. "They slump like this, and their eyes are closed." He slumped over, his wet lashes curled upon his damp cheeks. Rena laughed and rushed to hug him.

"Why, you're as tenderhearted as your grandpa Upton!" she declared. "The sun will fix it. Don't you worry. Feed the horses first. Wait for the sun. You'll see. I promise you, Gavin. Those chickens are alive. They love sunshine and must sleep when it's gone."

Relief flooded his face. "I love sunshine too!" he exclaimed and rushed out to finish his chores, his terror of death apparently appeased by Rena's words.

Harlin farmed, continued to build county roads when he wasn't working on the 66 highway, and sometimes worked the extra board for the Rock Island Railroad.

"You've worked yourself thin as a sapling tree," Rena cautioned. "You've no extra fat to live on."

"I want this farm clear of our debt for improvements," he said.

"There's always debt on a farm, Harlin, even in good years due to perpetual investment in repairs, cattle, purchases."

His silence said he would meet debt stress his way—not her father's way, for her parents headed for Colorado between harvest and planting "to get away from Oklahoma heat," her mother said every summer.

Rena felt sorry for the wives and children of the WPA laborers—that kind of feeling that turns an ordinary farmhouse into a mansion beside the canvas outside. "Where's your pride?" she chided when Harlin stayed with the crew part-time.

"Proud to do it," he told her. "It's history we're making. This route will eventually take us across America."

Rena couldn't get that excited about it. She just wanted her yard to look like one again despite her willingness to share it.

Would the child sleep all day? she thought irritably on the following Saturday morning. She walked nearer the couch where he'd fallen asleep again after chores. She stood above him, her longing look already drawing him into her arms. As if he sensed her nearness in his sleep, he stirred. She moved to the kitchen and tied an apron about her waist. She lit the kerosene stove and started a pan of water boiling there for his bowl of hot cereal. He liked it with thick cream, cinnamon, and sugar. She reached for a jar of apple cider, his favorite for breakfast. Gavin kept her sweet company until Harlin walked the mules in late at night.

There was no school today. He could feed later than usual. *The rest was good for him, for he too had long hours for a little boy,* she thought. A few farmers enjoyed the ease of tractors, and Harlin planned a second purchase in their near future. However, mules were used for the government road project, and Harlin earned extra dollars for feeding and watering more than a few at each day's end.

She heard Gavin's steps on the wooden floor before he called her. "Mom, Mom," he said a second time when she didn't respond immediately. Rena Lily popped the lid on the cereal and turned out the burner. It would steam softly now without more fire. Eagerly, she turned to him, his arms reaching up as always first thing in the morning. She squeezed him up against her ample breasts in a tight hug. Time flew by for her. *He would be an adult too soon,* she thought.

"Hungry?" she asked.

"For your cooking? Always."

"You look ready," Rena Lily said with a gentle laugh. Dark braids formed a circle about her head, and her blue eyes twinkled with happiness. She sprinkled the cinnamon on the crushed wheat, its bright scent filling the kitchen. From the cool pantry, she removed a small crock of cream, dipped a half pitcher from it, and returned the crock to the dark closet. She took the cream and cereal to the table, then set two bowls and spoons down for them. Suddenly, she heard a pounding on the front door. She'd eaten breakfast with Harlin before dawn as usual. Her Saturday breakfast with Gavin near 10:00 a.m. satisfied her lunch.

She walked to the door and hesitated there, her hand upon the white ceramic knob. From the start, she'd wondered what she would do should any of the crew approach her for hay, tools, or food. Their supplies were hard earned and harder still to replace.

They'd done well to get their twelve-bushel wheat crop last year. But the price for it was a dollar sixty, up from the forty-cent price of the crash, but short when they needed more equipment and new tires for their only transportation—their farm truck. Rains continued to be sparse. Crop prospects for '36 seemed uncertain. Rena thought that forty—or fifty-cent wheat could be in their future again despite last week's rain.

The county seat country store paid Harlin three to five dollars each Saturday for their cream and eggs. Still, it took all they made and more for seed and stock feed, for work clothes and tools. For cattle, chickens, and other stock required huge winter investments in feed besides the hay, corn, and oats that they raised.

If she bought fresh greens in the winter for a treat at their own table, as she often longed to do, they ran short of cash toward the end of the month. If there was cash left, it usually went for wire or lumber for their fence, water gaps, or corral repairs after windstorms.

Still, she felt uncomfortable at the thought of telling any of them she wouldn't share her wealth of provision, short of depriving Gavin. When she finally opened the door, she recognized the intruder immediately. A quick smile sprang to her lips. The man who had taken his wife's burdensome baggage and seen her to a better place for their tent stood before her. "Mornin'," she said, noticing that he removed his hat. His gesture of respect pleased her.

Gavin walked up beside her and stood with his thumbs inside the bib to his striped overalls like the man of the house might stand.

The tall visitor smiled at him before his glance turned to her. "Fine boy, Mrs. Rush," the man said.

"Thank you." Her eyes questioned, but she said nothing more. She had found that some men thought it an impertinence for a woman to question them. She waited, risking no offense that could incur anger in spite of this man's cordial demeanor.

With a little lift of his chin, he said, "Your man home?"

"Be home before long," she said. She always said that when Harlin was gone whether it was so or not.

"I'm a representative of the United States government," he said. "My name's Ray Swain, and I'm needing a formal hay contract for my mules. I noticed the stacks of it back of your house. I'll get you the top price for it."

Rena Lily's worry fell away. "There might be extra. Hard telling until summer grass and the freezes are gone for good. More clouds coming in again." She looked around him to the north and shivered from the draft that pushed inside the open door. We're feeding some already, but I'll ask. Bring your wife to supper tonight. Children too," she invited. "You can ask Harlin about the hay. If he can spare it, it'd be like him to let you have it. And if you'll be needing more than he can spare, he'll be telling you where you can buy it."

Ray Swain put his hat on again. "Thank you, Mrs. Rush. Until this weather improves and the 66 roadwork starts again, feed may stay scarce."

"Rena," Rena Lily supplied. "Rena Lily Rush, and this is our son, Gavin. It's true. Cattle are using up a lot of feed when there wasn't much to brag about."

"I've two sons," he said. "Tad and Jonsi. One girl we called Jenny, and an unknown in the oven."

"I've just the one," Rena Lily said, a warm flush rushing to her face at his reference to his pregnant wife.

Ray Swain smiled. "Looks lonesome." Rena Lily knew he meant her no harm, but she wanted him to leave now. He stopped smiling rather suddenly. As if he'd read her mind, he replaced his hat. Then with an awkward tip of it, he said, "I'll be telling the missus about the invitation."

"Come at seven, we'll be done choring then," she said. She closed the door and leaned against it. She'd almost died having Gavin. But she'd had him at last with the help of a midwife after more than forty-eight hours of labor. She could have no more children. She felt sad; her whole body felt sad.

"Mom," Gavin said, his tone concerned.

"Is your phonograph stuck on 'Mom'?" she repeated crossly. "Eat your breakfast."

So Rena Lily picked up her morning where she'd left it when Ray Swain knocked on her door. He wouldn't be with the WPA long—not that one. Mr. Swain would be moving on to better things just as soon as he could manage it. She'd not be afraid to bet money on that. People who cared about someone who cared about them usually progressed in this world, she had noticed, unless they had what she thought of as "the world owes me" disease.

She poured a cup of coffee, anticipating the company of a woman to visit with tonight. It had been a month or more since they had made time for socializing, even with family. She'd fry some fresh side meat and bring up potatoes from the cellar. She'd open several of her best quarts of string beans and a gallon of orchard pears. Suddenly, she wished she'd separated milk this morning and made fresh butter and cottage cheese. The old would have to do. She'd rinse it in fresh milk to sweeten it and make fresh applesauce from the last of the stored apples, too wrinkled now to eat fresh anyway.

There would be eight at her table tonight with the children. If there were leftover pears, she'd bake a cobbler tomorrow morning for Sunday dinner.

For the rest of this cloudy day, Gavin played solitaire, listened to the radio, and talked her into tic-tac-toe, slapjack, and a card game of books until it was time to chore again. Play, so rare during busy summers, brightened a late spring day such as this. Then as if some alarm went off inside his brain, he stood at the window about the time that Harlin was due in and watched the lane for his father.

"I'll start the evening milking," he told her. "Maybe we can finish choring before the Swains come." At barely nine, Gavin could milk four cows before she finished two when Harlin wasn't there to help.

Rena turned her mind to the company supper. Harlin would be late, and there was much to do.

"I've got a dream, so the work is pleasure," he'd said just this morning. "Good thing," she'd muttered, irritated at his chronic lateness.

Harlin was past seven arriving home, so Ray Swain helped Gavin finish the evening chores while Esther kept supper warm.

Darkness surrounded them by the time the three of them came in, tired and hungry. Rena Lily had heard all about the drought in South Texas from Esther Swain: they came here from South Texas to escape the rural poverty that follows drought. Yet drought still moved across Oklahoma and Kansas.

"The light snows of winter and sparse rains of this spring supplied no real moisture to ponds or fields of wheat," Rena told her. The talk depressed Rena Lily. Each day's trouble seemed enough for her, but she knew that the Swains only made conversation. Besides, they seemed to need for her to understand their reason for being here, doing what they were doing.

Ray told them he had worked in a milling laboratory near Dallas after his dad bought an elevator there. His grandfather was a Civil War veteran in Tennessee who had been given land in those parts by the government after the war. They had great prosperity in the beginning. Then with the drought, mortgaged land, and a weak economy, the banks called his loans, high taxes went unpaid, both farms and the family elevator business were lost.

Esther talked on while they washed the dishes and while Ray and Harlin settled on a hay price. "We're hoping he can find work at an elevator here in wheat country, buy into a mill—later, of course," Esther said.

"Be mighty nice," Rena agreed.

"There's no opportunity to buy in the east," Esther continued. "About everything's already owned. The stocks are all sold or sunk. Old towns, old companies. Ray says this valley's rough but new."

"Ray's right," Rena Lily said. She was a saving woman with words, and soon enough, Esther Swain would learn that living was hard but good here, whatever her man did, wherever they lived. The valley was no older than she was, not by more than a few years if at all. No need to tell her all about it and scare her. Not with her three living children playing cards in the next room with Gavin.

Towns had sprung up like bright cone flowers. Some had shriveled and died right away. Others quickly replaced them near the developing rail centers. Even now, all the sections of land weren't cut; all the roads weren't built nor the bridges—not half the businesses needed had been established. Half of the country's population hadn't indoor plumbing, a telephone, transportation, or electricity. But they would have power, and telephone cooperatives were already established in some communities. Hope thrived in those who stayed instead of heeding the call to California's fruit orchards.

"It's a good place to live," Rena Lily said. As an afterthought, she asked, "Do you have quinine with you?"

"Quinine?" Esther asked.

"Malaria," Rena Lily explained. "Never you mind," she added quickly. "I'll give you a good supply before you leave tonight." *Esther Swain might as well learn right away to look at the time and the place of her life, or she'd not have it long,* Rena Lily thought. *For a while yet, until there was money and time for more than grueling work to survive the times, quinine would have an important place in her life.*

"Boil all your canyon water, you can use from the well here at the house if you want. There's plenty. Tell the others too," Rena Lily offered. "Harlin carries some to them, but they may run out. Try to be in housing by summer, there's more danger of fevers then. Danger of cold and pneumonia now, so try to stay warm and dry—keep camphor."

"We'll be settled by summer for sure," Esther said. "Tad'll be starting to school next fall, and we'll not want to be moving him around then."

"That's good," Rena said, and the two women exchanged a quiet smile, a smile that confirmed friendship and trust.

*   *   *

Whether he walked behind the mule and plow, made garden, drove tractor, or cultivated the orchard, whether cutting and tying sheaves or pitching hay, Harlin sang. After work and supper, he usually took down Upton's fiddle and played a tune for Gavin and Rena Lily. "Turkey in the Straw," "Buffalo Gal," and "Red Wing" often entertained them.

"You'll play that violin someday, Gavin," Rena said one evening.

"Maybe," was his only response. He had no interest in music other than whistling or singing an occasional tune like "You Are My Sunshine" that Rena could see. He fancied "Birmingham Jail," "Little Brown Jug," and "I'm a Gamblin' Man." Rena knew that Gavin fancied activity that passed fast. Learning the violin sounded tedious and rule ridden to him, no doubt. Rules seemed mostly unnecessary to him, a concern that tormented her. Occasionally, he still mentioned those "stupid chickens" for eating in daylight but never in the dark. "As if they couldn't break a rule," he'd lament.

Rena had been raised on the classical music her mother played on their grand piano. Yet the bluegrass that Harlin sometimes played greatly pleased her. She liked the minor keys and the bold rhythms. She saw the amalgamation of world foods, music, and people in this new state as a miracle of adaptation.

"We've so much to be grateful for, Harlin," she whispered, her heart full of the day's goodness as they lay down together. When he didn't answer, she knew he slept, probably the moment his head hit the pillow.

At such times, *her* mind found time to roam over the years she had traversed. Her youth had known easy years that fed on her family's prosperity. They transferred wealth from Massachusetts to this territory when they participated in the land lottery.

Her adventurous mother and father still lacked for little, despite these hard times.

Their spirit infused her, one of reaching farther than your dreams and trusting a creator to fulfill it in His time. Reaching required planning. Planning required work. *Harlin dreams and labors toward his vision. I plan the immediate and do it. Harlin believes in the earthly powers of food, water, money, markets, and man. I believe in doing my best and letting God do the rest. After all, isn't He in charge?*

I'm little, but I'm strong, she thought. *And I'm willing.* As she curled her body around Harlin's backside, she smiled. *Best of all, I have Harlin and Gavin.*

The warning of Letti Pearl threatened to break through and spoil her rosy idea of her family: "You'll regret giving in to that boy's every whim someday, Rena. Why, he's so spoiled now, salt wouldn't save him."

What did Letti know of it? She could have had a dozen children though she had only Harlin and Mary-Mary. She hadn't lived in fear of losing her only son to these perilous times.

CHAPTER VI

Ray and Esther

The sun rose red in Central Oklahoma on June 20, 1936. A streak of purple cloud cut through it, giving it the illusion of a toy—a yoyo, a ball of red wood at the end of a purple string that Esther Swain could draw to her or shove away.

She awkwardly turned on her side, away from the window's view of a new sun rising. Ray slept beside her. Aware of her motion in his half sleep, he caught her side in his great hand and drew her nearer. The pressure of his arm sagged there across her, an added burden to her swelling belly, for she was in the sixth or seventh month (she wasn't certain) with their seventh child, three of them still living. Two boys had been lost to premature births. Esther believed that the third had died of heart defects for he had turned blue and died just minutes after birth.

In the wild plum that grew just outside the window, the brown wrens gathered to chirp the sun up among the hundreds of dangling fruit that turned pale orange and yellow in spots. She listened, her glance caressing Ray's face. He remained lean and appeared young at forty. She wanted to trace the fine laugh lines across his cheeks with the tips of her fingers as she often did.

Then he would catch her fingers in his own, kiss them, then kiss her.

Not this morning—not any morning until the child was born, for she sensed a need for caution. She wanted to carry this child full term, and passion could potentially trigger an early labor. So Esther lay very still, savoring the sounds and the promise of summer that entered their room through the thin white curtain at the small east window in morning's first light.

This little space in each day seemed exclusively her time, precious moments to muse about a dream or some special happiness, to plan her day before Ray wakened. For when the children wakened, usually about a half hour later, the day's demands pushed her through the hours like wind at her back until dark.

Ray yawned and snuggled closer. She brushed his forehead with a kiss and began to pull away. This was his day off from the flour mill where he worked as a chemist. He planned to walk to town for chicken feed and take Tad and Jonsi with him. They loved to see the young chickens and rabbits for sale there. Jenny would stay home to help her with the laundry. With all of them home for summer vacation, she must wash clothes twice a week.

Ray held onto her as she tried to turn and rise. Just then, her child kicked. He must have felt it, for he opened his eyes and smiled sleepily at her.

"Another lively one," he said, his dark hair rumpled on his forehead.

"Yes," she laughed nervously. "This one will surprise me if she stays where she belongs for another few months." She frowned a little. "I'll put the coffee on." He tangled his hand for a moment in her light-brown hair that shone with blond highlights, then he slid the back of his hand down her cheek.

"Git then," he said huskily. "You're so sure it's a girl. Maybe it's a boy."

With a soft knowing smile, she left him, drawing her soft wrapper of blue flannel about her rounded belly. The kitchen would be cool, even for June, because of the dirt cellar beneath it. Taking a few of the long hairpins from the dresser, she lifted her long hair off her neck and swept it into a swirl atop her head, pinning it out of the way as she walked to the kitchen. Until the wash was on the line, it would do no good to comb and arrange it. Wisps of its golden strands trailed her neckline and lay softly at her temples as she walked down the red-brick path to the well. Ray would pipe water into the house for her before winter; they'd saved enough to do it: a hundred dollars.

She brought enough in to start the beans she'd left to soak the night before. If she washed until noon, they'd have their lunch. By the time she finished her first cup of coffee, she heard Jonsi rump bumping down the stairs as he seemed prone to do. After that, no one slept. She added a pan of boiled oats to the other busy kettles on the stove, and the children ate them while Ray filled the great rinse tub for her and set the water to heat out of doors for the Thor washing machine on the screened-in porch nearby.

In the winter, she heated water with natural-gas fuel inside the small enclosed back porch. In the summer, it made the house too warm, so they relied on wood and a small outdoor fireplace. Jenny usually took her small personal laundry out beneath the tree quite near the porch to scrub her things clean on her small rubboard.

"There'll be time for you to do your own things first before I need your help carrying," Esther told her as she sat back down at the table to finish her coffee.

"I wanted to go to the library today," Jenny sulked, then took her empty bowl to the sink. "Ms. Ferber has a new novel out, and I'm just dying to read it." She flipped a thick lock of black hair off her shoulder before turning pleading blue eyes to Esther.

"Ms. Ferber?" Esther repeated. Esther had never had much time for reading, although she'd fought everybody including her eleven brothers for the right to learn.

She'd ridden a horse six miles a day to school and back to read the McGuffey Reader and do her figures before her life became an endless stream of youngsters, first her brothers and sisters and now her own, for she'd been born the oldest in a family of fifteen. If she ever found time for it, she figured she'd better start with the Holy Bible.

She exchanged glances with Ray, who had just stepped inside to tell her all the water was in. "You stay here and help your mother," he reminded Jenny.

Jenny's blue eyes clouded to violet, and Esther's heart softened at the sight.

The coffee, her favorite beverage, tasted good to her. She wanted another cup. Through the small north window above the sink, she could see the dust high in the air. "Is there wind?" she asked Ray, watching him get a cup and walk to pour himself some of the dark brew.

"It's a good day to wash," he said. "Dirt looks a ways off. I don't think it will be here for several hours."

Now both Tad and Jonsi had arrived from their upstairs bedroom for breakfast. Tad returned to the stove to dip another bowl of oats while Jonsi silently stuffed himself with toast and plum jelly. "Maybe you better make another pot of cereal," Tad observed. Jonsi turned his bowl up and drank the last of his like a chaser for his jelly sandwich.

"That's all there is. I've more to do than be an oat stuffer all morning," Esther teased them, then glanced at Jenny, whose bottom lip protruded in a pout.

"Take Jenny with you," she told Ray. "It's all right. I'll not fill the baskets but half full. Maybe she'll tell me about Ms. Ferber's latest novel. That's next best to reading it for myself."

She smiled at Jenny, who jumped and rushed around the table to hug her. "Wash and rinse the dishes for me before you go," Esther told her firmly, "and see you don't keep your father waiting."

"You're sure," Ray said.

"I'm sure." Suddenly, she craved being alone as if her earlier morning silence hadn't lasted long enough. She always felt like that close to childbirth, but she shoved that thought aside as not relevant. It wasn't time. She rubbed her puffy left hand. She had retained a quantity of water for several days, enough to make her gold wedding band too tight, but that didn't necessarily mean trouble yet. The child leaped within her.

—

78

"Why, I've had her dusting everything and sorting linens," she reassured Ray. "She weeded all of the tomatoes for me yesterday evening. She deserves her morning at the library." Besides, Esther thought, she'd rather Jenny not bend her life to other's children; she would have her own to take care of. She wasn't certain what she wanted for Jenny, a bit of ease perhaps. Ease and freedom to make independent choices eluded her own life. Her days filled with the needs of others and always had.

Jenny let go of her, then gave her a wet smack on the cheek. Her young face flushed with the excitement of going somewhere. Then her blue eyes opened wide as if in alarm.

"Oh!" she exclaimed. "I've got to do something about my hair. It's just awful!" Her gleaming black hair tumbled over her shoulders and down her back. Her younger brothers began to clown.

"I've just got to do something about my hair," Jonsi mimicked.

"It's just awful!" Tad joined him. Then they giggled and snorted together, having great fun.

Jenny ignored their fun, a thing that usually incited more tirades.

"You boys dry the dishes for her," Esther said sternly, and they quickly sobered.

When Ray began to strop his razor against the leather strip on the wall where he sharpened the blade to shave, the others moved quickly to clear the table and wash the dishes. Within twenty minutes, Esther could see them walking along the road that bordered the orchard on the north, a charming road that curved and was bridged and that trains ran over and a creek ran under—a dusty mile-long road that led to town. Esther walked it herself on market days.

She drew a deep and satisfied breath as she watched them. A tiny stabbing pain struck low in her abdomen when she exhaled. She touched the area lightly with her hand as if to secure the life there, then pulled her bonnet from the nail beside the door. She put the first load of white linens inside the gyrating tub of the Thor washer that Ray had filled for her. She'd felt that same pain last week. It had come and gone like this one.

She began to hum her favorite hymn, then she sang a few lines: "I've reached the land of corn and wine, and all its riches freely mine. There shines undimmed one blissful day, for all my nights have passed away. She sang "Beulah Land" the way she wanted to at home. At church she never sang for she wanted to hear Ray's mellow baritone as he led the songs.

He would bite the tuning fork, listen, hum do-mi-sol-do-sol-mi-do. Then his beautiful voice resonated as if it were touched by the fiddler's bow.

Another pain pried at her pelvis, but she ignored it. It wasn't time. She wanted this baby. Maybe if she ate a soda cracker. She went to the kitchen for one after she'd run the first load through the wringer to the rinse water. Yes. She felt much better, she thought, returning to work.

By midmorning, she carried the sixth small load of laundry to the line. Now the sun rose to quarter sky and turned into a fuzzy disk back of its dust screen. It reminded her of pasture puffballs in Texas she'd seen as a child when she ran the cows home at milking time, but those hadn't been bloodred with dust. She shivered in spite of the heat at the sight of that red sun as if it would drench the earth with its blood.

How she longed to see a clear day again, to feel its reassuring warmth. It seemed the dust never went away entirely or for very long. When the showers came to clear it away, they were sporadic little cloud bursts that left too soon or fell too fast to actually soak the earth. These recent spring showers never ripped chasms in the soil or washed it into the creeks and gullies.

"God forgive my ingratitude," she murmured, for even the sprinkles helped to settle the dust briefly.

Esther didn't remember seeing anything like this, not even during the drought that drove them from South Texas years ago and never as a child growing up on the banks of the Red River. Her father's farm had skirted the river, a place to swim and to fish. They'd farmed cotton mostly then before this craze for wheat. Farmers plowed up the prairie grasses that held the soil to plant wheat, so the wind carried it away.

She snapped the pins onto one of Ray's shirts, fastening it to the thick wire. With the stolidity that had seen her through to this day, she set her square jaw. She didn't miss dragging that cotton sack or carrying water from the river when the well was low. For even with water still outside her door and no inside toilet yet, her life grew easier though it seemed to take a long time. She had felt shocked at first to learn that more than half the homes and more of the farms here didn't have electricity or plumbing. Oklahoma was newer than Texas—not quite thirty years old. There were signs, she reminded herself, that public works, federal school aid, and fewer dust storms relieved the poverty caused by the Depression, which drought immediately followed.

Their acreage that grew vegetables and fruits besides supporting a cow, chickens, and a few goats wasn't far from being a small farm. They were self-reliant during these hard times. With Ray's job at the mill, she knew they could make it through the hard times if they held on and kept up the hard work and penny pinching.

Route 66 was now built through here and stretched east toward Oklahoma City. Soon it would snake into the former badlands of Oklahoma's recent past.

A few tall tales still reached Central Oklahoma from that previous Indian Territory. The recent fracas of Bonnie Parker and her Texan, Clyde Barrow, had even caused local folks here to lock their doors. *The badlands of Oklahoma, due more to its reputation than to fact,* she thought, *could still hide bandits. It remained a natural paradise of mountains and water and woods if they could believe the newspaper stories about Turner Falls and Robbers Cave.*

Its wild, varied terrain provided remote, unguarded areas for bandits and bank robbers from the east as well as the land's own. Hard times bring crime with it. Hunger too, she thought.

Her mind on safety, thoughts turned easily to the mill where risk seemed a given due to the height of the huge ivory storage cylinders that rose like castles, the chemicals, the grain dust, and rodent controls. She hoped the safety standards were raised soon there. Her stress would ease then. Air filters to help prevent dust explosions were recently installed. Equipment needed updating. Ray had confided that keeping old equipment repaired was becoming more difficult, though new equipment could also fail.

She brushed back a wisp of hair and bent for a pair of Tad's overalls. *Everything takes money*, she grieved. *Even safety.* Thirty-cent wheat already created unrest for both millers and farmers, but the market out of Chicago set the price. Ray felt helpless before it; he'd told her so. With low production and scarcity, the low price made no sense. Surely it would be at least $3 soon. The grain prices, the dry climate, the poverty, the rumbles of trouble in Europe worried her because of the boys, her Tad and Jonsi. How could she bear to see them leave, victims of others' hate, when she and Ray had taught them care and responsibility for others?

She didn't want to think about the restless workers, Ray's safety, of war, or of the destitute men that walked or rode the rails and asked for food. Lately, however, it seemed that she couldn't keep from it.

This lack of funds and the persistent drought across the wheat states meant shortages of bread for a hungry world. She sighed. Since the great depression of '29, wages remained frozen, polio still struck down healthy children, and jobs remained scarce despite the past seven dirt-plagued years.

Polio had even crippled the president, hadn't it? Her bleak mood deepened.

The lack of moisture, this dirt. Suddenly, it seemed unfair to bring another child into a hostile world. She rubbed her brow as if to rouse hope awake again.

Ray's dream of economic success exceeded hers of mere investment in the elevator. He planned to have the controlling interest in it. "This country will grow enough wheat one day to feed the world," he'd boasted to Harlin Rush one evening. The families had remained friends, though it had been several months since she had seen them. After Ray satisfied hay contracts with Harlin Rush to feed the government mules last year, he grabbed the unexpected opening at the elevator he'd hoped for though it paid less. *Ray acted on his dreams,* she thought, pleased that he hadn't followed the 66 highway crew farther east. She needed him here. Elevators provided him a work he knew and loved.

A little groan erased her quick smile. *This basket is almost empty,* she thought, not wanting to quit before the wash was hung. She had one last tub of heavy overalls for Ray, and she'd be finished.

With poorer working conditions and less products at the mill, these times made it harder to make the flour. Farmers worked harder too; they plowed deeper now before planting the grain, hoping to bring moisture to the surface. The wheat was still thin and full of cheat, a wild grass that plagued wheat growers, and bindweed that strangled and crowded it.

Her eyes scanned the sky, which had begun to darken. The dusters seemed to come less often, but today's sky grew dark gray—almost black instead of red. Rumor was that Texas dirt moved in on Oklahoma.

By evening, she thought, *a rain could come. Mud could streak the houses, clothes, and gardens but take the worry from Ray's face for a while. The children would be less likely to get the dust pneumonia or cough up mud.*

She scolded herself as she started back to the washroom. *Why do I try to gather life in wads of thought?* she wondered. She had a need to see its shape, she supposed; to get some rooted vision of it so that she could spring ahead from solid ground.

However much she wanted this child, she wanted it to be her last one. She felt squeezed out of the time to treasure anything before it ended. *When Jenny married, the grandchildren would start,* she thought. Jenny would be sixteen soon.

Esther's eyes clung to the blooming orchard until she turned inside the back door. The steamy area smelled of dirt, not the fresh sudsy cleanness of fresh laundry.

—

The moment defined her life that seemed made of shaping the land in her childhood, of fevers, of the Great War where her two older brothers died on foreign soil, of grueling work and loss to these dust days when the sun might show itself a few moments (hours at best). And now, this child she had conceived with what seemed the last of her courage and hope clamored within her with such eagerness for it all.

Tears shot to her eyes when it leaped within her again. She caught it fast there with both hands. *That was its bottom,* she thought as fists and legs shot out. She moved to the kitchen and sat down for a moment to quiet it and her thoughts.

For such a brief time, she'd felt guilty for her part in bringing another life to these times. She brushed quick tears aside with those feelings. There'd be rain by evening and water in the house next year. There'd be a child taking first steps and saying first words. This child would be her reason to go on.

She and Ray weren't church-going people, but maybe they would be. *A whole new life, past war and depression and dirt could open for us at this birth,* she thought. That's what they'd do; they'd go to church on Sunday. Decidedly, she straightened and stood to finish her work, energized anew with this sense of purpose. She lifted the hot breeches with the stick, now bleached and roughened by many wash days, and poked each pair to the lips of the wringer that gobbled them up and spit them out into the soap-filmed rinse water.

Her face, her body, her very motion revealed this renewed sense of purpose overtaking her. She and Ray were going to meet the better times halfway with a helper. She'd not seen to do that before. Too proud, she supposed, the two of them. Too proud to ask for God's help. A weight seemed to lift off her at the thought, and as the basket filled from the second rinse, her thoughts ran into new ones.

She no longer cared if relatives said that belief in a savior was a crutch for the poor. *What if faith was their power, like Ma Joad[3] believed when she said, 'We are the people.'* She knew this

---

[3]   From *The Grapes of Wrath*. Ma Joad's comment when it seemed that the only

mass of people would endure. She added water to the beans, her self-confidence surging. Ray and the children would be hungry.

She dragged the full basket of denim to the line rather than make two trips. It seemed to cramp her back and leg muscles to do it, but it put no stress on her stomach that she could feel. Yet as she raised herself to pin the first pair of overalls to the line, a low pressure alarmed her, and her eyes blurred.

The sun flamed almost midsky now. She squinted against it for it cast a peculiar glare through the dust. She clutched at the line until her vision cleared, then she drew a deep careful breath. The infant's foot suddenly jabbed straight down. A small explosion of warmth ran down her legs.

"Oh God!" she cried. But it wasn't God she wanted. "Ray!" she yelled frantically. She tried to see the road. Dirt whipped about her in little eddies, dimming vision and gritting her teeth.

There was no sign of him. It took an hour to walk both ways, not including selecting and loading supplies on the wheelbarrow. If he stayed and talked to Cyrus—her wondering about him yielded to her stout self-reliance.

She began to inch her way to the house, fearful of triggering any movement in the child by her own. As great as her alarm that she might lose it was her horror of a dry birth. She'd been through that with Jonsi. A trembling with nausea had attacked her the instant her water broke.

The infant must have thrust a foot through the sack, she thought.

"Foolish child," she wept. At the door, the hardest pain hit her. She grasped the wood facing, leaning into it for a moment. Then as it began to pass, she threw her head back in fresh resolve to make it inside. Carefully, she opened the screen door where black flies gathered. She stepped inside and closed them out.

As her next pain started, she knelt and stretched almost to a reclining position, for the child had dropped to the narrow birth canal, and she knew that she might injure it by more walking. She

strength left was in the human masses: ordinary men and women, but survivors.

—

waited there. She clenched her teeth against riveting pain, then slumped to the floor. On her side and with great reaches of her arms, she scooted her body along the floor until she reached her bed.

She had no phone. Fear now clawed at her mind, searching for what she must do, for she felt her body yielding toward the birth. The child could come with the next pain.

In desperation, she crawled to the dresser and dragged herself up far enough to reach her manicure scissors. She had the bed linens and the scissors to help her tear them. It was the best she could do, and as she felt the next pain start, harder still, she pushed herself up at the bottom of the bed and fell upon it.

"Ray!" she screamed again at the empty room.

Ray leaned upon the counter at Canadian Valley Feed and Seed. He'd made out his order for Cyrus, who measured his fall-garden seed for him while he filled his pipe.

"You'll need to order your sweet potato plants from Tennessee right away," Cyrus told him.

"Got 'em in the mail a few days ago."

"Are you waterin' at night so you get the most of your moisture?"

"Yep," Ray said, clamping his pipe between his teeth and firing it with a match. "Give me about a nickel's worth of them turnips, will you, Cyrus? I'm planting a large fall garden."

Cyrus dipped into the turnip seed. Just inside the seed store's door, a burlap bag of peanuts sat open. The scale for them sat in the front plateglass window. "And sack up about a pound of them peanuts for Tad and Jonsi," he said. "They've ate about a nickel's worth already."

At that moment, Tad and Jonsi busied themselves feeding lettuce to the rabbits. Their hutches lined the north wall of the store. Lately, they'd been nagging their father to invest in the commercial rabbit business for them so that they could earn their own spending money.

"When you gonna give in to 'em?" Cyrus asked, as if he could read Ray Swain's mind.

"I'm not!" Ray said assuredly. "They produce too fast."

"You've another young'un on the way, ain't you, Ray?"

Ray took the pipe from his mouth and gave Cyrus a long stare, but Cyrus's straight face didn't crack into the grin Ray expected. He didn't want jokes about Esther; he wanted this baby here and her all right. She seemed extra tired with this one; Esther had held up under a lot.

"I'd be obliged if you'd sack them seed up for me now, Cyrus. I ought to be getting back. Esther's looking to see us in time for dinner."

Suddenly, he wanted to see about her, to know that home and all that seemed best to him in life remained as he had left it.

"Yeah," Cyrus said, moving somewhat faster up to his register. He dipped his eyes to peer the long distance out the front window. "Hope you don't get caught in a duster going home."

Ray responded in his usual optimistic manner. "Duster's a long way off—tomorrow maybe. More than likely, we'll have us a rain this evening." He turned then, his pipe still between his teeth, and hoisted his sack of chicken feed upon his shoulder to load in the wheelbarrow. Cyrus had scurried ahead. Through the window, Ray saw him weighing peanuts. "Maybe another rainmaker will come to town," Ray chuckled as he stacked the feed.

"Get your peanuts, boys," Cyrus told them. With a nod of his head toward the counter when he came back inside, he said, "Got a flyer to post for a rainmaker up front. Glad you mentioned it."

Tad and Jonsi dashed to the front ahead of him where Cyrus added up his bill. "Is that enough for Mom to make peanut brittle?" Jonsi cried.

"Be two and a half," Cyrus said. "And there's more than enough, Jonsi," he added.

Carefully, Ray counted out the money. "Peanuts are free," Cyrus told him.

"Too bad about what happened in Chicago yesterday," Cyrus rushed on as if Ray knew it too. But Ray stood, deliberating free peanuts and rainmakers just then.

"Chicago?" he asked absently. "Let me pay for them peanuts, Cy."

"Board of Trade," Cyrus said. "You didn't hear the markets before leaving the mill yesterday?" he asked, refusing Ray with shakes of his head.

"I guess I forgot to check them, come to think of it. Everybody's restless there with the strike talk. It's all most of us can think of these days." He put his billfold away, dropping his change into his side pocket. "Safety issues."

"It dropped eight cents in less than half an hour. It's hurt the speculators real bad. I can't afford to charge their cattle feed for them this time. Don't know anyone who can. You're a paying customer, Ray. I appreciate it."

Ray knew what that meant; there'd be cattle sold or dying for there wasn't the pasture for them, and there'd be still less later unless they got subsoil moisture. For some ranchers, that meant the last blow in a hard fight. For others, it would make hanging on a while longer that much tougher.

Ray reached for his sack of garden seed, his glance falling upon the familiar local newspaper clipping tacked to the counter post that supported the ceiling. Cyrus had stuck the editorial from the local paper there May of last year. Ray knew it from memory now.

> A great thing has occurred amongst us. We have made a complete turnaround, and at last America's face is toward the future. Three years—1929 to 1932—we Americans looked backward. All our financial and political machinery was geared to pull us out of the Depression by the same door through which we entered. We thought it simply a case of going back the way we came. It failed.
>
> We now realize that the way out is forward—through it. Thanks for that belongs to President Roosevelt. Inauguration Day he turned the Ship of State around.

"What do you think FDR could do for them that they can't do for themselves? The poor sons a bitches," Ray said.

"Government borrows from gold to pay paper, ain't you heard? Peter and Paul be hanged! There'll be government in agriculture."

"Already is," Ray said. "That twenty million tons of soil that left us in May of 1934 to dump twelve million tons of it on Chicago and grew to 350 million for New York sparked the Hugh Bennet Crusade to save the land. Federal Soil Erosion Service is here now. But it's a darn good thing, I think. What do you suppose will take the place of the paper when that runs out, moving ahead the way it appears we're doin' now?"

Cyrus scratched his head. "Well, I'm hard-pressed. Are you sure there were millions of tons? Seems far-fetched."

"They'll be in the banks too," Ray interrupted. "That's what. Banks taking farms hasn't set well with FDR. More than two hundred thousand of them so far."

"You sure about that number, Ray? I sure didn't realize. Think cattle will bring more than $6 a hundred weight when they come off this dying grass?" Cyrus asked, as if to change the subject on purpose.

"I think more will die, that's what I think. Not that you'll believe me," Ray noted, giving Cyrus a sideways glance. Any time five hundred million tons of topsoil can vanish in the wind, cattle aren't all that will die. This heat wave's murder. Over 106 degrees in the shade. We've got to help our neighbor, we've got to hang on!"

The phone rang just then.

"Don't leave until I think on that, Ray. Let me get this danged phone." He turned aside to the desk a few feet back of where he stood at the counter. "What's that Government Soil Erosion Service?" he asked over his shoulder.

"It's a plan for terracing hill land, draining excess water rather than losing topsoil in a wash away. Farmers that had twenty bushel to the acre wheat have nine now—need a plan, need trees, need more wheat on less land."

Ray started a few steps down the aisle toward the door as Cyrus put the receiver down. He turned back and said, "I'll tell you what else they'll use when the money's gone: words. They'll write them on little exchange slips like IOUs in the legislature, and they'll regurgitate them in the news." The look on Cyrus' face stopped him. "What is it, Cyrus?"

"That was Dory Isaacs. She said she lives down the road a space from you." He paused as if hesitant to speak. "She says you're to get Doc Eber quick, the baby's coming."

Ray realized it was too soon. He rejected the panic trying to overtake him, yet he felt frozen in time. He knew that Jonsi raised the wheelbarrow and spun it, that Tad sat atop the sack of feed, and that people moved around them on the walk. Curious how life went on around the joys of another, around the griefs and urgencies.

Abruptly, Cyrus moved from behind the counter to Ray. "I'll load that barrow for you in my truck to deliver it—no charge. You git on that phone and find Doc Eber. If he needs transportation to your place, I'll be by for him."

The words jarred Ray into action. He rushed to the phone as Cyrus moved past him toward the door. He struggled against the great wad of grief in his aching throat. His eyes filled with tears. "Esther, Esther, Esther. I'll be home soon, Esther."

When Doc Eber himself answered his phone, hot tears of relief poured down Ray Swain's face.

"Oh, Doc! Am I ever glad it's you!"

CHAPTER VII

An Eager Life

"I saw her clothes basket sitting there unfinished under the line," Dory told them. "I knew Esther wouldn't let them dry out in wrinkles unless something had happened, so I checked on her." Esther's friend and neighbor stood wringing her hands.

"Thank God you did," Ray said, laying more bricks inside the oven.

Doc Eber came into the kitchen then and helped wrap them in flannel and towels. "They'll hold heat for more than four hours, then you'll need to heat more," he said. "And don't give the young'un to her. It hasn't much chance to make it. If I had an incubator." He sighed a long sigh, the sentence unfinished. "These damnable times!" His white shirt sleeves were still rolled, revealing curly gray hairs on his arms. His head had balded years ago, but his aging brown eyes remained bright and alert.

"My nerves will calm down if I can help," Dory said, lifting more warm bricks wrapped in flannel before disappearing into the bedroom with them. She lay them beside the tiny life that waited like a twelve-inch doll with papery ears and a wrist so small that Dory could have slipped her wedding band about it.

Doc Eber came into the room for a last look before rolling down his sleeves and buttoning the cuffs again. "I need to fill out the certificate," he said. "Esther's still sleeping, and the child isn't named."

"She named her," Dory said.

Ray stopped short in the doorway, holding another wrapped and heated brick to exchange for a cooled one.

"If it's a boy *or* a girl," she said before that last pain, "Its name is Teal, like that sky out there this morning before dust changed it to gray. Blue-green. That's heaven and earth packaged together for those strong enough to claim it."

"She said that, did she?" Doc Eber looked at Ray. "The blue of the sky and the green of this fertile valley when the rains return. They will return." He rubbed his chin stubble. "That's a mighty fine name. Well, go lay more bricks, Dory, then come back and pour us both some coffee before I finish and leave. You look like you could use a sit-down."

Dory smiled indulgently at him and beckoned Ray into the room with her. Esther wakened. Teal slept in her bassinet in the corner, swaddled in flannel-wrapped warm bricks.

"I never heard the baby cry," she said, fear flickering across her eyes.

"No," he said softly, then bent to kiss her forehead. "She didn't cry."

"She?"

"Teal Swain, a she," he confirmed. "But she's—" Ray couldn't go on. He swallowed. "You lost a lot of blood, Esther. You need to rest."

"She's alive!" Esther said, starting to raise herself.

"You lay back there," he ordered mildly. "She's alive, but she's a preemie. You knew she would be. Doc Eber says she can't weigh three pounds with her blanket and hot water bottle." He paused, not wanting to say more than that yet knowing he must. "There isn't an incubator in these parts, Esther."

"Where is she?" she asked, stretching her neck around him to see what Dory was doing in the corner.

"Dory's putting more warm bricks around her. Don't fret. She's wrapped them in flannel. Doc Eber says we're to give her drops of water every hour to rid her of the jaundice." Then he too walked to the bassinet and finished the exchange of warm bricks for the cool ones so that Dory could get Doc Eber's coffee.

"Doc can use that coffee now, Dory. I'll finish here."

"Jaundice!" Esther cried.

"Lay back!" he ordered, sternly this time. "She might not make it, Esther. You need to prepare yourself for that possibility."

Esther's bewildered eyes sought his. "I want my baby," she said quietly.

Ray dipped his gaze at her as if she were a child. He shook his head in a short, abortive gesture. "Doc says *no*. He says it'll just make it harder on you . . . to . . ." He couldn't go on. "You're to rest. Dory will stay tonight and help me do all that can be done. In forty-eight hours, Doc says we'll know."

Esther lay back and watched him like a cautious animal. When Ray turned to leave the room, she let him. She knew that everyone except the two of them would be gone soon, even Dory. She would see to it. As for the children, they would have garden chores of watering, gathering, and storing, then bed.

I'll know the right time to do what has to be done, she thought. Weakened as she was, she knew that the *right* time and the *right* thing could forge her physical strength. "Where are the children?" she asked him, and he turned back inside the doorway to answer her.

"I sent them outside to wait."

"Have Jenny bring in the clothes and fold them before it either rains mud or the dirt alone hits," she said. "She can hang your overalls on the porch."

"It's all done," he said. "I took care of it."

"Thank you," she said with a wan smile. "Tell the children to water, gather, and store the vegetables." She hoped he would go now to tell them her wishes. She must reach her Teal, warm her with her body, encourage her to nurse.

"I'll tell them," he said softly. Then he turned and started back to the kitchen for he couldn't bear not to hand her the child.

"Be sure they mask against the dust," she reminded.

"I'll be sure," he said.

"What if she gets up for it?" he asked Doc Eber.

Doc Eber took the last sip of his coffee, then turned his cup upside down in his saucer. "After that birth, she'll not be up for several days."

"You don't know Esther."

"I know what's possible!" he said emphatically. "She's a strong woman, but she's human."

"The times before . . . It almost kills her to lose anything, especially a child," Ray said, grave concern in his tone.

"Don't make it any harder on yourself than it has to be," Doc Eber said sternly.

Solemnly, Ray nodded. He dreaded this long night.

Dory finished making more coffee, then called in the children to beans and corn bread before going home to her own family. "I'll be back after I see to *my* family," she told him.

Doc Eber prepared to leave after the drops of silver nitrate had been carefully administered to Teal's eyes. "Two teaspoons full of boiled warm water by dropper now, every hour for the next forty-eight hours," he reminded Ray. "If the child's alive then, we'll give it every two hours and so on, increasing the quantity a bit as her color improves. She's as yellow and wrinkled as a persimmon," he grumbled and shook his gray head. Then he pushed at the center of his gold-rimmed spectacles, picked up his black bag, and left with instructions to call him "if need be."

"Is Mother okay?" Tad asked. Ray knew the boy at twelve understood today's mysteries. About halfway through his supper, Tad couldn't let the question die. "Is the—?" Ray sat with him and Jenny, finishing a cup of hot black coffee. Jonsi sat on the floor playing jacks.

"Your mother's going to be okay, but she'll need rest for about a week, maybe longer." *It was enough to say for now*, he thought.

Guilt over his pessimism that Teal might not live attacked. "We got us another girl in the family," he said confidently at last. *She could live,* he reminded himself silently. He'd see to the fluids all night himself. He rose to boil the water.

"Thank goodness," Jenny said, looking down her perfectly straight thirteen-year-old nose at Tad and Jonsi.

"Phew!" Jonsi responded, wrinkling his face. At eight, Jonsi's sandy hair and brown eyes reminded Ray of Esther more than his other children did, though Esther's eyes were that pale blue of dreams. He reached now and rumpled the boy's hair. "Girls!" Jonsi elaborated, as if to assure his father that he would have preferred a brother.

"You boys dry the dishes for Jenny. I'm going to see about your mother, then give the baby her drops of water. If your mother agrees to it, you can all have a peek at her. And Jenny, Dory will help see to your mother tonight, but we'll want you to learn what to do for her and the new one so you can help. I'll be needed back at the mill soon. When you finish in here, you're to mask against the dust and see to the garden. Water, gather, and store."

They made no smart remarks or argued. Rather, their faces sobered. He sensed their response reflected both their aversions to a baby in the house after eight years and a desire to help.

As he left them, he heard Jonsi say, "Drops of water! I thought babies nursed. Don't babies get milk from their mother?" He obviously struggled with the idea. Ray paused to hear any response.

"Sure they do," Jenny said. "But maybe they have a drink of water first. I don't know about such things, for heaven's sake."

"Well, you better be learning," Jonsi said, his voice almost breaking into a laugh. "Dad says you're to help." Then Ray heard his son run out the back door and slam it hard behind him.

Ray drew a long breath and entered their bedroom. From the expression on her face, Esther was waiting for him. "Give me the child, Ray. Hand Teal to me now, or I shall get up and get her."

"I can't, Esther. Doc's orders, and you know as well as I that he knows best." He pled with her with feeling, his caring in his eyes.

A muscle began to jerk at his left cheek as their gaze held one another's.

"You know I don't like to go against you, Ray. And I've trusted Doc Eber with my life more than once. He means well. But I know what's best here. Trust *me*." Now it was her turn to beg. It seemed that her heart shone from her eyes. He couldn't stand it, so he looked away—but only for a moment. For when she started to raise herself to a sitting position, he stepped forward with alarm.

"You're pressing too hard, Esther," he said. "You'd not make it to the crib. I tell you, you've lost too much blood! If you start the hemorrhaging again, Doc says we could lose you too."

"Too!" she exclaimed. "What are you saying? That you've given up on a child that is breathing?"

"Now, Esther, don't excite yourself, please," he begged. He felt himself giving in to her, fearing that she'd endanger her own life with an excess of feeling or movement.

"I'm just saying it once more, Ray. You don't have to understand. Just give me my baby, and don't wait any longer to do it. If you don't, I'm going get her myself, and that's that!"

He didn't look at her long this time; he dared not risk it. He yielded.

"I can't watch you all the time to see that you don't," he said and turned to get the child for her. He reached for her, then stopped.

Startled, Esther lifted her head from the pillow. "What's wrong?" she asked. Her usually ruddy face, already pale, drained of all color.

"Just one of my hands is bigger than she is," he answered helplessly. "I'm afraid to touch her."

Esther laughed softly as she lay back. "Just roll the basket here. See? On the legs, the rollers?" He stood there watching as she reached for Teal. Her hand held her tiny bottom, and the wee head rested high on her wrist.

"That's an incredible sight," he breathed in a husky whisper. "Her little ears, thin as paper. What if they grow crooked?" He heard Esther's soft laugh that labeled him foolish.

"That hair all over her looks funny. When will it go away?"

She smiled up at him, happy to hear him speak as if their child would live after all. He bent toward them, feeling magnetized by the sight of her bringing the infant to her warmth.

"That fuzz will go away in a few weeks," she assured.

It seemed for a time that she wouldn't nurse. Then suddenly, Teal's sluggish instincts wakened. The rosebud lips opened to grasp the nipple while her tiny fists pushed against soft flesh, and that natural rhythm of warmth and nourishment verified by the infant's smacks and sighs began.

"Ahhh!" Esther sighed, then laughed aloud. "You see. She's very strong. I knew she was very, very strong, and so she shows you."

"Such a bald head," he said, his voice cracking.

"You're to call Doc Eber in the morning and tell him, hear?"

"I hear," he said. "Can the children see her?"

"Let me have this time with her first," she answered softly. "And, Ray," she said quite seriously, "don't think me harsh, just trust me. I want everyone including you to wear a mask in this room until Teal reaches her nine months."

"Whatever you say," he said, his glance asking her forgiveness. She reached her hand toward him. He moved around the basket to bend and kiss her hair. "I'll go to the children and explain the situation."

"Yes, do," she urged. "Help them understand." And so he left her with Teal until he heard her call for him.

* * *

From the start, the children regarded Teal with suspicion above their tea towel masks. "She doesn't look, well, human," Jenny ventured.

Esther gave Jenny's opinion no dignity by responding to such remarks.

When shortages of oranges channeled the slim supply Teal's direction, Jenny whined the judgment. "It's not fair!"

Esther ignored her. Jonsi tried a different approach: reason.

"If she's such a miracle kid, why does she get all the special stuff? Looks like less would do. Besides, she's a year old now. She walks and talks like any other kid."

Esther had just stripped Teal to lay her in the sunny window. She began oiling her plump body with olive oil. Teal's skin turned golden and pink with health in the glow of the June summer and Esther's care. Esther felt that she'd shaped the living child with her own hands. She gave Jonsi her warmest glance.

"Darling," she pled softly. "This minute I want so to hug you. Come nearer so I won't have to let loose of Teal. She might fall if I did. See how wriggly and strong she is?"

Jonsi saw. Sullenly, he stared at Teal. "I hate her!" he yelled, then spun about and left. Esther told herself that it was just a passing mood.

After she'd finished sunning Teal, she bathed her, nursed her, and put her to bed for an afternoon nap before seeking out Jonsi. She found him sulking in the barn.

Between his feet was a can of rusty nails, which he cleaned one by one with a ball of steel wool.

She stooped and put her arm about his shoulder. He jerked away.

"Dad says I'm to clean these," he said, pitching his voice lower. "We're gonna tear down this old shed and build a barn by spring next year."

"I see," she said. "Where's Tad?"

"Minding his business, same as me, I reckon," he remarked. It sounded like the vocabulary of his father.

"Well, it's plain to me that you're growing up just fine," she said softly.

"Yeah," he said. She stood, wistfully observing him at her feet as his chubby fingers lay each nail aside. They turned orange with rust, which he wiped on the legs of his overalls with regularity. At the edges of his gleaming gold hair, she could see brunette roots. Half of her wanted to pull him up to her and clutch him as the child he wanted to be. The other half wanted to end this struggle for him and force him to confront his fear of Teal.

"I need to say just one thing to you, son," she said.

He didn't answer.

"Teal hasn't taken anything from you, not love, not oranges. She was born to the outside world too soon. She has a need for protection so close and safe as a mother's body because she left her safe place inside my belly too soon. Someday you'll understand that, and I'd like you to remember that I cared enough to explain it."

He stared up at her, his eyes older than his nine years. "Tad don't like it either, and neither does Jenny. We think she's over all that, but you're not because you love her, well, the most. It don't feel fair."

Sudden anger gripped Esther to think her children questioned her behavior and Teal's right to special attention.

"Well, young man!" she snapped. "I'll just find the two of them and have a little talk. I'll see that they begin occupying themselves as usefully as you are!" She swished out the door past Ray, hardly acknowledging that they passed. Angry that her children could be jealous and spiteful of one another frightened her. Adulthood brought unknowns to a family. They would need one another's devotion.

"Where's Jenny?" she asked, turning back toward Ray.

"She's tying up the grape and berry vines. Tad's hoeing the okra."

"Oh!" she said, feeling suddenly left out of the business of family and structure. An unaccountable feeling of missing something overtook her, and tears sprang to her eyes. She hurried into the house and made a compulsive check on Teal to verify she still breathed.

Teal's crib sat in the corner of her and Ray's bedroom where the basket used to be. She slept peacefully, her chubby fingers curled, her lungs clear and strong. Suddenly, Esther turned and flung herself upon the bed, her tears spilling fast in a hot stream of rebellion.

She needed to give up this fear. Oh, Jonsi was right, but fright seemed a part of her now—her fright and her hope struggling together since that day. She sensed that the guarding of her child's health preserved her hope for the future. Suddenly, she sat up and brushed away the tears. A year had gone by, and it was time to take hold of the summer and become a part of her whole family again, whatever else she felt. Could she change her mind and lose this anxiety? After all, life for everyone included some risk.

Esther went directly to her sewing machine, and by the time that Teal wakened, she'd sewn her two bonnets to protect her from the sun and dust. Together then, they went out to join the others in the garden.

That night when she and Ray lay together, their children asleep, they talked.

"I'll buy her a wagon," Ray said. "She can sit in it when we're working or toddle along until she tires. She doesn't tire easily." He laughed.

"The children enjoyed running after her, didn't they, Ray?"

"Oh, sure!" he said. "It's the first time they've ever given her much mind, I'd say."

"Teal loved it," Esther mused. "She's such a greedy little thing for life, was from the start. I knew it the moment she clutched her milk so and her fit to die."

"That's past, Esther."

"Is it, Ray? Is war and disease and depression and dirt—"

"Shhhh," he answered. "It all came too fast and filled the space of seven years. Now it's gone. Look around you, see your plump and healthy child."

Esther moved closer to him. "She was as shrunk and yellow as the times. I think that's what I saw when I looked at her, and I must have felt that if she died, I died. I think I must have thought the world was rolling downhill."

"She didn't die," he said, wanting her to hear it inside where it counted.

"No, she didn't die."

The shrill whistle of a freight train sounded up the curving track.

"It's pulling heavy," Ray said. "They must be moving out some sixty-cent wheat. If we don't get more rain for fall planting, the price and low yields have to make it hard on local farmers. Why, a man with a hundred and sixty acres is doing good to get three hundred dollars above his expenses. Fuel's up to almost ten cents a gallon some places. Who would have believed a price so low for wheat—wheat, a staple for the hungry world."

"The three-year mortgage moratorium will soon be over. Still, it's saved a lot of farmers from losing their land." Esther yawned. "Where they shippin', do you suppose?"

"Out to Houston. Europe will get it cheap—or China. Political turmoil in Europe can raise export quotas or kill them. Germany keeps stirring the pot toward trouble."

"Is the mill getting what it needs?"

"Oh, sure. Customers from a long time back bring it in. The question is, can they afford to keep bringing it in? It gets any dryer—"

"You mean the price can drop lower?"

"Even with a scarcity, prices could drop. There may be no money to buy. It's the stock too. There's less pasture all the time, less hay. Growers are forced to sell for any price. When a beef sells for three fifty, hogs too. When a farmer's wife gets a dime a dozen for her eggs and just a few cents over that for the whole chicken—"

"If they raised the prices at the store, let the consumer pay his share—"

She stopped. They both knew most couldn't afford to pay their share. The times had made the few very rich and most of the rest very poor. At dollar-a-day wages, they needed milk at five cents a quart.

Ray sighed. "Ah, the trains will be moving regular again soon."

"How's that, Ray?"

"Addis Ababba," he said flatly. "Italy'll get all of Europe stirred up if Germany doesn't, and the flatcars will start hauling army green tanks and trucks across the country again. That army green and the New Deal's billions for defense will roll right past our lives."

"If need be," she said. "Some of the New Deal sounds good, like a free education for the children and buses to get them there if we live too far. We didn't have that, Ray. I want it for Jenny and Jonsi, for Tad and little Teal."

"I know," he said sadly. "I guess I just wish there was another way. It took a man with paralysis to move a paralyzed country. All I'm wondering, Esther, is if there's a way for a man who isn't paralyzed to do it without taking from our gold, without becoming our caregiver. Government in the middle of education bothers me.

There'll be a time for reckoning, a time when paper money will shrink in value because of population growth and depleted gold supplies. There could come a time when government controls what our children learn and believe, and we might have no say at all."

"That's not fair, Ray. You know that necessity is the father of invention. We need this New Deal."

"Who said so? Ben Franklin said that necessity *never made a good bargain.*"

"Well, I don't know besides me who said it, I just know I figure ways around things I don't have and that you do the same."

"We make do, and I'm grateful. I'm just saying that I'm a realist, Esther, who wants gold bricks to show me the wealth of a nation. Sometimes the 'ways around,' as you say, aren't as top-notch, not as good a bargain as it could be with the better idea. I'm not a man who can see abstractions like New Deals and a philosophy for the common good and for the common man. *I don't feel like a common man. I feel equal, and I feel I am a child of God. I feel the terms common man and common good are condescending.*

"I want the wealth of this country to reveal itself in the health and independent courage of its people, Esther. I want to see it in the price a man gets for his product. I want to see it in the way a school teaches my children and others of any color or culture to earn a living and to solve a problem for themselves."

Esther yawned. "Oh, Ray," she said. "Those are such plain and ordinary things. Why, Mr. Roosevelt's looking at the whole world. He's looking at five hundred men at a time—five thousand. He says that old way of looking at things, seeing the individual, hearing the individual just won't work for a progressive time."

She heard him sigh again. After a long pause, he said, "Maybe somebody besides Mr. Roosevelt will find the way to have both democratic freedoms and free education. Then a work that pays a fair and competitive wage to a people prepared for work in a country that flourishes instead of a country limping along can be realized. It seems to me that both lost freedom and lost talent may be the price we pay besides higher taxes and reduced incomes. Good labor unions and the equal opportunity for health and higher education must come, or the *common man*, as the uppity Washingtonians call us, will be the slave of the industry owners, bankers, and Wall Street—maybe even *with* union organization if they're crooked with greed as well. Too many bright and talented Americans are kept under the foot of the wealthy. They writhe in that prison of obstacles before turning to alcohol, drugs, indigence, or crime. Not all, but too many."

"What on earth do you mean? Why, that's wild, Ray. You sound like a—what you just said is wild. Nobody can predict a thing like that from public works and government help."

"Nope. It will take a heap of doing to prevent an eventual world-leveling socialism where those that work take care of those that can't or won't. And if accountability from government doesn't back off greedy gangsters who grow wealth from others' sweat, these New Deal solutions will fall flat. They're already doing their dirt in New York and Chicago. Will Rogers says it costs the average taxpayer two hundred dollars annually to keep a government employee on the payroll. Where does that leave those working for a dollar a day?

"Why, in fifty years, half the population will probably be on its payroll, I'd bet on it. And someday, government jobs could be the only safe jobs. We can say 'Thank God Tad, Jonsi, Jenny, and Teal have safe government jobs with adequate health insurance and every holiday off besides sick leave and vacations.'"

"I don't want to talk about it. You sound angry. Let's go to sleep."

"You mean I sound angry instead of like a Communist?"

They were quiet for a long time.

"Are you asleep?" Esther whispered.

"No," he whispered back. "Why should I worry now that you women have the vote?" He chuckled. "You'll save the democracy. Introduce your cinnamon rolls to China, and we'll have a huge market for wheat that will make our farmers rich, deplete the reserve storage that reduces the price, and control the effect of hedgers whose quantity of owned wheat isn't capped to protect the market."

"They don't eat wheat in China," she said. "They eat rice, and don't be surprised if some woman doesn't clean up the corruption and greed on Wall Street."

"Wait fifty years, then tell me that. Tell me in fifty years that the government hasn't made commodity futures gamblers out of our producers and changed a supply-and-demand market to a funds market for speculators as well."

"We won't neither of us be alive then," she said, her voice fading entirely.

It prompted him to draw her close to him. Esther reached in the dark to see his face with her hand. Her fingers trailed his lips before he kissed her. But Esther's unease persisted until it broke through her need to set it aside.

"Ray," she whispered as his lips brushed her cheek. "If our farmers just plain couldn't afford to feed us, what then?"

"Dependency on others instead of ourselves puts us at their mercy for prices and for supply. With all the wonderful available land, think of imported wheat to balance trade. Think of canning industries that plant crops instead of the row-crop farmer. Several controlling corporations for grain would develop most likely, import some cheap to sell high instead of export our surplus for profit. They can always sell the cheap import for more and have a profit. They might maintain the surplus to force prices down. Don't think it won't happen if consumers and speculators demand it. The elected want votes. The government could continue to subsidize the farmer and to limit his planted acreage. Or they can pull the production limits and delete subsidy payments.

"There will always be those who don't understand subsidizing to the actual producers who can't get a fair price for his product due to market manipulation. If the government representatives who are out of touch with growers' production costs have a voice in the power structure, they'll call an end to *all* subsidy instead of ending that to nonproducers who collect on acres of sorry land for doing nothing but spraying for weeds.

"Eventually, food prices will go sky-high unless there's lots of competition and cheaper energy to transport and to produce.

"Until and unless the producer has access to all information and acts on it, he's at the mercy of the dozens of uncontrollable market forces surrounding him. Fact is that there is *no way* for him to know who holds how much grain, where or how they got it, or who gambled on it that never held a single grain. Political pressure may cause boycotts, strikes, imposed religion, loss of our freedom. Agricultural land could be confiscated or zoned for residences or business. That's progress that really costs because land would go fallow, probably with a payment to encourage it. Much of our arable land would probably be covered with concrete for city streets, airports, and industrial sites.

"Yes, if you want to consider something scary, consider this country dependent on another country rather than its own to feed its millions. Still, in times of drought, trade means survival. Bottom line, Esther, it takes both self-reliance and trade."

Esther sobbed just thinking about such possible misery. Her mind seemed to leap ahead.

"Without our healthy competition in this democracy, problems with distribution and corruption could leave millions to starve, even in times of plenty," she said. "There's people who will scam the government as easy as their neighbor." Esther's voice trembled at the thought. "Our control over our lives—gone."

"If we get out of this depression like Roosevelt says," Ray suddenly reassured, "there'll be money again. That capitalistic competition you mentioned assures that. I didn't mean to alarm you. Money means safety at work, comfort, space. You have a tender heart. Believe in tomorrow. We must make the most of each day, live with gratitude for it."

"If folks lose heart, both economic recovery and victory over enemies like those pounding Europe now becomes difficult," Esther agreed. "Wages will need to go up though. Forty-five cents an hour is slave labor. If I had the money, I'd pay for a little comfort, like a velvet chair and ceiling fans, wouldn't you?"

"I don't know. Depends on how many hours I had to slave for it so that someone else can have my dollars. I might rather be uncomfortable. Paper money that's paper all the way through has built-in inflation potential, Esther. A penny saved is a penny earned, I always say. But what makes me think I know more'n a president or educated economists? I apprenticed in milling and elevators for feed and grain, in the chemistry of baking, in the shipping terminals."

Ray's voice sank. Esther lay silent for a moment, then she kissed him first, and he kissed her back. "Make love to me," she whispered. "Maybe Tad or Jonsi will run this country someday while we run our own mill."

"I like both of those ideas," he murmured. "That's the best thing, besides freedom, of course, about this country. It dangles hope in front of you like it was a rainbow to follow to your sure and certain pot of gold. I just can't keep from believing in the goodness ahead. Why, despite hard times, I've blessings aplenty: a work I love, beautiful children, health. Best of all, Esther, God gave me you."

"And Ben Franklin," she added.

Then Ray Swain drew Esther Swain into his arms. "He gave us Ben Franklin *and* the Good Book," he murmured. "But I really don't know who said 'a penny saved is a penny earned' before my father said it."

Two weeks later, Tad began running a 103° temperature. Ray feared that he had eaten unwashed scattered strawberries from a stalled train's empty boxcar floor. No other exposure explained the mysterious illness that caused his delirium. After the diagnosis of typhoid fever by Dr. Eber, Jenny, Teal, and Jonsi could no longer be in the same room with Tad.

*   *   *

Teal's days were lonely as she agonized in the house's quiet shadowed corners.

Her days had fled the sunshine, it seemed, for Esther sat night and day at Tad's bedside. Women from the church arrived in shifts to give her brief relief, or Dory Isaacs appeared so that she could sleep for a few hours.

Her father seemed far away from her as well, working longer and longer hours at the mill only to come home and sleep in his chair as if to escape their common dread of hovering death.

She overheard her mother telling him for a truth that a loud knock had come to their door the night before Tad's fever finally broke and that when she opened it, there stood the Grim Reaper in all his grotesque ugliness and stench of death.

"I slammed the door in his face," she declared, "and retched from that stink until it seemed my sides would burst!"

Then Jonsi broke out in huge welts from the hives after getting the typhoid shot, and Teal ran a mild temperature herself, which further alarmed Esther and caused a fit of hysterics that prompted her father to lift her mother like a child, tuck her in bed, and order Teal and Jenny to bring hot tea.

Then as suddenly as Tad became ill, he recovered. The only reminder of the illness seemed his curly hair instead of his previously straight hair.

"Might have started curling anyway," he told them every time he tried a new product to straighten it again. None worked. Other than that, life resumed normally at the Swains.

CHAPTER VIII

Oklahoma City

Teal was eight when they bought the shiny new Chevy. It became a familiar sight to see Ray Swain withdraw the crank, and with the sprocket over the spindle shaft, he cranked and cranked. On cold mornings, he cranked still more, but once it started, a more-dependable vehicle was hard to find. That first summer he owned it and after he binned the season's wheat harvest, he woke all of them early.

"We're going to see Oklahoma City!" he announced.

"The zoo! The zoo!" Tad bellowed. A science major at the University of Oklahoma now, Tad wanted to research the primates for his paper on the gorilla.

Esther said there was some shopping that she might do, and Jenny immediately began to talk about visiting Browns and Rothchilds. They're exclusive," she said. "I'd like my wedding dress to come from an exclusive store like that." Her eyes rolled up in a dreamy stare, for Charles Huel of *the* Canadian County Huels had given her an engagement ring.

"Drama queen!" Tad teased when they all met in the living room.

"Then you'll see your fashions," Ray said, "and Tad will see his zoo, and Esther can shop." He paused a moment, his eyes bright as a boy's with a new red wagon. "How about Jonsi and Teal? What do you two want?" he asked, looking from one to the other with such open affection in his voice and his glance.

Teal's heart felt marshmallow soft before it. How she adored him! A stern efficient man, Ray Swain often gave tender moments to his family with a freshness that equaled the relief of dry-weather showers. Silently, she thought of her mother's single Sunday dress and her father's one gray gabardine suit slightly frayed at the back collar.

"Who cares!" Jonsi spouted in his usual sour mood these days. Jonsi had begun his senior year. Teal had overheard Ray and Esther's concern that Jonsi seemed in a quandary about his future.

"One of these days your face is going to stick all screwed up like that," Ray teased him, but Jonsi, who sat between Ray and Esther in the front seat, still sulled.

"You asked Tad first," he mumbled, staring at the floor.

"I want to see everything on the way," Teal said. "And the zoo and the shops too. Jonsi loves growing things. Aren't there gardens or farm shows, something like that in Oklahoma City?"

Ray nodded approval, lavishing Jonsi with a smile and giving her a wink in the rearview mirror. "We'll come home by way of Lake Overholser, Jonsi. I'll take you for a boat ride. There's boats for rent there, they say. There's considerable landscaping at the zoo that you'd enjoy." He tousled Jonsi's hair.

"Stop it," Jonsi protested, obviously pleased with the attention.

So they set out on their Saturday excursion the week before Jenny's wedding to Charles Huel, the eldest son of the valley's wealthiest farmer. Sadly, Teal sensed it was the last family trip she would have with Jenny before everything changed.

There were ranchers who owned more grassland for their huge herds of cattle than the Huels owned, but nobody owned more wheat land than the Huels. And the main difference in a farmer and a rancher in these parts was in the acres of wheat and grains and the number of cattle that grazed

—

"I'll bet Charles's mother has a charge account at Rothchilds," Jenny said before they were five minutes on Route 66 east of the county seat.

"I'll bet she gives you her old fur coats and buys all new ones on it," Teal said with a snicker. She turned her head to look out the window for distraction. She felt more like crying at the thought of Jenny leaving.

"You shut up!" Jenny snapped.

Teal slyly brushed a tear off her cheek. She felt ashamed that she should care since Jenny never seemed to care about her.

"They bought two new tractors," Ray said, "and a new Massey combine. Cut all of their grain with it this summer. Averaged thirty bushels, three higher than most farms. They had a section or two that made thirty-five. 'Course, they have migrant thrashers and haulers to get their crops out in a timely way. The rains didn't stall *their* harvest."

"That's what Charles said," Jenny agreed proudly. "Charles said we'll get to live in the big homestead house. He said his folks were moving to town when we married."

Glumly, Teal stared at the harvest fields. The yellow stubble looked almost white in the July heat. She could see the hard earth at the field's edge that needed rain.

She didn't have to know much about farming to see it wasn't going to be an easy job turning that stubble under.

"They better leave that stubble for quite a spell this year," her father said as if he had read her mind. "It's too dry and windy to plow it under. The topsoil that's left will blow right off."

"Charles says they're starting, uh, conservation, something new for the land the government sponsors."

"Charles says, Charles says," Teal mimicked.

Jenny stuck her tongue out at Teal.

Ray frowned a warning at them both from the rearview mirror.

From the county seat of El Reno on to Oklahoma City, the land stretched level. Owners had suffered drought effects and insects

—

like greenbugs, army worms, and grasshoppers. The wheat itself appeared spindly again.

"The new land conservation programs of terraces and waterways will help hilly land for sure," Ray said. "It's good that Charles is learning about it. That level land is begging for deep plowing to bring up moisture. They plowed too shallow before this crop."

"Lord help us if the grasshoppers are bad again," Esther said.

"When we gonna be there?" Jonsi interrupted, suddenly impatient. He must have asked that same question six times or more before the skyscrapers of the capital raised their rectangular heads like great slate-blue slabs of concrete. Teal could distinguish no details—not a window. She thought that if she saw it in a painting, she would believe the artist quite forgetful to leave off so much. They were upon the city before she could see the black-iron fire escapes, the hundreds of tiny windows, and the skyscrapers' identifying signs.

A terrible smell filled the air.

"Phew!" Tad complained. At twenty, Tad stretched six feet tall and had probably gotten his dark good looks from twice-removed Cherokee ancestors, though neither Esther nor Ray had bothered to trace it.

"That's the sweet smell of oil," Ray laughed. "Breathe deep. You may never smell it in our own county."

"Lord, I hope not," Esther said. "Who'd want an ugly sight like that in their backyard?"

"I would," Teal said without hesitation. She took a deep breath of it. It smelled black and slick and rich. It was the next best smell to earth she'd known.

Ray located Rothchilds and parked on the curbing right in front of it. Jenny acted as if she couldn't move for a moment.

"Get out, stupid!" Tad told her without ceremony. Esther and Ray exchanged a glance, which Teal interpreted as half concern, half good humor. They exited the car followed by their children. So Jenny bought her wedding dress for her marriage to Charles at Rothchild's in Oklahoma City.

Teal knew that her mother had saved back three dollars each week from the grocery money for a year to buy it. "Don't you tell her, Teal. She might feel bad about it. No one should regret a wedding dress."

The Huels have a high living standard," Jenny informed them en route to the zoo.

"What do you think ours is?" Esther asked, tucking a strand of her golden brown hair inside its comb. The afternoon had grown quite warm, and the sunshine burned through the front glass. She mopped her damp forehead with her handkerchief. She loosened the fabric of her lawn dress, a pale green that clung to her perspiring arms.

"Owning shares in a mill is good. You know I think a lot of you and Daddy," Jenny said. "But the Huels are rich, Mama. *Really* rich." Nothing Jenny was saying made sense to Teal. She shut it out of her mind to think only on Jenny's wedding.

"Then why is she baking and selling, making jelly and selling, picking orchard and selling, pickling, and pie baking for restaurants? I don't understand that," Esther said with irritation. "It appears to me that they need money like the rest of us in these hard times."

"She's artistic. It's a hobby," Jenny said.

"May be," Esther said. "Just don't count your chickens before they're hatched. It can be mighty disappointing. Farming's a hard life, and the more of it there is to do, the longer the days and nights and the harder you work."

"You're always throwing one of those sayings around like they're law. There's hired help," Jenny argued.

"For the women?" Esther responded, glaring pointedly over her shoulder at Jenny.

"Well," Jenny began, then paused thoughtfully. "I've not asked Charles that. I assumed."

"Ask it," Esther said. "If they hire thrasher and tractor drivers, there's likely a crew of twenty to cook for, to raise garden and leghorn chickens for. Going to Rothchilds once or twice a year between all that would be like living in hell and going to heaven

—

112

for an occasional visit—short at that. But don't let work discourage you. It's an honorable thing." Esther's voice had begun to grate, and her handkerchief fairly flew across her brow.

Teal hated the tense and bitter tone of her mother's voice, though Jenny's prattle annoyed her too. She longed to hear her mother speak more encouragingly about the wedding again. She had heard her mother mention *the change* and *hot flashes* when she had these irritable moods. Esther mopped her face again then shook the hanky out as if to find a dry spot on it.

"She probably doesn't go to Rothchilds very often, Mother," Jenny said apologetically. "Maybe she doesn't go at all."

"Ask Charles," Esther said, taking a fan from her purse and fanning herself. "Ask him."

"I will, Mama," Jenny said meekly. "I surely will ask Charles." Jenny's sudden quietness was as unsettling to Teal as her prattle. Teal figured she was considering all that work. Work wasn't one of Jenny's favorite things.

Teal stepped close to her and clasped her hand. She felt saturated with remorse and looked forward to a wedding. "Tell me again how your dress looks inside that box," Teal begged. "Oh, I wish I'd seen you try it on. I wish I'd known that you were. I'd have bought my popcorn later. Want some?" she offered.

Jenny reached in the bag for the few remaining kernels. "Thanks," she murmured.

Teal wadded up the empty bag after crunching the last of the hard tack from the bottom of the sack. She licked the salt off her lips and fingers. Outside the store, she threw the empty sack in the trash.

*   *   *

Perhaps it was the long drive over, the shopping, the anticipation of the zoo, and the boat ride, for a quiet settled over them. Ray Swain occupied himself by watching the highway and following the black arrows along the route to the Oklahoma City Zoo in Lincoln Park.

The July sun still hammered down in the afternoon's fullness. It glared white upon the concrete beyond them. It amazed Teal that pools of water seemed to lie just ahead, but when they arrived there, the water vanished.

"What is it, Mama? See the water, see, look!" As they passed over the hard dry surface, she twisted her head about to look behind, but it was gone.

"A mirage," Esther said. She slurred the word in deep and guttural tones as if it and happiness were the same word.

"Life changes," Ray said. "Like that mirage, someday Teal will marry too. The child will vanish, and the woman will appear." He tossed a smile over his shoulder at her. Teal tucked her chin down, but her eyes held his.

He was away more and more now, and Esther seemed in another place most of the time. She almost never included Teal by glance or gesture, not even when they spent hours together in the same room. Whatever Esther did these days, she did it in deep and pensive thought that discouraged interference.

"And," Ray continued expansively, as if a matter of another important change must be faced, "there's only so much resistance to Jonsi's request to join up that we're allowed. I'd rather sign for him than have him leave us, resentful and estranged."

"Thanks, Dad!" Jonsi exclaimed as if it was settled.

Teal's heart seemed to shrivel at the thought of *that* change. Tad was over eighteen; he'd signed up a few months after Pearl Harbor and was waiting for his orders. Jonsi, only seventeen in two months, required his parents' signatures.

Esther slapped her hand against her forehead. "Not now! I can't stand to think of it." Ray took his pipe out of his pocket and clamped its stem between his teeth. He did that when he was worried without ever lighting it.

"Sooner or later, Esther," he said quietly. "You will have to think of it." Teal looked carefully at Jonsi beside her. She wanted to memorize his sandy good looks, but he turned his head to stare out of the window as if to escape her scrutiny.

Just then, her father turned right and entered a huge parking lot. Before a wrought iron gate farther to her right, black enameled letters told her they had arrived at the zoo. Tad tumbled out from the other side, obviously relieved to have his six feet two inches standing again, for he stretched luxuriously beside Ray who held the door for Esther.

With her exaggerated dignity, Jenny followed, grumbling about a "dumb old animal farm."

"That's what you're marrying into, stupid!" Jonsi told her. He crawled out of the front seat behind Esther.

"Yeah, and who's going to war instead of college?" she shot back.

"There's a place in France where the women wear no pants," Jonsi sang.

"Now that's enough of that!" Ray told them sternly. "I've let it pass earlier, but the day and patience with it seems to be wearing thin."

Teal wanted to have a good time. But a peculiar emptiness inside her that had nothing to do with food made itself known as her father's words finally caught up with her.

"Things change," he had said. *No,* she thought, *that wasn't right.* "Life changes, Esther." That's what he'd said. Life—not things. People changed things like the furniture, their friends, or their clothes; life changed people. Suddenly, she realized her life would soon change drastically. Tad and Jonsi would be gone; Jenny would be gone. *She would be alone.* Her mind repeated. *Alone, alone, alone.*

It wasn't that hard to accept Jenny's leaving. Jenny bored her. Besides, she wanted their room to herself. And Jenny wasn't going very far away. Then there was the wedding. The wonderful wedding with flowers and organza dresses and little cookies with pink punch. But Tad and Jonsi . . . bombs . . . When that empty place inside her filled up with a scream that she must keep there, she thought she understood why her mother seemed in another world these days.

"Get out, Teal," Esther said.

She clutched the back of the seat in front of her. She heard the right front door slam with exploding force as Jonsi took out his anger at Jenny on the car. She didn't want them to go! Her brothers! Go where, and for what? She thought she might choke if she thought about it any longer.

"Stop dawdling, Teal!" Esther called, moving ahead. So Teal scrambled out too. She had to skip to catch up with them. The animals lay drowsy in the sun, each of them in their cage or cave and some of them in pairs. Beautiful animals, sleek and spotted and striped with black or white, with brown or gold—different. *Like people,* she thought, *but more interesting to look at for their odd shapes and colorful designs.* She giggled to herself. *People were more oddly shaped than animals,* she thought. To her, the animals seemed more perfect to their species in both behavior and appearance for she didn't expect them to use common sense instead of violence, gluttony, or dishonor.

They passed the park's lake. She looked long at the water, beautiful and brown and sun glinted. Small but beautifully shaped shade trees were along its bank. A turtle slid down the bank and submerged. Several swans swam by, their regal heads held high.

She thought of the tree she'd drawn last year for art class. Her teacher called it perfect and gave her a superior mark on it. She'd studied it, looking for a flaw to repair and found none. Then suddenly, she knew why she hadn't liked that tree. These were beautiful imperfect trees. Her tree, the tree she'd made, didn't look as if it had lived through wind and snow, through dry years and wet. Too pretty, too straight for this kind of beauty that was in touch with the elements and alive.

A little shiver ran over her. She smiled at the ducks and geese that paddled ashore for the popcorn and bread that children brought. She felt her father's hand upon her shoulder. "Next time we'll bring stale bread and feed the ducks," he said.

"And pop some corn to bring too," Esther added, her voice soft and allowing that future happiness to slide through like hope. Tad strode down the slope to the lake with manly motion. Jonsi followed, and then the rest moved near to stand together and watch the ducks and swans and geese in their stately rituals.

"There's a teal duck," Tad said with a side glance at his little sister.

"There's a duck named after me?" she asked, obviously taken with the idea. She thought it odd that everyone laughed heartily.

Curiously, it fused the day and seemed to prepare Teal for the anticipated changes. In any case, she felt both closeness and separateness as they stood there enjoying this moment's reality. She fell asleep on the ride home.

She wakened as Ray Swain gathered her up in his arms to carry her inside the house. Her lids fluttered open a bit, and she saw that darkness had fallen and that the sky was shot full of stars. No cloud tonight promised rain. She squeezed her eyes shut again and pretended sleep, for it was the first time in a long time that he'd held her as if she were a little girl. It felt so safe to be clutched warm and tight against him.

"Just lay her on the couch for the night," Esther spoke softly. "Jenny might rather be alone for a few nights anyway. A girl has things to think about before she marries."

"I'd best go out and water tonight or the garden will be gone. The squash are suffering the most," he said, placing Teal on the daybed in the dining room instead of on the couch. He drew the cotton blanket over her feet and legs after removing her shoes. She'll rest better here for the night."

"Beans too," Esther said. "Water them too. They might bloom again with water. A rain would be best." Teal heard their conversation through her half sleep. She heard the others hit the stairs for their bedrooms. She turned upon her side when he laid her down and knew that it was Esther who drew the light covering over her shoulders. "I'll be going out to help you, Ray," Esther said.

"That'd be mighty fine," he responded. "I've missed you not working beside me in things the way you used to."

"I only said I was going out with you tonight," she clarified, a slight edge to her voice.

Teal thought she had heard something new in his tone, something hard and bargaining. It was a tone she didn't understand, but she knew it was far more important than those few words. She felt it had everything to do with Esther's distance, with their failing closeness. *Dad might not have nearly so much to do nor Mother so much to think about if there were more days like today,* she thought, drifting toward the thick darkness of sleep.

To the north, Teal heard the train whistle, its departure from the roundhouse where trains could be routed east or west or north or south on the great track-slashed wheel of a floor. That's how she imagined it in her mind as if trains originated there.

They seemed alive to Teal, like great steel dragons, friendly dragons that breathed smoke and fire, gobbled coal, and whistled when they passed. She watched her father help load thousands of railcars with wheat or flour at the mill.

The trains brought the produce into towns, and it took their products out. They followed the rail farther than camels followed the Sahara. The rail ran to coasts, to ports at Galveston, New Orleans, and to Houston.

The chug-chugging grew louder. The whistle grew shrill, faded, passed by. The raucous clacking of rails and puffing of steam seemed to speak of struggle. Then after a shudder of jagged steam, like the chaotic beating of her own heart at times, the wheels clacked faster and gained speed and distance, their sounds fading into silence as if swallowed by her sleep.

When the cars returned, trucks would back up to them at various points along the line to unload oranges and bananas, coal and oil. They would unload cars and trucks and plows and a ton of P&G soap. She thought of the wonderful crisp heads of lettuce from refrigerator cars that arrived all the way from the valleys of California.

Inside those cars, she knew, could be rainbow-colored candy that filled the glass cases of every store in town, or peanuts, almonds, and English walnuts that nobody raised in this valley.

Wistfully, she sighed. She thought longingly of Jenny's wedding. It seemed a place past barriers, a place outside her secret center. On her fingers, she counted the years until she would be thirteen and nearer becoming a woman. She stretched luxuriously, imagining that glorious place of freedom where one could do as they pleased: adulthood. Then Teal sank into the silence of sleep.

*   *   *

The freight train roared along at eighty-five miles an hour downgrade outside of Chickasha. The fireman, a middle-aged black named Abraham Jones, turned to the engineer, Rory Leese. "Why are we short of wheat?" he asked, coming straight to the point.

"Trucks undercut us three cents. They're buying for Texas mills at two twenty-five."

"Good Lord!"

"We'd better hope so. It'll drive up the freight rates for sure," Rory said. "And more than three cents. Wheat freight's heavy."

"The layoffs is a comin'," Abraham said.

Rory gave the cord a "woo-oo-woo" up-and-down yank in response, and Abraham went back to shoveling the coal to it. "Folks have been without the dollar too long, so long that it looks like the whole world to them, like the difference in life and death maybe."

Abraham shook his head. His sooty brow glistened with sweat beads in the silvery light of the moon that crept through the cars. Now and then, a little gust of the night air hit him and seemed the breath of heaven. "It's the beginning of greed, and it could mean the death of the railroad. The less wheat we haul, the higher the rates will have to climb to fill the gaps until we'll not have the business to stick."

He wiped his brow and went back to stand beside Rory. His clothes were damp now, and the open car door let in the outside air that cooled him.

"Ain't it some night," he said.

"Yep," Rory agreed.

"Folks want everything in a hurry these days. Trucks mean one load and unload instead of two, direct routes at higher speeds. How do you think it'll all end, say, twenty years from now?" Abraham asked.

"Hard to tell with the mills wanting to make thirty cents a bushel on all the wheat they don't mill theirselves. Wheat's unpredictable stuff. They'll have their freight bills to make up, their railroad contracts to fill, or they'll get no cars at all. And that won't do either."

"Looks like truckin' could get damned heavy. Lots of volume."

"Damn right. Take thousands of them to haul what a train can," Rory said. "But like you said, they just load once instead of onto trucks or ships from rail. Saves time. The whole world's in a hurry."

"But the trains will be out of business."

"Crippled," Rory said. "But not gone. This country's not that damn dumb. It won't let its rail die."

"Hope you're right," Abraham said. He was one of the few blacks in the valley with a good job, one that paid him anything for his hard work. He made almost three hundred dollars a month, more when he worked on wrecks. Most all his "brothers," as he thought of them, depended on their gardens and custodial jobs. A lot of their women kept house, cooked, and raised the children of whites who could afford to pay for help. Their pay wasn't much. It helped pay the tuition at Langston for his boy, Leroy, for his own Sparrow to work. Andy, his younger son, had started high school last August.

Their chickens, their wits, their janitoring, yard work, junk dealing, and if they were lucky, their woman with a "house" job in one of the mansions on the east side of town saw the bills paid. He wanted this railroad alive so his two boys would have a job if they couldn't find one with their college degrees in the black-and-white divided world. He'd proved himself before them, paved their way to make it easier. It made him proud to do it.

Sparrow did their gardening and spread their table with its bounty, filled his house with plump and happy children, then scrubbed and cleaned her Saturdays away for "white folks" besides. She worked as long hours as he did and for the same cause.

She wanted to. The nights were worth it all. He took what she gave him, and he never thanked her; she'd be insulted if he did. She took what he gave her, and she never thanked him—not with words. With their lives, they thanked life and gave themselves to it and to each other. Most of all, they brought their bodies to it. Always, Abraham came back to this awareness of the reality of their physical power to love and to work.

He drew all the air into his lungs that they could hold and let it go with a small explosion. A shiver of pure pleasure coursed through him. He pulled out his pocket watch and turned it where it would catch the glint of the moon. He was on the extra board tonight, and the short run to Chickasha and back was the four to midnight shift.

They'd unwind the cars, stick an engine on the other end, and head back when the designated cars were switched. Then he'd walk the few blocks to Admire Street and be home, lying with Sparrow. Sparrow, whose hills and valleys were wet and brown and all of earth he craved. The day would come, he thought, when this power would break through the valley's walls of separate bathrooms, restaurants, fountains, and schools for his loved ones who would live beside these farmers and millers. Maybe his grandchildren would own farms, raise wheat instead of haul it.

There'd be work and there'd be worship and there'd be learning, the best learning possible for his children. They'd not thank anybody but the Lord for that either because it was due, because they had earned it fair and square, and the Lord's love had grown the power that did it all.

—

"I'll go give her a shovel or two more," he said when they'd crossed the Washita. "We'll be back by midnight for sure this trip."

"Yep," Rory agreed. Abraham grinned, his white teeth gleaming. He liked a man that didn't talk too much. He often told Sparrow that Rory didn't talk much, but when he said something, he best damn sure be listening because it was too good to miss.

CHAPTER IX

The Wedding

The following Saturday night, the night before Jenny's wedding to Charles Huel, Charles screeched around the corner of the Swain property in his new Ford coupe. Jenny leaped to her feet. She flew to the heavy curtains and pushed them back.

"You sit down! Finish that veil!" Esther ordered. Ray nodded approval of the reprimand.

Looking back over her shoulder, her cheeks high with color, Jenny said, "It's Charles! I know it is!"

"Do as you're told!" Ray scolded harshly. Reluctantly, Jenny let loose of the curtain. Her father relaxed a bit and began to smoke his pipe as if the evening might go on as usual. She knew that he wanted to hear his favorite radio programming, the *Fibber McGee and Molly* half hour. He liked *The Grand Ole Opry* too whenever he had the time for listening. He rested his head on the back of the stuffed chair and closed his eyes.

Esther, Jenny, and Teal occupied themselves with the wedding garments. Jenny returned to sewing tiny seed pearls and crystal beads onto her veil. Its sheer net of white cascaded over the edges of the sofa as if she sat upon clouds.

From one of the boy's rooms upstairs, the strains of "Don't Fence Me In" drifted downstairs. Both would leave for induction into the army within weeks.

Jenny would marry Charles Huel tomorrow afternoon. Teal sat shaping a white organdy rose to be worn at her sash. Teal could hardly bear the excitement of the wedding. She thought it the most important wedding in the world besides her own. "If you marry at twenty, Teal, I'll miss your lively presence. That's only a dozen years away," he said, "and after you finish high school, of course." His eyes fluttered open to look long at his girls.

"Jenny wants me for her flower girl," Teal exulted.

"Nothing could make you happier, I know." He roused to knock the ashes from his pipe, restuff it with Prince Albert tobacco, and fire it.

Teal sank to the floor beside her father's chair. "I thought you were asleep," she said. "I'm glad you're not."

Esther sat sewing the hem into Teal's new pink organza dress. White satin-threaded flowers embroidered its scalloped collar.

"It's beautiful, Mama," Teal told her.

"When I get the snaps on it, I want you to try it on," Esther answered.

The sound of the coupe approached again. Charles revved up the motor and squealed the brakes, then roared down the orchard road.

"He'll have dirt in the house!" Esther snapped. "I'll bet it's boiling up from the road, and the wind's in the south. Why doesn't Charles have to join the service?" Esther asked irritably.

"He's an only son, and his folks appealed," Jenny said. "Oh, Mama, he's just anxious." She hushed beneath the stern frown of her father. Ray Swain could pull his brows down into a V and look up with his blue, blue eyes in a way that froze thought or conversation.

"If I went out and sat with him, talked to him, he'd stop. I know he would."

"You don't move from this house!" Ray said gruffly. He banged his pipe on the ash stand, a move that settled that idea.

Teal said nothing. She didn't know why Jenny wanted to marry that Charles anyway. Soft and round and freckled, he didn't interest Teal except as a cause for the wedding. He looked nothing like the muscled farm boys she'd begun to notice. She went to the kitchen and poured herself a glass of cold milk. Out the tiny window back of the kitchen sink, tree shadows of the orchard didn't conceal the outline of the coupe.

The car lights snaked back over the narrow bridge. She had hoped he left for good before Jenny and her father clashed again over him, before Ray Swain decided there would be no wedding.

"Come try on your dress, Teal!" her mother called.

"Here comes Charles again!" Teal squealed excitedly in spite of her concern for her father's temper. She dashed to the front room, but this time, nobody acted as if they'd heard her or Charles. He blared his horn and screeched his brakes and roared through the neighborhood and was gone. This time for good, apparently, for after fifteen minutes, he hadn't returned.

As if Esther finally came out of her tense stupor over Charles's last episode, she finished with all her patting and fluffing and tying of threads on Teal's dress.

"Try it on," Esther said, handing the dress to her.

"They own thousands of acres," Jenny reminded her father, her expression begging him to like Charles for something.

"Go to bed!" Esther told her. "You can try yours on with the veil in the morning before breakfast if you want."

Ray clenched his teeth until his face turned red. "Let me tell you something, young lady. With two-dollar wheat and under, land is like talent or beauty or any of the other good things in this world. It's good because it has a good purpose. Having land in Oklahoma might mean money now because the tractor can cover five hundred acres and turn five hundred dollars into five thousand that way, but it might not. There is a certain price for the product and a cost to produce it. The war's pushed the price up—not high enough, but

—

wheat's got a better market now. But this war will end, and not soon enough for me and your mother. There's climate and bugs, cheat and fungus. There's trade agreements, speculators, and government policy. Mill people think a good market is a thing worth anticipating too. Mill people expect to pay their bills on time because of it, same as the growers."

He paused only to take a deep breath. He had laid the pipe aside and now stood in front of his chair.

Jenny started toward the stairs as if to escape his wrath.

"Wait just a minute, young lady," he said with a step in her direction. "There is hired help, truck drivers, railroaders, and equipment dealers—a whole herd of people made getting the Huels' crop down the road to a buyer possible. And not one of them is better or more important than the other. God help me, Jenny, I trust mill people, and you're one of them, will not act uppity. This country is based on people equality. Grow into it! Not money, not profession, not nationality or political party will change that ideal in my home!"

Jenny had begun to cry softly, but he pursued her. "I don't ever want you to tell me again that Charles is rich. I'll be wanting to know if you're happy with him or miserable, and that's all I'll be caring about unless you're hungry or sick. Is that understood?"

Jenny's face crumpled behind a burst of tears and gasps for air. "I won't ever be hungry!" she yelled. "Not married to Charles. I promise you that!" Then she ran from the room and up the stairs without stopping.

Teal wanted to touch her father just then, but she didn't. She started upstairs with her dress when Esther stopped her. "Use our room," she said. "It'll be quicker."

The gesture surprised Teal. Esther never allowed anybody there. Once in a while in the winter, company put their coats there across the bed, and she sometimes went to get them for them when they left.

"I think she only wants us to like Charles," Teal ventured, somewhat timidly.

"Teal, you always try to make peace: a good thing. But let this lie," Ray said. "Jenny may truly need a value—er, adjustment."

She nodded understanding and took the soft pink dress to their room, a place that felt cool due to the day shade of the plum tree outside the east window and smelled of the mothballs that protected woolens stored in its closet.

Over the bed, the sight of the large gold-framed print of a boy and girl crossing a bridge in a storm again mesmerized her. Her gaze always lingered on the beautiful angel with golden hair that hovered above them while the barefooted girl and boy appeared to help each other across the restless waters.

They'll never reach the other side, she thought. *Never.* Stopped in time and space, captured in color and framed there, constant danger waited to snatch them. Her pinafore bodice boasted buttons to the waist. Her fingers followed their hard round whiteness, unbuttoning. She laid the dress aside.

"Teal?" Esther called.

"Just a minute," she answered, forcing herself to focus on the organza dress. She lifted it and popped it over her head, blotting the picture from her mind. She snapped the side placket and tied the sash and looked at herself in the dresser's round mirror. It fit perfectly. She wore it out to show them that it did. Then she returned and put on her old play dress, as she called the pale blue cotton pinafore, before bounding up the stairs to tell Jenny "good night," and back again to join them.

"You go on to bed, Teal," Esther told her gently. "Tomorrow's a big day, but no cause for us to miss Sunday services. I'll want you up early to help me with the flowers and punch. We've still a lot to do before five tomorrow afternoon. It won't still be hot then, will it, Ray?" she asked.

"I want to listen to the radio too," Teal begged.

Ray didn't answer. Instead, he leaned into his radio so as not to miss Molly's response to Fibber.

Something akin to sadness crossed her mother's face and was gone. Teal thought she might have imagined it.

"Good night, dear," Esther said. "Perhaps some other night."

"Good night, Mama," she answered, then went to Esther and hugged her on impulse and kissed her on the forehead. Esther reached up and caught her about the waist in response.

"Jenny's in bed," Teal assured her. "She said she'd put the dress on with the veil before the wedding, and I said she'd sure better."

Esther laughed a little then. "You're a good girl," Esther said. "A good girl. Go up and sleep with her. She might like the company after all," Esther said with an encouraging pat on Teal's back.

Happily, Teal tiptoed up the stairs. She carefully slid out of her pinafore again. Still wearing a thin cotton slip that Esther had sewn for her from a white feed sack, she slid in beside Jenny. She supposed this was the last time she and Jenny would sleep together like this. Change seemed a wonderful and terrible thing to her. *I'll have this room, but I won't have Jenny,* she thought sadly. *She'll never tell me the Little Orphan Annie poem again that I love so before I fall asleep.* Her mind echoed the last line: "And the goblins are gonna get you if you don't watch out!" A single tear fell off her nose to dampen the pillow.

When her eyes popped open the next morning, it seemed to Teal that she had only slept five minutes. Esther called her from the bottom of the stairs. Jenny turned over with a little groan, her black hair spreading upon the pillow. Teal slipped out of the bed and dressed in her old dress again for the work ahead. Then she tiptoed down the stairs. It was the first time she'd worked side by side with Esther. They made a light breakfast of omelets and toast, then set them to stay warm while they made the huge jars of raspberry punch.

Teal understood nothing of formalities. She only knew that fifty relatives and friends from both sides of the families were expected. Esther arranged the napkins and cookies and refrigerated the tiny sandwiches and jars of punch. Then she and Teal went outside in the dew-moist morning to pick three bushel baskets of flowers for the great bouquets. They twined honeysuckle upon a trellis altar and placed it in the living room before the double windows. Esther soaked newspapers with water and rooted each long stem in shreds of it so they would not wilt. Then she arranged greenery about it all.

"It's a pretty sight if I say so," Esther exclaimed as she finished tying the last sprig of honeysuckle. "Breakfast is ready," she called.

Teal wasn't hungry. She went outside instead and sat upon the grass. She pulled stems of Bermuda grass and chewed on their sweetness. The scent of the honeysuckle she had gathered clung to her dress and to her skin. *Tomorrow,* she thought, *Jenny would waken in the Huel mansion, the most talked about house in the valley.* Teal had never seen it, but she'd heard Jenny talk about its ceiling tiles of shiny aluminum and its marble banisters. The living room alone was as large as their whole bottom floor, according to Jenny, and all the woodwork, cabinets, trims, and stairs was of thick oak.

"Even the globes on the chandeliers are hand painted," she had told her, "with little flowers of pink and yellow and blue—except those made entirely of crystal, of course. Oh! It's so beautiful there, Teal, like a world I've only dreamed."

"It's time to get ready for church now," Esther called through the south screen door. Teal twisted about and looked at her. "Some people don't ask other people anything when there's something they want, do they? I mean, Jenny doesn't care who likes it or doesn't. She'd marry Charles anyway because she wants to. And Tad and Jonsi just went fishing when maybe Jenny would like it if they'd stayed. Me too."

Esther shrugged. "What are you getting at, Teal?"

"If they didn't want to fish, they'd have said it was too hot to fish or too windy. Well, I mean, Charles's feet would have been too big or his ears would have stuck out too far if Jenny didn't *really* love him, rich or poor."

"You take that back!" Jenny shouted at her from the upstairs window. "There's nothing wrong with the way Charles Huel looks!"

Suddenly, Teal laughed. "See Mama? It's nothing, Mama. Nothing at all." And she jumped up and went inside to dress for church.

Usually they walked the dusty road to the small white frame building a dozen city blocks away. This morning they rode in the new Chevrolet. At the corner of the green lawn, black letters announced: the Church of Christ. They had begun to chip and peel.

Across the street, the Sacred Heart Catholic congregation worshipped in a red-brick building topped with a steeple and reaching cross. The physical difference in the two buildings glared a stark financial chasm.

It seemed to Teal, however, that their "congregation" at the Church of Christ took a special delight in the comparative simplicity of *their* building and *their* service, which also boasted a cappella group singing, often off-key. More often than not, the Sunday sermon dealt with Saturday night revelings or the error in other denominations' practices. Teal often felt guilty about the birthday and Halloween parties of her friends and the games of post office after school, none of which she felt willing to forsake at this time—not when a stamp purchase meant a kiss on her cheek from Heath Meriott.

She owned three Sunday dresses. Esther had sewn them all for her. The brown velveteen vest and skirt she never wore during the summer, and the lemon-yellow shirtwaist of soft cotton jersey needed laundering. So Teal wore her blue gabardine jumper with the pink rose-embroidered pocket. When she left off the blouse, it looked like a sleeveless summer dress, so she did.

As they started up the walk to the front steps, Teal looked dreamily at Jenny's gleaming black hair tumbling down the back of her white pique dress. The white rose she had made for Jenny's wedding dress temporarily adorned the side of her pompadour hairstyle. "I'm glad you like the rose," Teal said from a few steps away.

"I do like it, Teal. Thank you."

"Do you wish you were having a church wedding?" Teal asked then, skipping up to walk beside her.

—

"Heavens no!" Jenny answered. "Charles absolutely forbade it. He doesn't believe in going to church all the time. Besides, whoever heard of a wedding without music? No organ, no piano, I couldn't stand it."

"I won't be able to stand it either," Teal said with a sigh. "But I so want a church wedding. I want to kneel before an altar and light candles and wear a long, sweeping gown of satin. I shall carry a dozen red roses."

"You're so silly, Teal. How will you have all that? With all the money that Charles has, he doesn't believe in such waste. Papa hasn't nearly as much."

Esther threw her a warning glance as if she might have already forgotten her father's lecture of last night. But Jenny just tossed her head, an arrogant expression rushing to her green eyes. When Teal said nothing, Jenny pursued the issue.

"You're spoiled!" she snapped. "You always were!" Jenny's pretty lips drew down into a thin line. "Papa will play for me, and I shall come down our very own stairs. I'd much rather come down our stairs than that short aisle at church."

If Ray Swain heard any of their conversation, he didn't show it. Walking ahead, he opened the front door of the church for them to file inside.

"I shall have what I want, same as everybody else," Teal said pleasantly. "I decided that this morning. And thank you, Jenny, for asking me to be your flower girl. I'll never forget it."

First, Jenny frowned at such impudence, then she smiled at Teal. When she reached and gave her hand a squeeze, Teal's happiness overflowed. "I'm sorry I snapped at you, Teal," she said. Teal only nodded and smiled, for Ray frowned them quiet inside the building. Jenny loved Charles; Teal had pushed her to betray it yesterday despite all her talk of what he had.

She and Jenny sat together, but Esther went nearer the front and sat down among the matrons, easily recognized by "permanent" curls beneath fashionable hats. Teal sang the hymns her father led. He had favorites that he often repeated. He especially favored "When

We All Get to Heaven," his first selection this morning. He led "Shall We Gather at the River" almost as often, and one that Teal especially liked called "How Beautiful Heaven Must Be."

The only problem she had with any of them was that she liked things where she was, so it was hard to imagine anything more wonderful than here. An ordinary dandelion seemed a most extraordinary miracle to her. To Teal, God tracked over the earth revealing His beauty, humor, caring, and power to her in a multitude of ways. Still, she didn't want to discourage anybody's discontentment if it pleased them, so she cheerfully sang along, privately believing that Jesus's kingdom was here as surely as she herself.

With regularity, she became drowsy during the sermon. This morning was no exception. The minister, a wiry and nervous man named Harold Plummer, scrawled the Bible verses to be discussed across the blackboard: James 8:8, "A double-minded man is unstable in all his ways," and 14:16, "But every man is tempted when he is drawn away of his own lust. Then when lust hath conceived, it bringeth forth sin; and sin, when it is finished, bringeth forth death."

Teal decided that explained the cause of so many cold, quarrelsome people. They surely had become these walking dead.

Just to be safe from that demise, Teal rose and went forward at the end of the service. Esther stood and went with her.

"How have you sinned, Teal," Esther asked plaintively on the way home. "I couldn't bear your looking like a wayward child without me beside you."

"Everyone will be outguessing each other over their dinner tables about you two," Jenny snapped. "I'm embarrassed!"

In school, Teal wrote out definitions, but Preacher Plummer never defined sin with real words. He circled around it, he picked at it; it seemed to make him extremely nervous. Perhaps *he* didn't know what it was, and if the preacher didn't know, who did?

"What's sin anyway?" she asked at last. "I want to prevent it. I don't want it to kill me."

"It's going your own way instead of God's," Ray Swain answered her right back.

"How do you know the difference?" Teal asked. "Preacher Plummer had me feeling like a worm—like skipping or laughing out loud was wrong."

"Oh, lots of ways. You read and hunt for answers, you listen to your feelings, you learn from what makes you unhappy instead of happy. When you're in doubt, you ask yourself, "Does this nourish or destroy? If it serves no purpose, if it risks lives or property or the happiness of others, it may or may not be sin, but you do well to choose carefully the course you take."

Esther squirmed uncomfortably, a signal that she disagreed.

"You make sin sound—" Esther stopped. "I don't know. It sounds foreign—not like anything I've heard about in the pulpit. What about dancing and drinking? What about swearing and smoking?"

Ray Swain said nothing, and Teal didn't either. But what he'd just said made more sense to her than anything she'd heard about right and wrong. So she repeated the words to herself. She didn't want to forget them. To her they meant *Do no harm to self or nature or others. And if lust brought death, love surely brought life.* Her father's words freed her to return to her thoughts of more pleasant things than the living dead, than rules about habits instead of avoiding pure meanness in thought or deed. When they'd almost arrived home, another question popped into her mind.

"What's purpose, *exactly*, Daddy?" she asked.

"Oh, purpose is supplying a beneficial need to self, another, or society at large. It's a reason for existence and for behaving in certain ways. Purpose decides the quality of life for good or ill. So besides doing no harm, do as much good in this world as you can."

"Hmph!" Esther said, as if he'd finally blundered for sure. "Some people fill their need from other people's supply," she said with a bit of sarcasm. "They *never* give back."

—

"I think that I understand what you mean, Esther. You're probably speaking of taking before it's offered or without permission without ever expressing gratitude or generosity."

"That could be bad," Teal observed, really getting involved in this question. "Stealing's a sin for sure."

"That's right," Ray said. "Your mother's right about any inappropriate force or thievery being wrong, but there's not one of us that doesn't depend on others for some supply. It's no shame. It's a blessing."

"You saying it's right to just go after what we want?" Esther asked.

"That's exactly what I'm saying, and that's exactly what most people do, with good conscience or without. Others can always refuse. Most are happy to supply."

Ray Swain parked the car in front of the yard for he'd built no driveway for it yet. He didn't exit immediately though. He turned to Esther instead and asked, "What is it you've wanted and kept hidden from me, Esther?"

"You make it sound as if I've lied to you, Ray. I haven't. I don't."

"What?" he repeated, refusing to relent. "There was that edge to your voice as if I've willfully wronged you somehow."

"Well, I don't know." She paused as if searching her mind for what she could have meant. "I really don't."

"Think on it," he said crossly, then got out and slammed the door.

Jenny seemed to know she shouldn't speak, Teal observed, saddened by her parents' spat.

Her father said the blessing over the noon meal of cold beef and gelatin, things that Esther could prepare ahead and clear easily before the wedding. But he ate in silence, and Teal saw nothing more of him until time for the wedding when he took his place at the piano to play Jenny's request, "I Love You Truly."

The crowd soon gathered. Family and friends milled in groups about the yard and in the house. Letti Pearl Rush, who sold Teal her school tablets and candy from the neighborhood store, came with her family. Teal saw Harlin Rush and surmised that the tiny woman at his side must be his wife. Teal recognized him from his frequent feed purchases and payments at the office. She noticed the tall young man with her who looked vaguely familiar and who seemed to know Jonsi. She wondered if they would go to the army together. She wanted to recall where she had seen him but couldn't. Teal's eagerness for the wedding peaked with a case of hiccups. After almost a quart of the raspberry punch, they went away, but she thought her bladder would burst when it was time for her to be the flower girl.

At last, Preacher Plummer read the vows that Charles and Jenny repeated before sealing their contract with the ritual "I do's" and a kiss. Jubilant, Teal raced for the bathroom and relief. For the rest of the day, she could play. Until all their guests left, Esther would not call her to more work.

First, she ate her fill of cookies without her mother's notice or restraint for Esther stood on the lawn, sipping a cup of punch and talking with Mrs. Huel. Finally Teal joined others on the lawn.

She looked about her. Weddings seemed to be for adults; none of her cousins were here. As for Jenny, she and Charles left immediately after the ceremony for their honeymoon in Colorado. Teal felt disappointed that they wouldn't be in the Huel mansion tonight. It sounded more romantic than Colorado to her.

Not far from where her mother and Mrs. Huel talked, her rope swing dangled in the light breeze. It was a single rope, thick and knotted at the end. Teal ran for it. With enough speed and a tight grasp, it carried her over the yard's high bank.

"We're moving to town, you know," Mrs. Huel was saying.

"Jenny mentioned it, yes," Esther said in a distinct pronunciation that Teal thought sounded artificial. "Jenny's young, but she loves Charles," she added.

She sounds disgustingly syrupy sweet as well, Teal thought. She ran at the rope again.

"You've an attractive place here," Mrs. Huel said, turning her head from side to side. "Does it include the orchard?"

"Oh yes," Esther said. "The orchard too. Would you have more punch? I'd be glad to refill your cup."

"Oh, no. No. It was delicious though," Mrs. Huel said. They weren't really saying anything to each other. Why was that? Teal wondered. She began her third run at the rope. She caught it the same as before, but something went wrong.

In a split second, as if the rope itself had slung her off, she sprawled just past the embankment in the dust. She'd fallen flat, a belly buster from at least a dozen feet. She lay there stunned, unable to breathe past her mouth full of dirt. Helplessly, she twisted her face up to Esther, who just stared at her. Teal thought her mother would surely help her, but she had no breath to speak. Esther kept standing as if Teal should get up to properly dust off the new dress and pretend she'd never fallen, all for the benefit of Mrs. Huel. It couldn't happen, for her next breath wouldn't come.

She lifted her arm, desperate for Esther to realize. She tried to spit out dirt. If she could get the wad of it out of the back of her throat, she'd be all right.

"I believe she fell there when she swung out over the bank," Mrs. Huel said.

Their voices sounded far away to Teal. An uncommon ringing had begun in her ears.

"Are you out of wind, dear?" Esther asked in that same polite tone from where they stood. Neither had moved to help her. A bit of air redeemed her the very moment she thought she might die.

Esther didn't come to help her. Teal struggled to her feet alone. She grabbed half breaths and coughed up more dirt. "I'm sorry," she managed at last.

A bewildered look came over Esther's face as if she finally realized Teal's struggle and her inadequate response.

"I'm all right now, Mama," Teal assured her.

Esther met her as she climbed back into the yard. Tenderly, she smoothed back Teal's hair while Mrs. Huel fumbled in her purse for something. When she found it, she handed it to Teal. "It's a one dollar bill," she ingratiated.

Teal looked at it. Torn down the middle, its two halves lay in Mrs. Huel's palm. "All you have to do is to take a little tape and mend it. Here," she invited. "Take it."

Teal didn't want it. That tall boy with Mrs. Rush watched them. Had he seen her fall? She felt her face flush hot. She looked at Esther, who gave a slight nod as if she should take it. So Teal accepted it, thanked her, rinsed her mouth at the outdoor faucet, and went up to her room where she lay upon the bed and cried. When she felt finished with the tears, she took the dollar and stuck it under the edge of the congoleum flooring that she would walk upon. It seemed an acceptable solution to her. Now she needn't spend it, and she hadn't refused it or thrown it away.

She took a long bath when guests left, grateful she fell after instead of before the wedding; grateful too that her dress hadn't torn. She felt better, as if she'd washed off any Huel and Swain need to feel important instead of human.

She knew she had seen the possible beginnings of the walking death on Esther. *I'll never pretend to be something I'm not for anyone,* she resolved. It seemed risky business to her. Someone could die of it.

She sat at the dining room table that night reading some of the Uncle Remus stories when she heard Esther's voice from the adjacent front room: "I had a talk with Jenny, Ray. I asked her to promise me she'd take her children to church so they'd learn the truth and not burn in hell."

"Did you?" her father responded.

"I did. And do you know what she had the nerve to say?"

"What did she say, Esther?"

"She said that she believed the Bible, and the Bible said to allow the husband to head the house and that Charles would decide such things. The Huels are heathens, Ray. They don't even believe in God."

"They sure own a lot of land though," he said. Teal looked across the room and caught her father's glance. He must think that made a difference to Esther, more difference than belief or unbelief, she thought. She hated thinking that about a mother who had been so kind to her—before today. She wondered if Esther's values had changed over time. *Maybe money and stuff came first now. Could that be the cause of this recent wedge of indifference that she put between herself and others?*

She's good, Teal reminded herself. *She would help much quicker than hurt any living thing.*

"That's true," Esther said after a long pause. "And that's something to be thankful for. He'll take good care of her. She'll have security."

"I'm sure he'd better," Ray said. "But, Esther, the Good Book tells you that *you're* not to place judgment on others or—"

"Or what?"

"Heathen's a strong word, Esther. Remember that your grandchildren will be Huels. The Good Book says the judgment you use will fall back on you. The Huels may think less of their wealth than you do and more about God then we know."

Teal entered the living room just as her father knocked the ashes from his pipe. She supposed they would all retire soon.

Esther nodded and yawned as if he bored her, then vanished inside their bedroom, yielding the values argument. With concern in his eyes for her, he glanced at Teal and winked.

Teal smiled. She figured choosing God *or* security sounded plain foolish. She wanted both. God's about 95 percent of security anyway, the way she saw it. The other 5 percent of ordinary cash shouldn't be too hard to get with the Big Guy in her corner, she thought.

* * *

Ray Swain supposed where Esther's adoration left off, his began for Teal. He loved Jenny, no doubt about his pride for Jonsi and Tad, both of them, proud to serve their country in the army or out. Still, he wished them home again; he missed them already. Tad would take his drafting and mathematics skills to the Canal Zone—*his* boys: Ray Swain, a plain fellow with no particular education, had sons eager to serve their community and their country.

He stopped his thinking about his children and put his pipe and tobacco aside. The aromatic odor of tobacco pleased him. Where the unexpected and different qualities Teal demonstrated annoyed Esther, they pleased him. He felt younger, more alive around his youngest child. "Don't you grow up too fast and leave me too, kiddo," he called to her across the room, then rose and retired with Esther.

The following day, Ray saw that Teal left the formal orchard for the mulberry tree across the fence that separated the garden and the yard. The berries had ripened. He knew she had a weakness for that summer phenomenon of berries on a tree.

The staked brood cow's complaint when Teal cleared the fence near her space broke the morning's silence. She had calved again, a time that soured her disposition and made her dangerous to children who came exploring for the miracle berries. Her orneriness protected her calf from intruders, he knew, so he had warned Teal of her meanness at the birthing.

He'd vowed to trade her because of it, but a good producer wasn't easy to come by, so he continued to look for a fair swap. He started toward Teal in case the cow loosed the stake and lunged for her.

"Stay clear of Old Tab," he called. She had obviously forgotten his earlier warning. Intent on the berries, she didn't seem to hear him or notice the cow. He walked faster, alarmed by the danger Tab presented.

Teal reached for the berries. Ray knew her feet, fingers, and face would soon be stained with the wild fruit. Another time he might have smiled at the thought. Brown sparrows chirped high in the mulberry's supermarket branches. She caught the branch higher and pulled it down until its leaves brushed her arms. The branch creaked from the pressure as she plucked more fruit. When she released it altogether, it scraped her arm. She yelped with pain. Tab slung her head and snorted. Deaf to both her father's warning and old Tabatha's low mooing, she persisted.

Ray thought Old Tab might take account of their lengthy acquaintance and allow her the berries. Yet he knew that animal instinct to protect their young often betrayed former trust. He ran toward the pen as Teal's concentration fixated again on her gathering.

She popped a handful of the purple berries into her mouth and reached for more. She didn't look in Old Tab's direction as she turned to leave the tree. She focused instead on walking levelly to assure that no berries that she carried in cupped hands fell to the ground. Instead of going over the fence again, she headed toward the gate a few yards away. *She might trip the latch with her elbow,* Ray thought, *to prevent the berries from spilling. But she couldn't do it fast enough to get away from the cow.*

Ray caught the mad glint in Tab's eyes. The cow had struggled to her feet, her horned head lowered toward Teal, who ambled unaware toward the gate. She glanced aside to see her father's breathless approach. She lifted the berries with a triumphant smile in that split second that he yelled again, and she went sprawling headlong into a mixture of dried cow dung and scattered hay.

"Behind you, Teal!" had been lost on the wind. She hadn't had time to look back before Tab tossed her up, and she fell flat on her stomach for the second time in two days. She gulped for air, that horrible ache at the base of her rib cage causing her to cry out with the last of her available air. If she could get up, just on her knees . . . She felt as if she were outside herself, helplessly watching her struggle. She lay there, expecting to be hit again with horns or feet. For what seemed an eternity, she felt again that certain death surely held her. Then the miracle of air flowed in once more with rasping sounds followed quickly by that wail that's a combination of joy and tears.

She looked back and saw the swaggering hip bones of the Guernsey walking to her corner and the calf. Teal knew that the moody old thing could have killed her.

Her father burst through the gate, his expression apologetic. "I should have sold her!" he said as he reached to help her stand. He clasped her to him.

"I'm all right," she said, savoring the moment. Teal didn't mind falling so much. She bargained for that with her tomboy antics on her bike or her climbing of trees, hills—whatever she could climb. She looked at the berries, spoiled now in the dirt. "Why, I'd never harm her calf, the silly old fool," she said.

"She didn't know that," Ray reminded. She's a parent like me and your ma. You skinned your knees learning to bicycle brake expertly on gravel and to roller-skate downhill, remember? That fall at Jenny's wedding stunned you. None of these injuries were the same as this attack from behind, I know."

Ray lifted her shirt to check her back. "No skin break, thank God, but you'll be bruised."

"Teal," he said. "Experience is the reality of possible and actual defeat you won't bargain for nor always have the opportunity to avoid. Suddenly, you have glimpsed an unknown with dark potential for its being an unknown, and therefore, it feels unreasonable. Seeing this seems the reason for these accidents to me."

"But I had a choice," she said as her father fastened the gate behind them. "I could have let fear control. You told me why you fastened Tabatha inside the pen. Why you tethered her when you milked her as well."

"Fear feels loathsome, caution," he said. "Caution feels sensible. Try caution in the future, kiddo," he said, and he patted her head affectionately.

"In fact, I will *cautiously* trust both man and beast after this week," she said. "Even Mom seems a bit suspect now."

"You go in and soak in a hot bath," he told her. "Something like this makes your bones and muscles sore. The heat will help."

"Two falls in two days," she complained.

"You'll set more records than that in *your* life," he assured her with a chuckle and a wink. "Your mother loves you, don't ever doubt it. She's, well, bothered by aging and by a changing world. We must be patient."

*   *   *

Esther's hovering concern over Tabatha's attack seemed an exaggerated response to Teal, considering her lack of it yesterday. *Perhaps she has an emotional bruise not unlike mine due to her lack of response before,* Teal thought. *A conscience attack.*

Teal could barely move the next day. An enormous bruise appeared below her shoulder blades that turned brown and purple and green before it faded at last to tan after several days. It hurt less than the emotional bruise that could take much longer to heal. Like her father, she hoped to better understand her mother's behavior.

She supposed it had something to do with *the change,* whatever that was.

By the following Saturday, she went with Ray to the mill. She sat with pleasure upon the stool before the great scale and helped weigh the trucks loaded with grain.

They stretched almost a half mile like a great segregated animal, crawling and impatient. Their drivers knew that the combine bin could be full and waiting to dump before they returned. Time mattered. What if it rained or hailed? What if a tornado blew through? What if the price dropped or went higher?

She peered through the glass at the drivers, gave an authoritative nod of her head, then turned to prepare their wheat ticket. At her instruction, they moved on to return empty for weighing out. The repetitiousness of it didn't bore her because of new faces. This summer introduced her to her affection and interest in people of all ages and for work. How she loved their faces, all different, mostly smiling. What a good feeling this honest tiredness after work.

"Kindness is the best asset a body can have," she told her father decidedly.

"You're just a people person," he said.

"Is that good?"

"That's good."

"What's *the change?*" she asked him.

He hesitated before responding. "Why do you ask?"

"Mother." She didn't think it appropriate to expand more.

"It's only a different stage of life. We're a child, then a young adult, then we *change* to an older adult, followed by an old adult."

"That's it?"

"That's it."

She decided not to contrary him by saying that wasn't it, but she felt certain that Esther's lack of caring was not related to those changes. *More likely,* Teal thought, *her distances were related to changing attitudes.* Esther's thoughts were altering her feelings, and her feelings toward herself and others altered her behavior.

Instead she said, "When I feel ignored, I cause a stir so I'll be noticed, and when I feel sad, I often cry. I think Mom feels left behind. We leave for school, for work, or for war, and she's there. She makes it possible, but not for her. Know what I'm saying?"

"I do. And I'm glad you said it. That can make anyone feel like breaking out of routine."

"Lashing out at her—her jailers, you mean."

"We'll take her by the hand and lead her back into the sunshine."

Teal laughed. "Let's!"

CHAPTER X

Harvest

It rained across the valley for days, which damaged the grain in the field and delayed the end of harvest. But after her ninth birthday and toward the end of the first week of July, Teal sat upon that high stool once more, adjusting the weights on the scale and marking pounds into bushels, every ounce of it valuable for the dollars it would put into each farm family's larder.

Harvest's ending caused celebration, a time to replenish the closets with new clothes, to trade for the new plow, or to buy a new straw hat. The moment all the wheat filled the great storage bins, the shops downtown would see lively trade—not much of Teal's however. She regularly saved the quarter a day she earned. At two dollars and fifty cents for a five-day work week, she envisioned thirty dollars at summer's end.

When she didn't want more library books, she stayed home on Saturdays to help her mother. She went to church with Esther on Sunday. Sunday afternoon they took lunch to the elevator. By Monday, she worked at the elevator again.

The trucks moved slowly for the manager, Jim Whittier, tested each sample from each farm for moisture. The delays bored Teal, but the grain would spoil a whole bin if it weren't dry enough to store. When several trucks were told to move aside and wait on the decision, she hopped down from her perch and went outside for some sun. The bins could stand *some* 15 percent moisture wheat; the problem was how much to mix with the dry. If Jim didn't take it, another grainary might; he didn't like to cross good customers unless he had to, but he couldn't risk spoiling wheat either. His milled flour required 80 % grade A clean hard red-winter wheat mixed with 20 % soft from Kansas. He currently milled about thirty-six hundred bushels a day.

The front of the main office was solid concrete except for the plateglass window before the scale. Teal gazed down the block at the sweaty occupants of a half dozen pickups. Several ton trucks were dispersed here and there among them. Not many farmers owned big trucks, she guessed, noting that a few of the drivers were kerchiefed women with their babies whining beside them. Their faces, freckled and squinting against the afternoon sun, appeared flushed from the heat. The thermostat outside read 104°. She walked a few steps and saw the large red-ant den near the corner of the building. Her interest seized upon it.

She moved nearer and knelt to watch them transport grains of wheat inside the den. She had occupied herself there for almost a quarter of an hour when voices intruded upon her reverie, and she glanced up.

In an old black Ford pickup, about a 1938 model the best that Teal could determine, two boys argued. One had begun to look more like a man, but a very young man. She knew she had seen him before, then remembered the boy with Jonsi at Jenny's wedding.

"I been drillin' wheat since I was six, and I oughta know," he said. You can't drill a straight row unless you look to the end of it."

"You gotta watch right in front of your nose!" the other protested adamantly. They hung on the wooden grain sides, made to extend a possible load.

"Ah! You make me tired," the tallest said, crawling over into the grain. The obvious older of the two, he sported a deep cheek scar that curiously increased his rugged good looks.

"You got to keep check on your drill too, so's it don't plug up and skip."

Teal thought the boy tried to act as grown-up as his companion to impress him. They began to tunnel the grain like children.

"That grain could start moving and swallow you," Teal warned them. "My dad says so."

"You better pull that load over!" Jim called to the driver. Teal figured him the father of one or both of them. When the man pulled his cap off and wiped his brow, Teal recognized Harlin Rush.

The boys paid no attention to her or the man.

"Too wet?" the farmer asked.

"Fifteen. Just pull her over. We'll see what we can do, Harlin."

"I need to get back to my field," Harlin yelled with flushed impatience. "I'm short a tractor and driver."

Jim motioned the next truck up without recognizing the protest. Instead he said, "I heard about that. Seat fell off a running tractor and spilled Gavin. How is he?"

The man slapped his cap on his head and pulled off with a start that jolted the two young men who sprawled awkwardly onto the bed of wheat. They looked some older than herself to Teal. The tallest one drew her glance more than once. *He's probably about seventeen or eighteen now,* she thought since seeing him with Letti Rush at Jenny's wedding several years ago. In fact, she had learned that the Rushes and her folks knew each other years ago before she had been born. He would have been too young for the service then after all, for Tad and Jonsi had already gone and come home after their two years.

"He's here, thank God. He'll be over the soreness pretty soon. Pretty damned dangerous work sometimes," the boy's father yelled back. "Whether it's a tractor, a horse, or a mule, Gavin can make it fight back."

The pudgy blond boy looked younger, fourteen maybe. He kept insisting to his companion that a tractor driver watched right in front of his nose and behind as well until Teal thought she might scream. He glanced her way often. She thought he wanted her to notice him. The other one ignored her completely, an irritation to Teal.

"Go get us a bottle of cold milk from your grandma Letti's grocery on the corner, Gavin," the man driving yelled back, and she saw that the tallest and oldest slid down. His black hair glistened in the sun. A wayward lock lay above blue-green eyes that looked past her.

She wanted him to look at her. When he was almost even with her, she stood and smiled. She expected to exchange a hello. She locked her hands behind her, her whole self suddenly and unexpectedly intent upon his recognition. He had ignored her warning about the full load of grain; now he looked right past her.

Gavin Rush stuck his hands in his pockets and began whistling. He looked straight ahead as if he could see all the way to the grocery, the way, Teal supposed, that he looked to the end of his wheat row. Quick anger flushed Teal's cheeks. She hadn't known Letti Rush had a grandson so stuck-up. Teal visited Letti's store at least once a week for her Red Chief tablets and pencils. Letti sold her penny candy with a friendly smile.

She squatted at the ant den again, daring to glance toward the other youngster after what seemed a decent interval of time. Her pride wouldn't allow him to recognize her annoyance. *What do I care!* she thought. That Gavin Rush certainly had nothing to be stuck up about in her opinion. She threw the old truck with its load of wheat a disdainful glance, darting another look toward the grocery perchance he walked back already.

The space looked empty without him. She found a straw and began to flip small bits of gravel here and there, testing the ants' determination to surmount such obstacles.

After a moment or so, she glanced toward the store again and saw that he returned, his long legs reaching far ahead with jaunty and confident motion. Suddenly, Teal wanted to spoil that more than anything. She bet he would notice her now.

He deserves it, she thought spitefully and stood to search for a smooth stone. Lately, she'd become quite good at striking whatever she aimed them at. She stooped for one. As he neared, she watched him. This time, he looked her way with a scowl before looking away. *Deliberate snob,* she thought.

"Hello," she said, her tone daring him to ignore her further, but it wasn't easy to get a lot of message into one word, so she followed it in a hurry with a few more, for he walked very fast.

"Cat got'cher tongue?"

He tossed a look of disdain at her. "Squirt!" he shot back.

How dare him! she thought, moving the smooth stone between her fingers.

"I bet I can hit that jug of milk," she taunted.

That stopped him. He turned and looked straight at her. Teal looked right back, satisfied but snared in her own trap. "I bet you better not."

"Teal!" her father called from the door of the business office. Teal's pride smarted. How could she let him see her wilt under the authority of her father? She'd challenged him and now felt that she couldn't yield.

"I bet you can't anyway," he said. His eyes smiled a hard kind of smile that seemed to say, "You're already in a lot of trouble, and I'm seeing if you've got the guts to see it through."

"Bring that milk here!" his father ordered.

Teal smirked. "Take it to Daddy," she said.

"You said you could hit it," he baited.

Blood pounded in her ears. She couldn't think or hear clearly now. Her father's voice seemed distant thunder and not half the threat of *losing face.* She drew back the stone and let it fly. It popped against the glass like a plug on a pond. The jug split from the shock. The milk splashed and dripped from Gavin's shirt and ran down his trousers. Two irate fathers loomed upon them like angry schoolmasters.

Gavin's father whipped off his belt and let him have it twice across the rear in front of her as Ray Swain lifted Teal upon his hip bone and bore her, kicking and resisting, to the corner of the building where he trashed her with words. He shook his finger in her face until tears streamed down her dust-smudged cheeks. That seemed to satisfy him, and he stopped.

"You won't be back this summer!" he said at last. "Don't ask, it's final! And you can pay for that milk too, young lady," he said, fishing up the change from his khaki trouser pocket for Rush. "You owe me fifty cents, and don't forget it. That was a gallon jug of cold milk for a thirsty man and his boys."

Her heart dropped. With her chin down, she looked up from beneath damp lashes toward the old black Ford to see Gavin looking at her, his expression sullen but somehow sympathetic. She didn't want his sympathy. She stuck her tongue out at him. He looked away and didn't look back.

Ray Swain sent her home then in front of everyone. Feeling humiliated rather than victorious, she stuck her chin up defiantly and walked away with feigned spriteness. She thought of the incident with growing regret several times that week. Then Saturday finally arrived. When Esther allowed her visit to the library before her chores, she felt forgiven.

She and Sylvia, her best friend, went to the Sunday afternoon matinee at the local Rocket Theatre. At least for two hours, she wouldn't be able to think about Gavin Rush or feel puzzled about the pleasant sensations that rushed her when she did. How secretly grateful she felt that he had fallen clear of that tractor. What could his father have meant about horses and mules? She supposed farm boys could get kicked and thrown and stomped. Maybe just getting knocked down by a cow wasn't so bad after all.

*　　*　　*

Over the next three years, not much in Teal's life had changed except that Tad and Jonsi had both married after returning home safely from Hitler's war. Because of their jobs, wives, and college hours, she saw very little of them.

She liked Sunday school but endured church, allowing herself to daydream as she watched the great overhead fans, counted the round globed ceiling lights, and wondered, for perhaps the hundredth time, why there were no windows. When that failed to ease the strain of harsh hellfire sermonizing, she counted the women's hats over and over until a hymn or a prayer broke her ritual into bearable pieces like the communion bread, the passage of which signified the service's conclusion.

With Sunday's dinner of pot roast behind, Teal walked to Sylvia's house. This Sunday they met at the corner where they parted each school day.

"Do you know what's showing?" Sylvia asked her when she arrived.

"What?" Teal asked brightly.

"*The Outlaw*," she said, her blue eyes widening.

"Isn't that the movie where he rapes her in the hay?" *Rape* was only a brazen word Teal had overheard. She had no notion what it meant.

"Um-hmm. And there's more, Heath said."

"You told Heath we were seeing it?"

"He asked me," she responded as if that explained the revelation.

Almost every Sunday afternoon, Heath Meriott showed up at the movie to sit beside her. Now and then, he walked home with her after the show, and they sat on the front porch steps and talked. They had been sweethearts since childhood. At a fifth grade recess, they had exchanged what they believed to be marriage vows behind the lilacs next to the grade school building. Her mind gathered the days with Heath before today. Sylvia seemed to be in deep thought as well, probably about the same thing.

This twelfth summer, her world seemed a five-pointed star with energy as intense as her own. She sought its extremes. She pressed her bicycle, wandering miles from home. With a child's sensual pleasure, she observed and enjoyed everything while a new restlessness prodded her to learn all about what she saw or touched or smelled. Mentally, she craved adulthood; emotionally, she wanted to stay twelve forever.

—

A mile south of her home, she had found a long and narrow dirt road that led past a red brick mansion far back from it. It wasn't the house that interested Teal particularly, though she imagined proud and private people within; she never saw them outside enjoying the clipped and shady lawn. The bees there intrigued her. Their hives were situated next to the wrought iron and brick gate adjacent to the road. She went there often to watch them and made that summer's project an intimate study of bees.

She spent free afternoons at the Carnegie Library researching them. She quoted this impressive information about them to whoever would listen and returned again and again to observe and record with a thoroughness that eased her restlessness.

When this intensity left her, she pursued books. She read all of James Fenimore Cooper that she could locate, then started on Pearl Buck and Edna Ferber. Dickens occupied her now. She researched music history, composers, and various instruments. She studied world religions and books on the interpretation of dreams. She pounded piano scales and plucked the ukulele. She took Jonsi's accordion out of the retirement forced upon it when he'd left for the army after Pearl Harbor. She played a comb and paper, a harmonica; she whistled and sang.

"I think my mother hates me," Teal said with an abruptness that seemed to startle Sylvia.

"You must be imagining that, Teal."

Then Teal told Sylvia about her mother's changing disposition and recent rantings that had distanced them from each other. "'She's driving me crazy!' I overheard her tell Dad about me. She and Dad sat in the shade near the orchard. I checked a peach tree for a ripened fruit, then couldn't eat it for crying. The love she showered on me when I was little didn't leave all at once like a death. It slipped away unseen, bit by bit. I'll try to tell you her exact words, but I may start crying." Teal began as if she were there in the orchard again.

"'She's studying digestion now,' Mom said, as if it were a crime. 'Besides her classifying foods by fiber and color and vitamin content, she's memorized every minute detail of its passage through the body. And now she's experimenting, swallowing ridiculous things like seeds and string and—and—'

"Her irritation pinched her voice to a squeak, Sylvia. She sounded so upset, she could hardly talk. 'She drank a glass of milk and made a notation in her notebook,'" Teal continued. "*Citrus peelings are an irritant to the lining of the stomach. Any fool could have told her that before she—any fool.*' That's what she said." Teal's voice cracked as if she might cry.

"I'm so sorry, Teal. Is there more?"

"Lots! 'Now Esther,' I heard Dad scold mildly. 'I'll see if she wants to go to the mill with me. They can still use her help weighing the grain at the scales. Because of the rain, a few farmers are finishing their harvest late this year, but the flour contracts didn't wait. We can still use all the help we can get, and Teal seems to like it there.

"'More than likely, you'll miss her and be glad to have her pestering inquisitiveness around again.' After a pause, he added, 'Did you ask to see her notebook?' I thought that was a darn thoughtful question," Teal said.

"It was!" Sylvia agreed.

"A darkness in her that is more and more familiar to me confuses Dad, while I know that Mother needs for him to understand her, her—well, whatever it is. She often looks at him with a strained, closed look, as if she wants to tell him how she feels but can't.

"I think Mother resents growing old, don't you? Perhaps she feels cheated of something," Teal said. "She can't tell him because she doesn't know herself why she should feel so upset all the time. Oh, I don't know," she concluded, throwing up her hands.

Sylvia seemed to be absorbing Teal's revelations. They walked toward town without speaking momentarily.

Teal believed her father to be a good man. She felt Esther was blessed with a family from him. But that was done. *What do I do now?* her eyes seemed to ask. *They will all be gone soon.* Teal pushed that painful impression of Esther out of her mind. She wanted to run away from this conversation now; she wanted to enjoy the movie.

What is it that you want? her father had asked her mother that day of Jenny's wedding. Teal wished she knew what would help her mother. It would be years before her father retired.

"I'll be an adult and gone soon like the others, Sylvia. What will they do then if—" she stopped. "'Do take her,' Mom said. 'I would like to be alone some.' She wants me gone!" Teal lamented. "I have no doubt."

"I hope you're wrong, Teal. Maybe she needs those hormone shots that some women get."

I'll be sure to keep my notes hidden from her from now on, Teal thought. *Why, it would have been fun to share them with her had I known she cared.*

"Dad took his pipe from his shirt, then I saw his hurt expression from her comment about wanting aloneness. He still needs to be with her, but her walls have shut him away too."

"She needs hormones," Sylvia said with greater assurance.

What secrets did she think she would find in my notebook? Worse than her deceit, Teal thought, *is lack of trust. What dark side caused her to turn against me?*

Sylvia interrupted her melancholy by changing the subject. "I'll bet Heath won't be there. His mother." She stopped the sentence as if that one word, *mother*, said it all. "I'll bet she didn't ask to see your notebook, did she? Had you written anything about Heath?"

"If fathers could be home more, mothers wouldn't get so fixated on *us* instead of *them*," Teal said, shaking her head no. "She never answered Dad's question about it either."

1946 had seen the end of the Rocket Theatre's player piano and Wednesday night drawings for fifty dollars. The aluminum pan collections in the huge wire pen in front of it had ceased as well after the war.

Tad's and Jonsi's work, graduate studies, and starting their families meant that Teal saw less and less of them. They both bought homes in Stillwater. It seemed certain that they had no interest in the mill and elevator business. Sometimes they came home when

Jenny and Charles were there for Sunday dinner. Teal wished she could confide in just one of them.

"Will your mother be mad?" Sylvia asked her as they approached the ticket window of the Rocket Theatre.

"I don't think Mother knew what was showing. I didn't know until you told me, but I don't care."

"But *The Outlaw*—I don't want her mad at me." Sylvia grimaced.

"Don't worry. She wasn't angry when we saw *Duel in the Sun,* was she?" At that response, Sylvia's features smoothed.

"Because she didn't ever see it," Sylvia reminded astutely.

"She'll not see this either. She doesn't ever go to the movies."

"What does she do for fun?"

Teal thought about that for a moment, her ivory brow knitting below her dark auburn hair. Pulled tight at the crown, it cascaded down her shoulders. She wore a white peasant blouse and flouncy skirt of blue-and-black print above the ballerina shoes. Her thick black brows and lashes made her hazel eyes appear much darker than they actually were.

"She doesn't enjoy herself very much. She goes to church mostly." Teal shoved the white sack of butterscotch lozenges beneath Sylvia's nose. "Have another," she invited. "They're wonderful!"

"Honestly, Teal. Wonderful is a large way to describe candy."

Teal laughed cheerfully. "Butterscotch tastes wonderful." When she had extra dimes, she splurged them on butterscotch sundaes.

The sun warmed her bare shoulders and arms. She could see the poster of Jane Russell on the marquis just ahead that revealed the stunning beauty's figure.

"I hope I get a tan like that before school starts," Teal said.

"She's new," Sylvia observed.

Teal stared at the star. At twelve, becoming a woman seemed an unrealizable dream. Thirteen seemed an eternity away. She had no cause to wear even a beginner's bra. Lately, she had considered asking her mother to buy her one anyway. She could stuff it with cotton, couldn't she?

She laid her dime inside the empty half-moon cutout of the glass cage of a window. The cashier pushed a button, and the purple ticket popped up. Ticket in hand, she stepped aside to wait for Sylvia.

Sylvia already wore a bra. Enviously, Teal looked at her, standing there in her pale blue dress of lawn with its fitted bodice. Her yellow hair fell smooth and shiny as silk about her fair face.

Maybe I don't want to grow up at all, she thought. A part of her, a very real and fearful part of her, wanted to stay a child. A child just enjoyed life. She hoped she never felt as serious about everything as adults seemed to feel when she grew up. She hoped she enjoyed responsibility.

They bought popcorn at the concession stand for a nickel and went inside for the movie. Expectantly, Teal waited for the romantic plot to unfold. It didn't. She munched and watched and felt her soft dreams that started and ended with long kisses bend somewhat to further information. She'd never really wanted to think about why her mother and father slept together. Now it seemed that she must.

As the movie ended, Teal popped the last bite of corn in her mouth and wadded the sack. She felt disappointed as if something important had been left out. She preferred her romantic fantasy to the movie. Outside in the sun again, they walked along without talking for a long while.

"I guess Heath's mother wouldn't let him come today," Teal said at last. "*His* mother probably knew." Silently, she fumed over both his absence and his thrift.

Heath had a paper route, but he *never* bought her ticket for her. He told her once that he saved it for summer vacations, but Teal knew he never took them. She wrinkled her nose. She bet his mother kept his money for him.

"It isn't you, Teal," Sylvia said. "It's any girl. She doesn't want him out of her sight."

Teal shrugged as if it didn't matter, but it did. She missed him.

"You know you care," Sylvia said.

Teal's chin shot up, her pride trying to squash her feelings. Heath's mother would win. Someday when it was the most important time in the world for the two of them, she would win.

Straight and tall at twelve, Heath Meriott's face, the very scent of him moved her. From the first day she saw him, she loved him. She was climbing the steps to the slide at recess when she'd spied him through the ladder's metal strips. He waited at the bottom for her to slide down. They had been seven years old.

"Do you want me to swing you?" he asked her the moment her feet struck the dust. "Of course," she had said firmly.

They'd raced for the swings. Teal supposed they'd spent a thousand hours together since then. They walked to school together most of the time. They walked home together. They were constantly aware of each other, whether at play or in the classroom. When they accidentally touched, her heart pounded.

In the valley, summer lifted hot and white by late July. The sky itself paled in its brightness. Teal's body felt wonderfully akin to it, moist and supple—blossoming. She wanted to run or skip as she and Sylvia turned toward home from the theater.

"I have to forget about Heath," she said at last. "Things have changed. We're not sweethearts anymore after all."

"You can just decide that?"

"Change your mind, change you life," she confirmed, struggling against threatening tears.

"The things you say," Sylvia responded. "I swear, Teal, you'd be a great actress. Probably win a best actress award."

*   *   *

Unlike the metropolitan area to the east of them about thirty miles, El Reno did not thrive on oil but on wheat and the Rock Island Railroad. Essentially though, it was the land and ownership of it that provided the taxes for the schools. Marriage, the schools, and the churches were *the* essentials of these parts and had been since the numerous closings of saloons from the claim staking and lottery days when land ownership had been first decided.

The moral structure of the town grew still stronger after the dust days. Strangers easily surmised that these institutions were a strategic wall of defense against the several bars, the rumors of prostitutes, and other tales of immorality, usually sexual in nature. Even wearing shorts to town was against the law until the early '50s when the law was either banished or ignored.

In short, the community arose daily, in these transition years from dust to prosperity, in a state of suspicion in regard to a broad range of activities among which reveling, gambling, poverty, whoremongering, divorce, bootlegging, spitting on the sidewalk, and sometimes, even friendliness lifted eyebrows. Teal thought, though privately, that a lot more secret stuff probably went on around town.

The fact that there could be as much immorality here as most anywhere humans congregate, should one want to be judgmental, seemed best ignored or spoken of behind hands or fans or closed doors. Indisputably, gossip became the primary source of entertainment as the result of such pressures—for those above the legal age of twenty-one, at least. Teal tried not to miss any of it. As for those still younger, they certainly kept the wax out of their ears as well.

The township itself seemed easily marked off as east and west with the shops and supply centers in the middle. From north to south lay the sprawling Rock Island yards, the depot, and lastly, the large rail office itself and nearby Southern Hotel.

Farther north, south, east, and west than that were corn and wheat and cattle. Farms and ranches surrounded the town. With the two Canadian rivers to the north and to the south, their valley often enjoyed ample water. But when dry spells came, they were very, very dry. The valley's weather patterns favored extremes of hot and cold as well.

On this east side, the great white mills and grainery bins rose toward the skyline. This time of year, a half mile of trucks were lined, waiting to unload their summer crops to store or sell. It would go on all through the month of June and part of July or even later if showers came to delay the harvest. Everyone at the mill, her father included, helped where they could to relieve the stress. Ray Swain often worked eighteen hour days. Teal had been welcome help for several years.

Residents referred to the railroad as the Rock. Its numerous tracks of shiny steel bands bore trains in all directions: north to Kansas, south to Houston, west to Amarillo, and east through Oklahoma City to points beyond. Rail lay from north to south behind Swain Elevators as far as Teal could see.

She had walked miles of the rail, jumped ties, and picked armfuls of the buttercups along rails that skirted the east side of town. Mostly though, she bicycled east or west of the city, seeking the new and unexplored scenes. She especially liked her discovery of pastured horses northeast of town that she treated with garden carrots and orchard apples.

"If somebody from Mother's church saw me today," Teal said to Sylvia as they walked home that day, "they'll tell her, and she'll punish me." Momentarily, she imagined that possibility.

"You couldn't tell her what you didn't know," Sylvia defended legalistically.

"I couldn't have known," Teal responded, the fun of word games rising within her. "Why, when Jenny married, they went off in their corner and shut me out from learning."

"Remind her of it. She might believe you."

Actually, it was true. The movie didn't show all that much. What it left to the imagination, Teal was at a loss to put there. She felt extraordinarily ignorant about sex.

She wanted to avoid admitting to such a lack of genuine interest in it as well. For whatever feelings Heath inspired, whatever repulsion to ugly words or joy at the fantasy of a kiss, Teal did not *know*, in plain recordable facts, the reality of that mystery between a girl and a boy. She only grasped that to some, it was wonderful, and to others, it must be ugly, for they seemed so intent on snickering about it or hiding information about it. It. What? Love?

Did they hide information because it was precious and somebody might steal it? Was there not enough of it for everybody, or only so much and no more? She never saw anyone actually writing *that* word, and so, she concluded, they hid the facts from her for their shame. Such thoughts paraded her mind but did not stick there.

"Don't even say the name of the movie again, promise?"

"You are afraid."

"I'm not afraid. I'm not afraid of anything!" Teal asserted.

"Yes, you are, Teal. I wish you trusted me more. I know you're afraid she'll spank you." Sylvia's eyes looked more rational than troubled. Practical and intelligent, Sylvia Edwards never lost her temper, had no bad habits, and was the finest scholar in El Reno High School. If anybody knew the solution to a problem, Sylvia did. Teal had complete confidence in this fact though she would never confide it to Sylvia. Teal liked to think that she could take care of herself, whatever evidence to the contrary presented itself.

"You may not know *everything*," Teal defended. "*I'm* learning a lot this summer myself," she reminded her friend.

"You said you weren't worried. Teachers spank and many parents do, but my folks say that spanking is a poor excuse for thoughtful discipline."

"Aren't you afraid?" Teal asked.

"No, I'm not. I made up my mind to go, and it's nobody's affair but my own. I'd like to see them make it otherwise," Sylvia said.

"Sylvia!" But Sylvia didn't allow her to say anything more just then.

"If my mother dared to spank me now, I'd . . . I'd . . . I'd grab the stick! That's what I'd do, and that's what you must do, Teal. If she dares do that awful thing to you for your choosing what you want and paying for it, grab the stick. Promise?"

"What if I told her you said that?"

"Tell her!"

"Earlier, you said—"

"Earlier, I wanted her to like me. Now I want her to . . . to let you grow up. That's the root of the trouble, Teal. She loves you. She just doesn't want you to leave like the others have. That's exactly why she acted as if she did. You haven't stolen or lied or hit anyone. Even kids can go to reform schools for bad stuff. That's justice. You just saw a public movie. Use your head, for crying out loud."

Sylvia's voice sounded no faster or louder for the force of her information. It seemed to Teal that people solutions sifted down like ordinary sums to equations for her. Her suggestion that Esther might feel afraid she wouldn't be near her seemed a revelation that Teal wanted to believe. Her mother might even believe she could lose her father's love after *the change* when she wouldn't have more children. That much about the subject of sex, Teal did know. Old women didn't have babies.

"I promise," she said at last, imagining for the first time a world of possibility where she need not submit, where she risked the result of her resistance and took charge of change in her own life. Best, she knew how to talk to both of them. Her dad would tell her mother how much he cared again; she knew he would. He just believed she knew without the reminder. Teal would urge him to believe that her mother needed the reminder.

"Good-bye, then. I'll call you," Sylvia said. Teal's heart felt full as she watched her move away across the street, south. She walked on. She passed a thick clump of lilacs, their curly fragrant flowers hanging in nests of green. Their perfume followed her like a memory. She passed the corner to Heath's house and looked long down his street. She saw no sign of him; few people strayed outside their houses on such warm Sunday afternoons. She heard a lawn mower in the distance, the bark of a small dog.

Heath and summer lilacs and memories. A tear fell over the edge of her lower lid onto her cheek, but she brushed it away before running the rest of the way home.

—

Chapter XI

Becoming Teal

The road home curved down to the viaduct that covered the footpath below it and its steel rails. Teal liked leaving the world of square blocks and entering this place of paths and high banks, of slopes and creeks, of walnut and mulberry trees, which made where she lived separate from the middle space and from the west side.

She crossed the north to south creek on the narrow wooden bridge, pausing to lean over the handrails and stare as always into the running water, sometimes red from the red clay here after a rain, but on ordinary days past a week-old rain, it ran rather clear and beautiful like today. She pulled her blouse out of the waistband of her skirt and kicked off her shoes. She curled her toes against the old boards of the bridge before walking the rest of the way home barefooted.

Her father's ground, as her family referred to it, stretched like a flowering obelisk from the line of walnut and cottonwood trees at the base of the deep slope on the east side of the crowning rails to the snaking creek to the north. A narrow dirt road ran south. The two-story white house itself stood from the road, the design of it familiar from South Texas to Oklahoma. With porches on the south and east and flowering black locust trees surrounding it, it always seemed a welcome sight to Teal in summer. The large tree roots crawled down the high banks of lawn and jutted through the earth like tentacles. Cicadas usually clung to the rough bark by late July, and August's intense heat often arrived soon after to crisp the green leaves brown and crack the dry ground.

She turned up the path, soon stretching her skinny legs up the steep bank to the yard. The locust trees' branches shaded like green lace umbrellas; their clumps of white blossoms smelled sweet as cotton candy. She reached to pick a black-eyed Susan her father's mower had missed. They grew wild here and along the creek behind the orchard where the cherry and plum trees had bloomed weeks before and now made fruit. Apple blossoms remained, pears also, but peach and apricot trees now made fruit also. Pears stretched summer and called in the honeybees, wasps, and black bumbles until autumn. They never ripened all at once, but let her enjoy them until early September.

To Teal's left, a small flock of white chickens, the young Guernsey heifer, two goats (a nanny and a billy) were usually penned together. Tabatha, the old Guernsey, still had a pen to herself. She lowed at Teal's arrival home, then plopped down beside a partially eaten square bale of hay. Teal thought her father would sell the young heifer that Tabitha had birthed or butcher her. Now it seemed that he would keep her and sell Old Tab instead.

These acres that surrounded the grainary business were still rural housing development. Past the few developed acreages east of the rail route and the mill lay wheat farms. Farmers now turned over their land with plows to catch any showers before planting again in September.

The fresh-turned-earth scent on the air pleased Teal. She drew a deep breath of it.

The Swain elevator was only one of several along the rail's path for Canadian and adjacent counties produced enough wheat by itself to make bread for the world. That's what Ray Swain said. He said Canadian County alone had almost a quarter of a million acres in wheat. And if her dad said it, Teal believed it. The seasons usually saw enough business for them all.

Charles Huel had been right: conservation practices increased production, for it saved moisture and topsoil. "Six million bushels of wheat or more for the county became possible after 1945 thanks to Danne's Triumph seed, fertilizer, and conservation," he boasted.

"Thank God," her father always said when anyone mentioned these better days past drought. Yet now and then a duster still came, rarer and less severe than before. Now, a duster bore a haze of gritty dirt and sand. Before, its fine powder drifted against the outbuildings like black soot.

She could see her mother's vegetable garden. Planted in April, it sprouted yellow and green squash, bright tomatoes, and melons. The slow night watering grew tall cornstalks that eared well. She noticed that today's heat had wilted it. The garden fared better if they could get an occasional summer shower. Well water seemed to do it no good in late summer if there were no rains.

She loved everything about home as if it were part of her blood and bones. Here, she opened to and closed herself away from the world at will. Already, Teal understood that primary purpose of family choices that nurtured it.

Tom, her white Persian cat, sat in porcelain stillness on the south porch watching her approach. She reached to ruffle him about the head and ears as usual. He responded with a gentle slap of his paw, which he'd curled against a scratch.

Teal sensed that her mother waited for her return and that her father slept in his chair. Ray Swain had become a predictable man of schedule and habit, a thing that aged him to Teal.

He would waken after Sunday dinner in time for supper and plan his music for evening church services. Though Teal heard them talk of when they didn't know the truth, meaning they didn't attend or belong to a church, they now walked the mile to church Sunday morning and night, then again for Wednesday night Bible study. They took the car during very cold weather and stayed home when roads became treacherous with snow or ice. They walked on good weather days to save money.

Secretly, Teal preferred to hear her father play the old upright piano in their living room on those rare and gay occasions when he hammered out "Turkey in the Straw" or "Buffalo Gal." Such times shrank with every year that passed. It seemed to Teal that his critical frown and vocabulary of *do not's* increased at the same rate that his music decreased.

She shrugged, then caught Tom's paw in her hand in a quick and playful gesture that made his eyes harden and glint. Suddenly, he sank his sharp teeth into her thumb and forefinger just short of drawing blood. She scooped him up in her arms where he purred loudly. His body tensed, and his tail whipped back and forth.

"You're naughty!" she whispered with delight, then let him go. His sleek body slid like velvet past her fingers.

When Teal entered, Esther looked up from the round dining room table where she sat snipping fabric. The scissors' teeth moved like the snout of a shark around the edges of pattern pieces.

"You've been gone a long time," she said.

"It was a long movie," Teal answered.

"I heard," Esther drawled critically.

Teal didn't want to stay and make a tirade any easier for her mother. She turned toward the stairs that led to her room. The whole second floor housed only her since Jenny's marriage and Tad and Jonsi left. Teal stopped on the second step at her mother's next remark. "You might have told me it wasn't the usual musical," she said. Her tone inferred disappointment in Teal.

Teal backed down the steps to floor level. From the doorway that divided the living room and dining room, she faced her mother. "I didn't really know it myself for sure until I saw the marquee." She paused for a moment, hesitant to go on. With a little wry twist of her mouth, she continued. "I guess I wanted to see it anyway. Sylvia saw it too." She added the information about Sylvia as if that should qualify it, for she knew that her mother held her friend in high regard.

"Martha Milstick saw you. The whole congregation will know it by services tonight."

"Know what?" Teal asked irritably. "That I actually saw a man and woman lying together? I don't understand! What is it that I mustn't know, that you whispered to Jenny about when she married?"

"You shut your mouth! You know very well! It's that scene in the hay! Don't you think everybody knows about that?"

"Then why shouldn't I know about that too?" Teal snapped.

Esther's expression told Teal that she couldn't abide such confrontation from her. "Do you want the strap?" she threatened. She seemed suddenly half-crazed, unable to stand the thought of her growing up or seeing the world as quite sexual.

"Why is this physical mystery that men and women share like those buckets of dirt you sweep out of the house, Mother?"

Esther's face reddened as if gathering a moral mania inside her to keep out Teal's desires of the flesh. Teal thought that her elaborate defense could also have something to do with her fear of another pregnancy for she had figured out that whatever happened between the sexes caused babies for sure. In any case, Teal's own conscience didn't flinch.

"Everyone will know that Martha Milstick was there if she blabs," Teal reminded. "I saw nothing wicked in that movie, and if you dare strap me another time," she said with a jaunty tilt of her chin that Sylvia's encouragement prompted, "I'll take it away from you and—"

"And what?" Esther almost bellowed as if Teal had pushed her endurance to the limit. Her mother's nose had turned to a rich pink that pulsed with every heartbeat.

Teal thought her mother's voice would waken her father, but he snored there in his chair as if entering a deeper level of sleep. Esther's face twisted with rage. She dashed to the nearby window and drew a slender stick from the bottom of the cloth shade. Quickly moving to Teal, she caught hold of her arm and yanked her forward. With stubborn resistance, Teal struggled against her mother's strong hold on her.

"In the kitchen!" She hissed.

Teal's mind raced. With every step, she expected to feel the lash of the stick. Something Teal could not relate to was happening to her mother. She no longer cared whether she understood it; she wanted away from it or for it to stop.

When she faced Esther beneath that bare center lightbulb in the tiny kitchen, that farthest room of the house, Esther's challenging look spoke for her well, for Teal read her mother's response before she spoke.

"You grab this stick, and you'll get the worst beating of your life!" Esther warned, but she waited as if to test Teal's resistance.

"You won't beat me," Teal said. "You'll never beat me. No one will."

Esther didn't move for a long moment; she didn't speak. She stared blankly as if stunned that a child of hers should rebel. "I'm not a woman who can back down, and you know it," she said.

"Nor I," Teal said, her voice almost a whisper. "But 'spare the rod and spoil the child' is the most misread verse by your generation in the entire *Bible*." As the stick raised, she thrust her arms out before its lash to catch it. Teal bared her teeth, her hands gripping the stick with the intent of breaking it. She wrested it loose from Esther with rocking twists, but Esther grabbed it again and pulled Teal close with the thing.

"If you let go," she bargained, "I'll whip you this last time and never again. But if you don't let go, you'll be lucky to walk away."

Oh, why hadn't her father wakened and stopped this awful thing! her mind groaned. Teal's willful gaze clung relentlessly to her mother's. She desperately hoped for a concession, but Esther made none. It was her mother's authority at risk here today. Teal knew that she would never give it to one of her children.

"You swear it!" Teal breathed. Her throat felt dry. Her whole body ached with a kind of grief that thickened in her throat.

Her mother gave a short nod, and Teal let go of the stick.

When it was finished, Teal faced Esther. Tears streamed down her motionless face. "I hate you," she said. "I shall always hate you."

———

The moment seemed too much for Esther. Teal heard the stick clatter to the floor. Her mother's angry expression became shrouded with confusion. "Teal!" she cried. "I want you good and pure and perfect—protected from this awful world I learned about too late. It doesn't have to be too late for you. You have the advantage of the church to teach you right from wrong."

"You let that church lay guilt on you instead of grace. You spurn the whole purpose of Jesus's sacrifice on the cross: to set you free and to give you joy!" Teal said between her sobs.

Her tremendous cause to control seemed to send a surge of fresh energy through Esther, and she raised a fist as if to strike again. Then she dropped her hand to her side as Teal turned away from her.

Slowly, it would seep into her senses that the battle she'd intended to win with her stand, she'd lost, thought Teal. But the authority, she would justify. She'd saved that essential and godly quality that assured a forced obedience. As a parent, she must have that as her perceived Christian duty. Teal knew how Esther thought now; she was a receptacle for Preacher Plummer's *rules*—not scripture. Scripture promoted love, not law.

"I don't want you researching sex, Teal. Teal!" she called after her.

In her room, Teal flung herself upon her bed and let the hot tears flow until she felt emptied of them. The tears that cleared her mind left her soul with the naked grief. She remembered Heath's *different* smile last Friday afternoon. He'd looked at her as never before; she'd felt undressed. And the things he'd said. She hadn't sensed his affection; she had sensed a suggested activity to generate some secret shame.

They'd been walking home from school together, something that didn't happen as regularly as it used to, for Heath spent time now at the newspaper office and with his friend, Jonas, older than Heath and coarse, in Teal's opinion.

"Do you know how babies get here?" he'd asked her.

Teal couldn't bear Heath to think her stupid. She seemed to have been born feeling that she should know everything already, and what she didn't know, she deceitfully feigned the knowledge. That to know everything was an impossible task failed to discourage her efforts. So she proudly stuck her nose in the air and said, "Sure."

"A man and a woman marry and then a baby . . . happens," she said conclusively.

He laughed.

No," he said, a silly grin on his face. His eyes twinkled quite merrily at her. A few more steps and they'd be at his corner. They passed the lilac shrubs, still heavy with scent and purple flowerings.

"How then?" she asked boldly.

"It's the word that's on fences. You've seen it. They do that."

A panic arrested the moment. "That's a lie!" She didn't know what that word meant, but she knew it seemed despised and scorned. Making love and precious babies shouldn't be ugly. She knew that!

"Jonas told me."

"Jonas is horrible! I knew it! I wish you wouldn't spend so much time with him." She felt her face flush warm and seem to swell.

Heath frowned at her, the taunting smile not leaving his lips. "Ask somebody else if you don't believe me," he said. "It's the truth!"

"I'll not walk another step with you, Heath Meriott," she declared, and she had run off and left him to walk that last few steps alone.

She sniffed, the recorder in her mind recapturing his words. She would never knowingly make destructive choices. How Esther must doubt her, how she must hate that imagined side of her that didn't even exist.

Suddenly, Teal sat up on the side of her bed and wiped away her tears. When she was five, Sal Little, her young boyfriend who lived at the corner, had teased her. She'd felt confused then too, and wrongly.

"I'm going to catch you and kiss you," he'd said. She'd run, her heart pounding, but he caught her and smacked her on her forehead. Alone, she wrestled with that problem of what to say or do when her stomach swelled. For weeks that turned to months, she suffered anxiety over the episode. Then she won that fistfight with Joey Jacobs and got her Red Cross swimming medal and began crayfish creek fishing until so much time went by she realized that kissing did not cause babies.

Her body still stinging from the stripes left by the stick, she knew that seeing a tumble in the hay didn't cause them either. Something besides dreams and skin touching and feelings and romantic kisses caused babies.

Tremulously, she stood. She walked across the floor to the stairway with the carefulness of one stepping upon glass. Dreams were like glass to Teal. Breakable. She wished she could know in advance what lay on the other side of ignorance and dreams because she always chose knowing. She needed to know. She would deal with risk and any result by making choices of what to do or how to think, but she needed information. She now had the decided intention of researching sex.

Every creak of the stairs vibrated through her until her feet reached the bottom. Quietly, she moved toward Esther who sat at the dining room table, her head upon her crossed arms. Teal supposed she wasn't feeling well again. She found her in this posture rather often these days. At such times, her mother's face often looked a little swollen as if she'd been crying.

"Mother?" she asked, her voice as soft and unintrusive as she could make it.

Esther raised her head slowly. She looked very tired to Teal. Her eye contact seemed expressionless. Whatever Esther's mood and with whoever she interacted, her feelings traveled near the surface and revealed themselves with her expressive eyes. When she felt good, Teal usually benefited largely from her lavish smiles of approval.

"Where do babies come from and how?" Teal asked abruptly. "And I don't mean from the stomach. I know that," she clarified. "I mean, I need to know how they start and finish up." She paused, then blurted, "Heath says it's that . . . that awful word."

—

169

Esther's blank face registered surprise, an improvement in Teal's opinion.

"My god, Teal. The movie?" The exasperation in Esther's voice did not stop her.

"The movie showed nothing but two people, very close."

"Well, thank God for that!" Esther praised, then smoothed back her hair, almost silver now. "Sit down, Teal," she said flatly. "I'll explain it as best I can." It sounded to Teal as if her mother considered the conversation's prospects an ordeal to struggle through somehow.

Teal sat, expectant.

"I'll explain about becoming a woman," she began as if to introduce the subject. "Soon," she said, lowering her voice as if someone might overhear them, "you will pass blood monthly. You shouldn't be frightened by it, but it's a nuisance."

"That's all there is to being a woman?"

Esther regarded her vacantly, then added. "Well, your body does this when there's no child growing in it. Women have children."

"I know that," Teal said.

"But not until they are married."

Teal just looked at her; she knew that women had babies who weren't married. Still, she didn't interrupt her mother; she wanted to hear all that Esther had to say.

"You see, Teal, the man's body and the woman's body are made in such a way that the man can plant a seed in the woman's body and a baby grows."

Teal nodded. "Go on," she said.

"Well, that's all." Esther said, her face flushing with color. "Do you understand?"

Teal sighed. "I understand, mother. I think I'll go bicycling now if it's all right with you. I'll be back in time for church."

Esther agreed almost too quickly, and Teal sensed her mother's eagerness to end this discussion and have its reminder out of the house for a while. She felt oppressed here now—had since her return from the movie. Something besides the punishment divided her from her mother in a way she had not felt before. She wanted womanhood, but she rejected this shame of it that she sensed in Esther. She'd stay a child first for as long as she could.

Her need for Esther had diminished very little with the years and from those earlier times of exclusive attention. Jenny's notion that she was spoiled hadn't convinced Teal of that. Weren't all children in need of reliable kindness, support, information, direction, and respect from their parents? This change in their relationship created the first real unhappiness she had ever known. Her great hate and great love warred within her for she had heard of children who treated their parents badly also. Did this have to be the ultimate fate of all mothers and daughters? Teal thought it only a problem for those mothers who lost their confidence as if youth were *their* identity and all daughters who saved grudges because of it.

Wanting to flee, she bicycled far east of her house to the foot of her favorite hill. Its steepest point stretched south about three-quarters of a mile. She thought it a wonderful hill to coast down with no hands.

She trudged up its summit beside the rolling wheels. She leaned heavily into the handlebars and pushed. She sometimes arrived by the level east-west trolley route straight south of her house, then followed the tracks east to the top of the hill. That spared her the climb before coasting downhill. She felt the dregs of something that needed pushing out, so she pushed. By the time she sped down the slope as if in flight, her damp body cooled delightfully.

The wind tugged at her face and hair. She stuck her feet straight out the sides, the wheels purring like a cat as the spokes flew around and around. This hill was a place for deciding things, and as she reached the bottom, she thought, *I don't need details about sex yet anyway. I've lots of time.* So she postponed that area of her growing-up process by decision, feeling quite sure of one thing: she wanted good things for herself—education, career success, good health, dignity. She turned the bicycle toward home. *I will do things to make those good things happen,* she thought. *Until then, I'll collect information.*

—

Perhaps she'd lost something today, something to do with Esther. Teal wasn't certain of its nature yet. But she'd won something too. She'd won awareness of her will and separate identity. Esther would never hit her again. Nor would she martyr herself willingly for anyone or anything unless she freely chose to do so for a purpose she believed in.

The God she knew would not want her molded into a stranger to herself.

"I shall study quite hard on my books," she determined aloud, as if promising a listening God. "And make excellent marks." Jenny and Jonsi and Tad had their own lives. Her father retreated to late hours at the mill. He had a good crew, but he had begun a barley storage expansion that required later hours. *And Mother has entered a cave of fear, suspicion, and despair.*

Esther seemed afraid of her now. *Yes,* she thought. Afraid—of her and for her to grow up, to become a woman. She would have her books; she would have *her* search for *her* truth. Deciding it gave her back a feeling of security that she had temporarily lost and added a sense of personal power, the feeling that she was taking charge of choices and her responsibility for them.

At home, she rolled the bike to the side of the house and parked it. Broodingly, she looked out toward Tabatha's pen. She walked there instead of going inside. She crossed her arms upon the top wire of the gate and rested her chin there thoughtfully. Tabatha lay chewing her cud. The three-year-old heifer stood near her. Teal put her hand on the wire loop of the latch that hooked over a post, then stopped.

How she wanted to confront this fear, evidenced now in the sweat beads that popped out on her forehead and moistened her underarms. Tabatha had knocked her down the last time that she had gone near her babe. Would she do it if Teal forced her?

Teal dropped her arms away from the latch. Why open that gate? Tabatha couldn't care less. Her babe had become just another cow. She would face fear another way. She supposed life offered ample opportunity.

—

She dragged her feet a little all the way to the house. When Tom whisked about her legs, she shied from him. Hadn't he almost brought the blood that last time she'd held him? "Scat!" she scolded, then entered the house as quietly as she could. She preferred distance from both Tom and Esther and understood why one could distance themselves from another they loved. Enough hurt caused it. Would forgiving the hurt fix a person back?

Ray and Esther had become two people alone. Now they were three.

CHAPTER XII

Gavin Rush

On the following Saturday, Teal practiced croquet in her yard when the young man with those striking blue-green eyes passed by carrying an empty jug.

Later, she would learn that he had come in from the farm to spend the weekend with his grandmother Lettie, who still lived in the back of her store. He mowed her lawn and ran her errands for her whenever he could.

Teal still bought her favorite penny jawbreakers at his grandmother's store. The round hard and unbreakable candy lasted over an hour in the *jaw*, which accounted for its name. It had been three years since she had seen him.

She still wanted him to notice her, to say *hello*. He looked so . . . Her head had begun to spin as if she'd been spun round. Worse, her stomach felt as if she were on the downside of a whirling Ferris wheel.

"Hello," she called.

Gavin Rush stared only at the stretch of red-dirt road.

"Are you deaf?" she yelled, watching his backside moving away from her.

He made no response.

"Hello!" she called, still louder, knowing her persistence surely made her obnoxious rather than desired or adorable. Her insides churned as she watched him saunter farther and farther away. *I won't feel like a zero. I won't.* But she felt like a zero in this young man's eyes. This farmer boy from whom she could not take away her own glance—not then, not now. All reason deserted her. She only knew that recognition *must* be mutual, for good or ill.

His head tilted toward the sky as he gave her the back of it.

"Squirt" echoed from the past. "I'm thirteen and pretty," she assured herself between clenched teeth.

"If you don't speak to me on your way back, I'll break that jug of milk again," she yelled after him. Her voice cracked. She felt like crying. Why did it matter to her? She agonized over his rudeness. What was this mysterious force that propelled her toward this . . . this most gorgeous male she had ever laid eyes on and in this self-defeating way?

Teal thought she'd not see him return. *If it were me, I would go around the block the alternate way. He's doing this on purpose,* she thought when he reappeared, *to force his meanness on me. If he hadn't already seen me, I might have hidden in the house. Perhaps he would have felt ignored.* She knew she would have the devil to pay for spilling his jug of milk again.

"Hello," Teal called, unable to follow her best intentions. For she believed he knew she had seen him and that he would think her a coward or worse: that she cared nothing for his attentions. After all, he might say hello, even smile at her.

When that handsome nose aimed at the sky again, she threw a firm clod that she'd fetched from the road. The force secured a direct hit. Again, milk splashed over him with a thoroughness as complete as her own disappointment washing over her for the second time. What was it about him that tormented and attracted her very being? Agony seemed to grip her heart and squeeze.

"I'm going to tell your mother!" he yelled. "I paid for this milk." He wriggled his feet as if it had filled his shoes. Glass lay scattered in the road.

Terrified, Teal stood where she was as he stalked to the door and knocked.

"I'm not one bit sorry," she said, struggling to hold back tears.

"What if he had been cut!" her mother scolded. "Why, your father and I met the Rushes when I carried you. They are friendly, Teal. That young man was a visitor in our home then and at Jenny's wedding as well. He came as an invited guest. Upstairs to your room! No supper for you tonight!"

Still, Esther made no mention of a spanking. *Best thing about this,* Teal thought, *I moved through my* fear *of punishment to act on the need to cure a snob.*

She inched past Esther, going quickly up the stairs to watch from her south window as he walked spraddle legged to the corner, turned, and disappeared. In spite of her regret that he hadn't responded, she smiled with satisfaction.

"I'll bet I flipped over in the womb if he was in the room before mother had me," she told Sylvia, who responded with a rueful look.

"If you ever see him and I'm with you, point him out to me, Teal. He may not be a snob, you know. He may be one of those cold users like the cowboy in *The Outlaw.*"

"Not Jonsi, Tad, or my dad lack natural affection. Hollywood must invent those men for movies," she said. But Teal actually wondered otherwise and intended to research the issue. *Perhaps,* she thought, *deep down where it counted—in the soul—such men hated women. Perhaps they feared their gentler side and walled it off from consciousness. That is, if they really existed.*

It would be five years before she saw him again.

*   *   *

Gavin rode silently beside his father most of the way home from his grandmother Letti's. He brooded over the episode outside that girl's house. His skin felt sticky with wet milk, and as the edges of his socks dried, they stiffened wherever the milk had been. He could smell it souring in the denim.

Why hadn't he said hello? Such a simple thing, but he hadn't thought of it *first*. She had. What made the memory more tragic for him was that he *knew* she wanted his notice. *I'm an adult, she's just a kid.* Still, how powerful and desired he had felt to remain aloof.

Gavin liked thinking of things first; he liked being in control. Most, he reveled in the notion that this brat seemed mad about him. That's why he'd deliberately asked his grandma Letti if she would like him to fetch her a jug of fresh milk. He knew the Swain's lived there, and he remembered the girl from that summer after he graduated from high school but before his two years in Korea.

"Your mother won't be happy about your spoiling your clothes," his father said.

"It wasn't my fault," he said.

The old truck bumped along the dirt road. His blue-green eyes turned sullen and moody. His cousin Lester sat grinning beside him. "You're acting like a hog in the sunshine!" Gavin told him. "What's so comical!"

"You and that dumb girl. She was willing for punishment. You were willing to be her dope again." Lester said, shaking his head. "Wasn't your fault, hah!"

Harlin looked over at them. "You start the milking as soon as we get home. I'll take our fresh milk to your grandma tonight for making butter and cheese, and I'll bring the combine in from the field. We can start the plowing tomorrow."

"Better let me off at home then," Lester said.

Harlin stopped the truck at Lester's house. "I'll expect you tomorrow unless it rains, Lester." Lester was Rena's sister's boy. Their place was across the road from Harlin and Rena's.

"I'll be there. I'll cut across when I hear the Johnny Pop," he said. Gavin called the John Deere diesel machine a Johnny Pop because it "popped" and hummed along. Harlin had two tractors in the field now, an old Minneapolis Moline and the newer Deere.

Any of the combines reminded Gavin of crawling bugs, their teeth chomping up the straw and swallowing the grain that filled their bins like stomachs. The John Deere was a green and glorious sight to him in the middle of a gold grain field. But he liked operating the "Mini" better. He was used to her. Best, tractors didn't startle and thrust you into the dangerous equipment they pulled like horses could.

He reached to touch the cheek scars, remembering their horse, Red, that startled at a train whistle when he moved alfalfa near the tracks. The sickle blades cut his arm to the bone, slashed his leg, and stuck him in the face. At age seven, he believed he might bleed to death before a passerby saw the accident and got him help.

As for Red, he'd grown old and arthritic. After being turned out to pasture, he died the following hard winter.

Lester jumped out. When a safe distance from Gavin, he said, "She's the first that's outdone you, Gavin, and I'll bet she's no more'n twelve." He laughed loudly as he ran off toward his house.

"I'm gonna punch him good!" Gavin said, making a fist.

"You do, and you'll get the strap!"

"I'm almost twenty-one. Those days are past, and you know it." He turned bold and cool eyes upon his father, now half a head shorter than he but hard and muscled from his years of heavy work. Harlin had been too young for the Great War and too old for WWII. Gavin, on the other hand, served two years in the Cold War to stop communism and resisted treatment that inferred that he bore a minor status in his father's eyes.

"The day it takes more than me to head my house, I'll gladly give it up. But today ain't that day. You may be a man, but you didn't act it today. A man masters himself—not an adolescent girl with a crush."

Gavin heard a quaver in his father's voice; he saw no flinch in his stance nor softening of his expression. Instead, when they arrived home and Harlin parked the truck in the barn, he stepped sturdily to the wall and took down a strip of raw hide, soon to be tanned for halters and saddle trims. "Grab your ankles!" he ordered.

Gavin didn't move for a moment. Not even his eyelids flickered. "You think a strap still resolves the authority issue?" he challenged. His love for Harlin went far beyond punishment. He worshipped him. He had spent most of his life waiting for the sight of him. To Gavin, his father was as dependable as truth itself. He'd taught him loyalty to purpose. He'd taught him to work and to wait, to keep going despite cruel people and odds. He saw his future beside him on the farms.

Gavin grabbed his ankles. He could bend for his father. When nothing happened, he stood and faced him. They looked at one another as two men might who recognized the other.

"That's the last I'll ever threaten you," Harlin said and threw the strap in the corner as if it were contaminated. "God willing, you won't sass again but will address me as an equal. Older isn't less, young man. More important, without respect for authority, a family, a community, a whole country can be overtaken by anarchy." Harlin stared at the barn floor. His shoulders slumped as if Gavin had punished him. Yielding authority and asking for equality obviously humbled him.

"Every generation of parents looks for the best way to get respect from their children," he said, lifting his head to look Gavin in the eye.

"I apologize, Dad. I'll strip the strap out for a halter." Gavin started toward the corner to pick it up.

"No. I'm buying you a new saddle and halter for Blue, soon as the wheat's in. But so help me, God, Gavin. If you can still take your punishment like a man from me, why does that slip of a girl befuddle you so?"

"Damned if I know." He was thoughtful for a moment. "I've been thinking I'd sell Old Blue and put the money for him down on a car. I've not even ridden him since my discharge." Gavin waited for an explosion. "I've tired of taking dates out in the truck. I want my own transportation to go to the university ball games, to date more." He would have his own car on his father's guilt or any other way he could legally get it.

—

179

"A good crop was twelve to fifteen bushel an acre ten years ago," Harlin said. "Topsoil had blown it away, terraces were slowly being built, and rains were still infrequent. All our land averaged a twenty-five bushel to the acre crop this year, thanks to Danne's Triumph wheat seed. And it brought twice as much as that dollar twenty-five wheat. It's the improved seed and fertilization. Sell him. When I top-dress the next crop with nitrogen after it sprouts, we'll get an even greater gain. The researchers claim fifty bushel to the acre may be possible in this valley. I'll give you the cost of Blue's new riggings for your car instead. Could be as much as a hundred and fifty dollars more, maybe two hundred. You're a grown man, and I'll never treat you otherwise again."

Harlin smiled, a twinkle in his eyes. "She's pretty special to you, is she?"

Gavin glanced away without answering. Sara Jane was his personal business, not his father's. Instead he said, "They say that after fertilizing and when the sprouts are up, to top-dress with nitrogen does get an even larger crop. I read about that too."

Harlin turned aside and walked toward the house. "Maybe we'll top-dress," he called back. He walked like a proud rooster, his head high and his legs almost stomping the ground. Fine particles of dust stirred with each step. The evening sun's red orange slid behind the house. Night would fall soon.

He caught and held that image of Harlin walking away, the silver glint of his hair, the dust rising and falling about his scuffed boots and faded denim. He thought him a beautiful sight. They spoke as equals and agreed on how to manage their next crop. Perhaps their confrontation forced a healthy transition, he thought.

Gavin walked to the barn's corner and picked up the raw hide to hang it back on the wall. He'd probably need a job as well to pay for a good car. After wheat sowing, there wouldn't be much farming besides counting and feeding cattle or helping with calving and winter chores morning and evening before the spring vaccinations when they also made steers out of young bulls. Harvest next summer would begin a new cycle.

In the meantime, maybe Ray Swain would hire him part-time at the mill. Car payments and gas money could come to two or three hundred dollars a month. The two hundred from his father and the price of Old Blue would make the down payment. *I'd even say hello to that brat of his if he'll give me a job,* he thought.

After the milking that night, his mother went to the house to cook supper, and his father went in to help her while he washed the milk cans with antiseptic soap. Rena Lily insisted on sterile utensils before and after the milking. They milked the small herd of eight Holsteins each morning and evening. It took only an hour when they worked together that way.

Gavin carried the foaming buckets to the porch to fill the chrome cans. Each time he emptied one, he washed it promptly with fresh well water. They took only spotlessly clean buckets to the lot. Each of the spotted cows gave at least two gallons of milk each morning and night. That represented a lot of cream, cottage cheese, and butter for Rena to sell in town.

The cows stood waiting in the faded light of evening or in the pale light of dawn, their heavy bags going from teats stretched taut to the shriveled and relieved bags. Their hip bones jutted in spite of their health and glossy coats; that was the look of them—big boned and gangling. Holsteins were good producers that gave ample milk and light cream for both selling and for their own cream gravy and pancakes, the homemade butter and sour cream cakes his mother made. His taste buds spurted thinking of her chocolate brownies and puddings. The sweet butter she made melted over her hot breads fresh from the kerosene oven.

He grew impatient for supper thinking about it.

"Gavin!" his mother called.

"Coming," he called back, swinging the last of the clean buckets beside him.

He sure hoped his father didn't think he wanted to date that kid. She had the makings of a real looker someday, he supposed, but Sara was his girl. Sara left for college when he left for the army.

—

When she graduated, she would teach at the local high school, and he would farm with Harlin. Maybe they would marry—someday.

*   *   *

Harlin at forty-five still walked three miles to work daily. "Saves gas," he said. Cutting across fields, he reached the county barn in about an hour in the morning and another in the evening to reach one of his own fields or the house. When wheat-planting time arrived, they sowed at night. He and Gavin did it, with Gavin filling the drill or guiding the tractor so his father could doze at intervals. His mother milked his portion of the cows so he could sleep later on the mornings after he plowed or sowed at night; Gavin looked forward to that.

As a child, he had risen early to help before meeting the school bus at the road, a quarter of a mile from the house. Before he began high school at the county seat, he'd gone to the country school. In winter, he'd often gone early to build the fire for Ms. Tucker. Before spring of each year, he often prepared the flower beds for her. He would clean the blackboards before each term. He earned a dime a day that way, funds enough to allow him a few purchases when they went to town each Saturday.

He and Harlin loaded the cream cans and egg crates before seven every Saturday morning. That's when Rena also took any extra butter or cottage cheese to town to sell at the open market. Sometimes she had sand-plum jelly and fresh vegetables, fruit, or baked goods to fund their shopping needs.

He lay, remembering those things tonight when chores were done and the house fell quiet after supper. The pattern of their lives changed little after they moved into their own house and off the Indian land. Their farms provided for them and many others.

There were perhaps a dozen books in the room, among them a Zane Grey novel, a dictionary, and a geography of the world. There was an odd book called *Rape of the Lock* by Pope and Emerson's *Self-Reliance*. They were curious volumes that Gavin never took from the shelf. What had they to do with *his* life? "You're a mover, not a thinker," Lester had chided once.

But he opened the geography book often to read about the world he had not seen. He imagined its rivers and learned the directions they ran. He memorized capitols and continents;, climates and rainfall. How the world worked interested him in the same way that how a combine operated interested him or how a grain of wheat burst from its seed and stooled, stemmed, and ripened every June, hardened by the sun, changed into flour and cereal and feed and forage.

Gavin also liked to make things go. He liked operating the tractor alone in the field. Those hours were his alone. Unlike most of the other young men he knew, he liked *alone*. It pleased him to haul the wheat to town. He wanted to build roads and bridges, to operate big equipment like bulldozers and road graders. He felt one with the machines as if they were an extension of himself or, maybe, vice versa.

His room felt chilly tonight. He tore up a piece of tablet paper and lit a match to it, then tossed it onto the fireplace chips. They flashed and caught at the small pieces of dried sticks. He added a log. Gavin altered the damper on the chimney, sending the smoke that wanted in the room up the stem. When at last the wood coals burned brightly, he went to the small reclining reading chair beside the bookcase and pulled the geography book of the world free. He opened it to the chapter about Australia. He read about the untamed land they offered buyers for two dollars an acre until he fell asleep.

There, the untamed girl named Teal with the young breasts pressing against a thin white muslin blouse that looked too small for her swirled in and out of his dreams calling, "Hello, hello."

CHAPTER XIII

The Dance

Teal preened before her mirror, first naked then wrapped in a bit of scarf, then draped in a sheet or whatever bit of fluff suited her. The new suppleness and glow of her body pleased her. The sun-yellow dress waited in its lustrous pile of satin and lace across her bed. She anticipated the Beta K dance.

Annually, senior members of the exclusive girls club leased the country club for it. Teal's excitement grew as the dance approached. She invited Heath, her usual date for school functions. They were rarely together at any other time.

Since their freshman year, Heath had been preoccupied with his editorial duties on the school paper, the *Banner*, and the school band where he played the clarinet. Recently, the school yearbook occupied him. They would graduate in May. She hoped they could go to the senior prom together.

He'd begun to alarm Teal who felt that she came last or never in his recent schedule. She didn't care for his urgent preoccupations and deadlines. She hated everything that kept them apart.

She wasn't certain what she wanted or needed to fill this awful uncertainty about a future she had believed she would share with him. She only knew she intended to ask him why he never touched her anymore. When they were children, they walked hand in hand.

At last, she skimmed into the dress and pulled up the side zipper. The satin hugged her new curves and tossed back the light in the room.

She supposed that was what she wanted, she thought, mildly surprised. She wanted Heath to touch her. She smoothed down the dress, the fabric already warm from her body, the quality she liked best about satin. It had a special affinity for warmth. She wanted Heath to feel it tonight, to feel her body warmth and realize they were alive.

Esther had made this gown for her. Strapless gowns were the vogue; almost everybody had one, but Esther wouldn't hear of it. Small capped sleeves embraced her shoulders snugly and fell into a sweetheart neckline, which accented her bare throat. Teal left her throat bare; she wanted no bit of jewelry, no ribbon there to hide what skin she could show. *I want no gloves to cover my hands either,* she thought.

She'd caught the front and sides of her long hair at the crown and clamped it with a bar of gold. The rest tumbled down the middle of her back.

She inspected her flawless white teeth, pinked her high cheeks with rouge, and applied a rosy lipstick. After inspecting her appearance from every angle, she lay the hand mirror aside and hurried down the stairs. If Heath were his punctual self, he would arrive within minutes; she'd not keep him waiting. He rigidly planned everything. To keep him waiting would upset him.

She wanted some word, some gesture or feeling from him tonight that would let her know her value to him—what he hoped for them. *Heath hasn't really talked to me in a long time,* she thought. In fact, she now felt like one of his habits—a block in the structure he planned. Teal wasn't at all certain that she fit there anymore for she knew she could never be happy as his *afterthought.*

She would encourage him toward a closer relationship tonight. Then she would know if *he* wanted them closer in reality.

I might step near him on the porch when he brings me home and say lightly, "Don't you want to kiss me, Heath?" Or I could say, "I'd like you to kiss me, Heath."

She wrinkled her nose. She needed him to think of it. *I'll move near enough to feel his warmth and look up,* she decided. *He'll surely kiss me then, surely have sense enough to think of it himself.* But even as she daydreamed, she recognized his behavior as neglect. His ignoring her seemed avoidances that both hurt and puzzled her.

If she salvaged her pride with him, she must lie, she thought. She must tell him she loved him like a sister but without those other feelings. That wouldn't be entirely a lie; her strong feelings for him frightened her since he seemed not to return them. It provided some relief to pretend she didn't have them. Wouldn't she be forever safe from them then? For when she thought of him actually touching her, her whole body seemed her heart, her breath. She felt consumed by some power greater than her own, an energy she could only explain to herself as better than roller coaster rides or no-hands bicycling.

Heath seemed essential to her survival.

Though it was early yet, she looked out the front window each time a car passed. His punctual self, Heath arrived at seven sharp. A foot taller than Teal, he stood lean and blond. His blue eyes met her with that cool, intelligent gaze. He handed her the florist box, and she looked with delight upon the iris's beautiful lavender petals that crowned the gold throat that led like a cave to the flower's short stem.

"How beautiful," she said. "Thank you, Heath. Your first flowers to me. I'll keep it forever."

"I wanted an orchid, but I couldn't afford it."

His words wilted her happiness; even the flower seemed to turn brown about its edges. He had such a way of doing that. Or was it her? It seemed to Teal that her insides both frowned and smiled when Heath entered her atmosphere. Beautiful as he was, Heath spoiled things.

"It's beautiful," she repeated and let it end there. "Please come in."

"Aren't you ready?"

"Well, yes. I thought—"

"Then let's go," he said factually. Teal shrugged. "Well, step inside at least while I pin on my flower."

"I'll pin it for you," he said, his glance and his voice more aware and warm. The backs of his fingers lay warm upon her shoulder while he pressed the pin at the base of its bud. Esther entered the room from the kitchen.

"Well, Heath! I didn't know that you were here. Why didn't you tell me, Teal?"

Teal didn't answer.

"Won't you sit down?" Esther invited him.

"No thank you, Mrs. Swain. Teal and I are just leaving, aren't we, Teal?"

"That's right, Mother. Now don't wait up for us. I'll be home soon after the dance."

"See that you are," she said. "You know how your father gets when you aren't home before midnight."

"Oh, I'll have her back, Mrs. Swain. There's no need to worry."

"No need," Teal agreed. And there wasn't. She had asked Heath almost a year ago why he never called or came to see her. She wanted to just hold hands. How she craved time with him tonight.

"I'm waiting," he told her then.

"For what?" she had asked.

"For later."

She hadn't asked him since. Later had arrived long ago in her opinion. Perhaps he meant marriage; perhaps he meant when he could afford marriage. Perhaps he meant when he was old enough to afford the risks of real feelings.

Until she had hugged Jenny's children or squeezed a new puppy, until she laughed out loud or cried, even feelings were only thoughts. Delicious sometimes, always human, but not known with sound or taste or touch, and therefore, unreal.

—

The best of her life seemed the internal journey of her mind to some reality. Her life experience grew larger as the consequence and gained greater depth rather than changing to something unrecognizable. He still looked like Heath, but she no longer recognized him as that reliable life partner that she had once dreamed.

Life itself might be a thing in parts and seasons that she could not clutch and keep except in her memory. She hoped she never had to pinch herself to see if she was real because of a cultural redo. Somehow she must accept this change and adapt. For Heath seemed to be someone in the process of willfully becoming a self-made machine according to the popular concept of a Mr. Right.

She wanted to know where he stood regarding her. She felt outside of his plans for college or for marriage. He had put her there. *Connecting to the fringe of his life,* she thought, *compromises any integrity. It feels like self-betrayal.*

Her life felt like a ball of snow that grew fat with its rolling or like paraffin warms and dribbles down a candle with even burning until the light goes out. She didn't know yet if the whole of it would be snow or candlelight or some of both. Perhaps that explained this great chasm between them: Heath *must* know and plan each step as if he controlled the result of his life experience. She desired the revelation of her life. It lay within her like a continent to be discovered and developed.

The day Tabatha knocked her flat and could have killed her in the middle of her best-laid plan for berry picking taught her that plans get changed without permission.

So Teal's love of connection wrestled with her wariness of Heath's planned materialism: his ambitious struggle for the best that money bought. She wanted closeness to the earth, to the sky, to bodies and books, to work, and to everyone who wanted her close. Wasn't increase simply the natural result of a loved work?

Heath must not want to be close. Not now. *Maybe not ever,* she thought, catching his glance as he pinned the corsage. Closeness to Heath might never be more than repetitive brushes with the physical—when he had time.

"Thanks," she said softly, trying to hold his glance, but he turned toward the door. She followed him to the auto for he had rushed ahead instead of waiting.

Her fear clawed its way to consciousness. Heath might be incapable of real closeness, of being known.

He owned no car. Not many of the young men his age did unless their father bought it for them. Teal thought that odd for every day after school and on weekends, Heath worked as a printer and errand boy for the local paper. He bought iris, thinking of orchids, and he borrowed transportation. She would surely know who or what meant anything to him someday. Right now, she suspected his mother and his money could claim that distinction.

He opened the door of the blue Plymouth for her, and she got inside. She sat in the middle so that she would be nearer him. He didn't seem to notice but drove directly toward the club with sparse conversation.

"It was nice of your aunt to loan us her car," Teal said. Conversation seemed an awkward struggle.

"Yes," he said. "I have to have it back by ten."

Teal clamped her lips together in a wry expression. *That's why he assured mother of my arrival home early,* she thought. The evening she'd looked forward to seemed to be going rapidly downhill. His camera hung between them from a shoulder strap. It separated them. She started to shift it aside to clasp his hand.

"Don't touch it!" he cautioned. "I've got it set like I want. I have to get pictures tonight for the *Boomer*." The *Boomer* would collect their four years of high school memories into a hardback book to cherish. She cherished now—tonight.

"Can't somebody else? The dance!" she objected. "It's been months, Heath, since I've been with you at all. I want to hold your arm. You have another shoulder."

She felt without shame, for tonight seemed their last chance to recover something very precious. Her love for Heath felt visceral and exclusively his since childhood. It had grown with each year into a pristine and secret paradise.

"Nobody else can do it." He sounded irritated. "We'll have time to dance. I know what I have to do."

"Good," she said, her voice tinged with bitterness. "You could have as easily said you were sorry about the old pictures and wanted to dance with me."

"I do want to teach you the two-step tonight if you don't know it. Mother showed me the steps." He sounded a bit contrite.

"I don't know. I just like to move," she began.

"I want to teach you," he interrupted. "It's a right way to dance something that isn't a waltz or jitterbug. I don't like to just make up steps for you to follow."

How would he know, she thought. They had never gone dancing. Teal sighed; her attraction to him and her objection to him began a quarrel with her love for him. "Your attitude is—" She stopped. Tempted to lie, to compliment him, she balked. "Rigid. Why don't you pay any attention to me anymore, Heath? You hang on, but you don't really want to see me or you would! I don't understand."

"I don't want to lose you, and it's too soon to be serious. I've a lot to do before getting serious."

"Too soon for what? To be kind? To talk? To touch?"

When he failed to respond, she pursued him. "What are your plans? What is it that you want? I need you to tell me how I fit into them. Talk to me, Heath. Tell me."

"I've had to work, I've had to save. Why can't you just believe I don't want to lose you? Why can't you wait and know I'll tell you when it's time, when I know that it's time?"

"But we're graduating, Heath. I need to know. Can't you see that I need to know what's out there for me, for you—for us? I have a life too. It can't be all about you."

"There's no way to know that until we're there, past preparation for a life," he said. He glanced at her, his expression begging her to understand, but she didn't.

———

"I need to know!" she repeated, her tone begging him to communicate.

"I'm sorry," he said. "I don't know. I've *got* to live a day at a time. I've *got* to plan, then follow the plan."

Tears shot to her eyes. She wouldn't cry! She wouldn't. She intended to have a good time. For months, she had dreamed of dancing with Heath. She wanted him to say they'd go on to school together, that they'd marry and scrimp and save and struggle together. Heath was logical and practical and full of good judgment. He wanted things in their proper order, according to him. He seemed to be thinking of their life *without* her.

Shouldn't she be in on the plan? She wanted to hammer her fists on his chest and require it of him. What was age or money or what anybody thought compared to lost time together? She had been wrong to have expectations.

"I'll *never* have expectations of another relationship if I live to be a hundred and ten," she snapped.

He parked the car in the lot, then walked around to open her door. The expression on his face seemed a warning against more talk while his behavior remained courteous.

She longed to tell him that nothing seemed to matter to her unless she knew he would be beside her. *How could he?* she thought, stepping out of the car. Being with her seemed to matter so little to him. She walked beside him quietly as her feelings for him limped into a smaller place.

The dancing had started when they entered the ballroom. The dimly lit room smelled of sweet colognes and sounded of rustling taffeta and Harlem Nocturne, the favorite melody at almost every party these days.

Teal loved to dance to its lazy seduction, so like honeysuckled summer nights. She had hoped to hear its minor chords tonight. They walked to the second room back of the ballroom where games were set up on square tables beneath bright lights. The checkers and cards already clicked to the motion of the players' hands, a kind of music all their own.

She slipped out of her light wrap. Heath helped her, hanging it on a wall hook. "I'll get a few pictures first," he said, "then we'll dance." He began to look around the room.

"Sylvia must be out front," he said.

Teal didn't like his preoccupation with pictures and certainly not his arranging her evening with Sylvia. She wanted to dance, not chat.

"I'll find her. You go on," she said, realizing that she had grown tired of waiting for Heath to share her enthusiasm for their relationship. He took her for granted. "Maybe for the last time," she muttered under her breath.

She flipped her hair with the tips of her fingers and smoothed down her dress as she reentered the ballroom.

Draped satin fastened with glittering medallions decorated the walls. Gowns rustled around her. Dancers already moved to the dance floor or near the punch tables. A few sat in the circle of chairs.

Teal felt drawn and repelled by the sensations that the stimulation around her generated, as if she could be trampled by them. *There are forces, dark and unknown, forces much stronger than I am,* she thought. *Because Heath and I don't understand each other, some foreign chemistry has killed the joy and invited adventure.*

Her favorite maxim "Change your attitude, change your life" tempted her to accept Heath as he was rather than let him go, but the temptation seemed weightless and detached like her exasperating hopes for their future together.

Perhaps he thinks reality will spoil a childhood fantasy. She had believed it would make it still better. *Would it? It would change the relationship.* Perhaps the dream belonged forever in their childhood where no risk could destroy it. With the thought, the smaller place where her feelings for him waited closed its door.

Heath's slender form moved gracefully between the tables in the ballroom now. The gold in his hair gleamed beneath spraying beams from overhead lights that glinted over the dancers. The fun, the color, and music and smiles swerved into Picasso shapes before her tearing eyes. She forced a smile. She waved to those who recognized her, most of them classmates she knew from the first grade.

A brutal nostalgia struck her. Lost. Her childhood was lost, never to be recovered. She fought back the tears. Her longing for it seemed like the longing for the child she was and for her own child of the future, the two of them walking side by side into an unknown. Heath walked away. Lost. He thought her saved; she thought him lost for she felt no connection to him now.

She swallowed the growing lump in her throat and concentrated on keeping her chin up as she moved through the spaces between tables. Her mood fell into the minor tones of Harlem Nocturne as she glued Heath's and Esther's behaviors together. She had sensed an eagerness in Esther for her to be gone and no longer her responsibility. Heath seemed to think of her as a stone in his path as well.

Her leaving home after graduation suited Esther while waiting on Heath's plan suited him. She realized she had better be making a plan of her own. *Job training? College? The mill, perhaps?*

Teal knew that Esther could not live easily in the same house any longer with youth. When she got home, where she had been, had she started her period? These issues were now Esther's obsessions. Her mother had become as much a stranger to her as Heath. Instead of concern for her well-being, Esther now corrected how she walked, sat, dressed, or stood.

Saddened, she wanted away from home and from this party. The music sounded too brassy, too loud. She felt out of rhythm with it. The rooms seemed stuffy and hot. She did need to find Sylvia, she thought, as Heath had suggested. She must tell her about Heath's plans for the evening.

She stumbled over somebody's foot when Heath's camera flashed, momentarily blinding her. Her eyes mirrored two shiny spots that turned all the people and chairs circling the dance floor into the appearance of black construction-paper silhouettes. Her pride smarted at the thought of waiting years, months, days, and even the next hour for *his* readiness, *his* security. Tonight had become an unexpected crisis for her.

Teal moved toward the music, her vision clearing. She looked about for Sylvia. She would find her and tell her that she now accepted Heath's choices. Spoken words did that for her; they fixed decisions in her heart like photos in an album. Again, Heath's camera flashed through the darkness, but the white light's glare was behind her now. It couldn't blind her.

She spotted Sylvia seated and smiling, enjoying the music. Teal sat down beside her.

"Where's Heath?" she began.

"He asks me here and deserts me. I can't stand it another minute. I swear, Sylvia, that this is the last time I'll ever go anywhere with him again."

Sylvia looked hard at her. "I don't believe that."

Teal bit her bottom lip until it hurt.

"I won't!"

"Talk to him, Teal. Ask him what's most important and why. You always want him to read your mind. Worse, you think you can read his."

"I did, and I can't again. I practically begged him to tell me where we stood."

"You can't blame him. You can't!" she repeated when Teal gave her a sharp look. "College means a good job, more money, a better life for you, Teal. For you! You know him well enough to know he wants your future with him to be just so."

"He knows that doesn't matter, that we could do it together."

"Could you? On base wage? You're not being realistic."

Teal glanced across the room to see someone staring back at her. She vaguely remembered the good-looking young man. "I don't know how we would do it. I only know we could if he wanted that too."

Sylvia's eyes followed hers. "He came with Ms. Sara Jane," she said. "That's all anybody knows. Do you know him?"

"He looks old for a high school prom."

"Well, Sara Jane's a teacher with a hot date."

He kept looking at her so directly that Teal felt compelled to look away. She knew him from somewhere. His face called up the years and stirred her in a strange but comforting way. When she looked back, he hadn't looked away, so she didn't either. Then she remembered. He had even worked for them for a few summers. She had seen his name on the payroll when she logged costs, but she hadn't seen him again because she worked at the elevator, and he had hired on at the mill.

"I'll bet he's twenty-five, at least," Sylvia was saying.

Teal smiled. He smiled back, and her heart began to pound. She felt like the only girl in the room, and he seemed the only boy, except he looked older. *Twenty-two or three probably,* she thought.

"He's looking at me," she said. "He's finally looking at me." She heard the bit of arrogance in her tone, but she no longer felt deserted. Heath's camera flashed far to the opposite end of the ballroom, and she no longer cared.

"A lot of boys look at you, Teal," Sylvia said. "You never cared a hoot before unless it was Heath."

"Oh," she began explaining with a little laugh. "I was at the elevator—" she stopped and started again. "I was in my yard a long time ago when he passed by carrying a gallon jug of milk. I wanted his attention and couldn't get it. He wouldn't look at me then. He wouldn't even say hello, so I threw a clod and broke the glass jug. I broke another one years before that at the elevator when he brought a jug of it from the store for his thirsty father."

"Teal! That's terrible!"

"Well, I did it," Teal said. "Twice. He remembers it too. That's exactly what he's thinking about this very minute. After that, he worked a few summers at the mill, farmed with his dad too."

"I wouldn't be so sure that's what he's thinking," Sylvia said suggestively.

"Sylvia!" she mimicked. "*That's* terrible!"

Sylvia laughed.

"Heath's behaving like a jerk," Teal grumbled. "He said he'd take a few shots and then we would dance." She began to pick nervously at the folds of her dress. She wanted to forget that anybody was staring at her. In fact, she'd begun to wish he'd look away. *Maybe he made fun of her. Maybe he'd decided that if she wanted to be noticed, he'd make her uncomfortably noticed.*

"If he doesn't stop that," she snapped, "I'm going to walk right over there and tell him to quit it."

At that moment, the band director walked to the mic and announced, "Girl's tag."

"If you get to dance tonight, I'd suggest you walk right over there and ask *him*."

"Heath won't like it."

"Ask Heath first. If he refuses you, he'll have no kick coming. If you don't ask him, I will," Sylvia urged. When Sylvia stood, Teal knew that she meant it. "There's Heath," she persisted.

Teal looked about and saw Heath adjusting a new flashbulb within hearing distance of her. She got up and walked nearer. "Heath," she called before she reached him. She lavished him with her prettiest smile. "Can you dance with me now? It's girl's tag."

Surprised, he lowered the camera and looked at her. "What is it, Teal?"

"Please stop now, Heath. Enjoy the party with me. Let's dance."

"I can't yet. I'm not finished."

"How long will it be?"

"Half an hour maybe. Maybe a little longer."

"But the party will be almost over then."

"No, it won't. Nobody's leaving until midnight or past."

"You said we were. You said we had to, that you had to have the car back by ten."

"I'm not finished, Teal. Fifteen minutes. In fifteen minutes, I'll stop, and we'll dance a dance or two."

She turned aside as the band began a blues number. She especially loved slow dancing to blues. The lazy trumpet sounds pleased her, and anticipation for the dance drove her mind toward Gavin Rush, someone they hadn't grown up with or known. *What did that matter now?*

"Ask *him!*" Sylvia repeated when Teal reached her. "Sara Jane's in the powder room, or should I say Ms. Hood?"

"She'll be back, and *she'll* be angry."

"Well, Ms. Sara Jane can't give you an F in home economics because you've pounced on her beau. The grades are in. Gavin Rush is his name," Sylvia continued. "I just asked. He graduated eight years ago and lives on a farm west of here. He has to be twenty-five or six, Teal."

"That's right! His grandmother has that little store between the mill and town."

"So?" And then Sylvia gave her the slightest push that sent her two steps onto the dance floor. Teal kept going. With every step, she knew that she broke the unwritten law of regard for the date who brought her. Rather than her resolve weakening as she advanced, it increased, so that by the time she stood before Gavin, she said boldly, "I'd like you to dance with me."

His eyes had held hers all the long walk. "May I say hello." He grinned. Those eyes looked the color of the sea and held hers as he reached for her hand.

A rough and calloused hand he offered her, work hardened and twice the size of her own, but it felt warm and covering to her as they moved silently toward an unclaimed space for dancing. Teal felt as if half her weight fell away. An unaccustomed fullness crowded her throat.

She wondered if Heath watched her, if Sara Jane had returned. Yet she felt compelled toward this moment, a time that changed nothing into something for them both because she'd dared to keep walking.

Everything conspired to magnetize and to fly together into this magnificent force that drove her glance only to Gavin and left everyone else in the past. She forgot everything but her awareness of him, his warmth, his breath, his motion, and his touch.

—

They moved closer together, and his head bent near her ear. "I can't dance," he murmured.

Teal moved her arm up to hold him close. She smiled and moved with him in no pattern that she could discern, just one they made up as they went along.

"It doesn't matter," she whispered back.

He stepped on her toes. They began to throb. It didn't matter.

But it mattered to her that she didn't have to learn the two-step before they dare try or to wait until he finished something else. She didn't want the song to end.

"I remember you," he said, his warm breath against her cheek.

"I remember you too." She drew back just enough to look up at him. When the music stopped, she felt his lips brush her cheek. His hand caught hers very tightly as he said, "I want to take you home."

"You can't," she said. Why did she stop herself now? Why, when she didn't want to stop herself? Teal stared at the floor and moved away from him, his hand reluctant to let hers go. Their fingers clung until Teal pulled free.

"I'll call you," he told her.

"Yes," she answered without looking at him again. When she glanced up toward where she'd left Sylvia, she saw Heath's angry glare. Sara Jane Hood's face flushed a bright pink when she whisked past Teal in an obvious huff toward the cloakroom.

Heath's picture snapping had abruptly stopped.

A red-faced and furious Ms. Hood tore past her again, her coat flying behind her. She looked nothing like the perfectly groomed home economics teacher who had always seemed like Miss Congeniality in her classroom.

Teal knew that Gavin would be leaving the party now.

"If she sponsored this party," Sylvia said, "she could get into trouble over leaving."

Teal supposed she would gossip about her to administration to get her sweet revenge and herself off the superintendent's hook. She lifted her chin and faced Heath.

"Are you finished with pictures?"

"Does it matter?"

Does it matter? her mind repeated.

"I'm sorry you're angry" seemed the most honest response that she could manage.

"Let's dance," he ordered. "That's what you wanted."

Teal moved beside him onto the dance floor. She no longer wanted them to touch until they must. What stopped the wanting of impossible things but other possible things? Until now, it hadn't occurred to her that all the most important events in her life turned on moments in time.

Stiffly, she turned to him.

"You spoiled the dance," he accused.

"You blame me?"

"Who else!" he snapped.

She loved him still and knew it. Maybe she always would. But she knew for a certainty that she no longer needed him more than she needed something real.

"You dream of the future and ignore today," she spoke softly. "Reality is where I live. I don't want to avoid challenge or struggle, and I can't be a front for another's self-serving behaviors. If you love me, Heath, you should say so now. If you want me, we should be engaged."

There, she thought. *I finally said more than Sylvia suggested.*

Roughly, he pulled her against him.

Teal turned her face away and refused to speak. Her arm and leg muscles quivered. From tautness? From nerves? She'd become almost rigid in his arms, resisting, closed.

"Teal?" he asked once, his voice less harsh than before. "Why now? We've belonged to each other for so long."

"Another question instead of a declaration. Oh, Heath, where have you been?" she pleaded. "Where are you now? You haven't expressed caring. You're just angry because someone gave me the attention you wouldn't."

He looked at her strangely.

—

"If I wait to hear you say you love and need me, how long would that be?" she continued.

"He isn't right for you, and you know it," he said icily. "You're trying to force things, to recreate the world in your image."

"You've no right!" she snapped. "I've needed *you*—to talk to, to be with, for friendship. Where have you been?" she repeated. She pulled herself free of him when he didn't respond. The music still played as she left him standing there alone while she went for her wrap.

When he drove her home, neither of them spoke. Before he left her at the door, he said, "You're spoiled, Teal. Someday, you'll have to grow up."

"It's all about me, right? I finally get it," she replied acidly.

She and Heath had an attraction and affection for one another that nothing would alter—not time, not Gavin. The memories swept over her, bearing residual anticipation of great joy. Then the reality of Gavin rushed to drive memory away. She had chosen. To do otherwise caused her the agony of longing, doubt, and loneliness. They had grown up differently, she thought.

Now she need never trust Heath again to belong to her. Now, neither she nor Heath would ever need to fear touching, loving. They were safe now—from one another. Time preserved childhood memories. She wondered if bodiless spiritual love could ever feel as real as actual intimacies to her. Were they equivalent? Was she truly just spoiled and insecure to need proofs?

To love God had no equivalent, did it? The thought swept in and left like a hard-to-hear whisper before her awareness could answer.

Sylvia wasted no time telephoning her later.

"First you want Gavin to notice you, probably because Heath was busy then with paper routes and a neurotic mother who manipulated his life. Then you wanted Heath to notice you *or else*, escalating your demands for attention instead of talking to him sooner. Are you going to break his heart because he doesn't know his own mind yet, let alone yours?

"*Now* Gavin has *finally* noticed you, something you can flaunt in front of Heath, the poor jerk. Heath has no idea what's going on. He needs more time. A heart isn't a jug of milk, dear. He still hasn't a clue about what you want or wanted because of his own agenda. I'm thinking you could be real sorry someday."

"Who gave me that shove? Besides, I've not only told him, I've practically begged. You're wrong this time, Sylvia. I said it all, I asked it all. I don't know him now. He's more of a stranger than Gavin."

"Bubble, bubble, toil and trouble."

Then the receiver clicked in Teal's ear. She knew Sylvia as a true friend for she recognized the effort that only a friend would risk. She would tell her that when they talked again. Thank her. She would explain that her urge for life disallowed imposed recesses and rejection. She chose to move on and pay any price.

Why should Heath expect that his choices had no price? she wondered. *No one escapes costs.*

Whatever one's choices, a price must be paid in time, money, grief, perhaps even death. Time *was* life, and Teal had no intention of wasting it. Still, it seemed to her that both Heath and Gavin had similar traits that they revealed in different ways: they had to be *boss*. She thought Gavin probably needed to think of things first, while Heath needed to do all the thinking. This thought felt uncomfortable to her, so she dismissed it as unimportant. After all, one dance wasn't a proposal of marriage.

CHAPTER XIV

A Change of Heart

Teal graduated that fall. Gavin saw her every Friday night that following summer. The first week of September, he gave her a diamond engagement ring.

"You keep the wedding ring for me. I'm afraid that I'll lose it," he said. The second diamond flashed blue lights from the tiny wine-velvet box from Zales in Oklahoma City.

"Ask your mother to keep it for us, please, Gavin. It doesn't seem that I should have it yet."

Reluctantly, he drew it back, snapped the lid closed, and put it in his pocket.

They sat on her front porch. She stared down a red-earth path that led to everything familiar and dear to her that she would be leaving for her freshman semester at college. Gavin looked toward the creek at the north end of the road. Without looking, Teal already knew that cold, distant expression, that particular angle of his head.

At such odd moments he left her; his attentive and affectionate presence withdrew. She tried to reach him with touch or conversation earlier in their relationship. She repeated questions, persisted in trying to connect, much as she had as a girl when he ignored her. Though she still wanted to call him back to her, she no longer persisted, for the door to him usually opened again after a few minutes. He could have his way; she had grown accustomed to it over the past weeks.

When his attentiveness returned from these escapes from the world, his mood became quite jovial and full of fun.

She propped her chin up on her knees and looked long at a grasshopper, brown green on a brown-green leaf. She turned over a loose brick from its spot around Esther's chrysanthemums that were trying to bud. Six gray sow bugs immediately curled into tiny spheres. Teal picked up two of them and rolled them about in her palm.

Until he gave her the ring, she had felt happy when they were together. Odd things had begun to bother her since then that she'd never thought about. "I'm not—well, I'm not very big—" She stopped. "Up here," she'd said. There was no doubt in Teal's mind that the opposite sex preferred large firm breasts and that her own attractiveness was considerably altered by their absence.

"I'm not . . . voluptuous," she managed.

"I know."

"Doesn't it matter?" She dared look askance at him, thinking she'd see disappointment there. A faint smile played about his lips and eyes. His rugged good looks became classic Roman when a tenderness softened his expressions. She saw that tenderness when he responded.

"You're pretty. You're all-over pretty—what I've seen of you."

Teal flushed again at the memory. She glanced at him and let the tiny gray insects roll off her palm like doubts. She felt ignorant and unsophisticated—a child too eager to turn into the woman she supposed that she should be for him. What on earth prevented her? Thoughts of her wedding night bothered her much more than thoughts of her wedding day. What was the right thing to wear, to say, to do? How should she perform to please him, to make him glad he'd married her instead of . . . of Sara Jane, older, more sophisticated, and a college graduate.

"I wish I'd left with you as you asked the night of the dance. Oh, I wish I had!" she cried. "We felt so . . . so *one*."

Gavin looked a little startled, as if she had wakened him from his reverie. He reached and took her hand. "Let's make a picnic, take our swimming suits with us, and find us a place a few miles away to spend the afternoon."

He seemed close to her again. Until that moment, she had blamed herself—not his moods for the absences of that first feeling of wonder they'd known together. She leaned her shoulder against his, and he bent his head to kiss her. "Home again," she murmured happily. A quizzical glance crossed his face as she faced him and reached her arms about his neck, open for his kiss.

She clung to him afterward; she felt wanted by someone at last.

"I'm not rushing you into anything, Teal. Understand that. First times are important. They affect all the other times," he said softly when they drew apart again.

Teal felt at a loss for words; all she knew was that she would not be available for sexual intimacy until after her college commitment. How she wanted to say, "Rush me! Please rush me, Gavin," but she didn't. College tuition had been paid; she had enrolled. What she couldn't say and couldn't do she must reveal—probably today. *But not this minute,* she cautioned herself. This minute she felt desired and liked it.

Nothing—nothing—could prevent her from her destiny. Destiny seemed a terrible and wonderful unknown that happened as it could or happened as one planned. She had thought she and Heath would go college together. Gavin already farmed with Harlin. She suspected he wanted to marry soon.

"Could we go *now*, Gavin?" she asked. Her breaths were suddenly labored as if she were running some long distance. She stood before him, her recurrent dreams of an inability to walk across a bridge crashing through her consciousness as if that bridge led to her very life, to her responsibility to it as if life itself were God. She wasn't safe from the rapids below. No guardian angel hovered overhead.

Did the bridge lead to an art major at the university, or to marriage with Gavin? She doubted that she could have both immediately. *Later. She would get the art major later.*

"Now?" Gavin repeated.

"We can go to a movie if—" she hesitated.

"No. Grab your swimsuit. We'll pick up the food. Mom will keep the ring for us until our wedding. Is a September wedding okay?"

Teal jumped to her feet, her plans for school assuming a second place to the joy she felt at the thought of a September wedding to Gavin. Unafraid at last, she turned back to the door to tell Esther that she'd be leaving and to grab her suit and a towel. *He'd said that they'd be married in September,* she thought. *Had he forgotten she left for school two weeks from today? Did he want both for her? Couldn't she go to school any old time?*

"I heard," Esther said sharply. She stood in the door where she'd been listening

Abruptly, Teal stopped. Her mother's tone made it clear she either disliked Gavin or disapproved of her potential change of college plans. Feeling threatened, Teal slipped past her to snatch her suit from the back porch hook where she'd left it to dry last week. She darted off the porch to join Gavin, who waited in the car. The engine rumbled as expectantly as Teal's pounding heart. No one—not Sara Jane and not Esther—would keep her from having Gavin. She had decided it.

Twenty minutes later they drove up the long lane to Gavin's home. Blooming vetch flanked the lane with purple haze. Rena Lily hugged her warmly. She looked long at the wedding ring as if she held their future in her own hands. "I'll be proud to keep it for you. I'm pleased you trust me with it." Her faded eyes sparkled at Teal whose own eyes misted a bit.

How she wished her mother had been this kind to Gavin.

White curtains billowed at the windows, and a ginger smell drifted from the kitchen. The furnishings were simple country. "Harlin believes that land is all that pays its own way," she told Teal. "So that's where the increase goes—for now, anyway. We'll have this house paid for soon. Barns and land are clear, of course," she said with a wry smile. "Harlin built it all himself. Three bedrooms."

Teal heard the pride and love in her tone.

"It's a wonderful house. I think it's the most peaceful house I've ever been in." Teal spoke the truth. For the space, the light, the openness Harlin had achieved brought the outdoors inside in subtle ways. A split-level plan, it put the treetops as near as the fireplace. But there were no bright cushions, no pictures on the walls. Where were the vases of flowers, the green plants?

Teal saw the lazy cattle grazing beyond the south window, milk cattle that provided the family's sustenance with hard chores, morning and night. Beyond them, stock cattle gorged on still-green pasture for first frost hadn't arrived. The billowing curtains, the land and cattle and the warmth of home told Teal how rich they were; the austerity and lack of color told her how poor. Gavin reached his arm about Teal just then and pulled her against his waist.

Teal looked up at him, so rich and poor and smiling. She knew she should tell him the difference between her and Rena Lily. She must create beauty in any home they made. Home would be her priority as it had been her mother's. Esther and Ray established a home, then bought into the grainery. People of the land, like Gavin, bought land and raised barns before spending much on a home.

Not yet, she cautioned herself. Harlin still accumulated land; later the extras would be added. Farm income opposed by farm investments didn't allow for them yet, not with equipment costs so high.

"No need to get home to the milking tonight, Gavin," Rena Lily told him. "Celebrate your engagement. I'll explain to your father."

They left very soon then. Gavin drove to Sawyer's Lake about forty miles south of town. The water was rain soft and warm. Her skin soon felt as smooth and slick as satin. Teal dared the nearness she'd craved when he reached for her, their legs sliding against the other's. She locked her arms about his neck and moved nearer. The water wrapped them like one continuous skin, but Teal's desire for him did not quicken until he kissed her there, his desire immediate against her thigh for her to know, to think about, to anticipate. He embraced her legs with his own, the soft brown water like a surround of satin. When he released her she felt heady, breathless, as if her desire and will were one.

The longing that Heath had stirred in her from the time they'd been children was a desire that she commanded with her reason. *Heath was inattentive and chronically absent,* she reminded herself. Heath did not want to marry her. A shaky sigh left her, and she felt a little faint. Gavin still held her arm firmly in his great hand. "We're not going to make love today, Teal. We're going to swim for a while, lie together on the sand, then go back to town for supper before I take you home."

"All right," she agreed. For now, maybe for only a little while, Gavin could tell her what she wanted. This new kind of touching puzzled her. She felt uncertain for the first time about the nature of physical love. She had thought it a thing she could transfer from Heath to Gavin. Instead, love stretched and changed for her depending on its object.

Her response to Gavin felt urgent yet safe, a bridge she *could* cross as if it led home. Her response to Heath had seemed urgent also but unsettling—a focused obsession in which to lose herself as if she could drown there in her joy. No destiny had seemed greater; no goal or career plan outshone it. Leaving the security of home for the security that Gavin offered bypassed her fear of rapids and the great challenges of a bridge to some unknown.

She hadn't known until today that love for someone could alter reason and feeling as if love forged a life of its own. Nor did she understand the growing physical need that was more like the need for water when she thirsted or food when she hungered or home; home when she felt lonely. Her need for Gavin refused to localize in head or heart or pelvis. Her need for him seemed the center fire she moved toward for life itself. She might always seek to become one with Gavin—a thing that could keep their anticipation alive for a very long time and make each time they came together a first time.

———

She thought of Heath and the mystery that caused her to feel they would always be one whether they ever shared their bodies. She had no awareness of that until she gave up her hope for them. If that's what he felt too but couldn't say, the moment for mutual understanding had passed them by. Anguished at the thought, she wondered how she could go on and never know.

"You romanticize everything too much, Teal," Sylvia told her when Teal shared her most current internal conflict. "Heath will be a big shot someday with a lot of money, clothes, and cars because that's what he wants. Believe me, he's *not* brokenhearted over love. When you've analyzed this to death the way you can, you'll be over him. He'd be brokenhearted if his plans got changed for him—not if he got jilted."

Teal shrugged off Sylvia's commonsense response. She secretly enjoyed agonizing over lost love. What she couldn't shrug off so easily was Rena Lily's recent remark before their wedding that Sara Jane expected a baby in about six months. She easily buried the remote notion that Gavin may have fathered the child. *Change my mind; change my life.*

"Her mother's hoping to see an engagement ring on *her* finger soon," Rena Lily added. "That's a poor way to start a marriage, though. A baby is expensive business for newlyweds."

Teal's silence betrayed nothing. She kept her suspicions to herself. Gavin belonged to her now. He didn't belong to Uncle Sam or to Sara Jane. He'd done his time for them both.

*   *   *

In 1955, Central Oklahoma lay dry again. The scraggly wheat had been dusted in; the lack of funds had totally delayed college for Teal. The agricultural economy made yielding to Gavin's preferences easier, though she knew she would attend some way, someday.

"There's a recession to make it worse. I hate it, Teal, hate it for both your sakes just getting started the way you are." Rena Lily sat peeling potatoes for their supper at the kitchen table in Teal's farm home.

It was Friday. Each Friday, Teal and Rena Lily took their fresh eggs and cream to the market at the county seat. The money they got for them bought groceries for the week and paid for using the Maytag washers at the Laundromat there.

The cabin on the Indian lease that Rena and Harlin vacated when they moved into their own home became Teal and Gavin's home, rent free but with partial indoor plumbing. The kitchen had water, but there was no indoor bathroom or washer-dryer hookups yet.

If there were bills to pay, Teal also paid those on Friday, then filled the gas tank of the little blue Chevrolet sedan with what money remained. It took all day to get things to town, purchase groceries and supplies, and to do the laundry. But there was neither more time nor more money to run the forty-mile round-trip more than one day a week. Rena went along to help her for Gavin worked at building more county roads across the south river besides farming with Harlin and his own leased quarter of land a few miles from home.

Although rural electricity and phone companies were established now, rural water hadn't been developed. For ordinary use, such as bathing and dishwashing, she and Gavin collected rainwater off the roof into a cistern, then bucketed it to the house. For drinking and cooking, they bought huge jugs of Ozarka water. The well water piped into the house sufficed for all other purposes where very hard water could be used, such as for cleaning. Teal hated only one inconvenience—the party line. It seemed that she either waited hours for her turn to make a call, or someone listened to the calls she made.

Home now, she stirred chocolate pudding at the stove. Yesterday, she'd made fresh butter, cottage cheese, and bread. Ribs from one of the beeves they'd raised themselves sputtered in the oven.

"We're doing all right. You're not to worry," Teal assured her. "Harlin and Gavin will be in from the field soon, and we'll have our Friday night supper together as always. It's been a good day."

"You do your part," Rena said. "Time will come when Harlin and Gavin will partner to buy more land. The increase will help."

"More to lose in poor years like this one," Teal said. She dropped a lump of butter into the thickened chocolate. She felt that she wasn't doing enough. It pleased her to do the new things she'd learned—to manage with less gasoline and to raise their food herself: to can it, dry it, or freeze it. Almost everything she set on their table, she'd raised herself last year.

It pleased Gavin too, but they borrowed money anyway. Four thousand dollars to invest in cows that were worth no more than twenty dollars a week to them in cream and cheese and for a crop that they lost.

Crop failure! Dreaded words, and theirs this first year as cheatgrass grew wild in the stunted wheat field. Half of her spring planting of vegetables had burned in summer's sun. Dry days didn't encourage a full garden or a robust wheat crop.

Teal poured the pudding into small bowls before setting it in the refrigerator. She arranged the table while Rena Lily put the potatoes on to boil.

"I wish you'd just sit down," she told Teal. "You never sit down."

"I don't like to sit."

"I know you don't!" the older woman said as if half irritated. She slid a lid onto the potatoes and began to forage in the cabinet drawer for silverware. She placed them beside the plates that Teal set. "Now, change them to suit yourself," she snapped.

Silently, Teal did. She felt almost compulsive about forks on the left and knives and spoons on the right. If that was the appropriate way to do it; she wanted to do it like that. In a low voice that took Teal by surprise, Rena Lily said, "And what does Gavin think about the baby coming?" Teal was placing the last spoon just so.

"Aren't you smart! How did you know?"

"The blush of your cheeks, the fullness of your breasts."

"He's been preoccupied, or he'd have noticed too much time going by without a period." Teal avoided telling her that she dreaded Gavin knowing about another expense he could not afford after a failed crop on credit.

"He doesn't know?"

"He'll know soon enough. I wanted him to be happy about it. I wanted—"

"You wanted a miracle to happen and a new crop to fall from the blue. It won't, girl! It won't! Life moves on, and we have to let go of might-have-beens. I know Gavin. He's likely to think it too soon for him. This isn't a might-have-been. You've a baby on the way now. How are you going to stay in this business? Why, Harlin is still struggling in spite of farming a section of his own land and the leased Indian land besides."

"You've saved money. Gavin's told me."

"For emergencies on our own farm. There's always equipment needs, fuel, a sick animal. I'm tired. I'm plumb wore out. It's been a good life. I'm not saying it hasn't. But both of you deserve better."

"Better or easier? I like this life, Rena. Gavin hasn't an education. I haven't either. This is what we want. We decided it. We'll stay with secondhand equipment. I'll budget. It's a *good* way to live. Besides, he has a county job that he likes. You know he loves to operate that road equipment."

Teal walked to the stove and checked the potatoes with a fork. They felt a little coarse still. She looked at the clock. It was almost six. Harlin and Gavin were due in any minute. They'd been tearing up some of the wheat, preparing the land for next year's crop for there wasn't even enough of it in some fields to gather. He would not be cheerful, she felt certain of that. They would be lucky to cover the cost of sowing on their own leased land.

She poured a little of the water off and fastened the lid a bit closer to the potatoes so they would be tender when mashed with butter and cream.

"Fuel is almost forty cents a gallon. How will you put in the new crop?"

"I don't know. But we will. I'll get a job. I've been thinking I would before today."

"You can't. It isn't done. You're needed here. Farm women are the glue that holds farm life together. They care for children, cook, sew, can, and take care of their man."

Teal turned slowly and looked at her.

"I will," she said. Her eyes locked with her mother-in-law's.

Rena Lily didn't look away. Without saying more, without blinking an eyelash she said, "You enjoy that baby. Whatever else is laid on you now, you nurse it and hold it and enjoy it every day, because now's your time for it, and there won't be any other. Do you hear?"

"I hear." Teal walked over to her. She touched her forehead with her lips. Rena Lily's forehead was cool and moist. "I love you, Rena Lily," she said. "But farms are changing. They cost more. I've seen the figures. The need for volume because of inflation caused it. More women will be getting jobs, you'll see."

"There's one thing about you," Rena Lily said. "You try."

It was what she always said. Over and over, she said, "You try."

The canning, sewing, and cooking from scratch were new to Teal, a challenge every day, a challenge to learn something new, to bend and stretch her body and her mind. She was happy in spite of the crushing disappointment of a sparse first crop. She had learned to plant and tend her own garden, to make cheese and butter, to harvest their cotton and wheat.

She had sewn the new bright cottage curtains; she had woven the hook rugs in the kitchen and bedrooms from fabric remnants. She had even painted the pictures on their walls. Yet she could hardly contain her joy over their child that meant far more to her than her creation of this beauty and provision. Now that his mother knew it, Teal knew she must tell Gavin. She'd not thought it best so soon.

*   *   *

Either cool morning air from the south or the raucous crowing of her game rooster wakened Teal the next morning. Shivering, she rose to close the window. She pushed back the white sheers. The motion seemed to inspire the sportive rooster. He stomped and scratched and "er-er-erred" some more for his audience of one. Gavin still slept, undisturbed.

Teal stretched and looked across the creek to the walnut tree where a squirrel family usually frolicked in the mornings. Sure enough, they were up and about before sunrise. Without dressing, she headed for the kitchen in her thin muslin gown, her bare feet flinching from the cool floor. She put on coffee and started the bacon before slipping into her robe and house shoes.

She set a kettle of cistern water for her bath on the stove to boil then checked the curdled skim milk from last night's cream separation. She put it on a low back flame so the curds could set. She began to hum contentedly. She needed to draw cool cistern water to mix with the hot for her tub. The hard well water felt like salt water on her skin, so she rarely used it to bathe and never drank it.

It was Esther who'd insisted on their buying bottled drinking water. "That *gyppy* water will cause your food to go right through you," she warned. Teal didn't mind. She knew Esther and Rena Lily both had seen times when bad fevers like malaria, typhoid, and dysentery killed people here. Besides, she would want the Ozarka water for their baby.

When things were sizzling and bubbling on the stove, she grabbed the water bucket. Her thin gown whipped about her ankles. The dewy dampness chilled her bare feet. These late August nights seemed unseasonably cool while the days scorched the landscape by noon. She draped the bucket handle over the pump's nozzle and began to work the handle up and down until the rainwater gushed into the bright galvanized bucket. To the east, the burnt-orange sun peeked over the sparse but green rows of cotton. They had only a twenty-acre cotton patch; they needed more, especially now. *Unless no rains came and the cotton crop failed too,* she thought.

She lifted the full bucket, held it out from her gown, which she caught tightly against her side and legs. Water sloshed over the sides. *I'll never walk with the smoothness of a lady like Mama wanted,* she regretted

Teal wasn't a lady. Ladies didn't wear their hair loose and their nails blunted. When anyone mistook her for one, she felt threatened by what she thought of as a protected life rather than an "experienced" one. Teal believed for a certainty that a lady did not sway her hips when she walked, sweat, cuss, like tobacco smoke, break her nails gardening, or mow her own lawn. Neither did she relish sex, independence, or nakedness—all of which Teal enjoyed. That she liked fashion, benevolence, conversation, and the dining graces kept her from becoming a social reject. She loved going to parties and having them, for she enjoyed people, food, and laughter.

She emptied the hot kettle of water into the tin tub on the porch. Harlin and Gavin were in the midst of adding the bathroom, though water softening would be required for the gypy well water. Extra funds were slow now to finish it. She turned the bacon before drawing the two cool buckets of soft water from the cistern for the tub. She drew another for washing the dishes.

I'll scramble eggs and toast after my bath, she thought, *so breakfast will be hot for Gavin.* She turned the burners off. After lifting and pouring the dippers of water over her, she dried and dressed in jeans and a red shirt, happily anticipating her once-a-month Saturday library visit.

When she called Gavin for breakfast, he didn't respond. She walked to the bedroom door. "Scrambled eggs, toast, and coffee are ready when you are," she said.

He sat on the edge of the bed, his feet flat on the floor. He rubbed his fingers through his hair and yawned expansively. When he said nothing, she turned back to fill her own plate.

His irregular silences no longer made him a romantic challenge to her. Rather, she felt closed away, sometimes for days, often longer since the crop failure. After that loss, he hardly spoke to her at all.

He seemed a stranger she might never really know. Now he scowled at his breakfast from across the table.

"I'm not super gallant or anything like that, Gavin," she said, "but we took this on, and it's just something for us to go on with. I believe it's worthwhile. This county could feed the world its bread most years."

"You think I don't know that?" he snapped, slapping a pile of scrambled eggs on his plate. "I'm not about to quit like my grandfather did. Softhearted and weak, his quitting the homestead made things tougher for Dad."

She shrank from his tone and finished her breakfast without more words. What she knew of his granddad Upton she'd heard from his grandmother Letti. He may have given up the land to save his family, but he was a grand success as a man and as a pharmacist. She stood to clear the table and wash the dishes.

"Your grandma Letti said that funds from your granddad Upton's business and investments bought her the store and helped Harlin buy his first farm."

Gavin sat pulling on his boots. "Their business is none of yours. She had no call to talk to you about it," he grumbled.

"I suppose she trusts me," Teal said.

When he said nothing more, uneasiness gripped her. He had spoken to her as if she were outside his family. "Eggs were twenty-two cents a dozen at town yesterday. Their price seems to be holding." *That bit of news might please him,* she thought.

"Let it go, Teal," he said, rising. "A man must be driven and hard shelled to survive this life. I intend to be up to it." He pulled on a bill cap and left for the barn and chores. She thought the remark the closest to an apology for his rudeness to her that he had made.

She grabbed a pitcher for some of the warm fresh milk and followed him outside. She looked over the sunlit plowed earth she'd loved so from the time they'd moved to the country. Even as a child, she'd looked forward to the wheat harvests when the great trucks came to the elevator. They stored it, milled it, baked it, and shipped it. It seemed in her blood; she felt the power of the beautiful tons of golden grain that fell victim to the control of those who owned most of it. Already it seemed more of a funds market than a supply-and-demand market. Teal expected *only* a fund market someday for those who grew no wheat, the farmer be hanged! It seemed to her that the futures fired a gambling game for those who could afford the risk while it destroyed the family farm that required a fair price.

At this moment, she pitied it, pitied it for not producing in spite of no rain. She hated their lack of control over rain and hail and bugs and the power brokers. She knew that abundance meant lower prices more often than more money at a stable price that would pay bills and provide a profit. For supply and demand easily became only a political tool to control the price for the consumer's benefit, to withhold food from a hostile country, or to reduce a surplus in the face of a hungry third world when the potential for crop failures the world over always threatened the food supply.

She'd not planned the baby. She'd used birth control, but *she* was producing. He wouldn't be pleased about that; she felt more certain of it with each passing hour.

"Oh!" she sighed heavily. *When he finished tearing up the last of it today,* she thought. Maybe then she would tell him. *The torment would surely be over for him in a few short weeks when the new green shoots sprouted a new crop of winter wheat.*

Teal had never considered the variable market price of eggs, of cream, or of wheat before. She only knew price was necessary. Now she knew that price should be high enough to see country people through such years as this. Yet even drought and low prices seemed nothing compared to filling her lungs with this air, her eyes with this beauty, her body with this child.

Gavin's tall strong figure disappeared inside the barn. She heard him call "Yaoo! Yaoo!" to the cows that lowed and bawled for the feed that waited for them in the troughs back of each stanchion. Each lumbered inside before her. Although Harlin still farmed the land around the Indian lease, he allowed them the cotton, the corral, and a patch of hay for their cows.

She dallied outside in the vegetable garden for a while, searching for late tomatoes or pumpkin and finding none. Unaccustomed dread seeped into her awareness to dampen her joy. Eagerness to be with him fled, even as she moved nearer.

"How much is the sunshine worth to you in dollars and cents?" she asked him the moment she entered the barn. Her question startled even her. Until now she had not thought this thought—that Gavin, like Heath, thought of material cost first, but in a different way. Heath had wanted more to spend; Gavin feared spending as if profit and loss were his blood.

He whirled around and gave her an odd look.

"When it rains, Gavin, what price are you putting on the inches, or will you count its value by the drop?"

"You crazy?"

"Maybe. I'm pregnant." She hadn't planned to say it this way. Hadn't she planned to wait until he could hope for a new crop? *It will be weeks before the plains green. I will be showing by then. Waiting had been a dream.*

His face seemed to turn to stone. A cow pushed past him as he stared stonily at her. She imagined him calculating the cost of the child—not the blessing.

He set down the milk buckets. Teal knew the milk should be separated while warm. Perhaps it would stay warm. In any case, she acted unconcerned and set the pitcher down to pour it fresh from one of the buckets.

"Are you sure?"

She nodded.

He poured the pitcher full for her, then ordered, "Get out of here. Now."

Quietly, she returned to the house. Numbly, she set the pitcher in the window to cool before refrigerating it. She poured a cool bath though she'd bathed earlier. If she had a cool bath, she would feel fine, she thought. Water always soothed her. Tears streamed unbidden as she peeled off her clothes and stepped in. *He'll be a long time,* she thought, *without my help.*

The dippers of cool water streamed over her swelling body. She stretched for the towel on the rail hook nearby when Gavin pushed the back screen open. He jerked it down then wrapped her in it. She let him as if already giving him the control over her he seemed to need. He lifted her, feet dripping from the tub, and carried her to their bed.

"The cows, the milking," she ventured.

Teal didn't take her eyes off him. It seemed that the force of his body pressed out of the clothes that fell off him even as he covered her.

Dampness and the scents of soap and sweat mingled even as he filled her, their motion, the pulse of anger and need, the hammering against the earth for injustice and returning to it this passion for life.

Tears slid from the corners of Teal's eyes. She met his every thrust. Their sex was never for its own sake or only for him. They shared that mutual burst of pleasure, rarely given up with any grace and certainly not for the other's sake. Physical union supplied the closeness that their lack of communication couldn't. Teal felt that Gavin relied on it to say what he could not.

"I didn't hurt you?" he asked, an unmistakable tenderness in his voice.

"No," she whispered breathily. "You're always a considerate lover, Gavin."

"I'm glad about the baby."

"I know you are," she said. He wiped the tears from the sides of her face with his rough fingers.

"Feelings spill over," she said. "More than I can hold. I'm not sad."

"Are you sure?"

That question again. It had seemed an insult before. Now she felt it the result of his own self-doubt in the face of this drought that could last for years or end tomorrow. "It's a reasonable question," he said when she hesitated.

"I apologize for leaving you to chore alone this morning." She refused to feel sorry for herself and turned her thoughts to him.

"It's done. Besides, you'll need more rest now," he said softly.

Teal felt she needed to fill the vacuum his inattentiveness and his lack of optimism created, not rest. She wanted to more ably endure it with greater patience and understanding than she had. She had a child to think of—not just herself.

She had wanted him to be glad about the child despite earthquake or whirlwind or devastating fire. Expectations again threatened to undo her. Yet he knew; he knew. He responded with a behavior instead of with words. She shook her head as if to clear it of an unacceptable thought. *Down with expectations,* she thought. *I'm not climbing on that wagon again.*

That night she left the choring early to prepare for bed. She deliberately waited until Gavin was just a dozen feet away from her bath to stand, wet and shining. She stepped out and wrapped the white terry robe about her. She wanted her image in his mind like an invitation to repeat the morning's lovemaking.

"You're going to shrivel like a prune, Teal. In case you haven't noticed, I see you these days. No need for tricks or broken milk jugs. This morning wasn't just a hello. I'm more than plain foolish over you."

Her pride smarted, but she slept nude to assure him she held no grudge and welcomed his lovemaking. Actions, not words, she realized, were Gavin's language. Perhaps his silences said he wanted her to leave him alone, a need she would try to respect.

"His silences may be like his earlier aloofness, an invitation for you to persist, a game he plays to get attention," Sylvia said when Teal shared her concerns.

"I don't like games," Teal said. "I want him to tell me how he feels about our having a baby."

"Change your mind; change your life," Sylvia mimicked. "What if he's too insecure to play it straight? What if he wants all of your attention? He got all of Rena Lily's as an only child."

"What if?" Teal muttered. The question hung there, unanswerable.

Chapter XV

Working Girl Again

When Teal saw Jonsi's car pull in, her spirits lifted. By 1957, Jonsi forged ahead with a drive to alert landowners to dangers confronting their future. His concern for the environment both complemented and exceeded his focus on improving wheat varieties.

He obsessed over the degradation of nature to anyone who would listen to him. Teal thought that the recent contamination of the cranberry crop had set him off. She opened the door and greeted him with a hug. Within five minutes of that greeting, he made her his audience.

"Our vegetation cover is being destroyed by exfoliates and concrete. There's a decline in the world fishing catch. Oil and gas reserves face depletion, as do metals. There's overcrowding of national parks and beaches—"

"All right, all right!" Teal interrupted. "I get your message. Food and energy for a growing population *is* important. I'm concerned about pesticide and fertilizer poisoning myself because these chemicals are born by air and water."

"Licensing and limits help with wildlife preservation, but I've serious concerns there too," he agreed. He seemed depressed over the emerging problems as if the solutions weren't keeping up with them.

"What's causing all of it, Jonsi?"

"The main cause is overpopulation and too few laws to protect the environment from greedy chemical and energy corporations who spend on themselves rather than safety. There's room for some new career job descriptions, federal and state if you ask me."

"Problem is that no one asks us," Teal lamented.

"Reducing rapid urbanization would help. I intend to promote a return to the country wherever I can. People need it, and the rural economy needs it."

"Jobs. The cities have jobs, Jonsi."

"That's what highways are for, sis."

"You and Rachel Carson," Teal laughed. "Soldiers of environmental quality if not for fortune. Get your ideas before the public, find a way. Schedule some speaking engagements with local clubs, notify the newspaper that you have a cause that may interest their subscribers."

Jonsi regarded her thoughtfully. "I'll do it. I'll even keep a log of the speeches and publish a pamphlet. The university wants us to publish anyway. Thanks, sis."

"You're very welcome. Just because we've learned some lessons since the '30s doesn't mean we haven't a lot more to learn."

Then with a warm hug and peck on her cheek, he was gone. With him went her brief enjoyment, for the melancholy that plagued her before his arrival returned.

Early this Sunday morning, she saw Gavin off to pheasant hunt in the maize fields of Kansas. She expected him home late that night or early Monday.

"Spoiled," she heard those who knew her best echo from the past.

Where Heath's illusiveness had caused her to turn aside, Gavin's challenged her. Her trusting and open response to him became conspiratorial. He aroused a need in her to pry open his mind for that exchange of inner thoughts and beliefs. Wouldn't shared minds complete their physical love? Her marriage to him felt like the game of flower-petal pulling—loves me, loves me not—from childhood.

His hostilities and his silences that alternated with good humor and intimacy created this yo-yo effect.

She smiled and embraced him when he returned about two in the morning, but fresh tears started when she recalled Saturday.

"Stop that," he said lightly, tying her robe about her. He leaned and kissed her very softly on the lips, then turned away. "I must notice you, talk to you, agree with you—you're incurable. I've cleaned three birds and put them in the freezer in the barn. Had good luck with that game anyway."

"Love isn't a game, Gavin. It is or it isn't."

"Privacy has nothing to do with love. There's a private side to me you want to break through. I'll never let you, and you'll never change me. I'm going to finish tearing out this crop. I'll be in about midnight, so I'm going to grab a few hours of sleep now." Obviously, the conversation was over.

Teal rose early to pack him sandwiches and extra water. "I'll chore and wait up," she said. "We'll have warm pie and ice cream." When she separated the milk, she gave the whey to any roaming critters for she had enough cheese, then she stored the fresh cream. She decided to seek work at the mill again today.

With no wheat to sell, her income would help cover their loss and the work would distract her from her unhealthy obsession to know Gavin. It only annoyed him. He had no curiosity about her opinions or beliefs that she had noticed.

"Better to leave him alone than start quarrels," she told Esther over the phone that afternoon. "You and Dad always talked so much. I heard the hum of your voices into the early morning hours time after time, so I assumed all couples were like that."

"Have you told Gavin that you're going back to work?"

"I'll tell him about it if they hire me."

The mill and elevator belonged mostly to Ray Swain and Esther now, 55 percent of it. So after her library visit, she drove there.

Recently, her father had started smoking cigars—chewing cigars was more accurate. He never lit one. They slowly grew shorter and shorter until he discarded the revolting stub. He twisted the thing

—
222

in his mouth without answering Teal. At last he said, "Is this all you came into town for?"

"No. I got art books at the library. The history of painting and architecture, a how-to-do almost anything."

Bills of Lading lay in a thick yellow stack on his desk, the record of poundage and freight rates required to haul out his flour and his wheat. Teal knew that freighting costs had risen to about thirty-six cents a bushel. He'd talked before about trucking his own products or delegating to a trucking company. No one who shipped wheat really wanted to see the rail go, though delivery took longer when you loaded onto hoppers then again onto trucks when nearer the destination. They believed the same thing could go wrong with trucking—costs could increase or strikes could block transit. Rail could again be more economical, slow or not. A ship could haul 750,000 bushel, but you had to get the wheat there first, either by rail or truck or both.

It had seemed a good idea a few years back to go entirely to competitive trucking. A cheaper choice then, but not now when the mill needed more hopper cars for excess product.

"Got anything that tells about sculpting? I always had a notion I'd like to do that, chisel something beautiful from a piece of marble or wood."

He gave the cigar a hard twist and clamped his teeth on it as if angry. Teal stared at her father, seeing something in him for the first time. He'd wanted that but never claimed it. With her mom and the four of them to provide for, there hadn't been the extra time or money for it.

"There's a book on it too." She turned as if to get it for him, but he stopped her short.

"No. It's too late. There was never the time or the money. It wasn't meant to be—not for me. Maybe for you, Teal. Odd you should want anything like it too."

It didn't seem odd to Teal. It seemed a reasonable thing since he'd fathered her, but she didn't say so. What seemed odd was the fact that they had never talked about it before.

—

"It's never too late, Dad. Wouldn't you be this age anyway if you had become an artist?" When he only looked at her, she was persuaded to get on with her purpose there.

"Well? What about the job?"

"Gavin's crops that bad?"

"Worse. He tore the last of it up, all but the cotton."

"Took a loss the first year," Ray sympathized. He shook his head slowly from side to side. "Does he know you're here?"

"No. But he will."

Ray stared hard at her, and she stared hard right back. "A woman should discuss such things with her man," he said.

"I'll be having a baby, but I'll work directly up to the time, and I'll come back to work right after." She didn't blink.

Her father took the cigar stub from his mouth.

"You making garden again next year?"

"Yes, I am."

"Cannin' it all up?"

"Yeah." Teal looked aside now. He was making her uncomfortable.

"Where'd you get that dress you're wearing?"

"I made it."

"What is it you're trying to prove, Teal?"

Quick anger shot right back at him. "Do you treat everybody like this who comes to apply for work, or do you save it special for me?"

Teal expected to hear him say, "Now you can settle down right now, young lady, or I'll use my belt on you." He'd never done it. He'd never hurt her in any way, but that's what he would threaten to do to assure his authority.

"Just you. It appears you've plenty to do already, Teal, with the baby coming on. I want you to take care of yourself."

She felt like laughing out loud. He would think her mad if she told him why in response to his quizzical gaze. How wonderful to hear someone share a feeling so easily in conversation—a simple thing, really, unless it rarely happened.

"You don't need me here?" she asked cheerfully.

"'Course I do. Why, I've even harbored the notion that you might want to partner with me in the business, you and Gavin both. Incorporate."

"Oh, Dad. Just a job. Have you forgotten what it's like to need a job?" She started to leave. "I'll apply somewhere else. This seemed easy, and I guess I felt nobody would hire me knowing they would have to let me go for several weeks to have the baby. I guess I didn't think it would be fair to them. I thought you'd understand." She reached the door and had her hand on the latch when he spoke.

"I do understand. Sure. Sure. You be here Monday morning if you want. But you explain to Gavin that it was you who asked me for it. I don't want to come between you two in any way. It's gonna be hard on him, Teal, to see you take this on when he had such hopes for—"

"I know it," she interrupted. "But Gavin has eyes, Dad. He'll see the need. He'll see my need to help him."

Ray Swain frowned as if he doubted that, thrust his cigar stub back between his teeth, and pushed the weight on the scale to read the tons of sorghum on the semi that had just pulled onto the scale. He shoved the cigar to the other side of his mouth and began to write his ticket. She supposed he might be until three in the morning reviewing his costs against his profits today. The hauling and price depressions were working against each other to make things tough for both the elevators and the producers.

"Agriculture in Oklahoma generates six billion a year," he mumbled. "There's only 2.8 million farms in the United States. And bankruptcy is the reward for productivity."

Diversify: that would be her solution, she thought. Diversification would save small farming and elevators—that and more volume. If he survived, he'd have to do one or more things: sell his share in the mill and hold only the elevator shares, a thing that would almost kill business during the winter when the market was slow, or he would have to expand to sell more feed and to develop a fertilizer business—even spraying, perhaps. Risking more speculation would be her last resort. She wasn't much of a gambler. Teal knew he had not been much of a speculator until recently. It seemed more a necessity than an option, she supposed. The commodity market had become an international economic and political power tool for trade balance and political negotiations in her lifetime.

With a sweep of his hand, he waved the truck off the scale. Because farmers and semicommercial feedlots brought grains and forage there for her father to grind into their own mixtures, he had considered *his* own packaged mixture in the past plus advertising his feed mixing service. Already, he'd begun stocking franchised brands of calf, chicken, and steer feeds.

Teal liked his ideas and encouraged him in such growth.

"Monday morning?" he asked her. She hugged him tightly about the neck.

"Monday."

Genuine pleasure pursued her as she rushed home, eager to tell Gavin the good news that their bills would be paid. She might be able to save some money back to help pay the fuel bill for putting in the new crop, she thought.

Her news seemed of no consequence to him. He said nothing during supper or chores. She fell asleep waiting for him to turn off the TV and come to bed. When she turned to see him beside her the next morning, he wasn't there.

He's probably already in the field sowing the new crops or preparing the soil for it, she thought.

Teal stopped to ride a few rounds on the tractor with Gavin on her way home from the mill on Monday evening. He had almost finished sowing the new crop of winter wheat in this west field, she noticed. A wariness tempted her to go home, but she brushed it aside. *He'd be thrilled,* she thought, because she was thrilled with the hope that this new crop and her new job would solve their money problems. He knew he'd done his best; he knew it wasn't his fault that the rains hadn't come, she reassured herself.

She parked the car at the southwest corner of the field so the south wind wouldn't throw the drill's dust on the car. Her straight yellow skirt prevented long steps, and her blouse already stuck to her arms for the late afternoon sun hammered down. Her brown loafers quickly filled with the hot dry loam. She paused to shake out the dirt. In this rare early September heat, the roadside grasses leaned their seed heads to the ground in the dry wind.

She waved.

He doesn't see me, she thought. She shielded her eyes from the glaring sun and tromped on over some remaining clods. *He'll have a time with these clods if it doesn't rain,* she thought.

He wheeled around a corner and threw the gray dust back on her. It gritted between her teeth.

Teal turned her head aside and held her breath. She waited for the dust fog to clear. She yelled at him, whistled in her tomboy way of flattening her bottom lip against her teeth. The shrill sound became lost in the tractor's roar. Gavin's back moved away from her now. She would have to wait until he circled the patch again. She squinted against the sun.

The stockings, she thought, looking up and down the road for cars. Seeing none, she peeled off the nylon panty hose right there and felt much cooler. She shook her hair with splayed fingers to free it of dust and brushed it from her clothes. Squinting back at the car, she realized she'd walked quite a distance, almost as far as from here to where Gavin turned his corner at the opposite corner of the field. She decided to wait where she was, then walk up to where he couldn't help but see her. His corners were short now, for the field appeared finished except for jagged little spots to correct.

By the time he'd turned at the southeast end, Teal's clothes were so dampened by perspiration that the breeze cooled her. She swiped at the beads of it on her brow and felt the grimy coat of dirt on her face.

It would wash off, she thought, smiling at the thought of him reaching down to pull her up beside him. He would share half his tractor seat with her the way they shared their lives, and they'd go bumping over rough ground, feeling good just to touch.

She waved again.

He stopped the tractor, and she bounded forward. The late afternoon sun's heat burned between her shoulder blades. Her long hair whipped its dark auburn strands across her eyes and her mouth. She pulled it back with one hand and held it there as she clumsily ran over the ground where yellow clumps of straw splotched it like chunks of fallen sun in spite of being freshly sown.

She had heard her father say that some farmer's were "dusting in their crop" again. Did Gavin have to do that? Had he not been able to pull up deep moisture with the plowing?

She had almost gained the tractor when she thrust her chin up to squint at him. He stood, his hands holding tight to the sides of the ladder. He was sort of bent there, his face distorted from a rage that Teal had never seen in him. Fear gripped her, for she knew violence sought a target. Her mouth felt suddenly dry. She could hardly make her tongue move to speak.

"I came to ride with you, same as always."

"You goddamned bitch!" he bellowed. "Get out of here! Get out of here before I drag you out!"

She couldn't move. It wasn't Gavin yelling that at her—because she was pregnant? Had the pregnancy done this? Was it the failed crop and the pregnancy and the dry days, or did he despise her? He lashed out at her because he could, she realized, and because he had to have his way even with the land.

The stunning effect of her realization changed to revolt. She wheeled about, her vision blurred by tears. Her thwarted expectation of joy changed to grief as she stumbled over clods. He saw dry days without hope; she saw an eventual rain and a greening field. He saw bills; she saw increase. *Today's the cure*, she decided. *No more rose-colored glasses for me! Change my mind, change my life.*

The hot tears streamed down her dusty cheeks. She tasted the dirt—gritty, salty.

"I'm flat tired of tears over him. I swear these are the last." She shook her fist at the sun as she swore it. *If that's the secret side, he can keep it!*

She yanked open the car door, her anger chasing away her hurt as she spun the car back, then forward. Dust formed in a great cloud behind her that screened the sight of Gavin from her rearview mirror.

She wanted away, far away from where he'd looked at her like that, spoken to her like that instead of at least taking the responsibility for his mood if he couldn't cope with hard times. No one had ever spoken to her like that. She smashed the gas pedal to the floorboard and drove. She didn't know where to go besides home to her mother and father. She couldn't go there. She couldn't let anyone see her like this, know her hurt. She felt trapped by her pride and bound by her love for him and their unborn child. *I'm no one's victim,* she thought. *Not yet, am I?*

Abruptly, she pulled the car to the side of the road and listened to the pounding of her heart. She allowed the emotional pain as she had allowed the crop failure. *Why?* she asked herself. *Why must I allow this? This isn't a natural disaster. It's an unnatural one.*

Because I believe in tomorrow, I believe in Gavin. I believe in our life, she answered herself. *I must allow his self-absorption to take him where it will. If I can restrain him with behaviors instead of words that do no good, I will. If I'm unsuccessful, he and I both will have to live with our choices.*

She knew now that she wasn't going to live happily ever after. For all she knew, nothing lay ahead but unhappiness and feelings of entrapment. For the first time, she realized she could not rely on making her life with Gavin. Her family lived for one another; Gavin lived for himself. She had a life of her own to make that she could share with Gavin and their children. She could share his life—what he would allow for as long as possible, she thought, instead of the former forever after.

To Teal, self-absorption and self-destruction were synonymous. Life didn't allow one to always have their own way. Perhaps Gavin would *change his mind and change his life.* If he couldn't, life would always seem his enemy, an enemy that would not grow old and weak as he would someday. Therefore, life could break Gavin as it

—

did those with ingratitude and hopelessness. The thought saddened her.

She had learned from her failure with Heath that she could bend, adapt to change. Hadn't she always believed *change your mind; change your life?* What she hadn't thought of until now was that Gavin could do so as well. She supposed he had changed his mind about her.

She raised her head up and saw that she'd driven to a favored spot near the Canadian River, the shaded clearing where almost all the school parties had been held. She was only a few miles from home. For a long moment, she stared out at the water. The river was low now and brown from its slowness. Slowly, Teal became aware of outside sounds again. The roaring inside her head subsided.

Life is his best teacher—not me, she reminded herself. *Gavin is smart. He will come around. If he can't, life will thwart rather than fulfill him.* As she watched the free-moving water, the edges of her prison relaxed. Yet she knew her choices would come with boundaries as natural as this river's banks.

"I accept this change. For as long as we are married, to do otherwise perverts my own joy," she said aloud. *He makes his own choices, as I do,* she thought. *It can't be otherwise, or we're both lost.* That Gavin seemed lost had not occurred to her before today—lost in the jungle of a mixed cultural marriage and an uncooperative climate.

They valued different things.

A hive of bees worked a few trees away. Cicadas sang. With care, she turned the car around and headed back to him. She drove with a calm resolve. Could she show another person invisible hope? Genuine alarm for his well-being and her own seemed an issue. He could force much from others with an inflexible will, but he could not force the elements to obey him. *He had chosen the wrong profession for that,* she thought. *Agriculture required the cooperation of the producer with nature and his or her acceptance of the need to confront the problems as well as receive the blessings.*

—

At the end of the lane, she saw that he brought the tractor in. She turned up the lane before him, parked, and waited just outside the yard gate.

Their old yellow dog foolishly chased sparrows as if he would one day leap high enough to catch one. "Hey, Pup!" she called. She stooped to hug and tousle him.

Clouds covered three-quarters of the sun. Teal suddenly laughed and scratched him behind the ears, her emotional pain already behind her. She considered Gavin's pain—his brutal disappointment over the lost crop he couldn't control. She understood his frustration over nature not meeting him halfway when he'd done his best and spent so much of their savings.

Hadn't he said a man must be hard and tough to endure a career in agriculture? He probably thought macho and strength were synonymous; a lot of men and women did.

She looked at the yellow dog. "Instead of Pup, you're dubbed No-name. Go on now, No-name, and chase birds."

She thought of herself and the child she carried. Gavin had to deal with this recession and drought the same as she. He could do it in his own way, but he couldn't blame it on her. She wouldn't move beside him as his cross instead of his equal, but now wasn't the time to communicate that, she thought. Over time and from her behavior, he would figure it out.

She wondered if most farmers' wives dealt with similar behaviors due to the costs in time, labor, and money versus the uncertainties. Numerous past generations of daughters saw their mother's and grandmother's acceptance of debilitating farm accidents, crop disasters, and price manipulations by those in control, whether a landlord, a cartel, a hedge fund, a government, or any other owner of the commodity. They put on their aprons and bonnets and went on. She would do the same.

The tractor sounded like a huge purring cat to her as he pulled it up to park. Its throaty vibrations assaulted the air. He always idled it for a few minutes before shutting it down. A great silence wedged itself between where he moved to check its bolts and valves and where she waited for him. At last he turned and started for her.

He was about a yard from her when he looked up. His shoulders slumped only a little. For the most part, he still held himself straight. There was a faint smile, a softness about his mouth despite the smudges of earth on his face. Dried perspiration etched great circles of white about the arms of his gray work shirt. It was his eyes that Teal's gaze settled upon. An unveiled apology shown through their blue-green. She sensed by the loose way that he carried his arms, they'd be around her in a moment.

"I'm sorry, Teal," he said, lifting his arms in a helpless gesture. "I knew the minute I'd done it, I'd made a mistake."

"Not if you feel that way," she said quietly. *He loves me, he loves me not* shadowed the moment and altered his power.

He looked at her oddly, then pushed past her into the house.

She followed him inside and stood watching him wash the dust off his face and hands at the washstand on the porch before handing him a clean towel. "I was raised by the Golden Rule, but I don't feel it today, so you're not to expect it," he said.

Panic started back of her breast bone; first he apologized, then closed her out. She couldn't get to where he was. He stood near enough to touch. She wanted to fly at him, hit him, scream—anything but accept this apology that he had followed with the inference of more to come. *He has to know that behavior is unacceptable,* she thought.

"When I *want*, whatever the want, if you give it to me," she said instead, "it's best you want it too or it's a lie. So you did right if you didn't want me with you. I want us honest with each other. But tell me *no* with as much regard as you would give a stranger—never again with such hateful spite. I'm your wife, for God's sake."

"I'm tired, Teal. I'm going out to milk now."

Her throat cramped from the pressure of the growing scream. Words whispered from memory, "You're spoiled, Teal, you're—" *I analyze everything too much. Let it go,* her common sense whispered.

She swallowed hard, wanting to break through his walls. He could talk out his own hurt with her; she was there to hear it. Perhaps she

—

was spoiled and selfish. Yet her common sense told her that Gavin's iron will had been crossed by forces he couldn't manipulate, and that alone caused his obscene anger. Her knowing had to be enough; her speaking against his behavior had to be enough.

Unavoidably, Sara Jane crossed her mind as the potential subconscious cause of his unprovoked resentments of her. Heath neglected; Gavin resisted. "Women accept," came some echoed advice from the past. *What happens to a personality built by one's own will if that will becomes dispossessed by fate?* she wondered.

"I'll fix something to eat," she said, "after I've bathed and changed. My clothes and shoes are full of dirt." She didn't volunteer to chore with him or put his need before her own. He might not show regard for her, but she could show him she had regard for herself.

Teal's joy slept for days. She hid her blues behind songs and smiles. When she thought of the child, a little of her buoyant strength returned. Then because it didn't please her to consider the uncertain future, her thoughts returned to Ray Swain and her job at the mill.

After supper each evening, she retired to the bedroom to read. She had begun regular library stops after work. She knew that she escaped into books to avoid Gavin.

Over the following days, she thought less about him. She didn't try to tell him about anything. She controlled her physical need for him, responding when *he* needed her. She left him notes when necessary to communicate her whereabouts, and she hurriedly bathed and changed before he returned from the barn each evening.

Weeks dragged by. She felt safe from Gavin now, as if he could not draw her pain as if it were her blood. She prepared meals and kept the housework done. She separated the milk, made cheese, and churned butter. He sat at the table reading the mail. After supper she washed dishes. He bathed.

The methodical days that followed had their natural rhythm despite the quiet distrust that grew between them.

Then one night, she dreamed about Heath, the same dream she'd had a few nights after the scene in the field. They swam together

—

in a narrow stream, side by side toward the spring head. Just ahead she saw a bridge. They'd go *under* the bridge if she could just make it that far. She'd swim *under* it to a life on the other side.

Walking across it had no part in the dream. She paused to rest and looked back to see Gavin struggling to catch up to them, but the current pushed him back. His arms flailed. He couldn't reach them. He hadn't before. She turned in the water without ever touching Heath and continued on, the bridge always just ahead of them until she wakened.

She lay without opening her eyes for a long while, remembering the dream. She had wanted Gavin to reach them. She wanted them to touch. She wanted to tell him about her days away from the farm, about her dreams and beliefs.

Her eyes popped open. The mill. What time was it?

She turned her head, expecting to see him lying next to her, wanting to move into his warmth, but he wasn't there. His frequent absences made a vacancy in her nothing filled—not even the job. She rose without eagerness.

"See you after five. I'll be at the mill," she wrote. But before she left the house, she pulled the book about sculpting off the small shelf in the living room. It was overdue. She'd have time to browse through it one more time before returning it.

Besides, she wanted her father to see it.

Teal was halfway to town before it occurred to her that Gavin hadn't left her a note. Was it his freedom that she thwarted? Their notes seemed a mutual courtesy—not an obligation. She would ask him tonight about his day. She would remind him that it meant a lot to her to know where he was should she need him.

That first night they'd danced, being with Gavin seemed the ultimate freedom, the freedom to feel and to touch, to be their separate selves but cling together for joy and for sharing. When they'd married, she felt freer still, free of Sara Jane, free from Heath, free to go anywhere with Gavin, and nobody had the right to look at her as if she shouldn't as they'd done at the dance. In marriage, their love had the world's approval.

234

Teal reached to turn on the radio. Music would push aside this uncertainty. *I'll just ask him to leave me a note so I'll know how to reach him,* she thought. She made too much of things, and she began to hum along with the radio. *Gavin didn't have time for an affair,* she thought. *Still, his compulsion to control could require it. He may feel that he has lost control of me.*

For a fact, he had. Teal's instinct for survival controlled her now.

*   *   *

At the mill, Ray Swain had finished overseeing the loading of several grain trucks that would make the run to Houston. Others would dump this afternoon at the grain terminal to the north and be loaded onto hopper cars. Besides his elevators, storage cylinders of white concrete and steel now rose like skyscrapers. His mills, bakery, and their parking lot spread across the adjacent lot to the south. Hopper cars waited to be loaded on local track with wheat, flour, or baked goods to help fill the government's export contracts and their own marketing agreements both at home and abroad.

A train stood by the track for oiling. The steamers were all gone, both the sight and sound of them missed by all who love rail, including Abraham Jones who walked up and down the train. He had a special interest in the loading of it. Two trains had derailed over the past two weeks because of overloaded hoppers. A hopper held thirty-three hundred bushels or about 198 thousand pounds of wheat. A twenty-five-hundred-bushel limit would preserve track and prevent derailment. He intended to march right into Swain's Grain and give the proprietor his personal opinion on the subject if he found any more overweight cars. He knew that most of this grain would go to markets in the southwest, to mills mostly. The rest was priced too high at two thirty-eight a bushel for Galveston.

Abraham also knew that it cost Swain every bit of two dollars a bushel just to mill the stuff here because he had a nephew working for him. He'd seen freight bills too.

He supposed two dollars and thirty-eight cents wasn't so much for a mill in grassland Texas to pay for Oklahoma wheat. But the best deal of all was when the Texas competition mill trucks pulled in and paid Swain two dollars and thirty cents a bushel for his wheat just to get it. That kind of trucking sure dented rail. Didn't help the sale of his flour much either; ran the mill short, shot the price up. But it saved him trucking expense when he needed that savings.

Abraham watched his tongue. The business of moving wheat was sure up against it unless the man had a barrel of nerve and brain, unless he diversified with feed, a mill, corn and, a bakery like this Swain. Abraham knew he even sold dog food and birdseed now. He admired the man. He'd ask about the weights before he accused him.

If competition from Texas mills and transit concerns weren't enough, he had the government boys poking their noses into it for inventories and regulation and inspection. Lately, energy costs were up everywhere. *Turning that grain to keep it fresh probably cost a third more daily,* he thought.

Abraham had heard that if one hundred thousand to six hundred thousand pounds of wheat tonnage came into Swain's business by rail, the government said he had to void twenty thousand dollars worth of freight billing—money that rail would never see again. Surely such a policy didn't exist. He hoped it was a false rumor.

To Abraham, it seemed a calculation to not only do in wheat transit by rail, but to close small-town rural elevators and mills as well. *Why, rail and agriculture built this country. When both are gone and the huge elevators depend only on trucks, those trucks can't begin to do what rail can. He'd bet on eventual high prices and shortages, on trucker strikes and delays due to detours for road repairs or expansions.* In Abraham's opinion, industry needed both trucking and rail.

He crawled up into his engine. Rory Leese was there flipping through bad order cards. "Not much wheat moving," Abraham told him. "Hoppers just sitting full."

"There's a rush on to cover their 'flat' position with trucks."

"Twenty grand is gone, twenty grand is gone," Abraham moaned.

"Sweeter than Jesus," Rory agreed.

He didn't like Rory's irreligion, but he didn't feel commissioned to change it either.

"It'll push the rates up here. We need our gravy too," Rory persisted.

"Yep, and they done done it. Rates is up this last weekend, and it'll keep the trucks moving for sure, even if wheat brings in enough to cover the loss."

"Over the long haul—" Rory interrupted him.

"It ain't good."

They were silent for a while.

Rory put the cards aside and checked his gages.

"If the government had never stuck in their nose," Abraham said. "Maybe, just maybe, someday, unless more industry comes our way then we got, this wheat thing will hit this railroad in the worst way because of it being loaded to trucks instead of rail."

"You're probably the only person in the world that thinks that way, Abraham."

"The day will come when *either* trucks *or* rail will be trucks *and* rail—mark my words. I ain't lost *my* common sense. Either-or thinking can kill a country. Either oil or nothing, either trucks or nothing."

Maybe he thought too highly of wheat. *Bread. Why, bread was the staff of life, and cereal should start every kid's day. Wasn't anybody in this whole country that didn't enjoy bread every day. And pie and cake and cereal and pudding and gravy—why, there seemed no end to it. Macaroni and spaghetti and ravioli and—*

The train jerked. Rory slapped his engineer's hat on his head, and they rambled into the run to Texas, west as far as Tucumcari, New Mexico.

"Finally," he muttered.

Chapter XVI

Change Your Mind; Change Your Life

Teal returned all the art books for more. This time, she searched intentionally for more information on sculpting. She thumbed the volumes feverishly. A growing intensity for the subject added zest to her busy days.

The following months passed quickly for her. At Swains, she worked at the scale, at the files, in the bakery and laboratory—wherever she could help. She wrote the checks for the payroll and the taxes monthly and quarterly; she could hardly believe the time passed so fast. She was due to deliver within weeks now.

Her body felt clumsy and heavy, but her energy stayed high. Her mind leaned toward the child but just as strongly toward clay. She could get her hands upon clay and shape it the way she couldn't shape anything else right now.

"You're impatient, Teal," Esther told her one afternoon when she'd stopped by to visit her mother. "You've always been impatient. It's a bad quality when a person isn't willing to let things run their natural course by doing what you see to do in that order."

Teal regarded her mother with affection. "You've always done that. I remember you doing what had to be done hour by hour, day by day, with the materials you had to do it with."

"Well, I did the best I could. I never had much education—"

"You are a linear thinker—a 'one step at a time' thinker," Teal interrupted. "I'm a 'kind of a wheel' thinker. These ideas and activities seem to spin out like spokes from my hub, from, well, me. Besides, living is an education, Mom. You've done a lot of that. You've taught *me* a lot too."

"I mean high school, like you, Teal."

"High school isn't much of an education anymore, Mama," Teal said. "I'm not saying I don't appreciate having it. It's just that it's state provided for everybody. Hardly anyone apprentices anymore, so college or vocational schools seem more important than they ought to now that more people are either certified in something or hold a degree."

"I wanted you to go on to it," Esther recalled.

"I know. Maybe I will. Someday."

"Jonsi's graduating this semester. He wrote I should tell you. He wants you to come see him walk across the stage to claim that doctorate."

"Agricultural research? Did he stay with that? He's been so interested in saving our environment, I've wondered if he changed his emphasis."

"Essentially, still agriculture with lots of electives. He wants to show his daddy up." Esther smiled when she said it as if it were a source of pride to both herself and to Ray. "He's excited about this ordinary farmer who lives not far from you and Gavin. He says that farmer did scientific experiments with accurate records right in his own kitchen. Actually, all over his house and outdoors in specially marked-off plots. He's discovered things about wheat that's already helping this Oklahoma wheat belt grow enough wheat to feed the world, feed the millions overpopulating everywhere. Do you believe a thing like that's possible, Teal? Right here?"

Esther didn't wait for Teal to answer. "Sounds far-fetched to me. Nobody famous lives here. I'd know about it. Sounds like a daydream Jonsi's attaching reality to. He always did worry me that way. Now he thinks he's going to change things. He talks about fifty-bushel-to-the-acre wheat as if it were a regular possibility."

"He lives near us?"

"Ask Jonsi."

"I'll ask Gavin, he should know. But more wheat on less ground sounds fine. Still, too much of our aerable land gets covered with concrete every year. Those in charge of law and zoning in this country don't seem to know the difference in aerable land and sand."

"What's the difference?"

"Difference is that it's a rarer soil type and will grow wheat, barley, or beans when most other soils won't."

"Have you heard the news about Heath?" Esther asked abruptly.

"I'm never where news of him would come up, you know that."

"I didn't mean anything by it. I only heard he's a candidate for mayor. He's young to stretch his neck into politics, but Ray says he's heard some good indications he's got the best chance to win."

"How will he finish his law degree and fill an office?"

"Don't know. I suppose he's got some plan in mind. Ambitious, Heath is ambitious."

"Yes. He is that." A silence lay between them.

Teal rose to leave. "I have seed in the car for my fall garden. I asked Gavin to plow over and spring tooth my spent garden plot except for the green tomatoes and the sweet potatoes I haven't dug yet."

It was good to let her mind slide away from Heath and toward the garden. Just talking about it, she saw the thick green vines of the sweet potatoes. She thought of whether they'd need water tonight or wait another day.

"I'd better water our potatoes tonight," Esther commented. "They'll need to be dug before the first heavy frost. They can take a light one." Esther followed along with her, leaving their conversation behind. "You planting any turnips?"

"I planted turnips early. A few. Will you want some of them? They're dry-weather hot."

"Sure I will, and pumpkin."

"Might not be time for pumpkin now, but there'll be acorn squash still from spring planting."

"Squash is just as good. You can bring me any green tomatoes you won't use. I'll make chowchow. You still like it, don't you?"

"Yes. Yes, I do."

Teal knew there was nothing more for them to say today. She and Esther talked only of surface things. Now and then though, Esther was in a mood to recount things in her own life; past things, some good and some not so good. Teal's impatience was a source of trouble between them at such times. She was glad that nothing like that had come up today. At the door, she turned back and looked at Esther directly.

"Why did you bring up Heath?"

"Is there a reason not to?" There was an edge to Esther's voice that Teal didn't like.

"No, I suppose not. I love Gavin, he loves me. Past is past," she reminded her mother.

"Heath's going to be a successful man," Esther said. "Why, no telling how much he'll earn when he sets up his law office."

"That's true," Teal said. She wondered if Esther looked down on Gavin, an ordinary farmer in most people's minds. Teal didn't see anything ordinary about someone who provided food. Furthermore, she thought the same as her father that the culture had been contaminated by the term *common man*, a term generated for political advantage—not for the American working male. It left out women entirely. She thought it destroyed opportunity that elitists reserved for the few. Since there wasn't a way to be prejudicial about other Caucasians to hold them down, Teal assumed that the term *common* served the socialists well; they could appear beneficent while they developed the slave-labor class to work for the underprivileged via taxation. It seemed to her that both major political parties bore the guilt of it.

The profession of agriculture required much scientific knowledge, a fact not commonly understood by the public. As for

—

the underprivileged, she agreed with her Dad: more often they needed a hand up to help themselves unless disabled.

"He's engaged to marry. I didn't tell you that," Esther's voice whined. "Sara Jane Hood."

Heat rushed to Teal's face. She felt it flush. She had to change the subject before she fainted. *Sara must be six years older than Heath—more, perhaps,* she thought. She forced her mind to move away from thoughts of them together for she believed she might die this minute if she didn't.

"I'm liking my job at the mill, but I've been thinking lately that I'd like a class in sculpting," she said.

"Sculpting?"

"Shaping things with my own hands."

"Oh." Esther stood about two feet from her. "It's to spite you, you know. Heath, because you—well, dumped him, and Sara, because you got the man she wanted."

"I dumped Heath? Hardly, Mother. Heath showed no interest in me past an idea of us—nothing from his heart and no hint of physical desire for me. Yet he encouraged me to reject Gavin's attention."

"He broke your heart?"

"So I went on with my life, yes."

Teal's parents no longer lived in the same familiar place of her birth. They'd moved into a residential section of the city on the west side of the mill and elevator business. The spacious cool house centered great shade trees that grew over gardens and birdbaths. A fountain gurgled in the back; Teal could hear the tumbling water from where they stood. She focused on its soothing sounds that filled the sullen silence between them.

"Sculpting could be entertaining," Esther finally remarked. "But I hope you're considering a partnership in the mill. Ray said that he'd mentioned it to you already. He's expanding the offices."

Teal breathed a sigh of relief for she felt she could not bear to speak of Heath and Sara again.

"I know. I thought I'd order some college catalogs, see if they're offering evening classes in management. Sculpting can be an elective. Electives are encouraged."

"The roads are sure dangerous now, Teal. I hate to think of all that driving. You're almost ready to deliver, and you're working so hard both at home and at the mill."

"Be some driving, but that's how it is sometimes."

Esther's mouth tightened into little pleats over her teeth. "You've got lots of time, Teal. You're young. You better take care of what needs taking care of first. Gavin won't like your being away so much. Besides, who will watch the baby?"

"I thought you would, Mama," she said to disconcert Esther, for she hadn't thought it at all. But if Gavin couldn't take charge of her, Esther certainly wasn't a delegate.

Esther looked stunned and said nothing more.

"Bye now," Teal said cheerfully, then waved good-bye from her car as she pulled away from the curb. Her mother probably thought a degree wasn't necessary since she'd grown up with the business. Perhaps it wasn't, but she felt that management and supervision differed from knowing how to *do* a job. *Management either motivates or obstructs employee productivity,* she thought.

Gavin could help, or she could hire help. What had seemed devotion freely given to him before his walls and rage now felt like a martyrdom to avoid.

The baby would bring change she welcomed. She looked forward to the new experiences with a child. She recognized that lives moved into changed seasons; she'd heard dramatic life changes called new normals recently.

The loss of dear ones, of innocence, of illusions, even the loss of the town's soda fountain counters with those tall stools she had favored seemed unfair yet natural. She missed the church picnics in the park, the traveling carnival and circus—gone, all gone. Could that dear, dear past of her childhood culture recycle one day? Return to give enjoyment to another generation that played red rover, kick the can, and paper dolls? She hoped so. In the meantime, her Mia or Brett would have their memories. The name Mia if a girl, Brett if a boy.

It didn't seem that she went home now when she went to see her mother and father. She went to their new house—not home where she'd been born. The mill expansion bothered her; becoming a partner did too. With the influx of change, there seemed an outflow of good times and good memories.

Then it occurred to Teal that ten years from now, this day might be forgotten if she failed to savor it.

I'll choose to make these times good and memorable as well, she determined. *Because taking responsibility too seriously and worshiping the past could hurt a person their whole life.*

It was twelve miles southwest to home. In the rearview mirror, she saw the red dirt flying behind her. Clay—that red dirt was her clay. She would develop a recipe from it that became malleable for sculpting. Figures needed to dry slowly—no cracks.

The tightness about her heart gave way to the news she struggled to repress: Heath would marry Sara Jane. The news ripped through her thoughts of courses and clay.

His marrying ended all their possibilities. Wasn't that what she'd thought when she married Gavin? Yes, and it had been half true. Now it would be finished; everything between them finished, forever.

More than her own marriage, greater than the distance growing between herself and Gavin, this news launched her into feelings of isolation. What meaning would her memories have now? She supposed they would die. No, she would wish them dead, for already she sensed their torment.

She must accept this change or go mad. The peace of mind she prized above all else and managed to preserve through all her recent concerns over lost love and a lost crop seemed irrevocably lost as well.

The finality of their possibilities critically wounded her like a death wound. It seemed unfair. How would she gain control of her feelings? How could she cope?

"Oh, Heath, did you go through this when I married?" she murmured. A tear slid down her cheek. "I didn't feel your pain. How cruel of me." Abruptly, Sylvia's voice echoed from years past to wreck her romantic notions of Heath's broken heart.

His career plans remained intact, she thought. His bank account remained safe from her. No doubt, his heart had too, she reluctantly surmised. Her tears stopped. *Just love and let be. Sylvia is probably right. The only thing that would break Heath's heart would be if his plans changed without his permission.*

Like a pressed iris from the past, romantic notions for either Heath or Gavin were laid to rest. Oh, it wouldn't matter, none of it, when she held their baby. When she had her own small sculpting studio and let go of the romantic expectations she had nurtured for her and Gavin. How lucky she was to have so much, she thought, even the partnership with her father if she wanted it.

About a quarter of a mile ahead, she saw the farmhouse. Painted white, it looked stark there on the prairie. The August sun dried the yard they had planted to buffalo and Bermuda grasses. They couldn't spare the water to keep it alive.

The field had begun to blow. Dust almost obscured her view of Gavin stripping it for Harlin. He circled with the tractor in wide but shallow swaths to prevent the wind from carrying off more topsoil. That seemed the curious part to Teal, for within an hour, the dust would settle after these plowed strips interrupted its flight. They'd still need a rain within a couple of days, or their first disaster would be nothing like the second. Drought. That word was a thousand times worse to Oklahomans than crop failure or hail, greenbugs, or army worms. Drought could last for years. Today's methods of conservation ended the dusters of old but not the crop losses. Even the dryer times since the thirties hadn't brought them back.

Teal intended to ignore the possibility of more loss and continued trusting in the new crop. *Why not?* She hooked up the hose to the well nozzle as soon as she'd parked the car. She watered the sweet potatoes and moistened the small fall garden patch that Gavin had prepared. Too clodded for a garden, she knew it was the best he could do during dry weather. It would have small chance of sprouting unless it rained. Though disgustingly negative, that reality rang true. She'd need to till it a bit with the hoe and rake it in the morning while it was cool, then plant it in the evening after she returned home. By the time that Gavin finished his chores, she'd have finished hers.

They worked separately now more often than together. But then, he and Harlin had a partnership where they shared equipment and helped one another. She had felt set aside in the beginning, but she had decided to accept what Gavin and his father appeared to want, and she could not change.

Her life may have lost what she had thought of as their *magical* intimacy of their first dance, but it revealed itself now as uniquely her own and easily connecting to many others through art and the mill. For Swain, feed and food products were now trucked across the country and their grain sold to international markets.

She bent to gather the hose into loops that she could easily carry when the child flopped over inside her. The suddenness of it startled her. She straightened in alarm, the weight of the hose yanking her backward. She struggled for balance.

Something popped. A bone? A sharp pain cut down toward her pelvis and left. She felt all right again, but she waited without moving a muscle for several minutes. She dropped the hose. *I'll ask Gavin to put it away. If I feel no worse by morning, I'll finish the garden,* she thought.

She turned toward the house and saw him coming around the corner of it. They were often apart now since that heated afternoon when his lashing tongue had sown this doubt in her mind, doubt that he had ever truly loved her. Was Sara Jane's infant his? Had he hurriedly married to avoid the responsibility of it? The child had been a boy that Sara called Eric. She supposed he had had his third birthday by now.

Responsibility and Gavin clashed, she knew. Perhaps since her pregnancy, he felt he might as well have married that first love. She'd learned that the less responsibility he had, the better his moods. He simply didn't cope well. His negative mind-sets stressed him over almost everything. His sky seemed always falling.

"Some class catalogs came," he said before reaching her.

"Oh!" she cried. Forgetting to be careful, she ran to the kitchen where the mail was scattered about. He came in behind her and watched her slap back page after page.

"There it is!" she said excitedly. "A sculpting class and only a hundred-mile round-trip on a Saturday! Won't start until after fall break. Weeks from now."

"I can't let you do it. There's the baby, and you're already working."

Teal only laughed. This time she wasn't hurt or angry or surprised. She'd expected this. She'd already met it in Esther—that combination of distance and authority.

"I've a lot to deal with here, Gavin, and I'm dealing. I like life here with you. It's new, it's a challenge, the kind that makes me unafraid if you don't love me or don't want our child, for I'm happy with this choice, with the choice to go to college as I planned when we met and the decision to go into the corporation—with Dad—to partner."

"I could be afraid of you," he said.

"You're either changing, or I never really knew you," she told him outright. "I'm sorry that I can't please you. But *I'm* not your child to instruct, control, or tell to go away. We'll have a child. My decision to have a life feels better than isolation feels."

"I don't know what you're talking about. I just know that you're not taking a class a hundred miles away."

"It isn't, it's fifty."

The baby flopped again. "Oh!" she said. "It's different, Gavin. It did that outside." She caressed her stomach as if to calm her child.

"It? He," he corrected. He dared a smile, the first she'd seen since that terrible afternoon. "Can I feel?" he asked.

"Sure. I hope you like the name Mia if it's a girl, or Brett if we have a boy."

He moved close to her and slid his hand under her loose blouse. It was the same rough hand with the same warmth and gentleness.

"I like them fine," he said.

Teal put her own hand over his and moved it to where she knew the child lay. It turned beneath their hands, and she heard Gavin catch his breath.

The wall that guarded his feelings tumbled somewhere back of his eyes. Plainly, he wanted their child. Why wasn't it safe for him to say it now that the time was so near? Yet as easily as he'd moved close, he moved away.

"Gavin—"

She stopped. She'd been about to ask him to hold her, but the words crumbled into the space between them. In spite of their child, there seemed an awful emptiness growing within her that she must satisfy outside of this marriage.

The evenings stretched long and the weekends longer to her. Gavin usually went to bed around eight unless he read agricultural journals or *The National Geographic* for a while. Sometimes they watched television for the news and weather. Conversations grew rarer due to his longer silences that would not yield.

She turned her thoughts toward straightening the kitchen, preparing a simple supper for them. Then thought fell upon thought, and she knew that in the morning, she'd enroll in the sculpting class. She *would* live fully without his support.

She'd set up her easel and paints in the old washhouse behind the main house. They never used it. It had electricity for a small electric heater and a lightbulb. *Low overhead and just enough space,* she decided. Just to think of it eased her need to control something in her life, possess something, touch something that didn't slip away.

Even as she thought these things, she dared to think of Heath. As it was now, she never saw him, but she sensed that that would soon change. Her life had become more public since her return to the mill. Heath's would be too should he become mayor. Even if he didn't, he would probably open a law office here or join a firm.

—

Teal cleared the table, then lifted down two plates from the cabinet and set them on a freshly ironed yellow cloth. She leaned against the cupboard then, her thoughts moving out the window and across the patch of cotton. *He would be married,* she reminded herself.

"Oh!" she sighed aloud, hating Gavin's desire to restrain her even as he ignored her. She'd hoped that since he and Harlin farmed and ranched together, he would understand her accepting her father's offer. Why, she'd thought that . . .

Oh, she didn't know what she thought. She knew he would have long days with a full-time job plus the farm. He and Harlin had taken on more land—a thousand cultivated acres besides grass for cattle. She hadn't planned on this isolation. She wanted out that window, and her decision to grow her life while Gavin grew his seemed the only way to be free of these shadows and trouble and loneliness. She wanted to feel joy again. His mention that he wanted to build their own home thrilled her.

Gavin didn't really seem to notice or care about anything but his wheat and cotton and the quarter of land that Harlin recently deeded to him. He planned to mortgage it to buy another. If he had married her to avoid marrying pregnant Sara Jane, perhaps he worked these hours to avoid *her.*

He wouldn't be looking at house plans for their own quarter of land if he didn't love her and want their child, would he? How she wished she could talk it all out with Jenny. Gavin's behaviors constantly confused her. Understanding them seemed as impossible as identifying him blindfolded.

Calling Jenny for solace wouldn't help. Jenny loved shopping and clubs and bridge. She rarely had time for Teal. Closeness to Jenny lay lightly on her heart, still cradled in the hope she held for it when a child.

Who cared? If he couldn't be cheerful and accept the hard times along with the good, well, who cared? *This* farmhouse was a blessing, the quarter of their own land was a blessing, their child was a blessing.

She planted her hands on her hips and lifted her chin. She could love him, but she couldn't make him grateful or give him joy. How often had Esther told her she would make her own heaven or hell by the attitudes she chose. How could it be any different for Gavin?

She whirled to finish her tasks, moving with a lightness of heart and a brisker step for she finally accepted that she could only change herself. The weight of Gavin's misery slid off her despite her hope for his happiness. *Could it be that he refused joy for fear of losing it? Can't lose what you don't have,* she reminded herself.

If I'm more careful with grocery shopping, Teal's thoughts moved ahead, *I can save enough back from the cream money on Saturdays to buy my art supplies.* She put her salary checks in their mutual bank account each week to help with bills. While she finished setting the table and Gavin bathed and changed, the dollars stacked up in her mind like hope, and she began to sing again for the first time in weeks.

"One thing about a radio," Gavin grumbled, sitting down to eat. "You can turn it off."

She finished a chorus before she stopped, her eagerness for living still strong. She no longer felt vulnerable to Gavin's approval or disapproval. She only felt alone in the same room with him as if he walled himself in as a preferred state.

She wakened with eagerness for the day the following morning. She seeded her fall garden in dawn's hazy light, chunking the clods smaller and raking the soil until she could make rows or hills for the seed. She made tiny furrows for the fresh greens' seed and shaped the hills of loamy soil for the varieties of squash and melons. She planted more fine turnip seed near the surface of the sandier area. Her crowded body prevented the easy motion she loved.

As she bent over her rounded belly to plant each onion plant separately, she felt short of breath. By the time she finished, she panted for breath but began to breathe easily as she sprinkled the new planting with cistern water.

The sun rose red and warm to begin its climb above the red-brown earth that produced the crops and produce and pasture.

An hour and a half had passed. The mockingbirds she had watched hatch in early spring serenaded her as she finished watering. Her back ached from strain.

She stood stretching for a moment, her fingers massaging her stomach and moving to her center back. She returned to the house more slowly than when she had gone to the garden. But already, she envisioned it greening and growing, the plump produce falling into her gathering basket.

Why, there'd be plenty for them all fall after all with hardly any need for the grocery store except for flour and sugar, a bit of shortening, and seasonings, of course. Why had she allowed her optimism to escape?

The growing of things had become the thread that connected her past with her present. Sometimes as she stooped to plant or to gather, her mind flew back to the memory of a garter snake beneath a tomato vine in her father's vegetable garden where she plucked a basketful of okra for Esther to can. Or she'd rub dirt from the new potatoes from her own garden, remembering Esther's wonderful creamed new peas and potatoes. She could recall the voices of Tad and Jonsi from her past as they fought over who got "first dibs" on them before they were passed around.

The bounty of food and her own self-reliance to assure it seemed associated in some mysterious way to *all* of life's bounty. It gave her great satisfaction to know that her energies and effort could turn the possible into the real. She would always make time for it, she promised herself. Always.

For though Esther had taught her values and responsible choices (caring less for what others thought and more about what she knew about herself), her father had taught her that life's greatest partnership was with God, her Creator. "Go no place without Him in mind or deed," he'd said once.

She had bathed and dressed for work when Gavin sat down with her at breakfast "You really going corporate?" he asked.

"We are. Dad wants you in the business too, Gavin, if you want."

"I don't want. I like building new roads and bridges across the south river."

"That takes a . . . a . . ."

"An engineer?"

"Maybe."

"I was raised building these roads and bridges right alongside Dad. It's the way things were learned before college degrees. They hired me on my experience. Why, every road you drive down, I've helped build or surface or bridge.

"There's not much about water control that I don't know about either. Know where the divide is here?" His voice taunted her.

"What's a divide?"

He laughed. It was the second time she'd thought him cruel.

"You're making fun of me because you know something that I don't?"

He didn't answer; he just looked at her.

"I'm proud you have the job," she said. "We could have been happy together about what I'm doing too."

"That's why we're talking about it, isn't it?"

"I thought you were making fun. I thought you didn't want me to—" She stopped. Be best not to push that subject at him.

"I didn't really mean to." He said it like he meant it. She wanted to get up right then and hug him, but she didn't move. She refused to encourage him in his push-and-pull ways that betrayed sincerity.

When she shared the problem with Sylvia, her friend labeled it button pushing.

"He's located all your buttons," she told Teal, "and you probably aren't even interested in his. When he flies at you the way he can, you've pushed one of his. I'd make a note of each if I were you and avoid them like the plague. He sounds like a regular minefield."

"He's totally destroyed my trust in anything he says or does," Teal lamented.

"Are you proud of me?" she dared ask him later that night at dinner.

"About the corporation?"

She'd been thinking about the sculpting, but she said, "About anything?"

He hesitated as if he had to *think* about it. "Sure," he finally said.

"I wanted to be with you more, partner with *you*. I guess you and your father have wanted this for a long time—both of you, probably. I just didn't know."

Her tone sounded lower, full of more grief than she'd intended.

His eyes warmed upon her, but she glanced away. "Few husbands and wives partner like me and Dad. Men partner for fieldwork. Farm women cook and chore."

"I'll clear the table now. I'd better go," she said, puzzled at this new information. Why hadn't she noticed that? she wondered. Couldn't a woman do what farmers and ranchers do?

"So soon? I thought you opened later now that all the wheat is in," he said.

She paused midway to the sink to turn and look at him. Could he possibly want private time with her again now, now when she—?

Teal forced her mind to deal with her new reality. "It's time. We open at eight, some later now that summer harvests are past. Customers come in for fertilizer or feed. Most of the time, I'll leave still earlier."

"That's a hell of a note!" he spat, shoved back his chair, and left.

She supposed she had used Gavin to shield her from uncomfortable realities with Heath, she thought. Just as she had used thoughts of Heath to shield her from uncomfortable realities about Gavin. That had helped when she'd thought something must be lacking in her to cause their behaviors.

Why hadn't anyone told her that some men wanted distance, not connection except for sex. She wondered if this distance-loving characteristic typified husband-wife relationships for most couples. Was it how all farmers vented their career stress? Was it a behavior that would be profiled? It seemed to Teal that her only hope for connection would be submission to Gavin's control, which would make her an extension of *his* life without truly sharing it. Had she nothing he wanted but sexual availability and servitude? Logic responded "quiet." He clearly wanted her without verbal opinions, objections, or a cheerful melody.

All farmers may not cope with nature's fickle behavior by reflecting it, but Gavin certainly did, she thought.

Hold on! her mind cried. She grasped the steering wheel as if it were her life that she clutched. *Change my mind, change my life.* No longer would her life with Gavin smack of the martyrdom of someone left out, used, and belittled. Servitude, sex, and silence?

"I don't think so," she declared aloud. *There must have been women in past pioneer generations who found themselves in my situation or worse and coped, died, or ran away to who knows what. Their* options may have been worse than the blighted lives that they endured, but hers weren't. She loved Gavin. Because of that caring, she freely chose to endure his cultural ideas of men's and women's roles in order to be near him and to hold the family together.

Coping quietly with his histrionics might make her stronger, she thought. The question that loomed into her consciousness at that moment startled her. *But would it make her safe?* Her behaviors, however quietly pursued, would, undoubtedly, create great conflict in Gavin because they varied from his own.

She shook her head. Gavin would never escalate to physical violence toward her or their child. *Never!* she thought with a shudder.

Chapter XVII

Mia

Teal slumped on the edge of the hospital bed. She was alone in the room. Down the hall she could hear someone's baby cry. Hers? She drew a deep breath and looked about her. Her eyes fastened on the corner that joined the ceiling. It was a place where parts met and formed a vortex of sorts. She had let go of disappointment in her marriage and made room for the joy that this child brought.

I wasn't realistic about the pastoral life, she thought. *I imagined the life poets praised with perfect rain and sun and a ruddy-cheeked family living the abundant and rustic life of the Ray Swains.* For their little acre had been abundant. But there had been the lower living costs in town and her father's lucrative employment.

Moody pessimist that Gavin was, perhaps he only felt happy when he believed that God and the government were out to get him. She had just begun to understand that the agricultural life survived or died on a large volume of crop, land, and cattle and on reinvesting in the same, a proposition that didn't allow for giving up under economic stress or for requiring the comforts of home—not yet, maybe never.

Much of farm-family togetherness vanished into the changing picture of farmers' nine-to-five jobs that started their eighteen-hour days and of children who left the farm for more lucrative careers, like the farmers' wives who took jobs in town to help pay bills.

Her head throbbed. Gavin wanted his own home. He spent hours at night pouring over and developing plans for it. Now and then, he shared a thought with her.

"What price, prosperity to Gavin?" she muttered. She bet after the run for land, hope had given joy to some—not this stress. There had been almost forty years before drought, depression, and dust. Harlin and Rena Lily knew joy. Teal recognized it in them.

Down the hall the child kept screaming. Then the sounds seemed closer until the nurse stepped inside her room, a squirming infant in her arms. Steadily, Teal looked at them, the scene more real to her than anything she'd ever seen or thought about. She had a real baby of her own, Mia Emerald Rush.

"He's hungry," the nurse said brightly.

"She," Teal corrected.

"Ohhhh. A little girl. How sweet," she said as she moved nearer. "Just prop yourself back on those pillows. You are nursing, aren't you? I have that straight?"

"Yes." She had decided that before the birth. It didn't seem a thing to undecide now.

Teal looked at Mia Emerald, thin and bald, her skin peeling. She touched her cheek with the tip of a finger. It felt cool and waxy to her. The infant's warmth barely reached her through the blankets.

"What have you named her?"

Teal wanted her to go away. "Mia Emerald."

"I love to see a baby nurse," she said, then hurriedly glanced at her watch.

"Well, I'll be back in half an hour for her. Have fun."

Teal watched her go, then looked down at Mia, who already squirmed and nuzzled, searching for the nipple. Teal shoved the thin fabric of her gown down from her breast and moved her closer. Mia's pink lips brushed the waiting nipple. Teal's breasts were distended with the milk. Soon, her little mouth opened for the breast. Teal smiled as Mia grabbed hold, her small fist kneading against the fullness of flesh that comforted and fed.

Teal circled her arms more closely about her. Little smacking sounds surrounded them as the first colostrum rushed down. Joy rushed Teal like rain down a canyon. She leaned her face against Mia's bald head.

She pushed aside the blankets to examine her more closely as she nursed. "You're so lovely," she said. "And just look at those long skinny feet." But she touched them lovingly, lifted each to examine every little toe.

"I suppose," Teal told her, "that I must keep this bald-headed baby."

Yet inside, she knew that this child pleased her in every way. She was a strong child, fine-boned, alert, and responsive. *Aggressive too,* Teal thought with a smile, for now she nursed greedily. "You'll have hair soon enough, and plumpness too."

She heard a knock at the door and glanced up to see Jenny. "Better close the door behind you," Teal said.

"What's the No Visitors on the door?"

Teal smiled and pointed at Mia. Jenny's glance followed and she sighed "Oh," then closed the door for privacy and moved nearer to see the child at Teal's breast. "What did you name her? It says Baby Girl on her basket."

"Mia Emerald."

"Mia Rush," Jenny echoed. "I'll call her Mia. Both Teal and Emerald is too much green for me."

Teal leaned to kiss the top of Mia's head. "Emerald, like spring wheat fields," she said.

Jenny threw the fur piece over her shoulder. She never stored them, summer, winter, spring, or fall. "Furs are to be worn for show more than warmth," she told Teal once. "Whoever saw a fur out of fashion?" She opened a huge leather tote bag and drew out Emerald's gift. "Something for a child who needs *everything*," she said a bit mockingly.

Teal couldn't care. She laughed outright and took the narrow box and lifted the lid. There, nestled on soft cotton, lay a silver spoon.

"You may be right, Jenny," she said.

"You were always Father's favorite," Jenny kept on.

"The job at the mill?"

"The partnership."

"Weren't you asked? Weren't all the others asked?" Jenny almost yelped.

"Now, Teal. *Really*! Who are you trying to kid, kiddo!"

Teal replaced the lid on the box. "I don't understand."

"Well, it's easy really, and it's all right because it has to be. That doesn't mean I won't raise hell, honey. Charles too. You can get ready for it.

"Mom and Dad figure you need it the most, and they're right from the looks of things. You're living in a dump, and now you've got a baby you can't afford. Let's face it, kid, *you* married a farmer and *we've* got the price to pay just like we did when you were born weighing *less* as if *more* had to be punished. '*Everything* will go back to land and barns until he has volume—can't make it without volume,' Charles says."

"I beg your pardon, Jenny. Don't call our home a dump. A house and a home are not necessarily the same! And Harlin and Gavin are building volume. They've taken on more leased acres this year besides what they purchased last year at auction."

"Don't you try to infer that *we* don't have a home!" Jenny snapped back, then pursued her justification for what Teal presumed to be plain old green jealousy.

"Tad's away looking at wheat in Central Europe, and Jonsi's in agricultural research at OSU. Both are busy and don't seem to care. Tell you the truth, Charles and me have enough to do, but fair's fair. We're coming in for part interest. You can just tell Daddy that when you see him. Tell him we'll be seeing him at the next employee meeting, and we'll have our lawyer there with us."

"Why don't you tell him. He'd probably do what you ask without all that."

"I already tried that, Teal honey. He told me that when he was dead was soon enough for my share."

Teal thought she must have heard wrong. This Ray Swain that Jenny knew, she'd never known.

"You're his favorite, Teal. Didn't you know that?"

Teal still held her baby by a man who had turned on her when times turned. She looked at this sister whose tone spilled acid, then at the small orange-colored cardboard box that held the silver spoon inside, Mia's gift from her aunt Jenny. Would Jenny love this child, or should she protect Mia from this hate?

"Jenny, you and Charles lack for nothing. I'm *glad* for that. You know Mama's glad for it."

"Thank you for nothing," she said.

"I'll talk to father, of course," Teal said.

"Aren't you cool," Jenny responded, her glance not wavering.

"No. But I know what I want. What I want is as important as what you want. I can't change Ray Swain or you and Charles or Gavin, but I can accept a gift I want and count my cost as I go. You're not to plan on my trying to be in a partnership with you after today. Perhaps I would have yesterday before I saw this resentment that you've let override your humanity, or maybe I will down the years ahead. Situations change. We can rely on that from what I've seen of life so far. Your hate for me is your problem, Jenny, not mine."

Jenny stared at her. A stunned expression crossed her eyes as if she were either seeing herself, Teal, or both of them differently. Then her expression gave way to the more familiar arrogant glance. She grabbed up the fur and pulled it close. The fox head fell down her right breast as if to eat it. The thought repelled, and Teal looked away.

"Tad's in Europe to select wheat strains for grafts at the research station. He says the Danne wheat needs a shorter, stronger stalk to withstand Oklahoma wind. That's his dream." Her voice had changed to conversational as if she hoped to leave on a more charming note.

—

"Charles says it would sure speed up harvest. He has to combine like a snail to lift up the bent stalks that the wind lays on the ground. Too much grain shatters from the heads and lies in the field instead of going in the bin when he goes very fast."

"I didn't know. I thought Tad was in Europe to celebrate his doctorate. I hope," Teal said, "that he or Jonsi will find a job in policy making for ag research. Silence lay between them momentarily. "What do you want, Jenny?" Teal asked abruptly. "What did you really come here for today?"

"My fair share." She spaced the words like three-four-rhythm musical notes. "I never got it when we were kids, but I'm gonna have it now."

"You'll have it. I haven't lived very long, but I've noticed that life's fair. I noticed it when I planted corn like it was supposed to be planted and took care of it until it stalked."

"What do you mean?"

"I mean that I get corn when I know what I'm supposed to do and then do it, and I don't when I don't."

"I don't understand."

"I know you don't."

"Well, I'm going. Charles is expecting me. It's dance club night in Oklahoma City."

"Will you tell the nurse for me that Mia's finished?"

"Sure." And she was gone. Abruptly, her head appeared again around the corner of the door, those black curls coifed and her amazing blue eyes sparkling the way Teal remembered them from childhood. "Jonsi says he'll miss you at his graduation. It's summa cum laude, you know. He keeps his job at the university research station the moment he graduates—with a promotion, of course, because he will be Dr. Jonsi Rush. He has more travel plans abroad for study, all kinds of wonderful opportunities. Got a message for him?"

"Tell him I'll be in touch, and congratulations." She had his graduation announcements, and Tad had visited before leaving for Europe. But Teal knew Jenny needed to feel herself their brothers' emissary. Older than Teal, she always assumed the role. Teal felt it probably helped her cope with wounded pride when any of her siblings benefitted from their parents in any way before her. To Jenny, age alone seemed her qualifier.

"Will do," she quipped cheerily. Teal didn't see her again. Instead, the nurse returned shortly thereafter and took Mia back to her basket in the nursery. Teal slept.

She dreamed of the bridge again. Instead of swimming under it, there was a great wind all around it pushing at her car, but she held it firmly on the road. When she thought that she could make it safely across, an air pocket pulled her past resistance and plunged her through the concrete siding into space, unknown and unpredictable space, with the churning waters below rushing to swallow her.

She wakened in a cold sweat. Black night surrounded her like the watery depths she escaped. She felt disoriented, unaware of where she was for a moment before remembering that she lay in a hospital bed. If Gavin had come to see her, he'd not wakened her before nightfall. She lay staring at the shadowed ceiling shapes that her imagination created there. She reached to shift the miniblind slats at her window. The blinking neon across the street dotted the double-window shades with red and yellow. The dots changed as lights and shadows changed with the passing automobiles outside. Harlin left to locate him across the river where he built a new road with the crew; Rena stayed with her.

The life force that either arranged or changed things without her direction and offered her choices every waking moment, never slept. That was what the bridge dream meant. Unknowns. Choosing. Always the choosing. It only stopped when she slept. Becoming entirely real would require her to embrace unknowns as if making friends with the dark, she thought, and darkness never survived light. The thought empowered her. Her fear of unknowns felt transformed to raw energy. She turned upon her side to reach for a drink of water from the bedside table.

A slight stir in the corner of the room as if someone shifted their position in a chair arrested her attention. While trying to make some shape of the shadows there, she heard a deep sigh.

"Gavin?"

He stirred.

"Is that you, Gavin?"

He wakened fully then and moved his chair up close to her bed.

"You were sleeping, so I let you," he said. He switched on the bedside lamp and a pale glow illuminated his face.

"I wish you'd wakened me. Did you see Mia?"

"And what if I hadn't liked that name?" He bent to kiss her forehead.

"Do you? You said you did before when I asked you?"

"Yes. If you gave it to her." He seemed to have forgotten that they talked about names. One of his preoccupied times, she supposed.

Teal was silent for a moment. His intensities were as great as his distances and preoccupations. She moved her hand toward his and held it. His strong fingers caught hers so tightly she thought he might crush them.

"Oh, Teal," he said. The distress in his voice alarmed her. "The baby? Everything's all right, isn't it?"

"Oh, yes," she assured him. Then Teal heard a sob catch in his throat. The feeling she'd seen in him in their beginning now overwhelmed him. She had no notion what to say or do in this new situation, so she waited quietly.

"I thought you might die. For what seemed the longest time of my life, while that baby was being born and I was trying to get here, I thought—I cried like a child." He sounded bewildered by his behavior as if he didn't understand why he cared. "I'm sorry it took so long for me to get here. We're clearing blackjacks almost thirty miles south of here."

She didn't want to hear it. His inconsistencies stretched her nerves to the snapping point. Who was he? How was she supposed to feel

—

262

according to Gavin? No longer vulnerable to his manipulations, she chose objectivity.

"Birthing is familiar to you. It's a good time."

"It's not the same," he persisted adamantly.

"Oh, I know, but things almost never go wrong anymore."

"I know. I didn't understand it either," he confessed.

"Everything's all right now," she assured.

"But I don't ever want you to go through that again, Teal."

"But I want children."

"I couldn't stand it."

"*You* couldn't stand it."

"Shhh," he urged. "The nurse will be in. They gave me permission to stay, and I don't want them to change their minds."

"I had no real trouble, Gavin. Do you hear me? I don't know what you thought or what you heard, but—"

"It was your yelling. Mom said you carried on like you were in terrible pain."

"Of course I yelled. That didn't mean anything. You'd have yelled too."

"I don't want us to talk about it now. We have us a baby."

He had a way of getting his way dishonestly, she thought. What a performance. His charm at the prom dance—a performance? He had a real capacity for caring, all right. Gavin, Gavin—only Gavin. No room for her or for children.

And she, where had she been? *Stagestruck,* she thought. "I'm sorry, Gavin," she said. "I had a vision of you, the farm, our family. I'm just now seeing it with all its ups and downs, its human frailties, the lines I couldn't write, the part I haven't played well."

Teal pulled free of his grip.

Gavin said nothing. His expression betrayed nothing in the room's pale light.

Did she imagine that he manipulated this reality by faking grief at her pain to prevent ever having another? If he cared about her pain, how could he inflict emotional pain so often and so brutally?

If he adored this child, why was he saying "This is it. No more children?"

Silence again lay between them while her mind searched for answers. Perhaps he resented the cost of children. He might want land, not a family. Since she rarely got straight answers when she asked straight questions of him, she smiled and waited.

"I can't say things as well as you, Teal. But I'm here." He said. "Watch what I do, not what I say or don't say," he seemed to relay once more.

"Will the insurance cover the bill?" she probed.

"I don't know. Some of it probably."

"It's the money, isn't it?" she asked at last, her impatience winning despite her desire for harmony.

He moved away, back to the corner of the room. "Go back to sleep, Teal," he said, closing the subject. "I thought you would be glad to see me."

If she had misunderstood, misjudged; it was too late. Her impatience gave him the opportunity to twist her question and play the victim. She had asked about money, and money had become unmentionable since the crop failure. Consequently, the lack of it made its acquisition supremely important to Gavin. She felt an extraordinary fatigue and slept soundly until 3:00 a.m. when the nurse brought Mia back to her.

Gavin had gone.

If I'm to be happy, if we're to be happy, it's one day at a time with gratitude for it, she decided. Wasn't everything good for something—in time, in some way, large or small? Still, she wondered if Gavin were rich, would he be less fearful of living or just greedier? After they returned Mia to the nursery, she slept fitfully until dawn when her tray arrived.

She looked at her breakfast of one poached egg, dry toast, and prunes.

"Thank you, Lord," she said aloud. She thought that gratitude for prunes and dry toast a gallant beginning for her changed approach to living.

Chapter XVIII

The Boss

After Mia's birth, it seemed to Teal that the time raced by. She hired a housekeeper and sitter, Mrs. Jenkins, a widow who lived a few miles from them and whose only fault was an incurable nosiness. It kept her off Teal's party line until she returned home, and Teal and Gavin advantaged themselves of that fact with their personal calls.

She felt both challenged and pleased by her new responsibilities at the mill. The millers, bakers, truckers, and chemists all recognized her authority before she did. "That truck's overloaded, and you know it, Ted," was all she had to say, and Ted never overloaded again.

Ray Swain gave her a hard glance during the middle of her winnowing of the rule breakers.

"I want you to stop that, Teal."

"The weigh station will change its hours some evening, Dad, and you'll have the devil to pay."

"I know what I'm doing. It's not honest to prevent a man his living and force this ungodly expansion on me. We need the grain out!"

She ignored his exaggeration. "The expansion is a good thing—natural growth, improved productivity. You started it. Why stop now? I think we should add fertilizer," she said. "Survival is in diversification *and* expansion."

"Fertilizer!" he bellowed. "Are you serious?"

Teal held her ground. "I'm serious. It's increasing production, and our area farmers and ranchers are going all the way to Houston for 5-10-5."

"Not enough of them."

"The feed and seed store will stock it if we don't. Am I a partner or a bookkeeper, Dad?"

Ray looked at her. "We're borrowed to the limit here."

"I know that. I keep the books, remember?"

"Any suggestions?"

"Check out Houston, see if we can get the supply from there. I'd like to do it."

"Take it no farther than another fifty thousand. It's costing us two dollars and twenty cents to mill one bushel of wheat now. I can truck it out heavy at no more than ten cents extra a bushel, save a little on the gas."

He paused deliberately, but Teal did not defend her position on the trucks. She wanted legal runs. Already Chicago complained about more trucks instead of hoppers coming their way. Teal expected a weight scandal to break any day and force more wheat onto rail. The rates would do worse than kill their profit; it would create more debt and prevent more necessary expansion.

If fuel went up, trucking rates could exceed rail's. They had no guarantees. It made no sense for them to turn down the Texas mills' orders for grain by truck or the truckers who were willing to pay two thirty a bushel just to haul it to Houston. Such deals didn't resolve expenses, but they helped. The way Teal figured it, when everybody started fertilizing and production shot up from Kansas to Nebraska, Chicago would have its wheat.

The price of wheat at that moment was two twelve in Kansas with a base of two dollars here. It would cost them thirty-three cents more to get it to Chicago—not make them money. No question about it, they had to truck it to the coast.

—

"We're fighting for our life, Teal. There's mills closing all over Oklahoma now. There's some that think Oklahoma farmers should just as well throw in the towel on fifteen-bushel-to-the-acre wheat. Farmers need thirty-five or forty bushel to the acre. We all know Washington won't allow both surplus *and* a fair price. More consumers vote than the farmers who operate wheat farms or elevators and mills. They won't pay a fair price for bread without complaint or product boycott.

"Jenny said just yesterday that Charles was considering selling out to developers. They're both disgusted at having to go north with their combines to realize a decent profit. You and Gavin are working for salary so your ag business can grow, Teal. Makes no sense. Worse, the public thinks farmers get free rides with government payments when they see expensive equipment, pickups, and cars."

"Most of those are bought with mortgaged land loans," Teal said. "Land owners will lose their farms if they're not more frugal. I'd rather see Gavin and Harlin invest in more land than more equipment."

"More land takes more equipment," Ray defended.

"Or more time in the field with less of it," Teal argued. "*We're* not going under. We're going to sell fertilizer and buy more trucks of our own, and we're going to offer sorghum in our feed. We'll buy every kind of feed and hay and grain, and we'll sell it all back to them for more when it's mixed and bagged with our label. Our milling and trucking are already stable. But we can diversify the bakery products more."

"Teal."

"We've got it to do. You know it too. These are things that will pay back, Dad, not use up like a bigger house or car."

"Can *you* stand the pressure?" he asked. "Sometimes just the elevator and the milling are more trouble than a body can stand, especially when storms or ice short out the electricity, and there's problems with the backup generators."

"Are we or aren't we?" she persisted.

"Going to diversify? You know we are," he assured. "But allow for a larger generator. Maybe two of them for power backup."

"Fifty thousand will do it if we clean out that long metal shed back of the feed mill. We'll have to doze us a road up to it. Some crushed rock under chat will hold the trucks in wet weather."

Ray unwrapped a cigar without looking at her. "Think the boys at the feed mill can clean it up?"

"I'll go down and get them started on it after I make some calls to Houston," she said.

"You're gonna fly down, aren't you?"

"I've never flown."

"Time you did."

"Time we got us wire service in here too, then," she said. "I want to know the price without calling other elevators. Those calls take time that I don't have."

"I've been thinking along those lines myself," he said.

Teal thought about the 1960's increased energy needs and costs. Even a penny-an-hour increase in energy could affect a farmer's storage, for they offered the storage and handling of wheat for about two-and-one-half cents a bushel a month. They cleaned wheat and ground hulls and hay. They ran the feed bins to feed mixers and fueled trucks. They had to keep all the stored grain stirred and moved. If bills were this high now, what would they be in ten or twenty years? Unless the price of grain went up, how could producers afford to raise it or store it?

She wanted that marketing machine so that their customers could stare at that wire service. Price knowledge would get them in and keep them coming back because the best thing that could happen to them was to know exactly where they were by the price placed on their product at any time of the day. Then they could sell at the best price for it. When they did it, other elevators would provide the service too, but she knew the effects of being first as well.

Ray Swain stuck the cigar in his mouth and rolled it from one side to the other before he spoke. "I just as well get a hot plate and a supply of coffee too, reckon?"

She smiled at him. Then they laughed together. When she had made her calls for the necessary appointments in Houston, Teal headed straight for the old metal shed.

"Josh," she called.

Josh was the oldest of the mill's crew. Small and wiry, Josh could get into the tightest and toughest spots to make repairs or to free a stuck breaker to keep products and conveyors moving. Teal looked up at the equipment that bore the coarse grains to the exact bins and then on to the huge mixer after being chopped or ground.

"Yes, Mrs. Rush," he answered. Josh rarely called her Teal; none of the help did, and she hadn't encouraged a change. Josh had been with them the longest. She remembered him from her childhood when she came up to be with her father. She had introduced enough today for her father to consider. She'd save suggesting they raise Josh's pay for another day.

"We're moving in fertilizer, Josh. I'll be needing some help cleaning out the machine shed. It's junk mostly. I'll need a truck, several strong hands, and about six hours. Think you can get those for me?"

Josh looked at the thinning line of trucks.

"No more orders tonight for feed unless they come in without calling. Be about half an hour."

"I'll be down there getting started," she said.

"Huh," he responded. It sounded like a smirk to Teal. She dignified it with a glance, then gave her gloves a tug. She didn't wear denim to work. She wore pantsuits mostly. Today, she wore a bright orange jacket over khaki pants and an animal print blouse. She resorted to a ponytail and bangs for an easy hairstyle. It saved time.

She wore denim in the summer when she was needed to move up trucks or move them out of the way. Often she helped shovel the grain through steel slats to enormous traps beneath the elevators. It took everybody on the payroll most of the summer to just contain the wheat. Nobody ever pretended that they could control it.

"Pass the word along, would you, Josh? I'll be needing a few more hands to handle it, to sell, and to keep the records. I'll post openings on the information bulletin board. I'll need someone in charge for a percentage of the gross if it works out the way I think. They should apply for each position. If not filled in-house, I'll have to advertise."

She gave him a quick look and saw the sharp lift of his jaw, the glint that came to his eyes. He was interested all right. She tossed him a quick smile and walked on with a spring in her step.

Josh would be thinking of that managerial position, of a potential raise in pay. By the time she asked him, his decision would be made. He was certainly bright enough, stout enough, and energetic enough. Besides, he had a personal attractiveness that would help her hold and get customers. There was nothing in Josh to fear and much to admire.

The machine shed was dirty, and the work was hard. Mouse and rat droppings littered the floor. Bird droppings streaked the weathered board walls. Rodent control would be a must here, just as in the elevator areas. She would seal the holes and cracks, monitor the control.

She gathered the pieces of rusted tin roofing, the stray nails and wire and odd pieces of iron into a great pile in the center of the shed. "Rewiring and plumbing installation next," she told her dad.

When night fell, the crew had no light and stopped work.

She felt eagerness for tomorrow. Ideas about how to start, who to call to wire, repair, and equip the facility danced into formal plans. She sponged off the worst of the grime on her in the washroom off the main office and drove home. Her headlights failed to pierce the dense fog. Teal recognized it as the first sure sign of winter. There would be heavy dews now, then frost and ice.

She shivered and turned on the heat. Warmth fanned her legs. Outside the car, the clacking of branches and clicking of the dry autumn leaves announced the wind's change to the north. In a few short weeks, this winter's solstice would arrive. Another year would begin. She would need to finish the fertilizer business plans and get a crew onto them for she had not given up her idea of a sculpting studio.

She longed for a hot tub bath to stretch out in and soak away the muscle soreness. She bet the sides of that tin tub would be cold. She shivered at the thought.

The housekeeper, Mrs. Jenkins, usually left when Gavin arrived home. Teal found him alone at the kitchen table, the low ceiling bulb yellow-lighting the room with its harsh glare. Spread about were the scale drawings and envelopes of checks and receipts. Teal smelled the fresh coffee the moment she opened the door and immediately poured herself a cup and refilled Gavin's empty one.

"Where's Mia?"

"She's asleep," he said. "So I told Mrs. Jenkins she could leave. I hope you don't mind. She wouldn't eat—too tired, I guess. I'm planning our house."

"We'll have a house?"

"Our new house."

"You can't be serious. The farm—"

"Look, Teal, what I did with cattle. I knew it last week, and I've been thinking on this all this week. I'm not waiting as long as Mom and Dad did to build *our* house."

She looked at the cash receipts book. "A hundred and eighteen thousand," she gushed. Gavin had cleared over $50,000 on his steer investment.

She sat across from him, her mind trying to grasp their good fortune.

"Speculating on the cattle market will earn us still more. Buying and selling back. I've got a nose for it. I'm sure of it."

Teal still studied the long yellow sheet from the commission company. "My god," she said.

"Yeah. What'd I tell you?"

"You buying back? These cattle are some kind of miracle. Dry-wheat pastures and sparse wheat, but you fattened them anyway."

"Reject candy from the OKC factory helped most."

"Only you would have thought of it." She smiled warmly then, his gaze telling her he appreciated her response.

"Sure, but you don't buy back the same thing. That's where you make mistakes. I'm buying back stocker cows because they'll calve, then I'll sell them fast as they wean their young. Fatten the young on winter wheat and pellets and sell them and buy back the steers again for spring grass. It'll work right now because the market is good. But I'm going to back it up with a small feedlot of my own. I can do it with my cotton money. I'll buy scrap lumber, cut posts, and do the work myself. It will only take a long lean-to for feed, stanchions, rail corrals, and an arena."

"Oh, the cotton," she gasped. "How could I have forgotten?"

"We gotta get it out of there," he said.

"When?"

"Not before tomorrow." He laughed. "Not much of it survived the dry weather anyway. No more cotton. Can't get the pickers anymore for the relief checks coming in."

"Work's too hard," Teal said.

Suddenly, Gavin lay down the papers and walked around to her. Slowly he pulled her to her feet. "I've been a fool, a childish fool. It will work. All of it will work if I waste no chance and use my head doing it. It wasn't your fault, Teal, none of it. Life oughta go on in spite of everything—anything. Why, I'm gonna build you a house like you never saw on our own farm. I made a mistake here that I don't ever want to remember."

"I like this house. Why, you and Harlin made all the repairs yourself. Why can't we remodel, rewire, rock, whatever we want—you want."

She pled with him. "I'm a selfish person, Gavin. You know that. I don't want to give up anything."

"But this house sits on an Indian lease. It's not ours or Dad's really. We've only had the use of it."

Teal just looked at him.

"I don't want to give up this place."

"Well, I do," he said, letting go of her. "It's old."

"I'm tired, she said. Can we talk about it later?"

"I want you to look at the plans now," he insisted. "I want you to be happy about it. I want it for you! You never want what I've got to give you. You're always wanting something different," he accused.

The remark stunned her. *How horrible for him if he actually believed that*, she thought. She bet he griped until it was built and then blamed her if money trouble returned. He felt good because cattle prices were good. When they weren't, what then? With interest rates at 15 %, that money would gain enough interest for Mia's college.

"You've a right," she said, turning to put the kettle on for her bath. "Build it then. And, Gavin, I want a big bathtub in it."

"That all you care about, a bathtub?"

He sounded incredulous. "No. I want an extra room for a nursery, so there's plenty of space for another baby if we decide on it." She looked at him again after she'd turned the burner on. The flame leaped blue like petals about the edges of the kettle. Gavin didn't respond.

"Will you make the extra room?"

"Sure I will. I'll put anything in it you want, Teal. Anything. I've been obsessed with government sanctions, imports, and embargos to keep countries under control and consumers happy while they subsidize us to keep us on the string. I'd given up on actual profit until I saw the possibility with cattle.

"That's when I decided we should grab something for ourselves with this chance profit. We're in the government's pocket. They'll vote in or vote out whatever serves a political lever for *them*, not us. We're the people as surely as the consumer or the perceived enemy is the people. But we're the bottom rung because they don't know yet that agriculture is a science and costly and because we're only 5 percent of the population now. Most haven't realized that agriculture built Oklahoma before that first oil derrick. They haven't learned that any old patch of ground they plow up anywhere in the world won't grow hard red-winter wheat for bread."

For a fleeting moment, Teal saw his softness and vulnerability, the man behind those ocean-blue eyes who could open all kinds of possibilities for them. But she no longer trusted it. He had made her the brunt of his stress once, and he would again. Gavin coped by kicking someone or something. Still, she loved this rare glimpse of what he felt, what he thought about. This was the man she loved. It was the first time that she had thought of him as two people in one skin.

"I'm glad," she said, not moving any nearer to him. Then he turned back to his papers, sat down before them, and began again to push the pencil back and forth across the page in long columns of figures.

Teal finished her bath and went on to bed long before he quit counting the dollars down the months and years. Toward morning she wakened with a start for Mia cried out in the night. When Teal went to her, she felt feverish. The lymph nodes on either side of her throat had begun to swell.

She lifted her over her shoulder, but her breathing remained labored.

Teal made the tent of steam that Esther had relied on for them all. It saw them through all sorts of chest congestions, but it didn't help Mia. Her throat appeared quite swollen.

Mia's fever soared to 103°, then to 105°. Her tiny body jerked spontaneously. Teal crushed ice for plastic bags that she wrapped in soft towels and laid around her. She bathed her with rubbing alcohol.

When nothing helped, she wakened Gavin from a deep sleep. "Mia is very ill," she told him. "We must get her to the hospital."

Gavin rose and dressed.

"It's so cold out. Suppose a doctor would come here?"

"We could try. We can call and ask what to do. Nothing I've done seems to help her." Even as she spoke, Teal placed Mia back under the tent made of old sheeting where the vaporizer bubbled and steamed. "You call Dr. Eber for me. If we're to take her out of doors, she'll need to be dry and wrapped in blankets. If we are to stay, I'll leave her in the steam."

"It hasn't helped?"

"No."

"Then why are you still doing it?"

"I don't know what else to do."

"You had her in the ice a moment ago."

"I know. But ice won't help her breathe. It will only help keep the fever down."

"And the steam won't help the fever. It may only help her breathe. An antibiotic might do both," he said.

Gavin left them to phone. When he returned to Teal, he looked distraught. "He can't see her, he's had a heart attack."

Teal gasped. "Oh my, no," she said, her voice breaking. She couldn't cry. She must act. There was something she must do, but she felt too tired to think. "Try Dr. Speely. He's with the Valley Clinic. He might remember giving me an emergency tetanus booster a few years ago. They're so odd now. If they don't know you, they don't want to see you. If he can't see her, Gavin, we should just take her to the hospital emergency room. She feels hotter than before to me. I'm scared, really scared."

Gavin ran his fingers through his rumpled brown hair.

"He'll be here," he told her a few minutes later. "He'll bring penicillin. He said to tell you that he would."

"Oh, thank God," Teal said. Then she let go of the tears. She took Mia from the tent again, bathed her in tepid water this time, then wrapped her loosely in a blanket. *Such a little thing to be so sick,* she thought, *only a little more than a year old.*

She rocked her for a while, giving her ice water to sip at intervals when she asked for it. She dared not give her milk, though it seemed to Teal that the fever burned her plumpness off her bones before her very eyes. Again she bathed her in the tepid water. She put an ice pack at the back of her neck and at her temples again. At last Dr. Speely came.

"I'll give her a slow-acting but double dose of penicillin. She'll be on the mend by this time tomorrow, I promise you," he said. He was of medium build with medium brown hair and medium weight, but nothing about him seemed medium to Teal. He was human, someone who acted for the well-being of another. He seemed a marvel, a miracle in the middle of mediocrity and ineptness. For by 1956, no doctors came to the house as they had before. Large hospitals were built twenty to fifty miles away, and one could die during a long emergency room wait, often more than four hours in Oklahoma City.

"Thank you," she murmured over and over. "You're the last of a special breed."

"Surely you don't mean I'm an antique," he said with a chuckle.

"You're a tall man in *every* way," she said, looking up at strong but lined features graced by thick white hair.

He snapped the bag closed. "The temperature will be low-grade by tomorrow, gone the day after. That throat looks like strep—risky business. You were wise to call."

Teal held Mia until dawn when her fever broke. Then she laid her back in her crib with a light cover and in dry clothing. Both of them slept longer than Gavin the next day. She wakened to the scent of coffee and the sound of Mia's raspy breathing, but it was steady and deep, and her color looked normal. Teal touched her forehead. It felt cool.

She called the mill and spoke with Josh. She gave him the authority to select the electrician and the carpenter for repairs. "Select some basic secondhand furniture for a small space at the end. Just a file cabinet and a desk, that's all."

"Will do," he said, "but I'll want the okay from you."

"You can get that," she said. "And, Josh, I'm staying home today. Call you tomorrow." She put down the receiver, thinking that if

Josh handled this as well as she thought he could, he had the job as manager of the fertilizer sales. As for the rest of the long shed, she'd need it for storage. She would add more storage next year if their sacked blend sold the way she thought it would. As for the liquid fertilizer, she would need to invest in outdoor tanks for that.

She delayed her trip to Houston for several days so that she could oversee Mia's diet. She wanted to make certain she ate nutritious and healing foods. Between making chicken noodle soup, pureed carrots and peaches, and pushing fluids, she began arranging her art studio. Teal rolled the crib close to each work area.

By afternoon, Mia's alertness returned, and by the following morning, her bright responses and laughter cheered Teal. Nevertheless, Teal remained home to care for her for several more days. Tears sprang to her eyes when she saw Gavin bending over Mia and pulling up the flannel blanket. "You're our precious little pumpkin," he murmured. "We couldn't bear to lose you." Then he bent his head and kissed her.

Those rare moments of tenderness surprised and thrilled her. She felt they revealed his best nature, perhaps his truest nature. Like the bright flare that lights the sky above a stranded victim, such scenes gave her hope for a possible constancy in his personality when he reached his full manhood.

"Depends on the obstacles life throws at him and the choices he makes in those dire times," Esther said when Teal told her about these better times. "'Course, the choices we make in good times mean plenty too. But yes, it's encouraging."

—

Chapter XIX

Joseph Danne

Late evening several days later and the day before Teal's flight to Houston, Mia played on the screened porch. It was one of those Indian-summer days that come between the small northerners until autumn peaks just days before fall, the winter close behind.

While dragging in the heavy sacks of clay mix and forms, she heard a car pull into the drive. She intended to take the supplies to the studio later. Her corduroy trousers and shirt felt warm for such work. She shoved damp hair off her brow and squinted against the sun to see Jonsi crawling out of a new Thunderbird.

"Jonsi!" she cried and ran smack into him rushing to her. He hugged her tightly about the waist and whirled her around and around.

"Where's that niece of mine. I've never even seen her, and Mom tells me she's been sick."

"She's right here, and she's much better now. She's getting some sunshine today." Teal tugged his hand toward the porch, feeling more like a girl than she'd felt in days. "Isn't she beautiful?"

"Beautiful like her mother," he said.

"Oh, you sweet silly. I'm so glad to see you." Jonsi opened the screen door, and Mia toddled toward him with a step or two, then dropped to the porch floor and crawled the rest of the distance.

"She loves me already," he said with a big smile. His sun-bleached hair looked platinum, and his brown eyes warmed with natural affection at the sight of Mia. Teal hugged him again as he lifted Mia in his arms.

"Come in," she urged. "I've chocolate cake and cold milk, just like you like."

"Ho, ho," he responded and followed directly behind her, still carrying Mia.

"Just set her in her chair," Teal instructed. "I'll get her a bowl of pudding to eat while we talk."

"What did I interrupt outside?" he asked, sitting down at the kitchen table. So Teal told him about her new interests. When they'd talked about the mill and his school and Jonsi had finished two huge slices of the cake, he said, "I've a selfish purpose for coming here today, though I did want to see you and Mia."

"I figured that," Teal said. "It has something to do with this local farmer, Joseph Danne, I'll bet."

"That's right. We probably won't have his documentation for years. I believe he'll leave them for our research when he dies."

"Won't that be soon enough?"

"You're impatient too, Teal," he said, as if that justified his eagerness for the research.

"We have that in common, all right," she teased. "But I don't know him, Jonsi. Nobody really knows him. He's almost a recluse."

"He's a man obsessed with a dream, the dream of feeding a hungry world. That kind of obsession takes time. He can't lollygag around on Saturday afternoons shooting the breeze or—"

"All right, all right. I get the message, but I'm saying that I don't know how I can help you."

"I don't know how you can either with an attitude like that."

He rose as if irritated and stalked a short path back and forth behind the chair he'd just vacated. His short hair flopped boyishly on his forehead as he abruptly turned toward her. "Look, I'm not asking you to win the world for me at a raffle or anything like that. I just want you to walk up to the man's farm with me, say something like,

'Hey, I live down the road from you. Would you like a glass of my plum jelly I made last summer?' Something like that. Anything!"

He threw his hands out in exasperation. Mia, who'd been happily guzzling a sippy cup of milk, began to cry.

"He's sorry, baby. Aren't you, Jonsi?" She soothed Mia while she scolded Jonsi with her tone. She dampened a small cloth and wiped pudding off Mia's chubby face and hands. Mia displayed none of the lethargy of illness now.

"Okay. I get the idea. But don't blame me if it doesn't work. What is this anyway?"

"I intend to play dumb, ask dumb questions. But dammit, Teal, I've heard about that house. Tad has too. He's doing grafts on kitchen surfaces. They say he has test patches that have finally yielded enough seed to plant local fields that produced fifty bushel to the acre where they either irrigated or got rain. Do you know what that could eventually mean?" His face flushed with excitement. "Less work on less ground for greater increase. We have a mushrooming world population. Over half of it is hungry."

"What can you tell by looking?"

"Why, the size of the grain, of the stalk—the height and hardness. I might even recognize the strains he's crossing. He keeps improving his Triumph seed. Who the hell knows, but I've a sharp eye. I know what to look for, and I know what causes wheat to look like it looks. I'm not looking to duplicate his work. I'm just anxious to know about it. Science often builds something still better on past breakthroughs. This man has made a huge breakthrough in food production in a most remarkable and inspirational way. Millions thrown at sophisticated labs often accomplish much less, even with PhDs at the helm."

Teal shook her head. "I've looked at a lot of ours myself. I know when it's got a good kernel, when it's got the right hardness for storing. I know about how much sun or rain it's had by its color. But what you're saying is that this man has done this miracle in his kitchen and his backyard?"

Teal stopped. She didn't even know how to go on.

—

"You're in the marketing, sis. I'm in the developing, right where the grain's created. Like God. Yes, this man is living a spartan life and devoting it to God's work—food supply."

"Jonsi! That's sacrilegious!"

"Like God," he repeated.

He almost took her breath away with the look on his face.

"That's what God does with people: He makes us better. He directs us into meaningful lives. I wish there were more time to talk about it. I need to do it. Now, sis."

"Right now? I don't want Mia out in the evening air. It's too soon." So she called Mrs. Jenkins while Jonsi paced, eager to examine the Danne grafts.

"I'm glad you called," Mrs. Jenkins said. "She needs to stay out of the wind for sure." And she bent over, picked Mia up, and hugged her in her plump arms. Mia laughed out loud.

Then with a box filled with six pints of sand-plum jelly, Teal and Jonsi headed for the Danne farm. They saw Mr. Danne as they pulled into the long dirt lane that led to a boxy-frame house in need of paint. He unhitched a team of horses from his drill.

"Takes longer to sow 80 acres this way. Longer still, 160."

"How many acres do you farm?" Jonsi asked pointedly.

"Three hundred, when I'm lucky. Luck's been back now for about eighteen years."

Jonsi whistled. "That's a lot of work multiplied by years and hands-on labor."

To Teal's right and to her left, small plots were staked off with shaped sticks. Cellulose bonnets were fastened on various stalks of wheat. Each plot had labeled wooden stakes. The plots appeared to be in various stages. Some plots were only turned-over stubble while others sprouted green. Still others appeared to be freshly sown or in a preparation state, but some of the grain heads neared maturity, a stage called the dough stage.

Teal understood the nature of wheat—had to in order to store it profitably. Not-ripe-enough or too-moist wheat would spoil the whole lot of stored grain. Ripe wheat grains "clicked" when rolled in the palm and worked between the teeth.

The first frost would damage some samples, leave others undisturbed. "I'll collect those soon," Mr. Danne said as if he read Teal's thoughts. "I'll seed prepared plots this fall with them." She watched Jonsi, who wore a puzzled expression.

"What is all this?" Jonsi asked, contriving a bland expression.

Teal grimaced. Mr. Danne wasn't a stupid person, she thought. *Jonsi should level with him.*

"Just what is it that you want?" Mr. Danne asked.

"Want?" Jonsi asked as if affronted by the suggestion. "Must I want something?"

Teal stuck the box toward him. "Jelly. I'm a neighbor who's come to meet you and bring you a neighborly gift."

"Sand plum?"

"That's right," Teal said, smiling now and feeling encouraged by his interest.

"Made plenty of my own this past July."

"Oh," she said, genuinely disappointed. She liked him. She thought his observation about Jonsi deserved an honest response. She'd come here to please Jonsi because she wanted him to have whatever he wanted. She loved Jonsi even above Tad and Jenny. She couldn't explain it.

Slowly, Teal drew the box of jelly back. She looked from Jonsi to Mr. Danne, hoping one of them would forward this conversation. "You should go ahead and tell him, Jonsi," Teal said on impulse. She'd not meant to do it, but she wasn't sorry. She nervously waited for Jonsi's response, expecting an angry one.

He looked at her, his expression saying he reassessed his situation.

"Thanks, Teal," he responded. "I didn't know if you would be open to a college snob, Mr. Danne. I'm awed by your accomplishment and in research myself. I keep hearing on campus about a strain of wheat you've introduced to your own fields that's greatly improved."

"Almost half of Oklahoma farms are planted to Triumph now," he stated as if Jonsi should know that.

Teal relaxed.

Mr. Danne remained silent, then started the team toward the barn.

"Yes. Well, I find it the most . . . the most exhilarating discovery of the century, sir," Jonsi persisted, following close behind. "If what I've heard is true and what we believe about world population growth is true, you're providing hope for the world's hungry."

He unharnessed the team and stored the riggings. "I'll water them when they cool down. Could I offer you a cool drink?" their host asked, turning toward the cistern. Jonsi and Teal still followed the farmer's lead. He drew down a dipper that hung from a hook on a nearby tree, then pumped a cool drink from the ground tank.

"No, thank you," Jonsi said, but Teal moved nearer and waited without speaking. Before drinking himself, Mr. Danne offered the dipper, but her arms were full of the wild sand-plum jelly. She knew Mr. Danne was considering Jonsi's conversation before responding. *Others have approached him in the past, most likely,* Teal thought, *to steal his research. He might not trust us.*

"I'll swap for it," he said, the slightest smile brightening his glance. "Yours looks some clearer than mine." He took the jelly, and she took the dipper.

"Probably because you smash some of the pulp into the juice," she said.

"I reckon that's so," he said. He looked at her so straight and seeing that Teal's glance slid away from his to the water in the gray-granite cup she lifted.

She drank and handed it back.

"Sweet, isn't it?" he said.

"Yes. I use it myself."

"Do you, now? I figured such a modern young couple as yourselves would be drilling you a well and piping the water."

"You know Gavin, do you, Mr. Danne?" Jonsi asked.

—

"Since he was a little boy. Gavin Rush wasn't borned where his folks live now. He was borned up on the highway during the WPA days when they were building Route 66."

"Was he?" Teal exclaimed.

"Truth is, he lived and worked all over this county, him and his pa. Lots of land won't buy much these days. Dry—too dry. Can't even grow corn anymore without irrigating. They worked their own ground and hired out to work for others during harvest and haying and round ups.

"That Gavin helped build these roads plumb through the rock and red clay. When he was hardly out of the cradle, I saw him operating a tractor. He was no more than six years old." Suddenly, Danne raised a right arm as if alarmed.

"Watch where you're steppin' there, son. The first good cross I got came from one straggly but surviving seedling, number C7H. You never know what's going to give you the best results until all the growing's done. It's the same with people. To oversimplify, I did crossing with Blackhull, Kanrid, their hybrids, and a hybrid with Burbank until I secured complex hybrids. Planted the kernels in 1926, got encouraging results in '27.

"I taught myself wheat breeding and genetics, studied Burbank's work."

Teal greatly admired him. He was one of those rarely recognized heroes who changed the world for the better; the builders as opposed to the destroyers or leeches. "Seed from the same lot will give you same results, won't it?" she asked.

"No," Jonsi answered before Mr. Danne could, "that's the surprise. And even though you never know why a plant is sturdier or fuller kernelled or higher in protein, you take it and plant that seed and cross the best, and then out-of-the-blue you've got some predictable results from a line of seed."

"Or which will ripen first—a good attribute in Oklahoma. Much depends on your soil and rain," Danne added.

"Depends on that for sure," Jonsi affirmed.

Teal hardly recognized this zealot as her brother. *He sure chose the right work,* she thought.

"I don't often do this, and I'm not giving out more details of this work until I'm good and ready. I'm gratified to see fields of Triumph and forty-bushel-to-the-acre crops. I don't mind sharing the seed for more research either. I'm doing that already." He chuckled a little. "I can use the extra income from it. Besides, I want to see my wheat growing as far as I can see, as far as I can travel before I die. I will. I'll live to see it cover the aerable land here in Oklahoma's wheat belt and, hopefully, know it's helping the hungry of the world."

"It might cover the world, Mr. Danne, in one cross or another," Jonsi said.

"You see that, do you?"

"I see it. Your farm's an experiment station as surely as I'm standing here. You've achieved the stature of Burbank. Why, the world hunger everybody's been up in arms over, the population explosion that Malthus predicts, this quarrel over whether to clear more acres for production frightens everybody. Too much clearing without knowledge of conservation methods like terraces and contour plowing brought the dust. Bread is the food staple in homes all over the world."

Mr. Danne had turned toward a small rock walk that led up to several wooden porch steps. Teal noticed that a huge white Persian cat sharpened its claws on one of the porch posts. "True enough," he agreed. "Sloped land needs terracing, hills need to stay in pasture. There's already been harm to the land. Topsoil's been washed away or blown away. This land was new. It was Indian land." He clucked his tongue. "A lot of it still is. There's a few roads that still need to be cut through it on the other side of the south river. There's machines now that can do it. But what it needs is care, not more breaking out."

"Hard black clay and rock, but mostly blackjack timber as thick as snakes across the river," Jonsi said. "There's the ravines that the river cut before they brought it under control with Texas dams.

That's the south river. 'Cross the divide, that bottomland is as fine as any in the world."

"Yonder's the north river, dammed too, at Canton," Danne added.

"The divide?" Teal questioned.

"Sure. This land's got its high point so the water can divide, some to the South Canadian river, some to the North Canadian. That establishes a lot of an area's wealth or poverty. There's wealth here still, but not realized since the dusters because my wheat isn't over all of it yet. Triumph's right for this land. With the land Gavin and Harlin have, this wheat will finally prosper them in the good years when the weather cooperates and insects and molds let it be. I want to develop a blight-resistant breed."

Teal shaded her eyes and looked toward the high ridge to their north. She knew he meant that tender stage when the young sprout stools and tries to gain height and is as vulnerable as a bird leaving a nest or an infant about to be born. She craved to look at all this land, to see the routes of the water, to follow the canyons to the twin rivers, those to the south and those to the north.

"This is a rich valley between these rivers," she said at last.

Mr. Danne nodded appreciation for her remark. "More than that: there's a natural form of irrigation here that these creeks and hills provide. It's a powerful land, a land with an intelligence and a need to increase so bold that the damming of it is like the necessary reining up of a spirited thoroughbred."

Jonsi cleared his throat as if embarrassed by such poetry from a farmer. "I'll level with you, Mr. Danne. I want to see your seedlings. I'm not asking you to divulge your method or your results. None of the statistics."

"Then come in. I'll show you plots of plantings later. They're outside in specific areas. For all I know, all of the documentation will fall into your hands. You're in research, aren't you?"

"Yes, sir. For a fact, I am."

"He's Dr. Jonsi Swain, Mr. Danne," Teal said proudly.

"Swain, Swain. Related to Ray Swain of Valley Grain?"

—

"His second boy, sir."

"I store my own grain," Danne said. "I raise my own food too. You're blessed with education. Mine stopped at the eighth grade."

"From what I've heard, eighth grade then was more than some colleges now," Jonsi said.

Joseph Danne's smile was his only response.

"I noticed you use no tractor," Jonsi said.

"No. I don't. I use horses or mules. They don't take diesel or propane."

Teal looked around. A bachelor lived here, no doubt about that. It was clean enough, but cluttered. Unavoidably, she saw his note keeping stacked almost everywhere. Mason jars of grain samples with labels pasted on the outside crowded every available space and corner. She bet his cellar held still more.

"I don't mind telling you that I've worked hard. Like I said, it was in the '20s that I got the first Triumph. That's what I call it, Triumph wheat because it had a shorter sturdier straw that would take wind and wet weather better, and it had a dark gold grain that was high in protein. It didn't shatter as bad in Oklahoma wind. The foliage made fine pasture too. It raised my yield seven bushel to the acre the first year that I planted enough acres to tell. Took a long time to get seed enough, took seven years from one plant to get seed enough. Super Triumph is an improvement," he explained. "It ripens a mite sooner with a hardier, larger, more vigorous seed."

"You had a dream," Teal said.

"I worked."

Teal smiled. She'd been right about him. He wasn't a man that just sat and talked about a thing. Probably spent no time dreaming, actually. Mr. Danne planned, then acted, then analyzed before adjusting his plan and starting over. The conviction solidified back of her breastbone that action and dreams must partner with each other and with patience and persistence for the achievement of goals. "You wouldn't give up," she concluded.

He chuckled. "Often, I thought I'd get something different than what I got. I had to let go of what I thought. I even had to let go of what I found sometimes and just go on."

"It will go on and on," Jonsi surmised. "There will be constant improvement related to certain conditions that will produce a variety of new wheat strains."

"You might have a job for a long time, young man."

Jonsi grinned. "Yes, sir."

"Government pays you to do it?"

Jonsi stopped grinning. Teal felt she could read his thoughts for they were her own. Nobody had paid Mr. Danne. Mr. Danne had sacrificed what most other people in this world worked to have. He had no observable material blessing, no wife and children. Perhaps he never had. Relationships weren't a thing to ask about. Obviously no woman in the house supplied anything for him, and no machine helped outside.

Nothing they had seen except his own appreciation for his life and nights of deserved sleep could bring this man comfort.

"I have my faith. I want for nothing," he said as if he read her mind.

Teal looked from Jonsi, dressed in slacks and a sports shirt, to Mr. Danne, dressed in twill trousers and a sweat-circled gray twill shirt. He wore a short-brimmed fabric hat, dusty around the band. "You've a great regard for life, I'd say," she told Danne.

"That and agriculture. Agriculture is a road to economic growth here or anywhere," he said. "It's building Oklahoma despite its desperate climate and political struggles. It is and will be the foundation of growth that will continue to build Oklahoma. It and petroleum."

The blunt words of the realist complimented the poet in him that she had seen earlier.

"These two, wheat and petroleum, will draw business and industry here," he finished. "Cattle and milk production too, later on when the farm economy improves and folks can afford those investments."

"Improved wheat will increase production enough to supply the increase in population indefinitely," Teal observed. "Particularly if a reasonable surplus plan is effected that doesn't depress prices and discourage growers."

"If industry respects the land and preserves more than it covers in concrete," Danne observed. "But a reserved grain plan *will* depress a natural supply-and-demand commodity market. Plenty is needed, fair price is needed, but both are as fickle as nature itself."

"Thirty to fifty bushel an acre and better quality withal," Jonsi verified. "Farmers need the price of production plus price supports from Uncle Sam so folks can have food priced as low as possible. Everyone copes with gradual inflation. The consumer can't remain exempt forever."

"I'm stocking fertilizer today here," Teal said. "The farmers will buy it because wheat's two dollars a bushel. Their only immediate answer for higher yield is to fertilize. They have already complied with conservation techniques. They are progressive, Mr. Danne. Few are stuck in the past. They want to learn about conservation and ag science."

"Those I talk with are eager to improve their crops with your wheat," Jonsi added. "They do need a higher price for it though," he grumbled.

"They need newer tractors and combines to make their work easier. The dirt and sun exposure destroys their lungs and damages their skin. Too much machinery is worn out now. The answer is volume and storage until exports improve and the price goes up," he concluded. "It takes them all day and some of their nights to get the job done now.

"They have families," Mr. Danne, Jonsi said apologetically. "They *have* to work off the land for enough increase to support them. They *must* rely on machinery to yield them the extra time off the land for jobs."

"All you say is true but one thing. It'll take longer than ten years for all the people who need this wheat to have it," Danne said. "Oklahoma will be the second highest hard-winter wheat source

---

in the whole world before that happens due to government's trade agreements."

"Unless there's more embargos," Jonsi interrupted.

"Still, the day will come when food won't be used to lever power," Mr. Danne persisted, "because of world hunger and population. Maybe the day will come when Chicago doesn't set the price! Maybe the farmer will. Might be good, might be worse, unless and until there's better trade information available to each farmer."

"Wheat pastures cattle in winter for my sisters and their husband's ag operations. They say their bushels per acre are just as good if they take them off the growing early," Jonsi said.

Teal nodded agreement. "The Fort Reno Research Station proved that," she said.

"Some men are like boys, and the new equipment like their toys—costly," Mr. Danne said. "Unnecessary equipment can cost them their land itself, become self-defeating. That's the big pitfall today, wanting a hard job to be easier, to look easier and profitable to their neighbors." Deep lines at the corners of his eyes told of years in the sun.

Teal knew that such exposure to the elements could be costly as well, but she said nothing, for this man's years were now numbered. His generation would soon pass. She felt that farming would always be a challenging job regardless of better everything. Mr. Danne had his straw hat; Gavin had his air-conditioned tractor. The dependence on nature, on politics, and on economics would make farming a challenge whether the work itself did or not. Perhaps government's role in agriculture would become more progressive and creative as well. Weren't the USDA's conservation programs an example of that?

"Governments are quarrelsome, and economics can't be controlled no more than wheat," Danne continued. "More than thirty years, I'd say, for *actual* prosperity. It can take that long for growth to be stable. It has to be slow. Trade barriers need to drop. Ah," he sighed, as if discouraged by the choices of humans in the arena of prosperity versus greed and politics.

"Often, survival seems from the Lord," he concluded. "Men can make a potentially great gain impossible with politics, greed, or careless habits."

Teal stretched her mind to follow his words for she had gotten past really seeing the land for the first time to realizing it as a living, motivating, providing force in economics, politics, business, and life. She hadn't seen it as a player on the world's stage. Her own purely business enterprise now connected her to the land between these rivers in her consciousness and to the absolute value of wheat as power, sustenance, and a huge economic resource. Today's experience generated a new passion in her for the land.

Teal thought that the land seemed a utility to most farmers, not something to cherish. She sensed that she would sound quite foolish talking to them about it as a thing to love as they might love a woman or that responsibility and devotion to it, when driven by love, would cause it to flourish.

"Let's go now, Jonsi," she said abruptly. She turned to Mr. Danne. "Thank you. I feel more like I've been to church than I've felt in a long time."

He only smiled and thrust a jar of wheat seed toward Jonsi when Jonsi reached to shake his hand. "Take a sample of this back to your university lab with you, Dr. Swain. See what you can come up with before I do to deter wheat rust in the wet springs."

"I accept the challenge. Do you know, sir, what the odds were of your getting Triumph? They were one in one hundred thousand, sir."

"I was lucky from the start."

"You have a gift."

"I always cared about growing things. I always took note of their differences and of their likenesses. I'm curious too. What ifs have always motivated me. But most importantly, I worked long hard days and grateful for the opportunity to do so."

"I'll remember that, sir."

Mr. Danne walked with them to their car, muttering that he needed to water his horses and mules. Jonsi turned back toward the swarthy, lanky, and aging man. "You're a genius!" he called. Mr. Danne's hand shot up to wave them off.

"Kansas produces the most hard winter wheat for bread," she whispered to Jonsi. "We're second to them."

Jonsi chuckled. "He probably knows that," he said.

Chapter XX

Complications

They returned to the farm in silence. That night, after Jonsi had gone back to the university and Gavin and Teal sat at their supper table with Mia beside them in her high chair, Teal told Gavin about their visit to the Danne farm.

"He didn't tell you how he let me watch him graft new strains?"

Teal dropped the spoon she held and stared at him.

"OSU, Stillwater finally recognized his work publicly last year," he told her. "He didn't hire much done, and he didn't have a baler. But he hired me each summer to help swath and barn his hay that he fed to his horses and his cow. When I finished, he'd always call me up for a drink of his water. He's proud of that cistern. He built it, the house, and all the outbuildings himself. Then when it was cool, he'd light a kerosene lamp, and with a battery-lighted microscope he'd rigged himself and that pair of tweezers, he did the grafting."

"A pair of tweezers? He grafted with plain old tweezers?"

Gavin laughed. "Imagine the expensive equipment in grain research laboratories in comparison."

"But it's needed."

"'Course it is. That's not the point. The point is how work and a vision of what can be sometimes accomplishes what money and education never could without a special kind of dedication. That's how I intend to build a thousand acres from this one one-hundred-sixty-acre quarter. We need the volume—a lot of land to provide the increase for the good life without so much debt. Debt makes young men old and bitter."

"It's simpler than that. Jonsi said that it's plain acting on a good idea. That man isn't lazy!" Teal said. "Still, it takes a person who believes just as strongly in himself. Mr. Danne surely had skeptics criticizing his efforts, perhaps even making fun of his methods."

"That's right. They did, but they don't anymore, not since they saw that last thirty-five bushel to the acre harvest of rust-resistant wheat he had. That shut them up. And don't think I don't have ideas for some shortcuts to prosperity. He's hoping for both high production and rust resistance in his future grafts."

"What do you mean shortcuts? Share your ideas with me. Maybe I can help with more than just dollars."

"Don't pick my brain. Stay out of it," he snapped.

Teal's thought turned aside to her own life. She no longer wanted to hammer her way inside his closures. She had heard her art teacher say that an artist must be selective about brushes, water, pigment, and paper or canvas. But her artist friend who actually produced works that sold had told her she could use river water and a board, whatever she had that would work. He had said a good painting sprang from perspective, color, practice, and a good idea.

"Consider Van Gogh," he'd said. "Never sold a painting. Painted what he wanted the way he wanted. Painted most of his works in only a day, two at the most. He surely valued and loved each day. Those paintings sell for millions. But even better than the money, his life had meaning until that terrible day that he died."

Mia banged her spoon, and applesauce flew against the side of the refrigerator and dripped down. Teal laughed. "I don't want the refrigerator painted with applesauce," she said, moving to clean it off. She wiped Mia's face and helped her finish her food. "Jonsi called it a gift," she said. "I believe creative ability is a gift, but I believe everyone has it, plus the ability to recognize their achievement. Getting there by abusive means betrays both the lives it touches and any meaning for the creator. Someone like Danne reaps limitless rewards for himself and for others. His personal sacrifice, his purpose, his honest methods reveal such integrity."

She recalled the spark that came into Jonsi's eyes when *he recognized* certain things about those plants. "Some people can see a shape in marble or in wood and can take the material right off down to just that shape," Teal said. "I think Jonsi recognized progressive improvement in those grain grafts today. Maybe even how to achieve it."

Gavin looked at her oddly. "I can't admire his poverty."

"That's probably what you meant, Gavin, by a vision of what can be. Your shortcut ideas, I mean," she said, ignoring his remark about Mr. Danne's poverty for now. "I've always thought that some abstract art took a shortcut to the idea it represented."

"I guess that's what I meant," he said.

But he didn't sound as excited about her art as he had about Joseph Danne's new wheat or his own planned shortcuts. He sounded embarrassed. She instinctively felt that her remarks about abusive means *pushed one of his buttons*, as Sylvia had suggested relative to his abrupt mood changes. Yet instead of anger, she sensed the concealment of more than a simple need for privacy.

"You're that way about raising crops, about building roads and bridges. I've seen that in you, Gavin. I have," she persisted, hoping to brighten his mood. "It's there, that vision of what can be. I believe more in the goal than in shortcuts. A worthwhile goal can take two lifetimes, more than that even."

Gavin shrugged. "I believe in prosperity," he said, his lively responsive mood escaping into his shadowy self. "Prosperity is my goal, but I can't make rain." He got up then and went in the other room.

Teal lifted Mia from her high chair to wash her face. *Creativity gifted everyone in the form right for them,* she thought, *when they graciously accepted the gift.* "Made in God's image indeed," she said aloud, thinking of her father's vision for business, her mother's for new garments from her own patterns, her own for milled grain's end products and for art. There were no actual shortcuts, just better ideas or more effort unless one used unorthodox means.

Gavin's vision of empire must be his own with whatever shortcuts he chose, for he excluded her. Still, Teal felt no one could escape the costs; every choice had its price. Would he also exclude her from the rewards of success? Authentic effort from herself and the help of God was the only success kit Teal knew. She craved success for sharing with her crew and all her family—even the community.

Much later when she lay down in their bed beside him, Gavin spoke into the dark. "He never seemed to care much for anybody. He lives there alone. Rumor has it he gives his money away. You figure it, living with nothing."

"Prosperity means different things to different people." She paused. "Some people live alone in the same house with another person," she said.

A long silence lay between them. "I mean, I never heard him mention the need for anybody or for anything," he repeated.

"Everybody wants something from others at some time. Help, if nothing else," she said. "Perhaps he never had a want he couldn't either supply or do without. That's all. It seems to me he gave up a lot to do what he's done. I think he'd have to care an awful lot about all people to do that."

"I always thought he didn't trust others, that he felt they would steal his ideas and waste his time," Gavin said. "He's tried to patent his Triumph unsuccessfully. Felt he wasn't treated right, I heard."

Teal was quiet for she felt certain Gavin's own honesty rested in that remark. He might think of her as *his* outsider because of suspicion—fear that disallowed her insider privileges. She was city, and he was country. Every farmer had to sell, store, or buy something from Ray Swain, her father. Did they resent that or appreciate it? She longed to be more than the stranger to him that she seemed to be.

"Sometimes I feel that you don't trust me, Gavin," she ventured.

"That you think of me as an outsider to you and Harlin and Rena Lily." Teal hoped he would reassure her that they were one in his mind and heart before she gave up entirely on the possibility.

He said nothing but reached for her. She yielded to feelings she hadn't known before as if to fill the void she felt. She closed her eyes and allowed sensation without words. Feeling alone spilled over into life sounds of breaths and cries. Teal pushed her wet face against his. Gavin reached to wipe the tears away with his rough hand as before.

This physical closeness seemed the bandage on a sore that would not heal. Until she accepted her exclusion from the fabric of his life, she would not rid herself of this emotional vacuum her own activities had not filled. Esther had told her that sex pleased the man, and women suffered through it. She supposed her mother had either lied, felt guilty about her pleasure, or didn't know everything about it. For these times of physical union with him made all else tolerable.

"I'll focus on building our family," she told him. "I never mean to pry." Even as she spoke, she agonized over what felt like games that pulled her close then pushed her away. These uncertainties and her coping schemes warred against the oneness she craved. She despised the emotional pain when her natural affection resisted becoming a mere function called sex.

Change my mind, change my life, she thought, giving up resistance. She chose that night no longer to care whether Gavin truly loved her with any reliable constancy. The important thing, she decided, was the constancy of her own affection for him. Because she equated mutual trust and confidence with love, she made love's contract with herself and it instead of with Gavin, for he seemed to have deserted her.

She had already accepted the possibility of duty without martyrdom; now she accepted the idea of pleasure without mutual love.

—

I shall love him enough for both of us, she determined, believing that a possibility. *Besides, this thinking that he doesn't really love me feels neurotic.*

She shook her shoulders as if to sling neurosis off.

She'd begun to think of his behaviors as modes of manipulation rather than symptoms of a lack of love. She missed the authentic personality traits she'd known at home with her family and believed that Gavin could lose his real self that way, for he manipulated others also. He cajoled, ingratiated, charmed in order to use them for labor, for credit, for cash. She would rein in her feelings and take control of her pleasure and her pain, she determined. How could she blame him for what he could not or would not feel? In that way, she employed detachment from her passion for him. Her love for him became cerebral.

Teal caught the early flight to Houston the next morning. Gavin drove her to the airport. She hadn't thought that it would be this difficult to leave him for a few days. She sought the sight of him from the windows until they'd left the runway. What was it that she thought she would lose in this short separation?

She forced away thoughts of him to concentrate on the new banking interests and loan arrangements.

"How long will it be, then, before we see you?" she asked the representative, Damon Childress, after their first conference in Houston.

"The verifications we need can be completed in a few days. I don't foresee any problems. You've placed your confidence in us, and we'll certainly try to help you."

Teal knew that these expenses could be absorbed by the fertilizer profits or she wouldn't risk so much. She needed the warehouse and the bulk supply, the liquid nitrogen, and the tanks. One year's profits should return the investment.

The moment she entered the fertilizer business, she would attract competition.

They would do these same things, perhaps even make fertilizer their *only* business. She would need to invest in advertising, invent incentives to coax customers in and hold them.

"You take a chance with me, and we'll both profit," she told Childress. When this investment begins to pay, I'll want planes or access to that product delivery option if more economical for my increase or my customers. It makes sense to begin flight service for insect control, for certain fertilization possibilities, and even for transport of some bakery items."

"The records of Swain Elevator, Mill, and Grain are sound. But we'll see about those things when the time arrives, Mrs. Rush. You can always contract a spraying business, save yourself the cost of planes."

"I'll remind you that we discussed it someday," she responded. "We're a bakery too, remember." Teal thought in terms of satellite businesses for her progeny's economic future. She wasn't unaware of the chronic inflation eating at the American dollar like nibbling mice. Teal believed that diversification, like insurance, would compensate slumps in one or more areas. *I will never rely on one aspect only of this business, rely on others rather than myself to meet schedules, or expand too rapidly and lose control,* she thought.

He laughed a low laugh as she turned those thoughts over in her mind. The patronizing response arrested her attention. Dressed in the latest fashion, he looked immaculate from his trained sideburns to his filed fingernails.

Did she amuse him? She squared her shoulders, quite aware of her own split nails and of her hair in less than fashionable disarray. Standing in her neat pin-striped suit, she tucked a strand of wayward auburn locks back into the chic french roll. As if she required his assurance, he patted her shoulder.

"Now, now. All is in order. There's no cause for concern. We'll take a look at your business. I'll phone you when the board approves the loan. I look forward to this relationship," he said, rubbing her arm before releasing it. He locked his hands behind him and began to rock back and forth on his toes.

"Thank you," Teal said agreeably despite her aversion to his manner and, particularly, to his touch. She began pulling on her gloves as she moved toward the door, relieved to be on her way home. She'd begun to hail a taxi to the airport when one of the bank's limousines pulled up. The driver quickly reached her to assist her inside.

"The airport?" the driver asked.

"Yes, please."

He was a young man. *Probably a college youngster earning extra tuition money,* she thought as the glass dividing them automatically closed. It was the first time she'd ever felt less than something. She didn't like it. She felt small town begging money from a big-town financier who seemed to be testing (or cultivating) her vulnerability.

She pressed her lips together in firm decision. "I'm going to make a lot of money, so much money that I'll never have to ask for it from anybody, ever again." They'd ask her for it, banks included. With a jaunty twist of her neck, she watched the traffic fly past them. Then she gave herself a smart shake as if to sling off false pride.

"I'll more likely be in debt the rest of my life," she muttered, recalling that he said *when* we approve the loan—not *if.*

Damon Childress would not get credit for this vision. This vision of prosperity grew for Mia and for the grandchildren and great-grandchildren in her future. It had less to do with money and more to do with people whom she wanted to know God, to acquire knowledge, and whom she hoped that Swain businesses would shelter from any future economic downturns. If she could, she would protect them from her grave and pray for God to do the same.

A plane lifted into the air. Then as the limousine entered the terminal, she saw that another passenger plane landed. That's what businesses and huge corporations in this country did. They lifted and they landed. They expanded and they exploded, and every time an old one bit the dust, a new one soared. In her own lifetime, a mere twenty-three years, Teal had witnessed the rise and the demise of huge corporations and of small businesses. She'd seen others grow, like Swain's Valley Mill and Elevator.

She'd studied it from every angle, and the answer seemed simple. You had to have something to sell that people wanted and would want or need for a long time. You had to diversify, not put your eggs in one basket, or you'd go broke. And you had to be willing to take risks, to expand and experiment. Customers and efficient and prompt transport were a given.

She must trust herself and her customers, believe she had an eye for business and people, the same eye as Danne had for arriving at Triumph wheat, and the same eye as Gavin had for seeing a thousand acres in his future. Swain's would grow or change, whichever was needed or both. Teal knew she'd never close the doors unless she had to; quitting wasn't a choice. *But I won't live forever,* she reminded herself grimly, her mind already attempting to strategize the event of her death and the assured survival of Swain's should Ray be gone also.

She was going to put Swain Elevators from here to Chicago and points south and east, wherever they raised anything that needed storing and feeding. She wanted Swain Grain to become as familiar a name as Betty Crocker.

She exited the limousine and boarded her plane, but her mind was years ahead of the present: twenty-five years. That's how long it took Mr. Danne to get lucky with his grafts and both arrive at and distribute a significantly superior grain. She'd be forty-eight years old, and Ray Swain would be retired. Oh, she couldn't bear his retirement; fewer hours perhaps, but never gone.

Already she felt eager for the expansion. Perhaps she'd own an elevator chain much sooner than twenty-five years from now. *Perhaps in only ten years,* she thought. She would have help, she reminded herself. She could work twice as hard, learn to delegate more. Wouldn't three elevators be a chain? She leaned her head back and closed her eyes. She'd give herself ten years. If Jenny dared interfere, she'd make certain that she earned the right.

From now on, if Jenny wanted a voice in anything, she'd work for it. She'd get dirty and grow calluses. That ought to put a stop to any interference. She leaned her head back for a little nap. She felt quite fresh when she walked down the ramp toward Gavin.

At the sight of him, all thoughts of business dropped off her, and she quickened her step to greet him. He grabbed her to him just as eagerly. As if force would meld them, he kissed her hard, his iron embrace taking her breath away for a moment.

"Oh, I missed you," she told him breathily when he let her go.

"I missed you," he said. "And so did Mia."

"Is she all right?"

"She's fine."

"Everything went well, I think. We'll know for sure in a few days."

"I may as well tell you, Teal. It's probably better that it's me instead of your father." Gavin guided her toward their car as he talked, her tote swinging at his side.

At the car, he tossed it inside before he finished. "Jenny's raising hell. She's furious that you're expanding without the board's okay—"

"We've no formal board that *must* make these decisions," Teal interrupted.

"That's the problem. She's bringing in lawyers."

"She hasn't a leg to stand on. We're not *required* to have a board."

"She's family, and she's older. She's yelling blood and human rights and verbal promises and all sorts of things. Esther thinks she's got a good chance of screwing things up."

"Mother didn't say that."

"No. She said, 'Jenny's jealous, and she's gonna take it out on Teal because that's who she always took it out on. She's scared to death Teal will be richer than she is. She's never quit counting those oranges.'"

"I never knew."

"Mothers know that kind of thing."

—

"Did she tell you about the oranges? Blast her, worrying so over a preemie?"

"Yeah, but I think it's something else. I think it's a backlash from feeling unimportant to Charles, for the homesteading Huels thinking they're so goddamned much."

"Gavin!"

"Well, they do. They make a out of that first family in the valley garbage—"

"I wish you wouldn't talk like that. Your thinking it doesn't make it so." The look he gave her turned her unease to stone.

"It's the truth. I don't know how to say it nicer. Maybe you ought to figure some way for her to come into the business."

"Dammit, Gavin, I won't. I swear I won't. Jenny's the most extravagant person I know. I don't want her messing up my work until there's so much profit and cost success, she couldn't possibly screw things up totally. But I have been trying to figure a way for her to earn a voice in decisions. She doesn't like work, so it won't be easy. Someone else cleans her house. Someone else cares for the yard. Then there's her cook."

"You want my advice?"

"No."

"Well, I'm giving it to you anyway. Watch out for Charles Huel. He's back of this, Teal. Jenny's following his advice. I'll bet on either Charles's advice or intimidation."

Teal turned slowly and looked at him.

"Why?"

"He's wanting an easier way to make a living, and cream off the top of a good business is easy money for him. He's not going north next year. You've probably heard. And he's bought a lot of expensive equipment to make his farming comfortable and fast. I've heard he's playing the futures. There's no way he could have paid for all the equipment easily with today's market so depressed. Combines and tractors like that can set you back a quarter of a mil."

"Mortgaged his land," she said, realizing that Gavin was on to something. "Possibly to gamble instead of work. He's on the downside of thirty-five. Been in those fields night and day for twenty years."

"Probably playing the futures in hope of faster money."

"Could that be checked? There's always risk with futures."

"Wouldn't be easy. That sort of thing is supposed to be confidential."

"Suppose he's also out at the poker parties?"

"Coffee shop bunch says he's there too, but Jenny's not with him."

"Well, I want to know before she calls that special meeting. Perhaps a formal board with her on it would appease her. Who's her lawyer?"

"Heath."

The name hit her like shrapnel. Her whole body stiffened at the stunning news.

"He's just opened his new office as I understand it, also running for the Senate when he's only held office as mayor for a year.

"His main job now is with a corporation specialist's law firm according to Jenny. He has both an office assistant and a legal assistant that he can delegate to while he climbs the political ladder."

"I'll talk to Jenny," Teal resolved, "the moment I get home."

"You'll have no problem locating her. She's sworn she's going to talk to you. Watch out for her, Teal. She's fighting for her marriage. The quality of life she enjoys and her public image may seem threatened by you and even by Charles. She possibly feels put down, whether she is or not. Perhaps rivalry's the oldest sibling syndrome."

"Does being family authorize membership in corporations, or is it investment of self, of effort, and time? What about experience? Something. Jenny thinks that Swain blood should get her in instead of effort or an invitation. Blood's nothing when it betrays as an enemy would. Betrayal puts a family member on the outside as a natural result unless amends are made with a believable apology."

"There's people who don't believe that, Teal. Everyone doesn't look at things just the way you do. If you have a fault, it's that. You can't always see in time what somebody else is seeing. Jenny may be a threat, but don't write her off as your enemy too soon and become hers instead."

Something in his tone prompted her to ask, "Are you saying I'm not fair to you in some way?"

"I don't know anymore, Teal. I don't know what I have to give you that you want since our trouble."

She couldn't respond for a moment. She swallowed the lump in her throat. "I'm stunned, Gavin. I thought you didn't need me when you partnered with your dad and seemed so angry at the very sight of me. After that, I believed you married me to avoid the shotgun aspects of marrying Sara Jane, but I thought better of saying it."

"What I've had to give just hasn't been enough," Gavin persisted.

"Money?" He meant the money. He hadn't understood, so he gave up on the marriage. "But I've needed to do my part," she said, feeling frantic. "I thought you had no respect for me, puttering around the garden and kitchen. That day when you cursed me—"

He brushed that aside. "I guess we're different, you and me. Too different. I forgot that right after it happened. I knew I made a mistake, but hell, Teal, who hasn't? Do you know what you're doing with *your* partnership?"

"I'm building my life. You didn't seem to want me in yours—not just there in the field. I want a family, a work. I want a part in things. I want a part in the world. I've a right. What you do is a part—"

"Farming? Who the hell cares?"

"How can you say that, Gavin, when Harlin has carved it out for you? Who's going to unless men like you do? Do you mean that you don't know what you do? I know you love land, covet land, yet it sounds as if you don't respect it. Single-handedly, you raise enough food to feed hundreds of families besides your own. You're in touch with the earth—a link between it and the very lives of whole countries. You surely know that this valley is part of a wheat belt unique in the world. That Canadian County—our county—raises more of hard red for bread than any other. We could ship by truck or rail from fifty to one hundred million bushels of it any year, depending on our weather."

Gavin was quiet the rest of the drive. Teal didn't trust herself to speak. His words had hurt her, partially because she'd recognized them as the truth. Mostly because of his remark about them being different. She didn't always see like someone else; most of the time, in fact. She saw things in dimension with options and variables. There were times, though, that it was to her advantage to understand another's perspective. She sighed. This was a time like that. She thought that Jenny saw no farther than her own nose and that she lived in the moment without regard to consequence. Was she wrong?

She knew that she should use what she saw in this sister to the advantage of Swain Elevators. Manipulation would only waste time. For in the end, the same problem would be there: Jenny's jealousy and false pride. She would talk straight to Jenny—no games. She would be straight with her and take the consequences. Gavin was right; it would be rough.

She hadn't seen this thing happening with Gavin because she hadn't wanted to. Her thoughts turned back to him. "You're like water or air to me, Gavin. I crave being near you. I always enjoy you. Every time with you is like the first time—feelings so strong . . ."

Teal moved closer and stroked his arm. He didn't move it from the steering wheel. Instead, she felt the muscles harden. The thought of losing him turned her knees to rubber. That old urge to hammer her way through his walls erupted again. She wanted to rage at him, to scream that she cared and that he'd been unfair. He *knew* she cared; he *knew* her joy spilled over when they touched. How *could* he discredit her devotion like this?

To give himself a justification for betrayal! her mind screamed, a betrayal in his heart from the start that now strove for satisfaction.

Country tradition said that she was an extension of him, she thought, whose programming he would dictate—not necessarily as mutually desired. Noncompliance with this unknown automatically incurred emotional isolation or her acquiescence.

Or was he at it again? Sly, circumventing the past, inventing a new approach, escalating his game of "I love you, I love you not"? Have I been sucked back into the game? The boundaries of his games and reality had begun to blur.

Thinking that he escalated the emotional abuse, she dropped her hand. Instead of her typical grieved response, she refused to comply.

"I love you Gavin," she said into his silence, then looked out the window.

She needed her mind clear to confront Jenny. Moreover, she would risk his escalations rather than sacrifice the productive life she saw ahead for them both.

"Where is she, do you know?" she asked, changing the subject.

"Jenny?"

"Of course."

"She's at the elevator going over every record and every file that she can get opened."

Sudden rage tempted Teal at that thought. *Jenny could jumble or confuse nothing there,* she reminded herself. Teal knew every storage figure, every inventory figure on sorghum or barley or wheat or oats, on insecticides or pellets—anything. Besides her knack for remembering figures, she had backup copies in another building should storm or fire destroy the office records.

She knew the payroll tally and expense sheet balance against profits as well; they were holding strong. It was a good time for expansion. Due to the poor crops, there had been a lull. Still, storage dollars came in; feed still sold. The bakery thrived. *Still, expansion was the worst time for some leech to milk the company,* she thought.

Jenny, a leech? Teal shook her head as if to shake loose from that involuntary judgment. She couldn't. But a leech didn't have to stay one. Jenny was her sister. She needed to come up with some safe opportunity to offer Jenny, an opportunity for her to prove her actual interest in the company. *God help me,* she prayed, *to hit upon something right for us both before our confrontation.*

"She doesn't have Heath Meriott there with her now, does she?" Teal asked. To use his full name seemed to distance him from her. She needed that distance.

"No. She's scheduled a meeting for tonight though, and he'll be there then. She's arranged it at the Huels'. They've a 'just right' study," he said.

"She thinks her own turf will give her the clout she seeks. What has Dad had to say about all this?

"Oh, he just rolled that cigar around and said he figured it was coming, only he'd thought it might hold for a while. I think he wants you two to work it out."

"If he felt Jenny should be in, he would tell her. He would tell me, and it would be done. He doesn't, or I would know."

"He might change his mind if Jenny handles this well. If you could present something to her that she'd accept as her responsibility to the company, she might calm down. And, Teal, your dad needs to see that you can handle Jenny's aggression. He's bound to have concerns about what will happen when he's gone if you can't."

"I'm willing. I've already thought of that. I'll try. But I won't do it for her. I can't want it for her. She's got to do her own wanting and act on it. People usually wind up with what they want."

"Not everybody, Teal. Just the very strong."

"Everybody. There's always the choice. Always."

"People don't choose poverty or oppression."

"They do. Death may be the alternative, menial jobs, escape to beaches, to communes, or simple acceptance."

"You are spoiled. That's what Jenny keeps saying, and she's right. If you don't see anything else, Teal, for God's sake, see that sometimes people have no choice."

She just looked at him. She didn't believe it. She could only believe what she'd experienced or recognized as truth in some viable way for herself. How she wished she knew why Gavin insisted on

—

this no-choice stance that she saw as a way to rationalize away a lack of personal integrity, dignity, self-respect. If she were dying in spite of all efforts and accepted it, wasn't that a choice?

"I hope you never have to hit that wall, Teal. It's hamburger to the psyche."

"When a flame's too hot, I move, and when I'm cold, I huddle and seek whatever warmth I can find. When I'm hungry, I look for food. I've been lucky. Supply has never been very far away. But I could have given up. A lot of times I could have given up, complained, or run away, any of which would have been a choice. Maybe someday I will. Maybe sometimes I have without knowing I was doing it. But I'll tell you this, if I catch myself at that sort of thing, I'll have no respect for it. I'll have to do something, right or wrong, and take the credit or blame."

Gavin just nodded his head. She didn't know if he understood, agreed, or wanted silence again. She smiled to herself, pleased that they had a real conversation that let her glimpse the way he believed whether they agreed or not.

"She's doing all she knows to do, Teal. That's what I'm wanting you to see."

It was like a curtain lifting for Gavin to say that, and it took away a large chunk of her bitterness toward Jenny. She hadn't thought of Jenny like that.

"You're saying if she sees a better way, she may take it?"

"That's right. Be worth the effort," he said.

"Jenny's bright," she said.

"Of course she is. Maybe there's no reason—not wrongs from the past, not rivalry, and not Charles. Everything doesn't have to have a reason."

"But there is one. It's just that—"

"We who are blind can't always see it?" he finished sarcastically.

"Okay. That's enough. Thanks. I appreciate your help. Really I do," she emphasized. "I was just thinking that perhaps I haven't seen her *real* reason for hostility because of the reasons she's supplied when in her foul mood and those that others believe. I mustn't assume anything but stay open for the reception of new information."

His glance softened a little. She thought he had started to touch her, but he put his hand back on the wheel.

"I'll just check work orders, then we can get home. I'm eager to see Mia before any meeting."

"I've arranged for Mrs. Jenkins to stay with Mia until after the meeting," he assured.

"Thanks for thinking of that. She can get her needed rest that way. Besides, it feels unexpectedly cold. She shouldn't be out in the cold wind."

They approached the office and scales, located about five hundred yards from the elevator. Jenny's blue Cadillac sat parked in the front.

The elevator's large curved cylinders of cement towered beyond them. The office itself was in a native rock that ranged from white to brown in its colors. It was a low rectangular building that they'd roofed in corrugated tin.

Teal was barely inside the door when Jenny walked up to the front counter and slammed the huge ledger down upon it. Two customers sat back of them. Teal supposed they had decided to stick around for the free coffee and show after checking the markets.

"Nice to see you," Teal greeted her acidly.

Critically, Jenny looked her up and down. Her tailored pinstripes compared shabbily to Jenny's brushed suede and high-fashion makeup. Her hair was coifed in the latest cut, and she smelled of expensive cologne. Large diamonds weighted her ring finger, and her nails were long and enameled.

Again, Teal had that ridiculous impulse to hide her hands. Of all the beauty possibilities, Teal wanted beautiful hands. She'd been born with stubby, busy, short-nailed and freckled impossible-to-make-beautiful hands.

"You certainly look the executive," Jenny said. She arched a plucked brow and gave Teal that cool limpid gaze of the arrogant.

"You're looking pampered and kept as usual," Teal responded. She felt tired of being nice.

"Pampered and kept, is it? Visit me sometime, little sister. This is all for show." It was true; Teal hadn't been to see her since before Mia was born. But she didn't believe her. Those hands didn't reveal hard work.

"There's too much wheat in this elevator," Jenny snapped. It's full past capacity. Instead of this wild new venture of yours, you'd do well to build more storage north of here or west."

"I intend to. But we need to increase income here during the year that it's being built. Fertilizer will do that and ensure that new storage is full."

Jenny looked a bit startled as if she'd not expected that response, then forged on.

"This is a lot of money going out in a month. Look, purchases for wheat and corn, for fertilizer and insecticides, for pulleys and—"

"I know. I authorized it all and with Dad's approval."

"I'm not sure his judgment is what it ought to be. He's seventy now."

Teal slammed the ledger closed. "Rather than resort to those tactics," she snapped, "I suggest you address those you've asked to the Huels' with your business proposal and the part you want to play in its success. I intend to have an open mind at the meeting. But the meeting is to be *here*, and I shall have *our* lawyer here as well. We'll settle this objectively and fairly for the good of the company. I would like to move it from a family squabble mode to a business one."

Jenny had yanked her hand back before the ledger could sandwich it. "What you're not saying is you think I've done this for my personal gain, but Charles—"

"Charles has nothing to do with this business," Teal reminded her.

A startled expression sprang to Jenny's face as if she hadn't thought of that. She seemed to back down a little. "Well, I know

—

you're tired, Teal. You haven't even seen Mia in two days, and after she's been so sick and all."

When Teal said nothing more, Jenny brushed past her and out the door. The dust from her Cadillac foamed past the front glass where a trucker pulled onto the scale.

Ray Swain, who had been in his nearby office, answered the phone that had begun to ring. Teal stepped up to weigh the truck.

"Business as usual," Gavin said dryly.

Teal glanced up at him over the weigh ticket, then back at her work.

"Will you wait a few more minutes for me? I want to fill Dad in on the arrangements in Houston before our meeting tonight, *then* we can go home for sure. There are no work orders in the box. Dad's taken good care of things. I so want to see Mia and have dinner with you. Okay?"

"Okay," he said. "I'll be in the car." Despondency colored his tone.

"Would you check on the progress at the warehouse first? Please?"

"Josh in charge?"

"Yes." He seemed pleased that she'd included him, a thing Teal desperately wanted whenever possible.

He went out. She hoped he would bend enough to still do more in this business. But Teal doubted that he'd ever really want in. His feedlot and sale barn occupied most of his free time. Gavin would probably always seek the out of doors, the very physical. He'd almost finished building more lots, corrals, and barns. He looked for more land to buy.

They'd had their dinner and left Mia with Esther before starting back toward the elevator for the meeting with family and lawyers when the first hard northerner struck.

"This is damned icy for early November," Gavin complained. "It wasn't in the forecast." He turned on the wipers, but mushy ice kept falling.

—

"It's odd. I've seen sleet in this county and snow, but this slushy ice isn't either." Serious lightning streaked the navy blue sky. Slush kept falling in great globs, making loud plopping sounds on the metal and glass about them.

"This will be murder if it begins freezing. Even October can be full of early surprises in Oklahoma. I gave Josh so much to do, and Dad was left with the main office. The gates to the feed bins sometimes stick in cold weather. Breakers occasionally need replacing at any time. Someone can always get hurt in this kind of weather because of falls, and cattle always need more feed. I'll bet there's a long line forming right now for feed. This has to be covering pasture fast."

"Don't blame yourself, Teal. If you had been here, the weather would still be like this. I could blame myself. I was here. I could have thought to check and see if your dad needed anything, but I didn't. You need to build a crow's nest over the surface of the feed mill so those gates can't freeze. That would make it safer to work on at that height."

"You're right about that. I'll mention it to Dad. Usually, we're having Indian summer now," she regretted.

"I can't drive any faster."

"Try. I feel awfully worried about it. I wish I'd called Dad before I left the house. There's a crew there, but they expect to be told what to do—most of them."

"It may not be doing this in town," Gavin said. "You know how this part of the country is."

"I hope you're right."

But he wasn't. By the time they got to the elevator, ice had begun to form. The sun had totally set, taking any warmth with it. Light snow had begun to fall as well.

"There won't be electricity anywhere by dawn if this keeps up. Ice will get the lines, probably fell some of them," she noted. "We may need to go to generators."

They crept along the last mile, for their visibility of the road ahead was poor. The taillights of an occasional car helped from time to time. "I can't even follow the tracks," Gavin complained, leaning into the windshield as if that would help him see. "The tracks vanish beneath the snow as quickly as they're made."

"Oh my god. I wonder about the others. They have probably started too or are already there with the problem of getting home safely. It's come in so fast. The temperature must have dropped twenty degrees in less than an hour. Those clouds just looked like regular rain clouds. Who would have guessed."

The last mile was the most intense that Teal had ever traveled. At twenty-five miles an hour, they went into a skid at the company entrance and almost collided with an oncoming vehicle. At last, Gavin righted the automobile and aimed it at the drive.

"I'm so glad you're here," she told him. It wasn't like Gavin to be interested at all in company business, and Teal had never used him as her crutch. She'd not even thought about whether he would be with her or not; it had just seemed right tonight, and he had seemed interested in the meeting's results.

"It's so right that you're here," she finished.

"It feels right to me too," he answered. Neither of them mentioned Heath. Yet she wondered about his influence on Gavin tonight. When he stopped the car, they exchanged grateful glances beneath the glaring yard lights for their safe arrival.

"I'm worried, Gavin. I'm checking things at the feed mill before I come in. You tell the others for me, will you? I'm sure that Josh has things under control, that everything's operating. I won't be long."

"I'll tell them. You go on."

—

Chapter XXI

Tragedy

Teal pushed against the north wind, bits of sleet biting her cheeks as she crossed the mill and elevator yards to the feed mill. She shivered, glad to have the suit jacket on. A light flickered near the ladder to the feed mill's crown. Perhaps she imagined it, she decided, squinting her eyes against the blowing snow that almost blinded her. She stepped carefully for the ground had become slick where no layer of snow covered it.

Teal thought again that she saw a light gleam higher up the feed mill ladder. Then from near the top of the mill's surface, she heard a garbled yell over the howling wind. A voice called back from below as the lantern moved to the top. It swung back and forth like a light will when someone carries it.

"Oh, dear God, no!" she screamed. Her blood pounded in her ears. Who was on the ladder? Panic gripped her while sleet stung her cheeks. Her lips felt numb from the cold as she continued the arduous approach to the feed mill.

Was it Josh who now reached the surface? She couldn't bear for anything to happen to Josh. The ladder would be even slicker on the trip down. And on the top, that surface was surely as slick as the ground she walked upon and barely bigger than a large dining room table over a *hundred* plus feet above the ground. Fleetingly, she wondered if Ray Swain watched from the window of the boardroom. *He probably couldn't see through this snow,* she thought.

"Josh?" she yelled, hoping to be heard over the wind and distance. She tried to hurry. She slid and stumbled but kept her balance. When she almost fell once, she held herself off the ice with her right hand.

"Josh?" she yelled again, the light glimmering like a glowworm on a summer night. Then coming toward her from the feed mill and the snowy glare of a pickup's white lights behind her, she saw the shadow of a man approaching before she saw his face. "Josh!"

"I told him to wait for me when he called. It's the ice again," Josh said.

"Dad?" It was her father who had moved up the ladder to check the gate to the six feed bins. If frozen, the various grains could not be carried by gravity to the crimper that crushed it before spouts tossed it into the huge motorized mixer.

Josh put his arm about her shoulders. She leaned into him, her panicked sob lost in the wind.

The moisture fell thick and fast and formed a thick barrier on the floor to the bins. "There's two legs from the bins to the top," Josh said. He'll have to knock the ice free from the gate to let the grain in," he explained. "He's made it to the problem. He'll make it back down."

"Thank goodness he made it." Teal breathed a sigh of relief. Her breath fogged the cold air around her when she spoke.

"That surface must be slick as greased—" Josh stopped.

"That's all right, Josh. I'm worried too." Josh flexed his gloved hands and shifted nervously from one foot to the other, his head thrown back to watch for Ray Swain's descent.

When Ray started down, he either missed the rung or slipped. His lantern fell to the ground and went out like a bad omen in its bed of cold snow. He caught at the slick rung above, his legs clawing at the air for footing. Fear for him gripped Teal. His cry as he fell tore through her body. She felt critically wounded.

She and Josh stumbled and slid to his side. Josh started CPR while she ran back to call an ambulance. He had struck his head on the frozen ground and broke his neck when he fell; perhaps he had a heart attack before falling. No single cause was immediately known by the ER crew that pronounced him dead.

Jenny's face drained of color at the news. Teal wept uncontrollably. Both girls stayed that night with Esther. The company closed its doors until the funeral. "They'll have to feed hay. The cattle won't starve. Besides, most have already stocked up on pellets for winter," Teal said. They postponed meeting to establish a board-and-company policy. Teal felt grateful that all family members had gotten home safely that night.

At the funeral, Heath and Sara Jane seemed constantly underfoot to Teal. Wherever they were, Jenny was there also. Teal turned to Heath and Sara as they left the cemetery. Gavin stood by her, noticeably taken by Sara's young son, Eric, who did bear a striking resemblance to him. Teal wondered if Heath realized that also.

"I didn't know until returning from Houston that you were Jenny's lawyer, Heath. Gavin and I wish you, Sara, and Eric the best, don't we, Gavin?" They still stood on the grassy cemetery grounds after the funeral. Teal knew that Heath had accepted the boy as his own by adoption. By all appearances, Eric regarded Heath as his father.

Gavin pulled his eyes from the boy, hesitating only a moment. "Sure," he said.

Since he couldn't seem to keep his eyes off Eric, Teal walked over to the boy and asked, "Are you about six years old? You look like a big boy of six." He held her gaze. "I am," he said.

Teal took one of his hands in both of hers. "I'm very happy to meet you, Eric." Mia was with a sitter. Teal had thought it too soon after her illness to have her out.

Eric's young voice seemed to catch in his throat. "Thank you," he managed.

"You have a daughter now, don't you?" Heath ventured.

"Mia," she said, turning toward him then. "She isn't quite two years old and barely over an illness, so we didn't bring her today."

Sara Jane kept grinning at Gavin. "So good to see you again," she said, patting his shoulder.

Gavin looked uncomfortable, so Teal excused them both with the loose comment "See you at the meeting then, Heath," and they made their exit.

Teal had realized months earlier that wherever Gavin was, Sara Jane found an excuse to be. She often touched and hugged her hellos to him. Teal wondered if he felt uncomfortable about Sara's behavior when she wasn't around, or if they both privately indulged in thoughts of love lost to be regained some time in the future. A sane woman would not scream but would resolve this unseemly situation with reason.

Teal did not feel sane. She felt crazy with grief and emotional strain. She clenched her fists at her sides as they walked toward their mutual vehicles. She wanted to bloody Sara Jane's nose.

She knew that the moment she arrived home, should her house be empty of all but her, she *would* scream. Then more than likely, she would call Sylvia and vent. The third action would be prayer. Could she ever reach that goal of unconditional love where one prayed *first?* "I can try," she muttered aloud.

"What?" Gavin asked.

"I can try to go on without Dad, but it won't be easy," she invented, but meant it.

If all is choice as you tell others, her conscience indicted, *then choose like Joshua: As for me and my house, we will serve the Lord.* "I can try to manage things more like Dad did as well," she said, anchoring her resolve. For Ray Swain lived his attitudes of patience, tolerance, and forgiveness.

"You mean you're not going to have CEO put on your office door in gold leaf?"

Teal ignored his sarcasm and sat silently beside him en route home.

Ray Swain had lived loving like that: teaching her by example. The mill wasn't his greatest gift to her. His greatest gift was the example of his guileless and optimistic life. She bet Ray Swain wouldn't waste a minute of anger that prompted the desire to coldcock someone. He'd . . .

Teal stopped and smiled to herself. She'd almost thought that her father would forgive it on the spot then changed her mind. He'd do it or put a stop to it another way, than think and pray later, she bet. Ray Swain always expected appropriate behavior from his family. Maybe she wouldn't call Sylvia. Sylvia would just tell her she was analyzing things too much again. Maybe the next time Sara Jane slapped around on Gavin while just saying hello, she'd slap around on her as if she meant it and say, "Oh, I'm so sorry. I do hope I got that spider. It looked like a black widow."

After all, the false pride that made her pretend she thought nothing of it wasn't worth a hoot in hell as a way to put a stop to it. It seemed to Teal that Sara's lack of courtesy, her lack of respect, rather than the crossed boundaries aroused her anger.

The day for the family and employee meeting finally arrived. Teal chaired the meeting. Six weeks after Ray's funeral, Jenny stormed out the door of the elevator office when the newly established board of Swain Elevators approved Teal's decisions for diversification and voted her the new official CEO. She wasted no time before appointing Josh the general manager, which left the fertilizer division needing new leadership.

She chose to ignore Jenny for now, certain there would be a next time. Now she must think about the will. Her mother had privately shown her the safety deposit box copy the day after her father's death.

"The reading of it by Heath will be soon enough for Jenny to see it," Esther said, her voice strained with obvious stress.

"Relax, Mom, I can handle Jenny." Teal made her a cup of hot tea and gave her a warm reassuring hug.

Tad and Jonsi were joint executors. Twenty-five percent of the mill-and-elevator business would be in trust for Jenny, available to her at Esther's death providing she did not contest the will. Should she contest his decision, she would inherit one dollar. Esther would receive income above salaries and operational costs and development, for he had treated all children alike—25 percent shares at Esther's death.

However, the fertilizer business was willed to Teal in its entirety. In conjunction with this clause, he gave one half of his one-hundred-fifty-thousand-dollar life insurance policy (double now due to the accidental death) for the development and stocking of the fertilizer business. That clause would allow Teal to stock chemical to support crop health against the insects, weeds, and fungus that plagued the farmers' fields annually. Moreover, Teal had durable power of attorney to use all funds to manage and grow Swain Elevators until Esther's passing and the disbursement or purchase of assets. That dollar clause would control Jenny *and* the Huels.

Excitedly, she thought of her plan to structure the store differently than the rest of the business. She needed her employees to be her partners, all with equal shares and commissions on sales. That way, she would be free to oversee the elevators, mill, and bakery. Teal felt that if it were their business, they would grow it to their own benefit and hers. Ray had made certain that all his employees had health and retirement benefits, so within ten days of her assuming the helm, all ran smoothly.

Charles and Jenny requested Heath's reading of the will. Only family arrived at Esther's home for the event that lasted a brief half hour, even with coffee afterward.

Heath appeared uncomfortable in this setting as if eager for it to be over.

Teal shivered, recalling that horrible day at the funeral. *Get over it,* she told herself. *Let go of bitterness.* She would always believe that Heath married Sara Jane, Gavin's best girl for more years than he and Teal had been married, for revenge. Sara, needing a father for her young child, complied. Had Sara wanted to spite both her and Gavin as well? Sara Jane knew that Teal and Heath were childhood sweethearts. Why did she *paw* Gavin at every opportunity if not to agitate and keep alive a situation best left behind?

The story of Lot's wife haunted her. "I'll turn to salt, one of the walking dead if I don't focus on life past Heath and Sara. Jenny knows that. How she must hate me," she confided to Esther, "to bring those two back into our lives."

"How are you otherwise?" Esther asked knowingly. Teal glanced toward Heath.

"Feeling like a question mark. Dad is gone, Heath is an enigma that won't go away, Jenny's life choices are making us strangers—not sisters. Gavin works night and day at his partnership with Harlin and his feedlot. He's home no more than six hours out of twenty-four. I want to run away sometimes."

Esther put an arm around Teal's shoulders. "Look for the opportunity for good in each of those situations. It's there. You'll find it *and* self-discovery."

Teal brushed a tear from her cheek. "I can't run, can I?"

Esther shook her head. They stood then, and Teal gave her mother a quick hug.

"How you must miss Dad, and I whine instead of comfort. Thanks for the fresh perspective, Mom."

"There's more," Esther said. "Think of that poor girl. I'm going to say something I may live to regret, but I'm saying it because you need to know: a woman's heart won't break if she's prepared for the strike. It was money, money Gavin saw in *your* future, and money he neither had nor wanted to spend on a child so soon as—"

Teal refused to hear Esther's derision of Gavin or the inference that Sara did not love Heath. She turned away from her toward Heath. She saw his jaw harden as she approached him. "You seem uncomfortable, Heath. If it helps, it seems odd to me also that we should meet under these circumstances." Her remarks didn't appear to relax his tension, but escape from her mother's remarks helped her own.

"I hope you're happy!" he snapped.

Was there no escape from emotional chaos? Her mind struggled with this fresh attack. Determined to cope, she refused responsibility for *his* feelings. Would he never change? Her throat seemed to close; she felt unable to speak. "Your feelings are *still* my fault, I see," she managed. She swallowed. Waited.

"The years have been kind to you," he finally muttered. She thought she felt his breath on her face. "You are still quite beautiful." His tone had softened as her mind sought a safer place.

Did he not love Sara either? Perhaps he could not love. Were there people born without a natural affection gene? These questions with no answers spun around in her brain while she stared at him and finally uttered a squeaky "Thank you."

Suddenly, Jenny stood glaring at her, a brutal intrusion. "Well, little sister," she spat. "Your pie's been cut with an extra slice for your plate—Daddy's favorite."

Heath moved up beside Jenny to face her also, an unexpected reminder for Teal that he was Jenny's lawyer, not her own confidant.

"Yes," Teal said, squaring her shoulders. "And quite fairly. I work here for those nine-to-five wages you and Charles sneer at." Then she walked away. She would offer Jenny assistant manager of the business. Jenny would refuse for she wanted to be the proprietor via proxy and with CEO salary and benefits. Ray Swain had understood that.

She and Heath passed Teal on their way to the door, arms linked. Teal heard her say, "Let's get some fresh air, darling."

Heath disengaged his arm, looked at his watch, and said, "Sara expects me. Good night."

Teal faced her denial that both, however dear, had broken her trust. Heath had, as had Gavin. Perhaps most others in her life would also; perhaps that's how she seemed to Jenny and Gavin and Heath. Didn't Jenny think that she, Teal, had broken her trust? Indeed. Such beliefs occurred when people saw events differently. She recognized the pointlessness of making unverifiable judgments.

Her father probably knew that. It would explain how he overlooked and forgave with such apparent ease.

"It won't work," Gavin said that night as they prepared for bed. She helped him off with his boots. "She'll see your offer of assistant manager as a ploy. As the older sister, she could never swallow her pride to take orders from you."

"It's a boss's prerogative to change her mind if it doesn't. I believe it will. I'll need her help with the fertilizer expansion. There are big profits in fertilizer due to the constant need and the volume of sales in wheat country. It can change a thirty-bushel-an-acre yield to fifty."

"The right year only."

"Right years, all in a row. It happens, Gavin. As surely as drought comes eventually, it happens. "I believe in it."

"You probably believe they'll cap the tonnage of wheat that cartels, speculators, reserves, import or export schemes, and hedge funds hold, too. You must, or you wouldn't have offered assistant manager to her. If wheat ever brings a fair price of six to ten dollars a bushel, the economists will call it temporary artificial inflation to justify zapping the price."

Teal laughed. "Do bees like honey? Besides, I *must* look ahead, not back. I *must* be optimistic, expand, diversify, compete, and *share*. This gives Jenny an opportunity to change, to see me differently. I have a selfish motive too. I want to live, not turn to salt, not be one of the walking dead. I'm through feeling responsible for *her* feelings and attitudes too."

"Too?"

She didn't respond immediately. Her mind wrestled with how the wheat price could also change with fairer appraisal by an honest and knowledgeable representative in Washington.

"Farmers need to lobby Congress." With a fair price for wheat, they could raise storage a quarter of a cent a day—more perhaps. It added up with thousands of bushels stored over several years' time. *Salaries are my primary expense,* she thought, *with maintenance and energy running a close second.*

—

323

"Like Congress cares about 5 percent of the vote," he mumbled.

Change seemed the only reliable thing to Teal besides God. *Innovative product uses for wheat must be promoted*, she thought. Contests, awards, whatever might generate the ideas and investment in them for wheat. God had held an unshakeable place in her heart since childhood when she learned His name. She realized that an omnipotent power perpetually made this wonderful, natural world new each season. God authored creative change everywhere and for everything—living or dead (if there was such a thing as dead). Renewed felt more believable than dead to Teal.

"When we identify our marketing problems, solutions will come," she said. "New products and unclogged routes for distribution would help." She turned on her side, nuzzled into the pillow, and fell promptly to sleep.

Chapter XXII

Prosperity

The next ten years filled Teal and Gavin's lives with successful growth and personal joys in family life and prosperity—good years. Since the milk cans were old, Gavin just took them to his feedlot and sold them. Teal missed the fresh milk and cream, though she admired Gavin's new career focus on stocker cattle and diversification.

She picked at evening art classes, one here and there, often months apart. She completed basic drawing, watercolor, pastels, and an oil painting class. She gave her pictures away as gifts or hung them on her own walls. Mostly, she painted in early morning light before breakfast and work. Family farm life began its transformation from family farm income to outside income that supported greater volume and diversification.

No private class in sculpting had been offered. She realized college classes were where she would find these offered. The awareness frustrated. How could she find the time or the funding? No farm or mill budget could be considered. How could it when those incomes perpetually changed relative to climate and inconsistent costs?

In 1966 she saw an article about the teacher shortage. An Oklahoma-born Senator Moynihan from the east had fostered a bill to offer government loans for teacher education. She must agree to either teach for six years or pay back the loan. A major in art education seemed possible at last. Full-time enrollment had no appeal; she loved her full-time job at the mill. But she could schedule classes around her work there. She checked the catalog and saw that she could work a schedule around full-time employment.

She applied for the loan and got it.

Gavin bellowed, "Why don't you just become the college president! You're gone most of the time now because of those 'prairie skyscrapers' you call elevators."

Teal bit back the temptation to remind him of his own absences from her and Mia due to his land, cattle business, and wheat speculation.

"Mia's eleven and loves to be with me after school at the company or in charge at home. If it doesn't work out, I'll stop. She can probably do her homework while I have an art lesson. They are very informal there."

From Gavin's faraway expression, she supposed his thoughts ran elsewhere already.

*   *   *

It did work out. She graduated summa cum laude and walked across the stage quite pregnant with their second child. Brett was born less than a week after graduation. He crawled before he was six months old, walked at nine months old, and played happily whether at the mill or in Teal's sculpting studio.

Mia thrived on her freedom. At sixteen, she demonstrated grace and confidence beyond her years.

The sculpting, whether with wood or clay, transfixed Brett. He became obsessed with the watching until she handed him clay when he was only three. When he reached ten, his obsession changed to creating small animal objects from his rural observations of rabbits and squirrels or shaping the birds he saw seeking field seeds.

Their pieces sold well, and each second Thursday, she held an evening art class in her studio for fifteen avid artists. Brett always came to her class.

He and the clay seemed one from the start. His natural gift for it amazed and thrilled her. Before his sixteenth birthday, Teal entered his creations in the local art show where he won ribbons. At the Oklahoma City show the following April, he placed second with his stone sculpted piece, a mustang with her young colt.

To Gavin's disappointment, it appeared that Brett would not be a rancher.

Five years after her graduation, Teal invested in a kiln for Brett, who avidly took over the studio and the classes.

Wheat prices jumped to $5.80. Gavin seemed the man she had married again.

Then several years following her graduation, Jimmy Carter came to the presidency. While many presumed more land and equipment would make them rich by planting fence row to fence row, it didn't; the price for wheat fell to $2 a bushel when the glut of wheat hit the market. The lower prices and the Russian wheat embargo consumed previous profit for many.

Teal and Gavin prospered for they planted and harvested fence row to fence row without the debt of more land and equipment that others had who trusted the policy to persist. Nevertheless, Gavin's down moods returned, and he counted money lost in the depressed market instead of the two-dollars-a-bushel price that he gained.

At the company, Teal had already built the extra storage; no unmarketable grain lay in piles on the concrete at *her* elevator. All they purchased was stored, milled, baked, or sold. So when politics, prices, and the altered policy of allotted acres returned, the Rushes were in the black, and the Huels were in the red.

The great surplus caused by the fence-row-to-fence-row program continued to depress the market with huge reserves of grain. Moreover, the grain embargo continued to block sales to Russia, a primary market. Over time, the multiple barriers brought absolute calamity to the farm families who had purchased more equipment and land on credit to handle the new temporary demand on time, labor, and anticipated grain exports.

It felt as if they had swallowed the government hook intended to destroy them and their small farms and make the way easier for corporate agriculture. The post fence-row-planting government program restricted acreage planting again and closed the Russian market.

Those who had thought prosperity a permanent signal, who had not become skeptical of Washington's actual understanding and disregard for American agriculture, lost farms they'd mortgaged in confidence in order to afford the expansion of either more land, more equipment, or both. Some had even acquired their own grain storage and still owed the seller of the storage or building materials for it.

Others spent the next several years' profit paying off loans or selling their land. Most who also ran dairies shut them down and sold their milk cows for their dairy price supports also vanished while controls escalated. Poultry farmers fell victim to the same blight of low prices and failed supports. Government census reports required all vegetable and produce sales' information in order to secure tax data whether a large or small grower. There seemed no way to regain an agricultural foothold for many farm families. Those who found jobs off the farm felt lucky.

Teal missed the art studio, but the times required her full attention (with overtime) at the mill. Watching Brett's talent develop there excited her.

She had barely heard the rumor that Heath and Sara Jane expected another child when Jenny told her that Sara had suddenly developed uremic poisoning. Both she and the baby died before doctors could control the disease process.

Unable or not willing to restrain herself, Teal rushed to comfort Heath.

He seemed cold, empty. His eyes appeared glazed. "Why are you here now? Haven't you done enough? She wanted to give me a child. Too late, too late."

He seemed childlike to her, his face wet with tears. He seemed a dead man that still spoke, still moved. Heath and his perfectly controlled plans. The thought wrenched her heart. She fought back tears.

"Eric," she said, then stopped. "Where are they?" she asked him instead, struggling for control.

"Already at the funeral home."

"Eric also?"

"Outside."

He looked long at her but without any expression she could read. Did he also believe that Eric was Gavin's son? She wondered if Sara had revealed the father to him. "Please," he said. "See if Eric is all right. I've the business of planning the time, place, and burial. It would spare him that." Reluctantly, she turned aside to Eric.

"Come spend some time at our house, Eric. Take your mind off your grief for a little while," she invited. Teal felt both pleased and surprised when he accepted. A young man now, he barely knew them.

"I can't leave Dad long though, he'll need me later. Now he needs some alone time."

Teal nodded understanding. "That's thoughtful, Eric, and we'll get better acquainted in the mean time."

Teal stopped by the funeral home to see Sara and her child and to sign the register. "Come in with me Eric," she invited. "It may help us both to do it together."

Suddenly, she recognized Gavin's pickup at the curb across the street. She thought she might faint.

When they entered the room where Sara lay in state, Gavin stood beside her, his hands gripping the sides of her casket until his knuckles turned white. His back heaved with his sobs. Teal turned abruptly to Eric to gage his reaction to the scene.

"We can leave and come back," she whispered.

"I'm all right, but are you?"

Such perception and kindness at only, what? Early twenties? He moved her. She took his hand, and they walked forward after she gave him a grateful reassuring smile.

When nearer, she saw that Gavin's tears spotted the ivory satin lining. When he looked at her, Teal felt he didn't actually register her presence or her place in his life.

"I loved her so," he said, as if speaking to a stranger.

"I know," Teal said. She dropped Eric's hand, turned away slowly, signed the book by the door, and waited for Eric to join her before driving home. *How peaceful she looked*, Teal thought, *with the tiny infant there in the crook of her arm.*

"Dance with me, Heath," echoed from her past.

"Girl's tag!"

Then the mutual joy of that first dance with Gavin. She hadn't imagined it. She touched her cheek where she had felt his breath; she heard again his husky whisper: "I want to take you home." She wouldn't think about it now. The next move must be his. And beside her, this remarkable young man, Gavin's son and Heath's stepson, whom she easily loved already as a friend. She sensed his affection for her by his query. "Are you all right?" His touch had comforted and reassured her.

Mia shared her music and books with him. They went for a horseback ride, for a swim. Though she was almost four years younger than he, Teal noticed that he treated her as his equal.

Barely acquainted before, they all, including Brett, became fast friends. The following fall, they saw him very little except for summers for Eric had moved in with a grandmother at Norman, Sara's mother.

Heath threw himself into politics. Soon he had moved to Washington DC to serve in the nation's Senate. His running for the office and winning it surprised no one.

When Eric Meriott's senior year ended at the University of Oklahoma, Heath sent for him. But Eric often hopped a plane from Washington to Oklahoma to spend the weeks of spring, fall, and Christmas breaks from graduate school in DC with his friends and family in Oklahoma.

He spent considerable time with Teal and Mia the next few years, eager to learn about milling. "Every time I turn around, you're

—

at my elbow," Teal told him one day. "I need to put you on payroll. Here, enter these bills of lading in the books."

His quick intelligence didn't surprise her. His interest in business did. He transferred back to OU to finish his graduate degree so that he could continue at the mill.

"I've majored in business," he told her after the summer harvest and employment there with her.

"Really!" Teal exclaimed. "You be sure to stay in touch, now," she said, giving him a hug before he left them again. "Send me a graduation notice. I don't want to miss seeing you walk across that stage."

His face flushed when he told Mia good-bye, causing Teal's brow to furrow with concern. But Mia just blew him a kiss and waved. Teal wanted her to finish college as well. She suspected she'd see a lot of Eric soon. She would discourage romance between them—someday. The thought that she might have to reveal her belief that they were actually siblings repelled.

"Business," she mused. Fleetingly, she envisioned him here at Swains or at one of their other elevators now open in Kansas and Colorado. Josh had proved an invaluable entrepreneur.

Swain Milling and Elevators now required levels of management and supervision. *Eric is graduating just in time,* Teal thought, hoping to hire him for the Oklahoma facility.

* * *

When Letti Pearl started having trouble with her eyes and needed Mia to come on weekends to write her memoirs in the Big Chief tablets she still favored, Teal and Gavin allowed it. Teal drove her to Letti's this Saturday morning.

"She must have saved back a hundred of those tablets from the store closing," Teal said one Saturday morning driving Mia to her great-grandma's. Brett sat in the backseat.

"This may be your only summer for it, Mia," he said. "Graduate school will be demanding. Your time may get short."

"For a fact," Mia agreed. "We're almost finished. She said last week that there would be only two more weekends. Did you and Dad meet when you were kids because you kept breaking his milk jugs to get his attention?"

"She told on me, did she? What a memory!"

"She's ninety-two, can hardly see, but won't have the cataract surgery, Mom," Brett informed.

"Maybe she'll come live with us," Teal said. "I've thought my own grandma, Susanna, might need to do the same. Persuading her to come to America will be difficult. As long as they can take their baths and get to the bathroom, it would be great to have them with us for the few years we can."

"Daddy might not think so," Mia volunteered.

"We'll see. He'll be old someday. I'll remind him of that," Teal said with a smile.

"We were always going to Ireland to see Great-grandma Susanna and never have," Mia regretted.

"Never say never. Maybe we'll go, maybe she'll come back with us. I've saved all her letters. You can read them if you want. Write to her, she'd love it."

"Me too?" Brett asked.

"You too. The letters are one way of meeting her. She's from the O'Haly clan. Those who immigrated here during Ireland's potato famine spell it *Hailey* without the *O*."

"So, Grandma Esther was a Hailey," Mia said.

"That's right," Teal affirmed. "This country's made of every culture on the planet—probably."

"Probably not," Brett corrected. "I doubt if there are pygmies or aborigines here."

"Oh, you," Mia said. "You think you're so smart!"

"When Irish eyes are smiling," Brett sang in his baritone. Mia chimed in on the second stanza.

After dropping off Mia, she and Brett stopped for an ice cream before shopping for art supplies. Brett looked as if he were still an adolescent though he approached the age of twenty.

No adult in his art classes doubted his ability. He hadn't lost a student.

"I'm glad you have found this thing you love," she told him. "It doesn't look as if you or Mia have an interest in the mill. I'm mildly disappointed."

"Dad may be also, Mom. I don't really want to farm. I help him when I can because I think I should."

"Have you told him?"

"Not yet. It seems too soon."

"Not yet necessary, you mean."

"Yes. Eric loves the mill."

"I've noticed," she said.

"I think he likes Mia—a lot," Brett said.

Teal laughed. "I think so too."

*   *   *

When Ray Swain acquired the controlling interest in the mill in 1948, he'd required the upgrading of safety for his product and for his personnel. Dust and fire control, his major concerns, depended on loading and unloading rules as well as assigned smoking areas.

Safety measures for clean grain, for well-kept ladders, and for daily pulley and belt checks on all conveyors were Ray's doing as well. Even before he acquired full ownership, he implemented governmental rodent and insect control. The grain itself required protection from chemicals. He had walked a fine and costly line and succeeded.

But in the mid-1970s, Teal was faced with one new government regulation after another from rodent control, inspections, and new cleaning equipment to the unforeseen energy crisis. Her inflated expenses soared when energy rates increased even more in 1978. Her energy bill alone sometimes capped five thousand dollars a month for one elevator and flour mill during the month of June when the bins filled to capacity. The energy to operate the bakery, the feed mill, and fertilizer storage areas were almost as much.

By the 1990s, Teal projected the milling of fifteen to twenty thousand bushels a day, which meant bakery expansion. The energy costs would be astronomical unless they found an alternative energy source. She favored solar and wind.

Though the year of fence row to fence row wheat rather than the limiting acre allotments had not caught her unprepared, the Russian embargo had. Needing to keep the new crops of wheat off the ground the year after fence row to fence row, she'd had to use all her storage. Storage fees would not recover her storage costs for ten more years, a problem the embargo created.

"Implementing wind and solar will cost thousands initially, but save millions over time," she argued before her board.

"Increase the storage fees," her board urged.

"Not yet. Price needs to be better than $3.50 a bushel. I'll monitor the situation and give you regular reports. In the meantime, we'll buy and mill more, bake more, ship more. That will help."

"That will also cost more. We need open markets and more of them," Josh said.

"We've taught many of our markets how to grow their own, a benevolent act but an economical sacrifice," she said. "There will be elevator closings. Swain Elevators will take any loss, any challenge. We will not close."

The board approved her plan for increasing production and implementing the alternative energy sources. Still, Teal knew that government programs and independent intervention in markets via hedge funds caused economic downturns, a domino effect in agriculture from the product to the purchasing power of families and to the steel and equipment companies' losses. She couldn't control those things.

Ultimately, more farm and elevator failures resulted over the following months. The cost increases of fertilizer and energy plus the government rules for grain protection complicated the economics even more. Trucking costs continued to rise, chemical to control smut and insects increased in price, So Teal's price to farmers increased.

—

Most expenses in agriculture were related in some way to petroleum, another product smack in the middle of politics. It seemed to Teal that the government continued to block US elevators' profits and to dramatically reduce US wheat production. *To what end?* she wondered. The United States stayed on the short end of any trade balance. Wouldn't more grains to countries with crop failures or shortages help the trade balance? Better to give it away to third-world countries (where it wouldn't depress their markets) to alleviate hunger and diminish this grain glut.

Her plan to shift emphasis temporarily to the bakery division worked. They now milled thirty-six hundred bushels of wheat daily at the home mill alone. Teal searched now for an independent foreign buyer.

"I will find one," she promised Josh emphatically.

Interest on a six-million-dollar loan could cap 18 percent for her lender wouldn't agree to a fixed interest when it cost over six dollars to produce a bushel of wheat that might not sell for four dollars. At 7 percent and with lots of luck, she hoped to pay it off in under five years.

"Perhaps he wants me to fail," she confided to Gavin when she couldn't lock in the 7 percent.

He responded with his typical sarcasm toward her.

"You didn't just buy the bank?"

Instead, she persuaded the board to offer the fertilizer division to Jenny and Charles Huel. They actually needed the extra income now. The only division left entirely to her was hers to sell. Consulting the board seemed a necessary courtesy however. Over the past ten years it had consistently made a 35 percent profit. Valued now at 350 thousand dollars, the purchase would help reduce her overall debt for their Colorado expansion. She bet that Charles's folks would loan him the money to save them the potentially high interest.

Teal wanted to focus on wheat. The fertilizer business's profits that she had banked made that possible for her now. Wheat inspired her. She thought it a gift from God: the physical path to the mystical bread of life that Christ gave a person. She hoped she didn't profane Him to think wheat so necessary to the prevention and the resolution of world hunger. When it streamed from the auger into the truck beds or bins, it reminded her of semen, as if mankind and bread were one. As if sharing a life and breaking bread together were similar things.

The following years, Mia graduated summa cum laude in journalism and English and secured her dream job at Doubleday as a reader. They expressed interest in her writing as well. The exercise of writing her great-grandma Letti's memoirs from territory days had honed a writing and editing skill. Mia still spent many nights developing the stories. From time to time, she still called Letti to verify a date or place, all of which delighted her great-grandmother.

"She's giving my life a meaning, that girl," Letti said when Mia and Teal visited for lunch with her and Rena Lily.

"Your life has special meaning, Letti," Teal said, giving her a hug. "Every life could, if its owner allowed it."

"Allowed it?" Rena asked as if puzzled.

"Allowed it," Teal repeated without explanation, for she didn't want to offend the mother-in-law that she loved. Rena kept her life safe with repetitive activity, appointments, schedules. Letti had lived fully with adventure, change, and self-reliance. She felt in the presence of two great women, heroines in their own right whom the world might never know, for they had survived perilous times but in different ways.

"She's like a light," Letti Pearl was saying as she tucked up strands of snow-white hair and caught them again with a comb. "She made my stories come to life so folks born here can know more about the raw labor and sacrifice that started an undeveloped land only a little more than a hundred years ago. Think of it."

Teal laughed. "Almost makes my head spin thinking of wagon and cattle trails changed to Route 66 and rail that Interstate 40 eclipsed. Oklahoma agriculture built railroads and raised oil derricks, built industries, and fostered this progress."

"It was at the bottom of it," Rena agreed. "Provided the first prosperity."

"From sod house to skyscraper," Letti chimed in. "Hardly an original family without a rural background."

"Gavin called the mill and elevator storage prairie skyscrapers," Teal said.

"From dust to conservation in the thirties. These emerald terraces remind me of a tiered square dancing skirt in the spring," Rena said. Her tiny form had rounded over the years. Her blue eyes still sparkled though her black hair had faded to brown.

"The wheat itself is the gold at the end of my rainbow," Letti said. "How I wish Upton could just see how his dream fell on his son and grandson."

"You're building a Swain business in Manhattan, we heard," Rena noted.

"A bakery. We ship baked goods to our markets, but marketing from our own bakery is a first. Both Mia and Brett are there to oversee its construction. Brett has excellent art sales there. He independently studies various art mediums while maintaining his studio. Manhattan is where he and Mia found their doors to the world. We're calling it *Ray's* for their grandfather Swain.

"The bakery is like insurance—part of the diversification for the elevators as much as they are a result of them. When the economy shifts away from the raw product, wheat, other areas of the business can carry more of the financial load. Best, the business in Manhattan assures a place for them to work if they need to earn more to pay their bills there. It's an expensive place to live compared to Oklahoma."

"It may be the first bakery of many," Rena Lily said as if she liked the idea.

"Our other employees own a stake in the total corporation and its satellite businesses as well," Teal informed. "Their ownership assures their accountability, so that oversight is simplified. I only oversee the various locations these days. I'm home as much or more than Gavin."

With a forced lift to her voice, she said, "That home-cooked meal, the care of the home, as much time with me as he seems to want, he still gets."

When Letti Pearl and Rena Lily became quiet, Teal sensed that they knew Gavin needed little at-home time these days. Her bouncing back and forth from Manhattan to Oklahoma would likely be blamed for whatever this older generation believed about her and Gavin's relationship. Their early marriage years seemed from another world to Teal.

There, country and close family units that worked and reaped harvests together were a given. Most rural men and women were forced off the farm now to earn a living so that they could keep their land and a rural lifestyle. Though prosperous, Teal could not escape her feeling that her marriage ended the day Gavin stood weeping over Sara's dead body. The seed for its demise existed before her wedding day. She felt no regrets; she had chosen to ignore what she didn't want to see so that she could have him.

"Mia says she doesn't want marriage yet," she said brightly. "She's not worried about being called an old maid. It's a different time we're in." Still the women were silent. Teal now understood what the term *deafening silence* meant.

Rena spoke at last. "Eric spends plenty of time going back and forth to see her." Teal felt that Rena's deliberate stare and suggestive tone warned of something sinister.

"He and Mia are only friends," Teal quickly explained.

"That's good!" Letti emphasized as if the words were a double entendre.

Must I worry about this? Teal thought. *How could I ever reveal my concern that Eric is her half brother? What a shamble the emotional lives of both children, of Heath's life if he doesn't know—hers and Gavin's also. Sara Jane is buried. Nothing can hurt her now.*

"Gavin was no boy when I married him," Teal said at last. "He was twenty-two."

"No," Rena agreed, "and he's not one now. Is that why you're still put out and living on dissatisfaction? Because you didn't have him first?"

Teal whirled about, stunned at the remark. Rena Lily must believe as well that Sara's pregnancy was indeed the result of Gavin's premarital relationship with her. The old woman didn't blink nor pause a second from her paring of potatoes for their lunch. Her eyes seemed to mock Teal.

Teal posed no threat to Gavin's mother, nor did Rena seem a threat to her. She had loved her from the start. "I didn't care about Gavin's intimacies before our marriage. It's behaviors between the two of them *after* our marriage that upset me," she admitted. As for being blamed for their current problems, she recognized it as another generational difference: women of Rena's day assumed the responsibility for their "man" in everything.

"You think I'm getting too big for my britches with this career, I know. And maybe you think unhappiness drove me to it. I'm in it because Gavin and I had a need for income, and I could help. Dad knew I loved the business. That's all."

"I wanted no boy," Rena went on. "Not then or now! I wanted me a girl."

"You got me, Rena. You know I love you like my own Esther." She moved close and hugged her mother-in-law.

Rena seemed pleased; she rinsed the potatoes and wiped her hands on a kitchen towel.

Letti, who had waited motionless in the middle of the room as if in a shocked silence, smoothed her apron. Her face broke into a wide smile. "Well then, it appears you got some of what you wanted. Besides, Gavin's a man." Letti's smile left her face slowly as a steely expression moved to replace it. Teal sensed the old woman's wisdom, her awareness of time, and experience with people that makes life translatable. When Letti caught her eyes, Teal sensed that her thoughts were the same as her own: that Gavin had never loved her. He had used her to thwart Sara Jane for whatever reasons besides the child. Letti was his grandmother. She would know that

—

339

he resisted being pushed by a notion not his own, and the unplanned pregnancy of Sara's was that: a notion not his own. Besides, since knowing him better, Teal felt uncertain about Gavin's ability to be truly committed to anyone but Gavin.

The Swain's potential for eventual wealth that would trickle down to them could well have encouraged him as Esther had suggested, she thought.

"I'm not afraid to love him!" Teal said, meeting her gaze. "Enough for both of us." Teal knew the remark revealed her deepest awareness of her husband; he avoided intimacy while claiming it for his benefit at his chosen time. Sara had used sex to get his attention. She had broken milk jugs. She no longer had illusions about Gavin's lack of genuine devotion to either of them. Hadn't she learned that his behaviors revealed what words would not?

Letti looked away. She had dropped her lids the moment Teal confronted her. Her finger's reached for one of the oblong Irish potatoes and began cutting them in quarters. Finally, she looked up, her eyes soft upon Teal.

"Powerful feeling, love, when it's for a man."

A little tremor waved its way down Teal's spine. It embarrassed her for Gavin's grandmother to see her tremble.

"Feeling isn't a weakness to be ashamed of, Teal," Letti assured. "It's a woman's strength. Gavin has gotten himself lost. We all know it—may as well say it. Whatever happens to you, wherever you go, and whatever you do, let your feelings keep coming on. The harder the hurt, the more you'll need them. The stiffer the competition, the more you'll need them. Feelings that are good for loving are just as good for fighting."

Soon, their lunch of steaks, mashed potatoes, and salad ended. They finished with ice cream and Letti's famous angel food cake, a recipe Teal intended to leave with today.

"Your folks come to Oklahoma during the dust days?" Rena asked.

"My grandparents on my mother's side came in when it opened up," Teal said.

"Dad's side got as far as south Texas from Tennessee after the Civil War and stopped. They came here when things got bad in south Texas during the drought there, and tax debts lost them their land and elevator. Dad's maternal side stayed in Ireland. Mom's did too. Some are still there. Neither of them had more than a fifth grade education, but they never quit reading and learning about . . . just everything."

"Land?" Rena asked. "On your mother's side?"

"No land. My great-grandparents were teachers in Ireland and in Europe. They found menial jobs in the clothing industry in the north and in the east after coming here until they migrated south to work in tobacco fields. Dad learned milling chemistry at the mill near Chico, Texas. He did some farming there too before the Depression and drought. Came to Oklahoma to find work in a new state.

"All of Mom's folks like business, most of it small but substantial. They sold tailored clothes, they built houses, they carved furniture, they—"

"But they stuck here when it got rough?" Rena interrupted.

"I guess they figured by that time that, sooner or later, it got rough almost everywhere. Besides, my mother was only sixteen when she married, and Tad was born the first year."

"Depressed folk leave a spot, I reckon," Letti volunteered. "The optimistic stay."

"Maybe, maybe not," Letti said.

"What do you mean?" Teal asked with annoyance, for she felt Letti may have meant her parents should have stayed in Texas.

"I mean that if they had the courage to leave a spot razed by war or famine, by evil and the oppression of the poverty of . . . of everything, well, that's good. My Upton left a prime piece of land he had developed to save his family: me and the children. Upton had a tender heart. Gentle ways disguised his tough endurance. That's also courage: to turn your back on something past and done and strike out for a new life."

She locked her old eyes on Teals, and Teal understood their message.

—

"But those that stayed on the land, they're the strong who rebuilt, who took up the burden with the faith that it would be all right," Rena persisted. "That's my family history—both sides."

Letti bit her lip as if to hold back a quarrel with Rena. "Harlin picked up his heritage. He remembers the land of Indian territory and has his father's spirit for it. He passed it on to Gavin here in Canadian County."

"Wheat's all Gavin really loves, Teal assured, hoping Rena didn't argue that Gavin's love of the land came only from *her* East coast folks. If she did, Teal determined to remind her that Upton's folks were of the land in Ohio.

"That wheat pours into the bed of the truck like molten gold," she continued. "Wheat has shaped his life like nothing else has. His feelings are like that wheat. If the season's a good one, he's charming. If it's too wet or too dry, too cold, he thinks the sky's falling and seems to mold or shrivel like the grain."

"Wheat will curl back to the soil to save itself," Rena said. "I've seen the young plants do it. Sometimes that's what he does. I saw it in him when he was a child. He goes inside himself and sulks. Always did that when Harlin was late or if things didn't go his way."

Teal understood what was happening here today. The older women wisely foresaw calamity for her marriage and spoke in ways that would no doubt help her cope with the loss when it came. Hadn't her own life evolved in this marriage? The wealth of children, family.

Both his grandmother and his mother tried to help her understand him as if that awareness might save the marriage or her sanity—maybe both. The urge to explain herself seemed the natural sequel.

"I have wanted him—us—to share our lives. I needed him gentle and wanting babies, lots of them. I had hoped he would respect books and learning for the sake of the children and me if not for himself."

"Did you?" Rena asked. "A man is never what a woman makes him. He can only be who he is. Gavin was raised alone. He doesn't know how to be what you want. You were raised with brothers and sisters. Sharing and conversation seem natural to you. I've seen it," she said wringing her hands.

Letti didn't need to say anything. Her eyes rested quietly upon Teal's face. It was Teal who finally looked away, her face hot, her blood warming her neck and creeping across her breasts. She felt her nipples harden. *Damn that old woman,* she cursed silently. She clenched her teeth. Would her desire for him never depart? Just empathy for him aroused her.

The crone voice followed her, but she shut her mind against the criticism.

"I hadn't thought that my being different would hurt him. I would never deliberately hurt Gavin. I love him."

"You knew he was hard, a strapping farm boy, backward at love and learning all he knew about it in the backseats of cars when he got to the city high school. He had come from a one-room schoolhouse. Oh, yes," Rena dramatized. "He was supposed to go there to get that wonderful diploma, but *he* went there straight from that one-room schoolhouse that had few books one could call books and teachers with two years of schooling when they were lucky. Mostly, he went there where he must compete with boys, bent on books to make their living when he'd been pitching hay and hauling wood, milking cows in the morning's dark cold, bringing up the water to the house—all that before he could think of walking his mile to catch the bus to town."

Mia, who had been in the dining room preparing their table, returned to the kitchen. She acted as if she'd heard nothing, but Teal knew otherwise.

"Did Mom tell you I'll be working for Doubleday Publishers in New York City next month? They're starting me as a reader, maybe even an associate editor. I'll have my own apartment."

Teal smiled her gratitude for the interruption and rushed to reassure Rena. "Whatever Gavin does, he'll be all right, Rena. Believe it, for it's so." Rena began to sob. She turned to Mia, stifled the sobs, and wiped the tears away.

—

"Apartments can cost thousands in Manhattan. You might need a place outside the city. Use the transit system to get to work if you work there," she told her granddaughter cheerfully. She took a handkerchief from her pocket and blew her nose.

Mia hugged her. "Thank you for the advice, Grandma."

Teal hoped they left the dissection of her marriage behind and felt pleased to turn the conversation Mia's way. She bit back the temptation to tell her she'd set up a trust for her. It felt too soon to betray that information. She believed that Mia would grow stronger by doing what she could for herself and not expecting too much too soon. How she would love to help her up front—provide the apartment.

"I'll check it all out," Mia assured them.

"When you do, tell me the options if you will. I'll help you with a budget," Teal said.

"Maybe I'll waitress too, at a real restaurant where tips are good or at Ray's Bakery," she added elaborately. "Of course, I may want to take some manuscripts home to read evenings."

"Not a bad idea," Teal agreed. "*Real work* stretches energy levels and stamina."

Privately, Teal thought Mia's genetics and her inclination for books would lead her into more *writing* for publication. "Your book about Letti Pearl's life might be published in New York. You will be in the right spot for it. Then too, you might like to manage Ray's Bakery on weekends."

She glanced at Mia, whose auburn hair framed her porcelain features and gray-green eyes. Teal pried at her, but Mia seemed lost in her private thoughts. Just to see her willingness to take on her future pleased Teal, so she volunteered no more advice. Still, if money were short (and it could be), the bakery remained an option. Mia and Brett probably both knew she wanted it there as economic insurance for them if their careers in publishing and art wore thin. Trust money and time on their hands in New York City sounded like a route to their demise to both Teal and Gavin.

"Thanks, Mom, for you and Dad made my dream possible—for college, I mean. The rest is really up to me, isn't it?" she responded at last.

"Yes and no," Teal said. "There will be people along the way who will help. Others may try to hinder. Turn aside from those, go around them when possible. But, Mia, all of our lives are either made possible, difficult, or impossible by those who prepared the way."

"The way?"

"The values, the politics, the economics, the culture itself—you'll learn these things. And about the time you do, it may change. Don't be discouraged by change. Change is a sign of life. When some change feels uncomfortable or contrary to your life, give careful thought to your next choice and try never to sacrifice your own integrity for money, a job, or for another person, not even for a country. Your first loyalty is to God, who tolerates no gods before Him."

"Sometimes I recognize someone has been molded—like the clay Brett uses—into what others wanted or programmed for their own purposes," Mia said.

"That's true. People can overadapt," Teal said. "That's a dead end because of change. When it comes, they get lost. They have not developed the inner resources that compose and shore up their own identity. Still, it's never too late for anyone to be real.

"Don't get lost, baby. Discover yourself. Learn who you are and grow into it. If you should get lost, forgive yourself. We've all had that to do. Forgive and don't follow that crooked path again."

"You and your unconditional love, Mom. Be sure you wrap it around yourself."

Tears shot to Teal's eyes, and she hugged Mia to her. "What a wonderful thing to say to me."

"I have until the end of next month in paid university housing. I'll have my applications in and my research done on housing and transportation costs in the Big Apple by then."

"Well, sit down now, young lady," her grandma Rena said, "and have some lunch."

"Maybe you'll want several weeks at home before your launch into that future," Teal suggested as they lunched.

"Maybe."

"We're four generations here today—a rare and wonderful treat," Letti said.

"Indeed," Teal agreed.

Teal helped clear away the food and wash the dishes then took Rena home and Mia to her car for her return to the dorm at Norman. Teal gave her the usual warm hug and a kiss on her cheek before leaving.

"Thank God for you, Mom," Mia told her, returning her embrace.

"For you, love," Teal returned. She hoped Mia knew how lucky she was to still have Letti and Rena and Esther; Harlin too. All her own grandparents had died years ago. Stories of Indian raids, influenza, small pox, and war dotted their histories.

Her throat constricted with sudden grief. Ray Swain: gone but never far from her heart. She brushed the tears away. The children: gone to their own lives. Gavin: lost to her and, perhaps, to his own life.

Had she never found a life away from him, he would still be separate, alone. She believed Letti and Rena had wanted her to see that today.

"He was raised alone." Rena's words prompted Teal's acceptance of Gavin's nature. Gratitude for her full life with or without him seemed to erase any potential for bitterness due to love lost.

And Jonsi—in Bucharest at the World Population 1974 Conference. She could always talk to Jonsi, whom Esther had insisted despised her until she'd attained the ripe old age of three when he'd begun to adore her. She wanted him home soon and less concerned about so many immigrants and births the world over. She knew he felt they would face shortages of food, water, and medical care by 2025. She hoped he helped find the solutions that he sought, and the world could be at peace without warring over scarcities.

—

346

Her own predictions for inflationary growth of energy and other costs by the '90s would no doubt contribute to an economy in crisis long before the world faced such shortages.

Such shadowy thoughts pried at her tendency to see only the bright side of dire situations. *Must we always wait and live it? Must we be pawns of power structures?*

Jonsi no longer believed in passivity. Perhaps she didn't either. If people created the political and economic power, people could act to change it. The concept seemed too simple to overlook any longer.

She thought about the millions of bushels she transported north to Kingfisher and Enid, and then it shipped out of Oklahoma by rail to Minnesota, much of it to a relatively new gathering terminal called Cenex Harvest States. She thought it might move to east St. Louis from there. On the move—a golden cargo always moving and changing into amazing products.

Just realizing that she had a tiny part in that engine of supply energized her for action—for growth.

CHAPTER XXIII

A Different Harvest

In New York and at the art studio, Teal and Brett tagged and identified by label each of his paintings and sculpted pieces. Mostly, he still carved the natural wildlife he'd grown up with and observed.

Intricate pieces of birds and rabbits, of beaver, and of a horse and rider, even a bobcat and coyote interpreted his summers. For he had seen most while on a tractor or in the combine helping Gavin and Harlin.

"I'm thrilled for you and so very proud," she told him as they worked.

His paintings were primarily watercolor. "They go fast," he'd told her once. He loved the old barns, the paint-peeled disintegrating original farmhouses with sagging roofs and doors, the ponds, the fields, and fauna—old equipment rusting in the fields. He captured this historical transition in rural life on paper.

"So wonderful," she complimented. "And with genius. Absolute genius." He had been invited to show in Chicago. He waved graduate school good-bye after the basics for teaching private art instruction and creating his pieces in his own studio. At twenty-two, his shows drew respectable crowds in Chicago or New York.

"It was your example, Mom. You that I watched paint and mold."

"But *you* have the talent. What a great twist to our story. Perhaps art will be your *only* career, Brett, not just a place to exhale after a day at the elevators the way it's been for me."

"Depends on whether I keep showing and selling. I'd like it to be. I'm willing to burn midnight oil for it."

She tousled his hair. "That's what it takes: persistence. I'm wheat, but you and Mia are emerald. I'm not sure I've got that idea right, something I read a long time ago in a book called *So Big* by Edna Ferber."

"Mia really is Emerald," he laughed.

"Guess I had a premonition when I named her Mia Emerald."

She reached to take down Upton Rush's violin that she had placed on a top shelf above his easels.

"Grandpa Harlin was the last person to play that, wasn't he?" Brett noted.

"Yes. Gavin was never interested, though Harlin hoped for it when he gave him the instrument. I want you to have it if your father doesn't object. It's *his* family's heirloom, made by hand by your great-grandfather Upton, according to Letti. He proved-up land in eastern Oklahoma. He hoped for wheat but got cotton. He wanted the land but lost it to find his future in business. Gavin and Harlin inherited the dream of Oklahoma gold when that business sold after his death. Seed money came to Upton," she said, "from his mother, Maddy Hines Rush. So she 'passed it on' to Harlin. 'Seemed only right,' she said.

"Letti has gifted Mia with the diaries of their life together. These were your people, strong and gifted people who endured, provided, and progressed in lives of service, Brett."

"I'll ask Dad if I can have it. Maybe I'll even learn to play it myself someday. But, Mom, you've given me the gift of art that I love so."

"You may father a child who will play it if you don't. It has a wonderful tone. Your granddad Harlin used to pick it up once in a while. He loved to play 'Listen to the Mockingbird.' Your dad and I two-stepped to it more than once. In any case, I hope it never leaves the family."

"Dad danced to 'Listen to the Mockingbird' when he shot them off the windmill and out of trees to shut them up? What's that all about? I always silently rooted for the birds, wanting them to get away alive."

"It's their optimism, baby. It depresses him." She laughed. "I'm not certain what that's about either," she said with a shrug, "but I've decided he likes to worry."

Eric Meriott surprised them, arriving at the studio door unexpectedly. "Hey!" he said, immediately reaching for the violin. He drew the bow across the strings.

"Hey yourself," Brett said. Teal knew they had grown fond of one another. Eric had even ridden buses all the way to New York City and back to Oklahoma to spend weekends with Mia and Brett and to see Manhattan.

"Maybe Eric would like to learn how to play it," she said. "It's Gavin's, but no one plays it now. I've promised it to Brett if Gavin agrees. *Someone* should play it."

"Yes," Brett agreed.

"You sure?" Eric asked, obviously thrilled. "May I borrow it?"

"Sure," Brett said.

"In fact, Eric," Teal said, "I've been wondering if you'd like to train for assistant manager of the elevator and mill. You've a degree in business management now and always seemed interested in the business. You've worked part-time in almost every department. You grew up with the business. I can't carry on here forever—might not even want to. Charles and Jenny have their hands full with the fertilizer and chemical division."

Carefully, he placed the instrument in its case. "You bet I would. I love that place. I care about its future for our area."

"You see that, do you? I'm impressed. Then it's settled. I'll see you on Monday morning, eight sharp." She reached to shake his hand. "But now, let's go to the apartment for a sandwich and tea.

—

Brett has news about another Chicago show to tell us. We've been getting ready for it."

Eric took her hand in both of his. His grip felt warm and strong.

Teal smiled warmly, pleased at his acceptance and thinking that he'd grown quite tall over the years. *He must be about twenty-eight now*, she thought. *A man.* "You're a man now, Eric." She smiled. "You grew up when I wasn't looking."

They closed the studio, and after a brief visit and a snack at her apartment, Brett went home, and Eric found space on Teal's flight back to Oklahoma City. The flight was uneventful, serene, and quite smooth.

Before they recovered their autos and headed west for Canadian County and home, Eric invited her for a coffee in the airport restaurant. "This was a good idea, Eric," she said. "Thank you. Caffeine will see me home."

"Thank *you*," he returned. "I'm looking forward to working with you, Teal."

That he addressed her by her first name surprised her, but she didn't correct him.

"As am I," she agreed. "You've become a fine, accomplished man. You'll have a great future at Swains, I promise."

He regarded her in silence. His strong features around those gray eyes and that thick shock of brown hair trying to curl at his neckline arrested her attention in a strangely different way. Long strong fingers circled his coffee cup.

She glanced away, disconcerted. When she looked back, she said, "Who would have thought you, not Brett, would be with me at the mill?"

"Who would have," he said softly, then drank the last of his coffee. "Would you like more?"

She shook her head. "Thank you, no." So he took their empties and tossed them in the trash.

"I'll see you to your car," he said, touching her elbow lightly when she stood.

—

*   *   *

Within two years, wheat moved from $4.40 to $5.00, a price that exceeded the target price of $3.40. So no deficiency payments were made. It had cost Gavin over the five dollars a bushel to raise the crop because of fuel and fertilizer costs. However, the lush summer native pasture had fattened cattle before the time to transfer them to the winter wheat. Their gain increased to weights of eight hundred to nine hundred pounds each. He made a huge profit on the steers and cleared almost a hundred thousand *after costs* for his last hay and wheat crops on the two farms he owned and the two that he leased—a section of six hundred forty acres, some shy of the one thousand acres he planned.

Taxes hadn't been paid as yet, and the investment for the next crop could easily be thirty thousand. Still, Gavin's prospects for ag-business growth looked good.

A few oil and gas wells now dotted Canadian County. Gavin coveted one to offset costs and pay for improved equipment that could easily cost a quarter of a million now.

After taxes and all bills for the '83 crop—fuel, seed, oil, insect and fungi treatments, equipment repair and depreciation, cattle vet bills and inoculation costs, fencing and water gap restoration—he had forty-five thousand for living expenses, the unexpected, and to put in the next crop.

"We need a baler we can't buy. I'll need to pay again to have hay swathed and baled. The rains brought needed moisture but damaged the terraces and fencing. We could use another hay barn. Hay rots in the field.

"There's the expansion we need," he went on. "We could sell hay to Texas at a premium if I had a way to store it. If we have a crop failure at these prices, Teal, we're bankrupted."

"But if we can reserve as much as twenty-five thousand for a cushion," she said, "we'd make it to sow another crop, at least. Can you negotiate with Texas truckers to come get the hay until you can build the storage?"

"Can we live on less than two thousand a month? Insurance ad valorem," he reminded. He lifted his bill cap and scratched his head. Bald on top now, his hair fringed the cap when he slapped it back.

"We can always use my salary. You know that, but I think we can live on less than that."

"You've covered the education costs for Mia, Brett's art lessons."

"Whatever it takes, Gavin," she said. "Besides, those costs are going away. They've launched their careers," she reminded, "and the loans are about paid off. They're helping with that debt besides being self-supporting."

"One of these years, I'm going to plant it all to grass and forget the rest," he swore.

"And if cattle prices drop while feed prices go up? If chemical to control the weeds goes sky high, what then?"

"I've never respected being paid for planting nothing," he said. "But there's a program for it."

"Nor I, but land does need a rest. Let's rotate. We'll make less profit, but it will reduce the risk for a while. With Harlin's and Rena's ground and what we own and lease, you're cultivating over two thousand acres now, aren't you?"

Gavin didn't respond. She'd never been able to persuade him to rotate acres, rest the land. He and Harlin pushed land hard by drilling thick rows and fertilizing heavily.

At last he said, "I farm for profit, and I'll have profit any way I can get it."

*　　*　　*

Over the next few years, Swain Elevator profits paid for the added local storage and allowed expansion of storage into several other Oklahoma counties. The Kansas operation functioned well. It broke even after two years before clearing a profit of $250,000. Teal now considered extending farther into Colorado.

Eric had introduced terminals at rail sites and maintained trucking to Houston. He utilized trucks, barges at the Port of Catoosa, and rail to keep wheat moving.

"By 1986, Eric and I hope to add milling to the Colorado sites," she told Gavin. "Instead of reducing acreage and planting improved grain only, more volume with the same philosophy may be *your* answer, Gavin."

"Stop now!" he complained. "I can lease instead of buy. You can't. Businesses and banks are still falling out over the oil bust. Believe me, more and more farmers will throw in the towel instead of increasing volume. Few young men not born into it want it now. Half that are born to it want out. The land belongs to them, but they don't want it because no one on the outside understands their cost. Many are land rich and dollar poor without cattle and gas wells. Consumers probably believe we get rich on the government price supports for just playing with our trucks and tractors. Their food comes from grocery stores, not a farm. The typical citizen may be disassociated from Oklahoma's history and their own rural backgrounds.

"The government has never clarified agricultural programs for the public, probably because of its inequities, their own confusion, and the market's volatility. Tax dollars should never have gone to subsidize thousands of acres of sorry land that could never produce a crop of anything but cactus or sagebrush. Commodities don't belong on the board of trade any more than in a money fund for gambling. We need a national cooperative with state satellites and a network of marketing and transit specialists.

"If we got ten dollars a bushel tomorrow with no price support, one failed crop within the next two years from flood, bugs, drought, or freeze would ruin us without good cattle prices and second jobs."

Teal had listened in silence once more to his doom-and-gloom word assault. This time seemed different. He named some of the problems, and he suggested a solution.

"Another elevator or another baby," she laughed. "We're still standing, Gavin."

But Gavin didn't laugh.

"You're in a fantasy world, totally oblivious to this economic jungle."

"I wish you were here with me in my ivory tower, Gavin. Farmers must accommodate change, stay flexible perpetually just as we do at Swains. That's a good idea you have, that national co-op and all the rest."

"Too far to fall from," he said.

"No. You grow or shrink there too, for nothing stays the same," she said. "And you hang on during tough times as if they were a hurricane."

"Then count me out. I've had it. Marriage makes me economically responsible for my ag crisis—not yours and not the challenge of an ag movement for other farmers. When Dad retires, I'll have the volume I need."

"I'm salaried. You're not at risk because of me. The children are now self-supporting. What are you saying, Gavin? I don't have a Swain business crisis."

"I'm at risk *because* you're a salaried nine to five. I need more volume or more cash than that nine to five pays you. You could take out more. You're the CEO of a multimillion dollar company now, for Christ's sake, and you sink it all back in the company. All of this would resolve, even with the worst scenario, if I had the volume Dad's retirement will bring now. Another child," he scoffed. "You're almost forty-five years old, for God's sake. I'm not about to raise another child when I've been waiting for these to grow up."

"Waiting for what?" Trembling overtook her until she felt she could not stand.

He gave her a cold glance, turned away, and left the house. But not before he'd tossed an insult over his shoulder.

"You'll never change. Same old, same old. I've outgrown you, Teal." And he was gone, his pickup roaring down the lane, the sound fading like feelings dying.

She hadn't known that the most important events in one's life were captured in mere moments—birth, death, marriage, loss—all just moments in time. Perhaps she had been just a convenience for him at an inconvenient time in his life even in the beginning. Hadn't she wondered about that but never convinced herself of it because she hoped for a dream come true: of crossing the bridge safely with Gavin to the happy-ever-after life on the other side.

He needed his father's and her increase besides his own, then he would have enough? That seemed to be his insight. She didn't believe it. Enough would never be absolutely enough for Gavin.

She slept fitfully, an anger she recognized as fear raged without subsiding. At dawn, she rose and drank black coffee. He hadn't returned.

Letti's admonition years ago to use her feelings to fight crossed her mind. She believed in free choice, in freedom, in equality. She would fight for those values. So how could she fight Gavin for changing his mind about both his marriage and his partnership with Harlin? She couldn't. Her youthful notion of coldcocking Sara Jane died with Sara and inexperience. She must survive this crushing emotional upheaval that assaulted her life without her permission.

She wondered if Harlin knew that Gavin wanted to take over his land and probably just pay him lease monies—a pittance to his actual partnership profit. How wounded he must feel to see a son become so ungrateful.

"I do love my life," she said to the wall. "Thank God for the times with family, for the work, for Mia and Brett, for the best of times with Gavin." Yet her usual energy lagged. Tempted to call Eric and say she wasn't coming in, she resisted, arriving at the usual time.

"Are you all right?" he asked her, midafternoon.

"I didn't sleep well last night," she said. "I'll be fine tomorrow."

She wasn't. Within weeks, Gavin revealed he wanted a divorce on the grounds of incompatibility. "We're too different now," he said. But she had heard he had someone else. They had been seen together at restaurants and hotels in Oklahoma City. Teal didn't know her, wouldn't want to.

—

"It takes two," she told Jenny. "But if the woman had principles, the man would remain with his wife. Good women send married men home." They were having lunch together at Teal's.

"Good men may divorce, but it ought to be because their wives betrayed them unless they can forgive and forget," Jenny responded.

Teal shook her head. "I'm venting to you. Pay it no mind. Thank God Charles hasn't wandered."

"He just pays a hooker," she said. "That's what Charles does."

Teal didn't shock easily. But the idea of the elite Charles Huel and a hooker shocked her.

"We've done something wrong," Teal said.

"Maybe we just don't know how to pick them," Jenny said.

"I'm right about the obvious," Teal concluded. "When something ends, something else begins. And that always interests me. They're both good men, just human ones."

"Bullshit!" Jenny said. "We got shafted by them. Well, little sister," she added, "your ideal world isn't so ideal any more is it?"

"I think I need a trip, time to absorb this—"

"Humiliation," Jenny volunteered.

Teal wanted to deny that her pride had been gravely injured. It seemed pointless. "Humiliation," she agreed.

Past the pain, Teal knew Gavin's aura would never leave her so long as Brett and Mia were in her life. There would be grandchildren, extensions of them both, born of common genetics to them both. The thought slowly eased the anger into a decision to accept her new reality.

The harvest of family and prosperity they might have shared remained a harvest nonetheless.

"Bet his new conquest has land, little sister."

Teal nodded, yielding to the probability. "Bet you're right. Enough to add up to one thousand owned—not leased—cultivated acres."

*   *   *

Teal planned a long visit to New York City. After a Broadway show and museums, shopping, and Central Park, she landed at Mia's apartment. She kept her reservation at the downtown Howard Johnson Hotel however, for Mia had a one-room walk-up with a bath down the hall. There wasn't really room for two to be comfortable.

"Bring an inflatable bed next time, Mom. We could have more time together."

Teal loved Mia's unaffected ways. This, she thought, she had done right.

Brett still commuted from Oklahoma City to Manhattan for shows and points in between to realize the sales that supported him quite nicely. He phoned them from his Chicago show.

"He thinks he can afford to stay at his New York City studio by '88," Mia said, putting back the receiver. "He doesn't think he can sell enough from there yet to give him the lifestyle he wants now. He's short of time but expects to be back here in a few days. Said to tell you he'll call again later."

With that bit of information, Teal told Mia about the trust. "Yours will be available to you on my return home. When Brett is twenty-five, his will be too. Perhaps you can work part-time and polish that novel that's still waiting in your desk drawer with the rest of Grandmother Letti's memoirs."

"There's enough there for several novels," Mia agreed.

"Your father has filed for a divorce," she revealed to Mia before returning home two weeks later. "He'll get the house, for it sits on land in his and Harlin's name."

Mia sat silently, her hands folded together.

"You don't need to say anything," Teal told her. "I'm all right. Nothing ever stays the same. I've always known that. Only sure things are—"

"God and change," Mia finished. "Does Brett know?" she asked.

"Not yet. Most people would have said death and taxes," Teal noted.

"Not you, Mom."

Teal smiled then. "I'll tell Brett when he gets back to Oklahoma. He'll be between shows and projects. Eric knows. I felt I had to tell him to justify these weeks away from the Oklahoma division of Swains."

"Good idea," she said.

"What if I came here more often, helped you locate a larger place? You can afford it now. I'd like to come here every few months for a weekend, anyway."

"Yeah, maybe I can. Then you *can* stay with me when you're here."

"One of these days you'll marry one of your suitors, career girl. So don't let me get too accustomed to being around that much."

"But for now, Mom. Okay? You'll need it, I'll love it—really."

Teal hugged her, her heart full of joy for this child. "Thanks," was all she could manage. "Do I need to call a cab?"

"They're almost always around," Mia said.

Teal looped the small valise over her shoulder and left the walk-up. Within five minutes, she had hailed a yellow cab and was en route to John F. Kennedy.

She would call Heath, she thought. They were long overdue for that talk that could heal their communication breakdown. He'd surely heard or read about her divorce. She wondered if he would prefer she wait until after the settlement and final decree. *Heath was always proper,* she recalled with a grimace. Would he feel it inappropriate to help her with her legal questions?

Heath is still Heath, she reminded herself, deciding to get as much in order as possible first, then call. Still, he could certainly be her divorce lawyer. They could be friends now, for no spouses would make their friendship impossible. They might even talk honestly with one another about the things left unsaid.

Suddenly, Teal realized that was all she wanted: to say the things she should have said. She no longer wanted intimacy with him. She also realized that she had wounded Heath by not helping him understand her. Even now she loathed explaining herself. *To be understood might not change anything, anyway,* she thought. *He may remain rigid and angry, but I will at least have tried,* she reasoned. The risk to her pride seemed negligible now—the result of growing up, she supposed.

It brought a smile to her lips to realize it. She thought about how life had cycles that reminded her of economic and weather cycles. Did all of life spiral from its beginning to repetitive cycles that simply appeared different in their sameness?

All news suddenly seemed the bad news related to nuclear energy, wars, poverty, recession, aids, fuel scarcity. How had her forbears felt when they saw Vikings at their door or knew Alexander plundered nearby? The eons had seen huge volcano eruptions, floods, earthquakes, droughts, hail. Weren't dark clouds always over fundamentally free people to claim or destroy? She gave herself a little shake. *Relative to real problems, I have none. After all,* she reminded herself, *I'm no longer a child!*

Change! Change! And more change!

When I see Heath, she thought, *I'll discuss the US trade policies with him. He has accomplished so much in Washington, perhaps he can put his expert skills to the problem of trade imbalance and inadvertently help agricultural exports in the process.* The thought immediately lifted her mood for the reported trade deficit of 2.1 billion invited creative plans for wheat.

CHAPTER XXIV

A New Life

Two days after the final decree, Teal picked up the Sunday *Oklahoman*. She'd taken a six-month lease on an apartment near the elevator complex until she could relocate. She sat at the outdoor table on the balcony, the sun rising. *Good coffee this morning,* she thought, opening the paper. Around nine o'clock, she had gotten to the obituary pages.

There, the handsome face of Heath stared back. Gone. Heath, gone. She couldn't move. The paper fell to the floor, the rest unread. *Why?* Her mind screamed. How could he have been ill without her sensing it, knowing it?

She phoned Eric. "What can I do?"

"I'll need time off for a few days—legal things, arrangements."

"Of course."

"Auto crash," Eric said. "A drunk crossed the median, began driving in the wrong lane. When Dad swerved, he overcorrected, lost control, and rolled the car. Instant, they said. I'll call you when I know the arrangements."

"I've a new number." She gave it to him and replaced the receiver.

Nothing was the same. She had thought she could recover a bit of the past. Now it too had vanished. Memories, she had memories. Somehow, some way, she must make more memories.

"Good ones too!" she said aloud, like the memories behind her. She poured herself a brandy. "To you, Heath, wherever you are." No longer confident of the mortality of those she loved. She checked on Esther's well-being.

Teal signed the papers that allowed Gavin's new life. She walked into a future that felt mutilated by others less committed to loyalties. Her days just passed by like the rail cars that moved beyond the elevator. She often felt lifeless as if her life had no center. Like rock music, harsh and without melody, the active-filled months turned into years. She longed for joy. She sought it in trips to New York City, in films, and books. She took a trip to Central Europe, to the Middle East.

To distract her from work that now seemed grueling instead of challenging, she escaped to Manhattan. She stayed with Brett or with Mia, often for weeks at a time. She returned home only to go back again for the infusion of sunshine her children brought to her. She planned and implemented wider bakery franchise areas to add both interest and length to her workdays. She met new people and saw new places by such enterprise and soon felt alive again.

"What do you think?" she asked Mia. "Should I call the new bakery items Swain Wheat Treats?"

"You've enough bakeries and bakery items, Mama. Go home and marry Heath Meriott. He's alone, you're alone. It's a logical match now. Dad centered your life, and you haven't followed your own advice and changed your mind about that now that he is no longer that center. Heath can be that center for you."

"Mia!" Teal said, startled. "I've dreaded telling you. I thought Eric surely had."

"Eric's so busy, Mom. He's worried about you too. Told me what? Eric hasn't been here in over six months, and he's mentioned nothing about Heath in our phone conversations. Isn't Heath well?"

"Bad car crash—he died instantly. It happened three months ago. Eric just followed the plans Heath himself had made: a private cremation. He plans a public memorial service soon though. I'll notify you. I should go home, I've left too much for Eric. Winter snow and ice will catch me here if I'm not gone soon." She gave Mia a hug.

"I'm so sorry, Mom. Tell Eric I'll call him, will you? And go by Brett's studio apartment first. He's done some new abstracts that are *so* good. Seeing them will be good for you, I promise. Mom, will you be all right about, well, everything? You've dealt with so much: Granddad, Daddy, and now Heath's passing."

"These visits have helped me, Mia. You and Brett are like a tonic. I've probably overdone it. Eric and Josh encouraged it, but it's not fair to them to keep up this every-month visiting. I've so many great people that manage almost everything everywhere. I only oversee now, actually. So don't you worry about me. I needed your advice, and I'll give these new franchises my best shot. Your father just can't be replaced, that's the problem. But perhaps I can find a less prominent spot in my memories for him."

"I arranged this place for two, Mom, for me and you from the beginning. But you may be stuck with it if you want it."

"Eric?" she asked, holding her breath.

"You silly, Mom. Eric Meriott's my friend. I've told you that."

"You've someone else?" Teal asked, surprised.

"Yes, finally. I thought I'd never meet anyone I wanted to see at breakfast for the next fifty years."

"I dread telling Eric," Teal said, breathing easily again. "He'll be hurt, Mia. But thank goodness he has our family. Perhaps you want to tell him," she said as an afterthought.

"You do it, Mom, please."

Teal's heart seemed to skip a beat. The thing she'd feared had not fallen on her; neither Mia or Eric need ever be told that they were possibly half brother and sister. Both Sarah and Heath lay buried with any secrets. Gavin's exit from her life might leave a vacuum

—

for Eric, though she doubted it would ever occur to him that Gavin could be his biological father.

"Well, who is he?" she asked, brushing her concern for Eric aside for the moment. "When can I meet him?" she asked.

"Maybe Thanksgiving, Christmas for sure. He's a playwright named David Wynn. He says he sees Great-gran Letti's life on the screen. He loved it, especially the parts about territorial days, thugs, and the hanging judge. When *you* tell Eric, find some way to casually say how I love him like—like a brother."

"Like a brother," she mused.

"Don't fret. I'll find a way," she said, feeling like smiling for the first time in months.

From the airport, the shuttle took her to her off-airport parking. A fine mist dampened Meridian Avenue as she headed west toward home. By the time she reached her apartment, the temperature had dropped over twenty degrees, and a thin coat of black ice had begun to form.

There were no messages for her. *All must be well*, she thought. Restructuring had been a good idea. The change forced her to move on, to create, to think about franchises instead of Gavin's public plans to remarry as soon as their six-month waiting period ended.

As the QA overseer and CEO, Teal had restructured the company to accommodate their growth. She'd made Eric president, Josh her one vice-president, and all assistant managers became managers. Eric hired out-of-state managers, supervisors, assistants, shippers, bakers, bookkeepers, chemists, elevator help, and millers, all restructuring done with board approval. She delegated the hiring of office personnel to Eric also, for she planned to stay on the go, personally visiting each operation at every location to stay in touch with the product from grain to marketing.

She hoped to invest in their own hoppers for a shortage caused a backlog and operation-systems plans to fail. Moreover, the economic problems with the Rock Island Rail Company caused her worry.

Keeping her bags packed for frequent trips seemed therapy for her.

Eric contracted an advertising firm to keep the Swain name before the public via contests, sales, and sponsorships. The brand name, Esther Ray, for breads and desserts would soon be partnered with Swain Mills and Ray's Bakery-Restaurant chain.

Four more months to freedom, she thought before drifting into sleep. She slept well at last, grateful for her own bed. She sprawled over onto what might have been Gavin's side, allowing herself to enjoy the space. With the morning, she murmured to the pillow, "No more being crowded to the edge, no more blanket stealing." A tear slid onto the pillowcase. *Perhaps the last one,* she thought.

She had set the coffee on automatic. The alarm had barely gone off before its aroma reached her. She swung her legs off the bed, eager for a cup. It felt great to be alive again. She stretched luxuriously. The day felt like a miracle. It seemed that when Mia identified her emotional stagnation, Teal released it. Now, like an amoeba, she explored, seeking to give her life greater purpose than mere function and existence.

"Bergland's announcement that the farmers are making plenty of money is downright inspirational," she said to the wall. The remark stirred her blood and put her back into a fighting mode. She realized the problem of an eighteen-billion-dollar trade surplus over the United States (even more than the year before) would not dislodge the stubborn protectionist mentality in the United States of late, so a fight for fairness in the marketplace seemed an absolute necessity. Agriculture accounted for over a fourth of the nation's income, some twenty-six billion to eighty billion dollars, depending on who you talked to and what was included in the statistics.

To neglect agriculture would *always* court disaster everywhere, including that of world hunger.

First snow had begun to fall outside. She sipped coffee and watched it past the open drapes.

The fog of emotional trauma now lifted. She saw that her love for Gavin had generated many of her past goals, her hope, and her energy to succeed. The mere transference of that affection to herself couldn't cause this morning's joy, she thought. The power of love itself filled her center as if a room were made for it by that great love once there for Gavin but redirected now to her community and beyond.

"Praise God," she said aloud. Because Gavin lived, she had learned through experiencing her love for him what power that caring gave a life to grow, give, create, survive, renew.

She had just spread her toast with raspberry jelly and taken a big bite when the phone rang. It alarmed her to hear Josh saying that the feed mechanism that mixed the grains had stalled again and no feed could be mixed. *How could such a problem be brought to a screeching halt?* she wondered. She knew no solution but climbing that ladder. She grimaced, thinking of the disgruntled line of farm trucks. They would be needing feed this morning.

"Oh my god! I'll be right there. Don't let anyone go up, Josh. No one!" She chased the toast with a last swallow of coffee. She felt as if it could come back up. She put the cup down and headed for the elevator. All this expansion, she condemned herself, and she hadn't built a crow's nest over the feed mill to make any needed surface approach safer.

She felt shaken by the news and angry with herself for the oversight. The ladder and spherical surface would be iced over as before. Over a hundred feet high and as tall as a ten-story building, the climb there made Teal's head swim. Worse was the thought that one of her people might fall to their death as her father had.

She stopped by the hardware store for a can of defrost accelerant. She dropped it into her jacket pocket in case she needed it. She grabbed her pigskin gloves, a fur cap, and an extra sweatshirt. Her sport shoes were felt lined and cleated, but she purchased spikes that she could pull over her shoes for more secure footing. Suddenly, she realized that she had decided to go up.

"Think of it as an ice castle with your prince charming waiting at the top," she muttered, driving away from the hardware.

Act in charge. Act unafraid, she tutored herself, pulling into the lot nearest the office. Eric met her. *If I act the part, I'll surely begin to feel more sure of myself.*

"Hey, boss!" he greeted with a warm smile. "My job just got interesting."

"I'm sure I don't know what you mean, my good man. You're not going up there. It's simply not *your* responsibility. I've been lax by not building a crow's nest over the top to shield the surface from ice. Surely that would prevent frozen gates and floor spouts. We need that same solution for any feed mills in Kansas and Colorado as well."

His smile vanished. He shook his head. "I'll do monthly breaker and loose wire checks twice monthly from now on. I'll do one now to make sure there's no jamming of feed in the mixer. You go on inside. There's fresh coffee for you," he insisted.

She pulled on the pigskin gloves as she made eye contact without blinking. He must not guess that heights bothered her so, that she felt pulled back to earth when she looked down, that she loathed herself for fearing anything, wondered if she could force herself past this sickening dread she must face down. Hadn't she overcome that fear of crossing bridges when she accepted chaos in her life? That had been in dreams, but still applied.

Reluctantly, he handed her the ax hammer.

"I've de-icer," she said, reaching for it.

"That won't knock that thick ice free. Believe me, you'll have to use some muscle and an ax hammer."

She turned toward the feed elevator and pushed ahead against cold wind. Eric caught up to her. "No way! You're too important—" He stopped.

"I'm not more important than a single one of my employees. We're all in this together, remember? Like family. Which reminds me, we need to hire a person to oversee cross-training, travel. Do it seminar fashion so that all employees develop an awareness of the job descriptions across the spectrum. It will grow mutual respect within the company's divisions. Prep them for learning another position!" Teal yelled over the wind that tried to steal her breath.

"Not before I build a ten-foot-tall accessible cap for this feed mill!" he declared. "I've seen enough of this."

—

They had reached the ladder. Eric pulled an ax hammer off his tool belt. She would think of detailing those plans as she climbed, she decided. If she didn't think about the climb, if she didn't look down, she could do it. She reached for the tool, but Eric held on to it.

"Teal." He grabbed her. "Don't."

"Eric, for heaven's sake. I'll be fine."

"I shouldn't have waited for you. I'd have done the job by now."

She grabbed the slick sides of the steel ladder; the pigskin gloves helped.

"I'll be here," he finally said, yielding to her. "I'd have to knock you out to stop you, and I haven't the heart for that."

She took the ax hammer from him then. "It will take a while. I'm in no hurry. Don't be alarmed if I'm slow to take the surface. I'll be slipping into spikes."

Between each rung, Teal counted to ten. *I can't look down,* she thought. Her neck ached; she trembled inside. *Deep breaths. Deep breaths. Count to ten,* she reminded herself. The cold air crept inside her warm clothes. Her chest ached with every breath.

On the top, she paused. She didn't know if her shaking was caused by the cold or her nerves, but she must stop it. She struck at the thick ice repeatedly to release the frozen area. Wind tore at her as the grain again began to slide down the metal legs into assorted bins to be chopped or ground. Her shaking subsided.

Still, she knew that the problem wasn't resolved. She'd write a work order immediately for the whole feed mill to be checked and serviced quarterly and for the crow's nest to be built over its surface. The motor oil could be checked then too. Thinking calmed her. She began the slow descent. Her feet felt numb from the cold, so she focused on every step's resistance. An eternity seemed to pass before she approached that bottom ladder rung.

"Won't do to stop the traffic until this freeze ends," she called to Eric. "Then the motors to the grinders should be serviced." She thought herself calm, relieved, and safe; so why didn't her legs support her? "Cattle need feed," she said as if anyone needed reminding of that. Her knees felt like Jell-O.

He caught her from the back. The moment her feet touched the ground, he spun her toward him. She stumbled into him, startled at his nearness. When she slumped against him, he lifted her.

"Put me down, Eric. I'm all right."

"You're not all right. You're almost frozen."

He put her in one of the comfortable customer chairs inside, took off his coat, and wrapped it over her own, then poured her a cup of hot coffee. "Off with those gloves," he said, holding it toward her.

Teal reminded herself that Eric was only three years older than Mia and fifteen years her junior for he felt like her peer when he took charge as he had taken it moments before. The involuntary replay of Eric's embrace generated a delayed response as she warmed her hands around the cup. She felt on the downside of the highest roller-coaster loop. *Any feelings he could possibly have for me are because of Mia*, she reminded herself. *Foolish older woman*, she thought, *vulnerable to the younger man*. Did Eric need to be kept or mothered? Knowing him disposed of either motive. Stable, strong, and intelligent—that described Eric. Good looks and a genuine personality frosted that delightful package of traits.

She felt a warm flush rush her senses. She averted her eyes to avoid his gaze and the betrayal of this altered way of seeing him. She'd not appear a fool to Eric. *Yes, of course*, she thought. She had always been fond of him. Only that, she assured herself.

From the time the feed mill operated again, the typical day seemed anything but typical. For every time Eric came into her office or when the moment arrived for her to ask him a question about some customer's order or a bill of lading, this altered awareness of him threatened to break out of containment into their reality. She felt unhinged.

She called him on the phone. "I need to tell you Mia's news," she told him. That should close the door on this confusing awareness, trap it on the side of youth, and set things straight as before. She would witness the pain of rejection in his eyes at the news of Mia's engagement to David Wynn.

To Teal's surprise, he expressed gladness over the news of Mia's engagement when they spoke. The familiar relationship they shared as friends remained, but this unfamiliar unrest that disturbed her in a pleasurable way grew stronger.

One afternoon a few weeks later when the day wound down and the only employees left were she and Eric, he walked through her office door. She glanced up at him.

Why hadn't he married? she wondered. Handsome, healthy, smart, and personable, he had surely waited for Mia to commit to something more serious than friendship. Yet his cheerful acceptance of her fiancé seemed genuine.

"Eric," she greeted, first standing, then walking to meet him. "Sit down." She gestured to one of two blue-tweed customer chairs and sat down next to him.

"Thank you for all you do," she said first. "I don't think I adequately show my appreciation. Do you need more office assistants? You have my approval to hire more help if you need it."

He only nodded. A little smile played across his lips. "You have authorized enough help."

"I need to tell you more news about Mia and David. They're relocating."

He nodded. "Don't think you can just deny reality. Send me away, Teal. You'll regret it."

"Of course I wouldn't do that, Eric. This isn't about a job transfer."

He seemed to be looking at her strangely as if he didn't understand something.

"Let me explain. She and this playwright, a David Wynn, will be leaving the Manhattan apartment."

"I don't understand. Why should that bother me? I know you thought I hung around until I wheedled my way into your life because of Mia, but what are you thinking now?"

Teal stared dumbly at him, aware of what he might say next. A hot flash raced to her scalp from her toes and then drenched her like a wraparound blanket of steam. However, she recognized that her *change* and Esther's bore no resemblance. She felt far more for Eric than friendship. She thought it incredible that her response to him differed from feelings she had for Heath or Gavin, yet they also sprang from love. Her feelings for Heath had seemed the same as for her own self, for Gavin—like home or safety, even water. He had seemed a source of life for her.

"From the first time I saw you, Teal, I've wanted to be near you, any way I could be. You are the only person I've ever seen then to now who does things a hundred percent, supports others a hundred percent, who acts authentically. You either overlook the rudeness, neglect, and mediocrity of others, or don't even see it."

"Oh, Eric," she began. But he didn't let her stop him.

"I *was* a child when Mia was born and only an adolescent when Brett was a child. But I'm a man now. You are one of those rare individuals who want the best for everyone, faults or no faults. Otherwise, you *never* would have asked me into the business and treated me like someone special—me, the bastard."

"Stop right there!" She stood and faced him, her voice tinged with anger. I'm *not* all that and never can be. Please, don't require it of me. I'm as flawed and struggling to be mended as anyone. And don't *ever* call yourself a bastard to me! Never!"

"It will never be said again." His tone softened. "I think you wanted me to know it, though, because of Mia. But because of the scandal to Gavin or to me, even to Mom, you would never have told." He reached for her hand and drew her back beside him again.

"You knew? What if it isn't even true, Eric? I've never felt certain of it."

"Mom told me before she died. I have no feelings for Gavin. Sorry! Gavin thinks of Gavin. I have no respect for his desertion of Mom and me, and don't ever expect me to regard him in anyway but civil. Heath was my father. Heath accepted me as you have."

She nodded. "We finally understand each other, and I'm glad." She smiled at him, pleased with the honesty of their exchange.

He seemed surprised.

"Don't you be surprised. I'm the one who has had a surprising day. If I understand you, you love me—not Mia. You also believe Gavin's your biological father and couldn't care less. But the biggest surprise of all, I'm in love with you, my junior, so I hope you aren't saying you love me like a mother or idolize me for the image you imagine me to be. I'm human, older, and have faults *and* wrinkles."

"Teal, I'm thirty-two years old. Please don't hold age against me."

"How could I not have known all the ways I love you?" she said, tears starting.

"You're a proper person. It didn't seem appropriate. Therefore, it didn't exist," he said.

"You got it," she laughed. "You know me pretty well."

"What were you going to tell me a while ago about Mia and David Wynn?" he asked.

"That I was taking Mia's apartment in Manhattan. It's larger, and I love it there. It will simplify my trips there whether they are for business or for pleasure."

He stood then and drew her to her feet.

She leaned her head upon his shoulder. He held her there a moment before kissing her.

"We'll keep it for a getaway now and then," he said. "But we're building our own place. I have plans I'll show you. You'll love them."

"You were that sure of yourself, were you?"

"How about a burger?" he asked abruptly. I'm starved."

"Me too," she readily agreed.

They talked about everything from Manhattan to business expansion, from where to live to wheat markets, prices, and the effects of inflation. "Our business just generates carloads, not trainloads. Trucking plus rail *must* be our course," Teal said.

Eric nodded agreement. "No problem. I'm not an either-or thinker unless it's a life-or-death situation—usually."

"I've seen all of Manhattan, yet I'll never tire of it *or* of these hills and canyons," she told him, finishing her second cup of coffee. "I suppose I'm not either. I enjoy so much of everything, everywhere." At last, she approached the subject she dreaded. "Eric, you'll surely want children. At forty-seven, I'm not sure I could—"

"I've thought of that," he said. "If you could, and you probably could, it might not be wise for you or the infant to do it. What's wrong with a surrogate? We can negotiate through an intermediary and never even meet her."

"You're so casual about something so important."

"It seems so, because the notion of us and why it can work is new to you. I've had *years* to think about it, to plan for us."

She dropped her chin in her hand, smiling across at him. Her elbow rested on the table. "People will say all kinds of things about us—that I'm a gullible older woman, that you're after my money."

"I couldn't help but notice Gavin's schedule that constantly kept him away from home. In his way, he loved you, Teal. He just loved money and land more. If he and this wife think alike, that money is worth more than people or personal integrity, they'll be compatible. When he partnered with his folks instead of you, I thought his values would end the marriage years ago."

"Perhaps it did," she said softly. "Perhaps it died a natural death." A frown creased her brow as she spoke again. "Another child around may keep me young enough for you."

"I couldn't care less about your age. It won't matter unless you let it. Don't try to make me feel more or less than you because of it. I'll only think you doubt me."

"Sorry."

"Sure." He reached to clasp her hand. "Let's get out of here." He took her back to her car, planted a good night kiss on her, and helped her inside it. "I'm so grateful for tonight, for the way the day ended. But next time, Teal, we'll not be in separate cars going separate ways." He flashed a smile, then said, "Tomorrow night?"

"Tomorrow night," she responded breathily.

CHAPTER XXV

Teal and Eric Marry

Soon after Teal and Eric returned from their Las Vegas wedding, they were at Harlin's funeral; then only ten years later, Rena Lily lay beside him.

Gavin stood before noon at their grave sites at Rena's passing then anxiously watched the futures at the elevator with a furrowed brow that afternoon.

"Gavin's the primary futures' informant around here," Eric told Teal one evening that same September. "Since you're at the bakery these days, you may not have noticed how often I see him. I suppose we've finally become friends, Teal. Does that make you uncomfortable? If it does, I'll back away," he hurriedly added. "Why, he even wants me to get out of the office and help him on his farm's feedlot when things are slower here during the winter."

Eric paused as if to give her time to consider his information and respond on the spot.

"Do you want that?" she asked momentarily.

"Harlin's gone. I think Gavin is losing his fortune plus his inheritance on the futures and may lose all of the land. Gossip at the coffee shop is that his wife is out of the house and in an apartment. Speculation is that she plans to file for a divorce. I guess I feel sorry for him, Teal. For a truth, he needs help."

"The futures probably looked like another shortcut to greater wealth. Gavin's always looking for an easy way while he works eighteen hours a day at hard labor. He's like two personalities at war with one another. This may be something you both need, Eric. Don't think me too unkind when I say this though: Gavin is a shrewd, cold user who only cares about Gavin."

"Now, Teal. Everyone cares about someone."

"Not Gavin. You watch your back, Eric. Promise me."

"Oh, all right. I promise. I probably wouldn't do it if Brett partnered with him."

"Brett loves his life in the arts. He'll be glad for you to do it, believe me."

The following April, Gavin sent Eric on an equipment evaluation trip to Salina, Kansas, where a crew that retired advertised a gleaner for $25,000 and a used wheat truck for $20,000. Both sounded like bargains.

"He has a big spring sale at the feedlot," Eric explained to Teal, "or he would go. And at those prices, they could sell fast."

"I'll cover for you here. It should just take Friday and Saturday. I'll bet you're back Sunday afternoon. Besides, I want to watch this market. The board of trade stopped all trading on March wheat. A small group of traders are trying to corner the market, due to the tight supply in Chicago, probably. Fourteen million bushel were involved, almost six times the 2.4 million bushel of deliverable wheat."

"Call me with any news. I'll get a number to you as soon as I find a room."

Friday afternoon as she entered the morning feed sales in the books, Gavin came in to review the grain news. After watching the ticker tapes for a while, he poured a cup of coffee for her. "Looks like the market scare has passed," he observed.

"One teaspoon of sugar and a creamer, as I recall," he said, setting the cup down beside her. Standing behind her, he rested an arm across her shoulder and leaned into her for a moment. When she shrank away, he moved back.

"I drink it black now. Thanks anyway," she said.

"I've missed you," he persisted. "Big mistake. I made a *big* mistake letting you go."

Teal's mind raced to formulate what Gavin's ploy might be. She spun about on the swivel desk chair to face him. She knew now why Eric assessed equipment in Kansas, and she understood precisely why Gavin didn't go.

"Don't tell me," she said calmly. "Let me guess. We are made for one another. I still love you, and you never stopped loving me." But Gavin seemed not to notice her sarcasm.

"I knew you felt that way still. You'll always belong to me, Teal. Brett and Mia will be so pleased. Eric can work for both of us—nothing need change for him. He's a swell person, a good hired hand."

"A hired hand?"

Silence lay between them as they exchanged a knowing glance.

"*Eric's my husband,* Gavin, and I love him deeply. I have no regrets for our life together. But I would have huge regrets if I betrayed him.

"What a monster you are!" she accused. "No act is too low, no betrayal beyond you. Get out! Leave now, or I'll ring for Josh to throw you out. I may have seemed a shortcut or perhaps a responsibility bypass once, but never again!"

Gavin's bewildered look quickly changed to a smirk. "Miss High and Mighty. Energy's going up, the economy is beginning its cyclical downslide. You'll lose all this any day now, mark my words. Then you'll come crawling—"

Teal reached for the emergency cord, and a loud buzzer roared through the yards and buildings.

"I suppose you'll paint me the devil to Eric," he bellowed.

When she regarded him with steely silence, he left. She had no intention of telling Eric. It would only hurt him. What had Eric and Gavin's relationship to do with her and Gavin's? Nothing that she could see. She felt that Eric would see how Gavin used him

in his own time. His own time seemed the best time to Teal, who despised the idea of assassinating Gavin's character for him. Their relationship started in Sara Jane's womb before she and Gavin married. *And though he believes that means nothing to him,* she thought, *he could be in denial.*

The following weekend, Eric volunteered to help Gavin break ground again on a farm that had stayed too wet to sow. With these dryer days, perhaps all the wheat would be sown before Thanksgiving.

"Eric's helping Gavin plow this morning," she told Esther when she stopped by to deliver a few grocery items to her.

"That disturbs me," Esther said. "I don't trust Gavin any farther than I could throw an elephant after the way he treated you."

"Now, Mom," Teal said, giving her a hug. Yet the longer that Teal tried not to think about Esther's comment, the louder it nagged her to check on that situation in Gavin's field.

"I think I'll surprise the two of them with lunch in the field," she declared, springing to her feet.

"But it's only ten o'clock," Esther said. "Stay and have an early lunch with me."

"I'll pick up Kentucky Fried. They'll love it."

"On second thought, that's probably a good idea," Esther agreed. "But keep an eye on Gavin. He's a sly one."

Nervously, Teal repeatedly checked her watch. By 11:15 a.m., she entered the field Eric had mentioned during their breakfast together. She felt an uncommon urgency to reach Eric for Gavin had locked the main gate to the field. Disturbed to the point of panic, she recalled a wire gate to the grass pasture that Gavin never locked. She backed her jeep, stirred up a flurry of dust, and sped the quarter of a mile to the pasture. She would have to climb over or under a barbed-wire fence to the plowed field, but she didn't care so long as she got there.

Glad that she wore boots and jeans today, she moved quickly over a terrace and spied the two of them several terraces away. She ran now, her ankles trying to turn in the soft plowed ground. Breathless from the effort, she realized they hadn't seen her.

Gavin motioned to Eric to stop his tractor. He yelled at him to pull some jammed straw free that had wedged midway the length of his plow.

Gavin's tractor's engine rumbled while Eric got off his tractor that pulled the spring tooth behind him. He followed Gavin with his tractor to break up the clods the plow left in order to prepare the soil for sowing wheat.

Gavin reboarded his tractor, and Eric, who didn't question why he didn't free the blocked implement himself, moved trustingly to comply.

Teal screamed for him to stop, but he couldn't hear her above the tractor's rumble as Gavin began to back up.

Eric's hands slipped on the straw that wouldn't budge, and he fell backward. The plowshares behind Gavin's moving tractor caught his legs in spite of his fortunate slip.

Gavin stopped and started forward, then killed the engine and stepped off the machine.

Alarm twisted his face at the sight of Teal who already pulled Eric off plowed ground onto the cleaner stubble nearby. She tore off her shirt and ripped the sleeves and the back of it into strips to tourniquet Eric's wounds. She slapped straw onto the bleeding gashes and tied it there so that Eric wouldn't bleed to death.

"Do something!" she ordered Gavin. "Carry him to my jeep and then get to that gate and unlock it—Now!"

Gavin, whose face had blanched while he stood as if paralyzed, said, "It was an accident. I meant to gear forward."

"Move!" she yelled again. "Help me lift him!" For she had begun to try to lift Eric up by herself. "I know you, Gavin, but this mistake, as you call it, is monstrous."

When he saw she wouldn't relent and would get Eric to her jeep by herself, he seemed persuaded and moved to help her. "I'll get him. Start the jeep."

With Eric beside her, she sped to the gate. Gavin had already opened it for her. At the emergency room at the county seat, she paced in the hall while medics treated Eric.

When Gavin arrived, she spoke to him plainly. "You self-centered animal!" she said "Not your son, not me, or Sara. You would use us all to satisfy insatiable Gavin! Eric's legs were cut to the bone in four areas! The right one is broken. You might have killed him except for providence and his fall backwards away from the shares."

Gavin stopped short. The rigidity in his stature, so new to him, the twisted mouth and steely eyes he had acquired with age stared back in cold indifference.

She shivered at the sight when he abruptly clutched at his chest and cried out as if in great pain. There outside the emergency room, Gavin Rush died as Upton Rush had died, three generations before.

They coded him to no avail.

Despite what Gavin had tried to do to him, Eric, who was still on crutches, wept at his graveside. Teal stood by, wordless before the scene that traumatized her best memories of Gavin and numbed her responses. Both of them received the news that day that Gavin's will left all the land to his children. He had named Eric along with Brett and Mia five years before at the document's inception.

"Perhaps he didn't hate me after all," Eric said softly. "The only problem is, he's broke," Eric revealed. "I've thought it for some time. The futures got what his ex-wife didn't gamble away before running off with her lawyer. I hoped he would recover with my help."

"We probably have the resources to resolve the debt and save the land," Teal said. "We'll look at the mess together. Land is too dear to lose. Besides, I'm not sure that I didn't kill him with my words. So much had built up for so long. I lost all restraint with that tongue lashing that I gave him just before his attack."

If a man couldn't love, he probably couldn't hate either, Teal thought. "I'm sure he didn't hate you, Eric. Who could hate you?"

"And who could blame you." I never will," he said, embracing her.

Yet in her heart of hearts, Teal believed Gavin felt nothing for any of them apart from their usefulness to him.

He had intended to back over Eric, his own blood, and not for love of her, but for her resources that could bail him out of debt.

She shook her head. *God, forgive me if I've misjudged him,* she prayed silently. Apparently, Gavin hadn't intended for this new wife to have anything—not even the house until her own demise. Teal glimpsed at last what he valued: the Rush bloodline on the land. Their inheritance of it guaranteed his life after death so long as they planted and harvested.

She hoped they saw as she did that if you eat, you are involved in agriculture and that it affects every single living thing on earth by creating jobs and supporting numerous other industries, itself the largest industry in America, perhaps the largest in the world. She knew that Gavin felt powerful as one of the few who controls the food supply and, therefore, became an integral part of banking and the huge investments made there toward supplies, land, equipment, and storage.

Teal believed that very power that created wealth, when managed well, required generosity and humility to balance rather than inflate egos.

She supposed the populations of the world would not regret farmers making a profit as long as food remained cheap—100 percent of parity (what their wheat crop cost farmers, relative to the target price set by Washington) meant they survived but meant nothing to those who didn't go to the fields or endure the losses.

The question that plagued those who knew the profit and loss facts regarding food production was how food could remain cheap without bankrupting producers and retailers, even those with the volume.

CHAPTER XXVI

Teal Enters Politics

Although there had been many times with family, with nature, in meditation, and with Gavin that Teal experienced unmistakable joy, her time with Eric brought consistent happiness.

The years slipped by in their home on a hill overlooking the south river. They saw that family members interested in the survival of local American elevators and mills sat on the local boards for each area in the three states: Oklahoma, Colorado, and Kansas. The members all related to the real possibility of the demise of American agriculture and willingly lobbied in Washington DC for its survival at all levels besides grains: fruit growers; vegetable growers; the milk, pork, beef, and poultry industries.

Then they moved those lobbyists who wanted personal investment into leadership positions as officers, employees, or board members, depending on their interests and résumés. Teal admired those growers willing to exit government payments for independent sales that often brought them profit rather than loss.

"Look!" Teal exclaimed as Eric sat at breakfast that first week of November. She held the *Daily Oklahoman* article toward him that told of Langston University's $525,000 grant from the federal government to seed an agricultural program for aspiring farmers.

"The program launched last month and is especially directed at those with some experience. It's bound to give minorities a leg up."

"Perhaps there is fresh insight for a creative approach to agricultural support from this administration, particularly by the secretary of agriculture."

"Time will tell," Teal remarked. "It is encouraging to see such a complement to price supports. It smacks of innovation, which is sorely needed. Our own business needs it to survive."

"Innovation *and* diversification plus the supports might keep us going for sure," Eric agreed. "I intend to learn more about international trade laws and pass the information on while we approach innovations."

"Do you think the idea of an agricultural county cooperative is a good innovative idea, Eric? Won't we need to study the World Trade Organization?"

"Put the idea to the board. If they agree, then you can take it to our customers. Frankly, I think a national wheat cooperative outside the hedgers and programming is a good idea. When you think in terms of the whole world, there's bound to be room for a supply-and-demand market, a fund market, and an independent one. Can't all three function to more efficiently deliver food where it's wanted and needed? There must be more restructuring and a planning committee with business and marketing plans agreeable to all members. There will be pros and cons to work through."

"Charles and Jenny's fertilizer business has grown without my input," Teal said. "I'm very encouraged by that innovation for it helps us indirectly by providing almost twice the product. When I'm gone, Eric, I want the businesses that we generate to provide for our own family for generations to come."

"If you could be their mother hen from the grave, you would be."

"I would be," she agreed.

"Nothing will save us soon enough unless farmers get a minimum price of $7.50 a bushel for their wheat. Good managers might break even with enough left to sow the next year's crop. They sure better buy disaster insurance for that threat of crop failure. Two failures in a row can ruin those without several jobs outside the farm. Good cattle prices or income from oil or gas wells," he concluded.

"All aren't financially liquid enough to afford many cattle, and most don't have mineral checks. Some have only one other salary besides farm income." She felt discouraged.

"Some have *no* other income," he reminded. "They've aged unprepared for this economy. A professor from Rutgers recently published the remark that there will be no farm on the Great Plains soon, that we have a history of influx and flight—a Professor Popper."

"Let's prove Professor Poppoff wrong," Teal said, apparently bouncing back to the fight response.

"Popper," he corrected, but Teal only smiled.

"We're going to face obstacles. There will be powerful blocks to the idea of national food cooperation with satellites. Where money is at stake, there's corruption and greed," Eric reminded.

"Suppose the co-op satellites could specialize?" Teal asked, her thoughts racing past blocks. "Like Idaho potatoes, Kansas wheat and corn, California and Florida citrus. What do you think?"

"The idea, if it generates profit with accountability, will most definitely be contagious."

* * *

As Eric and Teal had wanted a child of their own, Teal supplied the ovarian egg and Eric the sperm for implantation in their surrogate as Eric had suggested. Their twin boys, Lincoln and Gregory, resulted.

The twins kept them going to competitive sports games throughout their elementary years. They played T-ball, then football. They wrestled and shot basketballs, batted tennis balls, and swam.

But as they entered middle school, it became obvious that Gregory focused on science projects and Lincoln immersed himself in instrumental music.

After fifteen years with Eric and with adolescent boys to monitor, Teal declared her life gloriously ordinary. Others ran the businesses; she ran the home, gardened, fished, and delegated. A good catch from the river pleased her as much as a good day at the mill had years before. It seemed incongruous to her, for 50 percent of all farm wives were now in the nation's workforce.

"You're a consultant," Eric accused. "You haven't *really* retired."

"It's fun for me to help unsnarl problems. I still feel important to the company when someone calls."

She had private time alone in summer to walk down the grassy willow-screened banks, shed her clothes, and skinny-dip in the river. The warm water felt like wearing loose silk. She often fished for the golden perch and catfish the river yielded to clean and fry for their candlelight dinners.

This summer afternoon, the sun reflected its own image across the ribbon of water that stretched as far as she could see. Tree shadows played around her as she swam for over an hour. Then she dressed and climbed back up the bank to the house, cleaned her fish, stashed them in ice water until dinner, and curled up with a suspense novel.

"This is *your* harvest, these heaven-sent days," Eric told her that night, encouraging her enjoyment. "Yours and mine." Over fifty, a few gray hairs now graced his sideburns. At sixty-eight, she remained energetic and trim.

Then too soon, their boys were adults and at the university at Stillwater. Their uncles Jonsi and Tad had influenced Gregory, through their careers in agricultural and environmental research, to seek a science degree as well.

Besides grain research, Gregory became enamored with food enhancement and the improvement of its quality, quantity, and distribution. He belonged to the current "green revolution" fathered by Borlaug. "He effectively combated starvation all over the world and saved millions of lives in India," Gregory explained. He idolized him as Jonsi had revered Joseph Danne's achievements for grain.

Their holiday dinners were almost always at Teal's house. Lincoln usually treated them to violin selections at such times. He had been drawn to the homemade violin of his great-granddad Upton Rush, completed a major in music with emphasis in violin and a minor in environmental sciences, particularly the science of water quality.

"On my concert travels, I intend to promote the idea of still more independent control of our grain markets in the face of world hunger. It won't hurt to tell them I'm from the country." He laughed. His black eyes sparkled with humor. Besides his musical talent, Lincoln had his great-grandfather's dark auburn hair. "There's bloggers now to pressure and to engage opinion."

"Distribution not product gets food to people. We can't give up on the solution for it. And until a better idea comes along, caring people are the answer," Teal said. "I'm proud of you, Lincoln."

The family gathered for Esther's ninety-fifth birthday party on Christmas at Eric and Teal's home. They celebrated Lincoln's and Gregory's graduations the following May. Teal called them Dr. This and Dr. That.

"With four children and now grandchildren, we'll soon be celebrating something every month," Eric said as they lit candles before their guests arrived.

Lincoln, her Dr. That, grew a huge organic vegetable garden that spring north of the house and away from the river. The year before, he planted the orchard of fruits, nuts, and berries. "To make you think of me often when I live in New York like Brett and Mia, and you're slaving over the canning kettle," he told her.

Harlin, Rena, and Letti had been gone for years while this new life of Teal's with the births and marriages increased with the years.

Mia and David gave her two granddaughters, Lacy and Maureen. Brett and his fiancée, Alice, focused on art. Teal kept hoping for their wedding. "I love weddings," she confided to Eric. "I'm still disappointed that Mia and David followed our example and escaped to Vegas."

"You just like to celebrate," Eric teased, putting a large baked ham on the table. He opened the drapes to reveal the river beyond. "Here's where I used to watch you swim in the buff," he said.

"You'd have been down there with me. Don't kid me."

"How about it, soon as June warms the water?"

"You've a date," she said. "If I can hobble down there."

"You don't hobble!" he scolded.

"Any day now," she said. "I'm apt to be like that one-horse-shay poem and just fall apart all at once."

"Not before I do, you don't," he laughed. "I'll want a good woman to look after me when I pass sixty-five."

Eric's hair, though still full, had quickly grayed entirely over the past year. Ironically, Teal's had not. It had faded to a light auburn instead. They did not appear to be years apart. Perhaps they never had, she thought, because she liked to think it. Active still, they both enjoyed health, wealth, and very visible happiness.

In the kitchen where Brett and Mia did their familiar sampling of hors d'oeuvres, Teal asked the question that had preyed on her mind. "Did your father ever visit?" she asked Mia. She glanced at Brett for a response when Mia didn't answer. "I've been concerned about your loss of him and wondered how close you may have become. I want you both happy. I need to know how you're handling that loss."

Brett broke the silence. "He called, sent Lacy and Maureen Christmas presents, didn't he, Mia?"

Mia nodded. "He said that they hated the city, or they would visit. The noise and traffic made them nervous. Lacy and Maureen were so little, they don't remember him. We visited him when we were back. We called first though. The children's crying made them nervous too."

"I visited him often, Mom," Brett said. "I accepted him as he was. He talked about their natural gas wells and checks for a new one or for damages *all* the time. Pretty boring. They leased out all the land, gambled at the Lucky Star, and watched TV. They seemed happy. I had more regrets about him when he lived, to tell you the truth."

—

"I wish it could have been different for you both," Teal lamented, then embraced them. "I probably should have asked about it years ago. I just couldn't. First, you dealt with our divorce, then with his death less than ten years later."

At dinner, Brett, Mia, Alice, Mia's husband, David, their two daughters Lacy and Maureen, Jenny and Charles's family of four, Tad's and Jonsi's families, Esther, and their own Lincoln and Gregory surrounded the long, long table to celebrate Esther's birthday. The blessing had barely been said by Eric when the talk of ten-dollar wheat came up.

"Your ninety-fifth birthday may introduce a grand year for wheat, Mom," Teal told her. "Had it come twenty-five years ago when it first cost six dollars a bushel to raise it, we would have saved more family farms from residential and industrial zoning."

"Ten-dollar wheat that's already sliding to five dollars while economists call it a false inflation fluke," Eric said, "and no farm program out of Washington soon enough for intelligent fiscal planning. Probably because the price passed target price, as if that plan still applied to profit."

"It was an election year," Esther reminded.

"Hey, Grandma," Lincoln said. "Did you know that tractors can have GPS systems now and come equipped with sensors to tell us if we need more or less of, well, just anything for the crop or soil? 'Course, you have to know how to program and read it."

"It's definitely a changed scene for farm families," Teal agreed.

Both Lincoln and Gregory enjoyed working family land or helping with harvests, but neither wanted agriculture as an exclusive career. They leased their land to hired operators in order to follow their other career pursuits. Eric and Teal supervised operations. Most rural families pursued various roles now, so Teal accepted that the life she had loved with Gavin had vanished for her and Eric.

Letti had said once that she liked remembering that her life in Oklahoma was from scratch. "I had seed and a stick to scratch a spot and plant it," she said. There was nothing here for her and

Cory before Upton joined them but a land to clear and develop. "We worked together for it," she told Teal.

"Of course you would," Esther finally responded. It had obviously taken her awhile to absorb the information about GPS systems for tractors and other farm equipment. "I was lost *once*—on Oklahoma City's south side. I rolled down a window and asked directions. You could save a heap of money if you just did the same and tested the soil like in the old days."

Teal laughed. "Remember that, son. It's information you may need more than a GPS system if this economy doesn't recover."

"Saves money," Esther repeated as she often did these days. "And without money, you can't even have a tractor. Put your common sense and initiative to work like your grandpa Ray and I did."

"This recession will pass," Charles Huel said. "Wouldn't it be good to know that someone in government understood recovering the cost of just the basic equipment? The cost of fuel for three or four ground preps before sowing a field with wheat, the cost of fertilizer and chemicals for mold and insect control and more fuel to apply it can cost well over two hundred fifty dollars an acre. Put a pencil to the math. Even if it makes fifty bushel to the acre, a farmer better buy that twenty-nine dollar-an-acre insurance for every crop, or he can be out of business in one season."

"Put a pencil to resowing costs plus insurance and the loss expense too if the crop fails," Teal added, remembering the trauma of her and Gavin's first lost crop.

"They need savings for a cushion, and savings are hard to have for a young farmer just getting started. Too many start-up expenses."

"Try no-till," Jonsi was quick to advise. "And please pass the ham." He took the platter and forked a thick slice. "Farmers will struggle as always, even with $10 wheat if they don't have other income. Necessary investment grows faster than profit these days. Their debt is for new equipment to keep up with the growing demand for grain and changed farming practices."

"Many are still in debt for land mortgaged years ago, Jonsi, or because of surpluses and the resultant low price. Land is increasing in value just as equipment is increasing in price, but farmers don't want to sell it, they want crops on it. Fuel and seed, storage and insect control, fertilizer—costs are blitzing any increase in price."

Jonsi took a bite of the ham. "The price will drop down again, sis, always has as if three or four dollars is all a bushel of it is worth. Name a product that's priced the same as fifty years ago besides wheat if you can. A farmer must save a little in the planting, save a little in the use of older equipment and in longer hours and less hired help. No-till might save some—not a lot though."

"What it saves is the land," Charles said. "There's less runoff—saves topsoil. Everybody talks about it. Most are afraid of it due to lower yields."

"What about the milk producer?" Eric added. "It costs a dollar-fifty a gallon to produce, and they get a dollar. How will those that hang on survive? Where will we find the product, and for how much when those producers all quit or die? A farmer's average age is forty-two in this country and growing."

"Oh, Eric, let's stop this talk right now," Teal admonished. "Hope and innovate, hang on. Land and survival are synonymous the world over because there's food on it and water under it."

"They're not making more land," Eric quipped.

"Because of dollar inflation, there's no difference in three-fifty wheat and seven-fifty wheat anyway," Charles said.

"Teal's right," Eric agreed. Talk is futile, and inflation a reality. We just keep going. Except with a crop failure, we'll be even deeper in debt, and loans may not come. Forced sales seem more likely than loans since the banking scandals. Their necks are on the block too, and they are afraid to lend money. Seven-fifties only break even because of inflation. There's no profit without price support. Government payments are still needed. I feel trapped in the need myself. Crop failures could finish all of us off, the elevators included." He reached to cover Teal's hand with his own. "Hanging on wouldn't help for long. If they suspend payments, the price either must be $10 a bushel, or wheat allotments must become grass and hay. That's the reality."

"You talk as if you walk in our shoes," Charles said.

"We do. If farmers don't succeed, elevator operators don't succeed. We're in it together. Teal and I don't farm a lot of land, but we farm some—manage more—enough to understand and recognize the problem. We invested in some of it for our retirement from the elevators."

"Independent marketing and innovation is probably the answer, but the initial sacrifice of money and time will be huge," Teal said. "Change will come slowly because stable growth happens that way. It must be the independents first, then the organized satellites and chartered headquarters. I hope I live long enough to see it. It's off to a good start. We're part of that beginning—the Rush, Meriott, and Swain families."

"I beg your pardon," Jenny said.

"And Huels," Teal laughed. "I apologize, Charles."

Charles just winked at her.

"Willing suckers to take the risk will be too scarce," Jenny said despondently.

"Cattle and jobs off the land have kept *us* going, the cows and calves mostly," Charles said. "Not the wheat price. There's some natural gas checks, but we don't rely on them. Gas and petroleum are as fickle as wheat in Oklahoma. The 1980s bust is the best reminder of that."

Dishes and silverware clinked as they finished their meal. Teal rose to serve dessert and replenish beverage glasses.

"Your party needs more cheerful conversation, Mom. We'll change the subject."

"So now because consumers may pay three dollars for a loaf of bread in some stores, eight-fifty wheat would probably decide *no* price support?" Esther asked.

"So that's what you've been so quiet about. That's right, you've got it, Mom."

"Time will determine that, Teal. I never wanted subsidies," Charles said. "They've just been a necessary evil. My older equipment instead of new helps me, but not the implement dealer.

He needs sales, his investment is in the millions. Consumers don't have the facts, they just hear about the government payments without knowing costs or realizing the difference in producers and nonproducers. When the producer and the implement dealers fail, jobs are lost, steel mills close, and on and on past the banks and retailers—a domino effect. Nonproducers have no cost but weed control, and only when that is actually monitored."

"I'm glad you've not mortgaged land to buy more tractors and combines, Charles," Esther said. "At these fuel and fertilizer prices, that could break a budget in a bad year even without a crop failure."

"I learned a hard lesson when I overbought thirty years ago," Charles told her.

"Someone's *got* to buy them," Teal said, "or implement companies will go out of business like Charles said. A new combine can cost $165,000. Just a baler can be $65,000 or more."

"Combine crews buy them, those that come here and go north to cut for farmers that own no combines or wheat trucks," Jonsi informed. "I think that's the way to manage during this economy. That's their business."

"But prices are driving old-fashioned self-reliance away," Esther said. "It's all so backward. Hire wheat cut, hire hay swathed and baled, delegate labor to hold down a job—I guess whatever it takes," she concluded.

"Ranchers and farmers with volume, several thousand acres in production can buy them," Eric said. "But even they need a financial cushion as well as stored grain in a bad year. Then they can finance the next year's crop."

Charles nodded agreement. "When it cost six dollars a bushel to sow wheat twenty-five years ago, wheat hardly ever brought five or six dollars a bushel for over five or ten minutes for the speculators' benefit—not ours. We were in the field and didn't know it. Three-fifty or three-eighty priced it most of the time. It will cost three times that this year," Charles complained. "That's why Washington will finally vote more innovative programs. Not one of them wants to be hungry. Sooner or later they'll see their own need for change."

"Washington better be reducing the free money for idle acres," Eric said, "or we'll all be losers someday. Some politician will drop us all in the same sack and stomp it, as if actual producers milked the economy instead of supported it."

Teal began to fidget. She wanted more frivolity for her party.

"We're consumers and tax payers besides farmers and elevator owners," Jenny said. "I loathe such waste of tax payers' dollars to fatten already fat pockets." She and Teal exchanged a smile. It pleased Teal immensely that they had finally formed unexpected common interests through the family businesses.

"It's an evil thought, but if farmers plowed up wheat ground to plant it all to Bermuda, if all the farmers in this valley did it and raised their grains to mix for feed and forage—" Tad began.

"Just raise cattle because that market's good? The government would import beef," Teal said. "Wheat too, probably. They've done it before. Then beef prices would drop due to a glutted market to drive you back to whatever they wanted you to plant, raise, or change."

"Why? Why does any government thwart its farmers when farmers feed them?" Jonsi complained. "Farmers help the trade balance with exports."

Teal sighed. "Bottom line: because they can. I think they believe any soil anywhere will grow wheat that mills into flour for bread when it won't. True, we mix a third soft Kansas with our hard red winter. But good bread requires hard red-winter wheat like Oklahoma's aerable land grows. Too, they want consumer votes. Consumers want low prices. Worse, they probably think anyone can just go round and round with a tractor to plant and reap. They may not grasp that our young need evidence that a career in agriculture is worth their pursuit."

Charles began to shake his head. "I'm a Republican, but this new Democratic government is getting involved by—"

If we don't raise it," Teal interrupted, "they will just import it from another country. Speculators can hedge with imported wheat

—

as easily as with homegrown. They have no calluses. They haven't a clue that aerable land is priceless and *not* very plentiful, or that agriculture is a science. They surely think that just owning land and equipment makes you rich—not earning money by eighteen-hour workdays in all kinds of weather."

"Worse," Tad warned, "food can become a political tool in the hands of other countries too. The worm can turn. We stop growing, another country can refuse to supply. I've heard that there's already a tragedy in China's sandy areas that's worse than our dust-bowl days because conservation solutions for sand aren't known. They've plowed up more and more for more and more just as we did. It's blowing away. Almost nothing can grow on it."

"They must find the plants to hold it, pipe in water to irrigate. Trees, perhaps," Teal lamented. "Lincoln," she said, "get your great-granddad Upton's violin and play for us. I need some music."

Jonsi nodded. "Not a bad idea, sis. I hope we're wrong about Washington, though. I'm becoming a cynic myself. To some of them, Teal, we're ignorant and unsophisticated Jesus people who don't know that the real world of Wall Street, and industry maintains the world's economies," Jonsi said. "Well, they don't. Free unprotested trade does that."

"Now listen to me," Charles intervened again. "This new agricultural secretary seems in touch with some of our problems."

"It didn't really change much to take the tractors all the way to Washington years ago," Teal countered.

Eric nodded. "Find me a history book that recorded it."

"We need a 'Take a Senator to Break Pond Ice' Day this January," Teal quipped.

"You're on, Mrs. Meriott," Eric laughed. "We need senators in touch with farming, not disassociated. Still, I'm as encouraged as Charles about some of the interest in agriculture that's coming out of Washington. We can hope that our young people aren't so discouraged by past negatives that they can't be recovered for the country's future."

This business was in his blood now, Teal thought. He felt the goal; he felt the pain. Teal loved him as she loved her children, her parents, her very self. She had loved before Eric, but he was flesh of her flesh—a oneness she had only dreamed of and never expected to have.

"Tomorrow is another day," Jenny mimicked. "But so far, none of our own want to carry the torch."

"I disagree," Charles said. "What I've heard tonight tells me we're a family with the torch."

"Time to sing 'Happy Birthday' to Mom," Teal said. "Consumers will get behind agriculture in the same way that voters of all races got behind the civil rights movement, and the tea-party groups are becoming activists for Constitutional principles. There aren't enough of us to be a threat, but that can work for us. The world cannot get on without growers and food producers. Communication, communication, communication is the key."

"Blog, blog, blog!" Gregory translated.

Teal laughed. "You're right. Let's celebrate. This clan will survive. I'm back to organic gardening with Lincoln and Gregory myself."

The singing, with Lincoln accompanying them, seemed to cheer everyone. He followed with the announcement "Now, one of Mom's favorites: 'Listen to the Mockingbird.'"

"The land and the grain that has fed the world from this county will survive," Lincoln announced with a flourish of his bow when he finished. "Americans will see to it, the support will come. We haven't worked and sacrificed this long for any other result. The problem is the same as your old feed mill's problem before you put the bird's nest over it—distribution. The legs to the channels of distribution *must* be unclogged."

Gregory nodded as he helped himself to chocolate cake. "Did you know, Mom," he added, "that China will still take all we can send them as well as grow what they still can themselves?"

Lincoln lay the violin aside and helped himself to the cake as well.

She didn't know. "Wheat, not rice? Perhaps they sell it for more somewhere. I thought they raised all they needed for themselves and their exports. I didn't even know about their dust storms."

"Sandstorms," Gregory corrected.

"They may sell it," he said. "I'm lobbying against rice to Africa. Those people can grow their own to help their own economy. It's immoral to sell Africa rice unless their rice crop fails and they are hungry. We'll destroy their agriculture that way."

"It's just as immoral to import wheat, but that happens here."

"You sure about that, Greg?" Eric asked. "Be interesting if we sell to China and they sell it back. Is there a way to investigate that?"

"Sure, I'm sure," he said. "Check the government stats. But about China, I don't know."

Their voices seemed to fade as Teal allowed herself to consider how these gatherings had changed. Rena and Harlin could no longer share their hospitality even before their passing since Gavin had made other commitments. They had buried Letti Pearl beside her Upton almost thirty years ago. She was one hundred and three years old. Too soon, she could lose Esther, who would lie beside her Ray.

Here were those of the old blood and the new: her grandchildren, her Mia and her three boys (Brett, Gregory, and Lincoln), who had persuaded Eric to invest in land. As if time turned back on itself, they planned a small ranching operation for a pastime that included horses, cattle, and what Lincoln called Oklahoma gold—wheat.

"Greg agrees we need a sideline that gets us out of the office and off the concert-tour schedules," Lincoln announced. The twins were the last to excuse themselves from the party.

"And you think that Pop needs to take care of it for you, right?" Eric laughed and waved them off.

Teal felt grafted into this love of land by living on it, benefitting from it.

June came quickly with its first day of summer like a promise as full as the rising moon. Before the elevator rush began, Eric reminded her, "We have a date at the river."

"Indeed we do," she said. "Why do you think I've tanned and toned all winter? Believe me, I've had to work twice as hard as I ever did to look a fourth as good."

Eric just laughed. "Good thing I didn't marry you for your body."

"Damn good thing!" she agreed.

That first harvest of the combined farms of Eric's and Teal's included his inheritance from Gavin and the land they had invested in for Lincoln and Gregory. They renamed the mix the T and E Ranch. That month of June, all the children and grandchildren camped out at Eric and Teal's place on the river.

"We'll make this an annual tradition at harvest. Put in for a June vacation, arrange your schedules or vacation days," Teal suggested as she served up the meat loaf and mashed potatoes.

"And if it rains?" Gregory chided.

"It rains," Teal said.

Esther joined them to be with family and the children again.

"These past six months since my birthday have gone by so fast. It seems only weeks."

"For me too," Teal agreed, clasping her to her breast warmly. "I'm so happy you're here for such a long time."

"Such a long time," Esther repeated tiredly. "I'm off to bed now, dear."

When Esther didn't appear at breakfast, Teal went to waken her. So still, so peaceful, that expression on Esther's face. Gone. Both her parents: gone, yet with her forever in her mind and in the resemblances of features and behaviors she saw in her children and grandchildren. *Was there even more to eternal life than this?* she wondered.

—

CHAPTER XXVII

Letti Pearl's Life Resurrected on Stage

It was David, Mia's husband, who, as a playwright, seemed more informed about current agricultural issues. His stage play, taken from Letti Pearl's early history in the territory near Winding Stair Mountain and Briartown, followed her life to Upton's farm on the south Canadian near McAlester and to their store at Ardmore before her move to Canadian County where she opened her unique store. It played only in small theaters for several years before one producer suggested a screenplay.

He stopped briefly by Swain Elevators to visit with Teal, Eric, and the board of directors about it. Since most of the family attended the board meeting, he received a warm greeting with their unanimous approval.

"Besides the fictional screenplay about this country that includes the farm and ranch struggles," David said, "I want to do a documentary film on the history of wheat across this section of wheat belt from Enid to Chickasha, south, and points east and west. The Great Depression, the dust-bowl drama of the thirties, those tractors in Washington, the embargo that caused low prices, farm policy that caused the glut of stalled grain to today's burgeoning population and grains diverted to ethanol, farmers plowing up wheat to plant corn or Bermuda rather than deal with Washington, bugs, and drought—the whole reality struggle really interests me."

Teal could hardly bear her excitement at the idea of Mia and Letti's story on the screen. The idea of such a documentary pleased her even more. "There's so much more to say about the blizzards and the other disasters that destroyed homes, crops, and outbuildings: hailstones like baseballs, fires, grasshoppers. We've had even dryer times, but conservation practices have prevented the dust storms of the 1930s."

"China's still buying all we can ship," Eric said. "Price is seven-fifty today." The news ended the meeting on a pleasant note. Several family members and Swain Elevators board members stayed after dismissal to chat and drink coffee.

"Seven-fifty may be break even for resowing at these fuel and fertilizer prices if no equipment breaks down or needs replacing. Some farmers have said so. It's still costing two hundred fifty dollars an acre to sow," Charles said. "If we treat for fungi, for insects . . . I guess I'll give in and buy certified seed at over $6 a bushel. Better crop if it's a good year. Fewer problems." Still, he shook his head at the price. "Not less than $6 for sure," he muttered.

"We're lucky, though," Jenny seemed quick to remind him. "Because of our fertilizer business, we can afford to store it until the price goes up or set our price on the futures—the wheat will be there."

"There's always a risk with the futures," Charles reminded. "Always. What about all those who need the money to live, to pay hospital bills, or to put in the next crop?" Charles didn't sound very optimistic.

"Too many of them can't," Teal said. "If they mortgage land to invest in a crop, pay bills, or purchase new equipment and then have a crop failure, they'll be ruined due to the high price of sowing. Does nothing ever change about farming? I so want Lincoln and Gregory to make a profit rather than incur debt in their experiment with small farming. They plan a cow-calf start with grass, grain, and hay programs. Jonsi says they will double-crop with beans to help replenish the soil on two hundred acres of cultivated land. The one hundred twenty acres of pasture is Bermuda grass. They'll need to hay some of the wheat, pasture the early growth. I'm glad they have careers that will support their efforts should the weather thwart them."

"Sounds like a good plan," Jonsi said. "For the survival of both the producer and the land—"

"Yes," Teal interrupted in an impatient tone, "we know, you want them to try no-till. Farmers aren't eager to change, Jonsi. It really doesn't seem to increase production though I realize it saves soil, moisture, nutrients, and some fuel. No doubt it's great for conservation and a potential debt reducer—once the different equipment is free of payments. I'm just tired of hearing about it, I guess."

"With the cultivated acres some producers have, it's a win-win situation, Teal," Eric said with a wink toward Jonsi.

Charles's eyes widened as he spoke. "You've got a point, Eric. We've almost six hundred acres in cultivation, four hundred in pasture. Tough as the economy is right now, I'm thinking we could easily slide into land redistribution again like in the 1920s when the lenders wound up with most of it if we don't innovate to conserve both time and money."

"If the land benefits besides, that's a real bonus," Eric added with a nod. "Save the land, save the producer, Jonsi."

Jonsi smiled at Eric's play on words.

"All right, I know when I'm outvoted. Do you remember that day we went together to Joseph Danne's farm, Jonsi?" Teal said, turning toward him. "I wish he were here now to tell us his ideas about this new technology and the direction of American agriculture, don't you?"

"I do, sis," he said. "Just think of how far we've come since then to feed nations and teach them how to produce their own food. Yet we still battle the same issues over and over. Walk me to the door. I've a long drive back to Stillwater." He rose to leave.

She took his hand in hers as they moved to the door. "Someone always thwarts, but someone else always forwards the goal toward an

---

ultimate good," she said optimistically. "That isn't going to change. Takes guts to stick to land, but it's the best life there is."

"Oh, I almost forgot. I brought you a book. It's in the car, I'll get it. Forwarding goals and mentioning Joseph Danne reminded me of it."

She waited under the porch light for him.

"Oh, I've heard about it, the biography of Norman Borlaug," she exclaimed, thrilled with the gift he handed her. "The father of the green revolution you mentioned to me months ago."

Jonsi gave her a hug before turning toward his car again. "I thought you'd like it," he tossed back over his shoulder.

Soon all had returned home, including Teal. Eric helped her clear away the supper trash and dishes they'd left before going to the meeting. "Deal with the rest tomorrow," he said.

Teal's mind still turned over the economic problems for agriculture this recession created because gross inflation accompanied it.

"Support payments on leased sections might only be enough for someone to barely pay bills and eat for a year, only ten or twelve thousand dollars after costs, rent, and taxes," she noted, saddened for families who kept hanging on without the benefit of alternative resources. Cattle costs aren't affordable when you can't risk loss. "What will the aged and uneducated who know no other work but the land do, Eric?"

"No one talks about that. I don't know what the small farmer who is too old to risk more can do besides keep his cows and calves. He can lease his land out for a few thousand a year and live on that small farm income and his social security. The farm he leases out for $3,000 a year sells for over $2,000 an acre—insane!"

"Out of touch," she concluded. "Salaries here haven't really kept pace with price increases for food, fuel, and home repairs. Most folks will need to downsize."

"As Jenny says," Eric quoted, "tomorrow is another day." He flipped off the downstairs lights. "New administration, fresh ideas. We can't solve the inequities with all this talk. We have to trust that our present state, federal, and local governments truly care and will become still more concerned about our survival. For our survival secures their own. The awareness of presidents affects agriculture more than the weather. History and FDR tells us that."

"Some folks didn't like what FDR did. My dad was one of them. If there's such a thing as a blue-blooded capitalist, Dad was." Arm in arm, they climbed the stairs together.

Programs aren't products, my dear."

"No more expansion, Eric. Agreed?" She recalled her father saying that to her a long time ago.

"I'm glad to hear it. Let those who follow us take that on, whoever that may be. I'm not that much against sharing the wealth, capitalist that I am."

Laughter and banter reached them from Lincoln and Gregory's room.

"I'm not glad to hear that," she said. "They're supposed to be at the elevator tomorrow so we can stay home. Get to bed," she urged, knocking on their door to back up her order.

"Video games. Let them play like children. They'll have their noses to the grindstone soon enough. They're back at Stillwater next week for that last semester before their graduation."

"Poker, more likely. How I wish Upton Rush and Ray Swain were both around to see what they started when they came to Oklahoma. Imagine this state being just a hundred and two years old."

"America's an adolescent itself," he said. The whole nation still has a lot to learn."

"Women couldn't vote until Mom's generation. Hard to imagine that truth."

"Not to mention the lack of the black and Indian vote. Not many Latinos here yet in those days. A few," he responded.

"No use to worry about these oil prices, Eric. The future's in coal and natural gas. If South Africa makes gasoline from coal, so can we. We've always invented what we needed. We'll find the way to clean coal energy and the reduction of CO_2 emissions. Energy costs for business and industry *must be* reduced, perhaps with natural gas and wind. Then there's corn for ethanol—lots of cellulose in those cobs and stalks too."

"I'm looking into wind for our business," Eric confided. "I like the idea. What do you think?"

Teal nodded agreement. "A few businesses have already put up windmills for an independent energy source, used them for years. Housing has utilized solar for decades. Perhaps it's time that we innovate rather than expand."

"It's called exhaling," Eric said. That's a challenge for Lincoln and Gregory. They admire the wind farms west of here and all of the solar energy housing. They said farmers who go to no-till will be paid for the carbon they sequester when they don't break land with the plow. This is rapid progress to promote multiple levels of conservation that may pay instead of cost. I'm encouraged by all of it because I choose to be, even when I don't understand it all yet. Jonsi says that the hope is that carbon sequestration will reduce global warming."

"I'm confused," Eric said. "Why is it already so cold the world over this winter if there's global warming?"

"That isn't all that's new, though," she digressed. "At the Dollar Tree Store yesterday where I was picking up some stationery supplies for the office, I saw canned peaches and strawberries from China. What's that going to do to the Colorado, Texas, Arkansas, and Oklahoma peach market or the Eastern Oklahoma strawberry market?"

"Unless they cost less than canning your own, nothing," he responded astutely. "Competition, Teal. Pricing and quality are at the heart of it, especially if it is a desired product."

Upstairs now, Teal prepared for bed. Eric turned down the bedspread and top sheet. "You still haven't explained the blizzards and snow across several continents yet, Teal."

"Well, who can!" she snapped. "You had those strawberries and peaches in the fruit salad tonight. They're delicious, beautiful, and competitively priced. But you know how strongly I believe in local markets for *everything*. Trade is good. I won't argue that.

—

But self-reliance prevents scarcity and inflationary pricing while it promotes local elevators and milling, local dairies, and local farmers' markets."

"Like Brahms Dairy south of here," he interrupted. "A brilliant idea for fresh milk and cream products and a business that provides jobs and buys local farmers' hay and feed for their dairy cows."

They shared the shower, another commonality in their marriage. "Better for back washing," they agreed as she soaped his back.

"We have local vineyards now too, Eric. I haven't seen one yet, but they're here because the wine is here. Local organic markets like the farmers' market at the stockyards off Agnew Street in Oklahoma City are healthy for the local economy. They've sprung up everywhere. Scarcity and inflation may meet their match in the independent spirits of Oklahomans."

"I agree. They've got my support and the new administration's support as well," Eric said. "It's in the agribusiness news."

"Really!" she exulted, obviously pleased. "Then the trend is spreading across the country."

Eric chuckled and reached to pull her close. "So I ate peaches from China tonight instead of Colorado peaches or Arkansas peaches or Stigler, Oklahoma, peaches."

"Stratford, Oklahoma, peaches," she corrected. "Stigler strawberries, and don't you forget it. And, yes, you did eat beautiful delicious peaches from China. Heaven help us when they're selling us wheat as well."

"Well, hold on to the blanket, baby," he said, tucking her in. "They are. They plowed up a lot of land to do it. Speculation, speculation, speculation. It's the new game in town, and it's dangerous to our business because it can drive up or down the prices of our product faster than we can know what the insiders are doing.

Most pivotal years this country has seen since 1968 were 2008 and 2009. Not because of cold wars and assassinations, but because of the economic attacks on energy in '08 that produced a trickle-*up* effect on everything in '09 from an inflated dollar to the housing bubble that burst."

"Then it all fell down." Teal sighed. "And when it fell, the corrupt participants robbed their neighbor. Energy prices are falling now, but the inflation of clothes, groceries, automobiles, parts, and building materials aren't and probably won't. Do you feel weary of the struggle, Eric?"

"No. And don't you quit on me either. Cyber attacks are next, mark my words. And all local production will probably be monitored by a census so all sales can be taxed. Some of our excess tonnage goes north to Enid and from there by rail to Minnesota and on to Cargill for trade, but this great wheat belt stretches from Texas to the Dakotas and points west. Kansas is the production giant. We're second to it in the hard red-winter varieties.

"All this propaganda about protectionism is part of our trilogy too, as if we can't be self-reliant and have free trade at the same time. The either-or mentality destroys motivation for some here at home. We went west because of self-reliance. We opened this Oklahoma territory because of self-reliance. The mills exist because of it," he said, giving her a big smack on her cheek. "But without trade or without our terminals and ports of departure for the product, all effort would be futile."

She snuggled closer. "Thank God for the Port of Catousa and at Houston as well."

"Seriously, Teal, you need to come out of retirement from the mill. I need you there at my side. We must get more rail going again. I need you to lobby for it."

"In Washington?" She sat up in bed.

"Rail must come back more forcefully in this state to compete with the trucking. With the right fuel development, it could stabilize pricing for freight," he insisted.

"Are you saying it wasn't just Freddie Mac and Fannie Mae that scrunched the world's economy?" she asked, propping herself on her elbows and peering down at him.

She never looked at him without the awareness hovering over her senses of how wonderful he looked to her. Oh, not that Eric was so perfectly featured, but that his looks were masculine: the strong nose, the firm lip line, and high cheekbones. Tanned and white haired, his appearance had changed over the years. He had become more muscular from physical labor at the elevators besides his office duties, and he had developed those becoming laugh lines at the corners of his eyes and lips.

"You sound almost turned on by our challenges, Eric, instead of pessimistic."

"I am. It's true that energy costs will go up with farmers holding grain longer for the $9 plus they hope for. We need to keep storage low for them. Fuel prices will go up and down, but our fees for storage need to remain at two and a half cents a bushel a month to undergird their hope for the better price.

"I read that one oil company alone has been paying 27 billion in taxes annually," he said. That's about $4,000 a second in taxes and $15,000 a second in expenses most likely. They have their own money crunch in today's economy."

"Lobby, huh," she mused, dropping an arm over his chest. It felt good to nestle her head into the crook of his shoulder. She looked up at him. "I'm not retiring my rod and reel."

"Nor am I," he said, hugging her close to him. "I have always loved the history of this state and especially this wheat-rich area." As he held her, his voice ran down the years of struggle and growth here like those settlers that first year gathered and counted their animal bones. *They sold them to dog food companies to survive until their first harvest while others counted their cattle or sheep,* she recalled. The care of the land, the building, the losses, the drought and hailstorms, the dust and poverty—none of that mattered when a few bonanza years that still came now and then made this life possible. "I'll fight for it to my last breath," he vowed.

"What I don't understand is why. Is it for the connection to the spirited people, to the land, for the challenge?" He cradled Teal's warm body against his own.

"It was for you, my Oklahoma gold," he said, as if surprising himself at the realization. "So like the wheat you direct, you seem its conduit to the world. Yet your management philosophy makes not only all your company people conduits as well, but the community of growers: the cooperative of mutual ownerships that insures the survival of Ray and Esther Swain's elevators and the small farms. For as long as the sun rises over them and blesses this sea of Oklahoma wheat, so green in winter when the rest of the world turns yellow and brown and so gold in summer when the rest of the world turns green, this rebel crop, hard red-winter wheat will continue to build Oklahoma and grow its self-reliant families. It won't surprise me if I learn that most grain grown in many countries bears some of the genetics of Danne's Triumph."

*   *   *

The producers wanted Mia's play to open in the spring as *Upton's Legacy*. The family congregated in Manhattan for the opening.

"Maybe someone will make a musical out of it and bring it back to the civic center in Oklahoma City," Greg exulted after the production.

"You write it, I'll produce it," David laughed. All that country music, dancing, and fiddle playing could be great."

"You're the writer," Greg reminded.

David slapped him agreeably on the shoulder.

They met at Ray's after cocktails with the actors and crew. Mia opened Ray's bakery-restaurant especially for them at 3:00 a.m. Teal fell gratefully into her hotel bed at the Omni Berkshire and slept until noon on Sunday, Eric beside her.

Over afternoon coffee at the airport and before they flew home, Eric asked her, "Why don't you tell Mia *your* story, encourage a sequel?"

"Everyone is a book. My story of fighting to survive after a husband's desertion is all too common these days to be of interest."

His face flushed as if she had embarrassed him. "I meant a story about building an empire to preserve land, family farms, and a rural lifestyle."

—
406

She fixed his gaze and reached across the table to cover his hand before she spoke.

"From where I sit, the heart of my life is simply . . . you. I plan to live it as long as I can, not write it. I'm in the middle of a heavenly harvest of all that's gone before, years as golden as grain, if you'll excuse the pun."

"It's called a bumper crop," he agreed, squeezing her hand. They leaned across the table and kissed, then walked to their airline gate and boarded.

"I've never told you the story of Mary-Mary, Harlin's sister and your great aunt. Upton and Letti had only the two children." So she told Eric more about a side of the family made strangers to him by Gavin's desertion of Sara.

"How I wish all of those great souls that have gone on could see their story and meet their new family that just keeps coming on. It really is a bumper crop isn't it, Eric?"

"Mary-Mary's gone?"

She died before Harlin died. She was only sixty-five. We weren't together then." She smiled over at him.

The Fasten Your Seat Belts message interrupted their moment, and the flight landed them at Will Rogers World Airport *and* home.

"I've an idea that can reduce our own costs, Teal," Eric ventured as they lay together before sleep. "And that of our area farmers as well."

"What's your idea?"

"Well, we've quite a volume of our own wheat now—the family's own wheat, I mean. Why not use it, advertise it as organic, for it is? No chemical touches it once it heads. We could market our flour and baked goods strong in local markets here at home, then take them to the states that touch our borders. It's a different model." He hesitated. When she didn't respond immediately, he added, "Cattle sales might cover farm expenses."

"It's a wonderful idea, Eric. So obvious, I hadn't thought of it. It's more innovation, yet it may create some expansion."

"It could maximize profit. Perhaps we can create a co-op of owners, investors."

*   *   *

It did maximize profit and infused the whole family with hope for the future of their operation and of all the other wheat and cattle farms in the county.

It was after one of Lincoln's violin concert performances with New York City's Philharmonic two seasons later that Gregory announced his engagement to a fellow instructor at OSU, a Dr. Jenna Jones.

"Is she as avid about saving the world as you are?" Eric asked him. He lavished Gregory with an approving smile that said he pleased him immensely.

"When's the wedding?" Teal inquired.

"Soon! That's all I know."

Their wedding drew a somewhat small intimate group that gathered in a chapel near the campus. Their mutual families and friends saw them off to a safari in Africa for their honeymoon.

After the ceremony, Teal had a long visit with Sylvia, their first in years. Then in one year to the day, Eric and Teal welcomed their third grandchild, Upton Meriott, Gregory and Jenna's firstborn.

"Four generations have come full circle to our beginnings with Upton Rush," Mia mused.

Teal smiled at her indulgently. "Upton is a wonderful name for him."

"Mom," she said thoughtfully. "When we get our son—and we will!" she emphasized, "I'm going to call him David Ray, after both Granddad and David."

"Oh, please do." Teal reached to clasp Mia Emerald's hand. "It's been a grand trip. My life, I mean. My losses be hanged!"

"Because you welcome the two constants: change and God," they said together, their joy spilling into laughter.

—

408

"Knowing that gives cause for hope," Teal said, embracing Mia. "I've an e-mail from Jonsi for you to see," she said.

"A USDA sign-up for grants to develop innovative products, grants for creative ideas that combine technology with agricultural products," Mia read aloud.

"I only dreamed such things," Teal said. "A government program to generate ideas that can infuse life into farming."

"Like that one that is funding agricultural education to minorities as well as to the status quo."

"Are we the status quo?" Teal said, her eyes widening.

"We're in 2010 now, Mom. Status quo is out, opportunity for all is in. Not all the way—"

"But we'll get there if this is an indication."

"What about med school and greater opportunity such as for us poor USA folks that can't claim a minority?" Teal mimed. "Us status quo folks, I mean. I hear there's a doctor shortage in this country. Can we squeeze in some crack before we import thousands more from other countries? Think of the wasted talent in the status quo majority due to class distinctions now commonly known as minorities and the relative poverty of all groups."

"Well, when you lobby for agriculture, expand your horizons, Mom."

Teal flashed a brilliant smile at the thought. "Of course! I can do that."

BIBLIOGRAPHY

1. "Food Problems in Germany Serious," Associated Press, *The Daily Oklahoman*, Oklahoma City, OK., Nov. 12, 1918, pg. 15;16.

2. *History of Oklahoma*; Dale, Edward Everette and Wardell, Morris L., Prentice-Hall, Inc., Englewood, NJ., 1948

3. Document No.8: Series No.2, USDA, "Some Landmarks of Department of Agriculture History," June, 1953, pg. 1-45.

4. *Law West of Fort Smith*; Shirley, Glenn, University of Nebraska Press, Lincoln, NE., 1968.

5. *Directory of Oklahoma*, (1977) State Election Board Staff: "Agriculture," pg. 11.

6. Pamphlet: "The Farmer-owned Grain Reserve Program," USD staff, Washington, DC, Feb., 1978.

7. *The Daily Oklahoman*, Oklahoma City, OK., Maize, Kennedy P.: "Politicians 'Milk' Dairymen's Lobby," Nov. 24, 1978, pg. 18.

8. Railway symposium: El Reno Junior college, El Reno, OK., Moderator: Dr. Duane Anderson, April 20, 1979.

9. The Oklahoman; Blossom, Debbie (business writer): "Langston Gets $525K for Agriculture Program," pg. 4B.

INDEX

E

education. *See* Oklahoma State
    University; Oklahoma City
    University (formerly Methodist
    College of Oklahoma)
El Reno, Oklahoma, 52, 63, 110, 156
El Reno Hotel, 50-52, 54
Emerson, Ralph Waldo
    Self-Reliance, 183
Enid, Oklahoma, 347, 397, 404
Europe, 45, 82, 101

F

Fannie Mae, 404
Ferber, Edna, 77-78, 151
    So Big, 349
Ford (automobile), 51
Fort Reno Research Station, 290
Fort Smith, Arkansas, 22
France, 45
Franklin, Benjamin, 102, 106

G

Galveston, Texas, 118, 235
Germany, 101
Great War (WWI), 45, 84, 178
Grey, Zane, 182

H

Harper's Bazaar, 30
Herefords, 44
Hitler, Adolf, 149
Houston, Texas, 101, 158, 235, 277-78,
    354

I

Indians, 8, 401
Indian Territory, 1, 7, 10, 81, 342
Interstate 40, *336*

J

Jennings, Al, 13
Jesus Christ, 132, 167, 335
Joseph, ix, 3, 48, 278-79, 281-92, 294-
    95, 301, 384, 399-400

K

Kansas, 7, 158, 221

L

Las Vegas, Nevada, 374
Longfellow, Henry Wadsworth, 29
Lot's wife, 321

M

Macintosh County, Oklahoma, 63
Ma Joad, 84
malaria, 7, 53, 58, 72, 213
Manhattan, New York, 337, 350, 358,
    406
McAlester, Oklahoma, 397
McGuffey Reader, 6, 77
Moynihan, Daniel Patrick, 325
Murray County, Oklahoma, 48

N

Nazarene church, 58
New York City, 350, 358, 362, 385
New York State, 103

O

Ohio, 6-7, 14-15, 22, 58
Oklahoma City, 45, 51, 60-61, 81, 110-
    11, 158, 358
Oklahoma City University (formerly
    Methodist College of Oklahoma),
    46
Oklahoma State, 45, 51-52, 54, 71, 81,

CPSIA information can be obtained at www.ICGtesting.com
Printed in the USA
LVOW090509260512

283420LV00001B/232/P